NOT MINE TO GIVE

A Scottish Historical by

This is a work of fiction. Names, characters, places, and incidents either are the product of the author's imagination or are used fictitiously. Any resemblance to actual persons living or dead is entirely coincidental.

NOT MINE TO GIVE
Copyright © 2012 by Laura Landon
First print edition
ISBN 978-1-937216-33-7

All rights reserved. No part of this book may be used in the context of another work of fiction without written permission of the author or Prairie Muse Publishing. Contact info@prairiemuse.com
Cover design by Prairie Muse utilizing selected photos from
© Michele Loftus | © Denis Tevekov | Dreamstime.com
© Brian Jackson | Fotolia.com
www.prairiemuse.com

Dedication

*To my best friend Petie, who's like a sister to me.
Thank you for being so special.*

Prologue

Kilgern Castle - Scotland
July 21, 1314

She pulled her wrapper tighter around her nightdress and ran down the stairs of Kilgern Castle, the words of her frightened maid still ringing in her ears. The priest from clan Ferguson was downstairs, demanding to speak to her.

She raised the candle higher as she crossed the wide entryway, then ran to the other side of the great hall. Her heart pounded in her head while her mind raced through the myriad of possibilities that would bring a priest to Kilgern Castle in the middle of the night. She rejected the most obvious. Ian could not be dead.

"Lady MacIntyre."

The priest quit his frantic pacing before a hearth that had long since given out any heat and extended his hands. She grasped his fingers and kissed his knuckles as she bent her knees. When she looked at him, her breath caught in her throat. Dried blood spattered the front of his gown, and the look in his eyes raged with fear.

"Is something wrong, Father?"

The priest wiped the sweat from his brow. "Aye, milady. There is much wrong." The priest lifted one hand to the cross that hung from his neck. "Is it true that you are English? That your father is the Earl of Wentworth?"

She swallowed past the lump in her throat. "Yes."

"Swear to me, milady, that you will protect with your life what I am about to give you and you will give it to only one man — to your father. Swear that you will do what you must so that no more Scottish blood flows to keep what does not belong to Scotland."

The priest gripped her hand almost painfully and she couldn't stop her heart from thundering even louder.

"Swear it," he repeated.

He reached into the pocket of his robe and lifted out a book. She didn't have to be told that it was the priest's well read Bible he placed beneath her hand.

"Swear before God."

Her heart skipped a beat. "I swear."

With an audible sigh of relief, he made the sign of the cross, then placed his Bible back into his pocket. Carefully, he opened a large velvet bag, then lifted into the air a round object covered with white satin. His movements were slow, reverent, as if he held in his hand the most precious object in all the land. With great care he removed the covering and handed her a crown.

The Bishop's Crown. The crown that had adorned the head of every monarch in English history.

It was magnificent. She stared at the priest in confusion then brushed her hand over the emblazoned metal. It was cool to the touch and a stab of strange power pulsed through her.

She held in her hands the Bishop's Crown. A crown that belonged to England.

Chapter 1

KILGERN CASTLE - SCOTLAND
JULY 29, 1314

Duncan Ferguson closed his eyes in an unguarded moment of exhaustion, then clenched his teeth, unable to hold back a harsh breath when his jailer's blunt club struck him in the ribs.

"Keep them eyes open, Scot." The toothless guard they called Crites brought the club down again, this time striking Duncan's right shoulder from the back. "You know his lordship won't take kindly to you nappin'. He don't intend for you to be enjoyin' his hospitality so much you won't be wantin' to leave."

Crites jerked on the cord that bound Duncan's hands behind his back.

Duncan sucked in his breath but held his body stiff as a fresh stab of pain shot down his arms. He separated his mind from his body, a trick he'd learned long ago. As waves of pain sliced across his shoulders, he registered every moment of agony; every burning slash. He would never forget.

The dull clang of keys from outside his cell alerted his guard and Crites straightened his foul smelling body as if he considered himself more important than the ignorant lackey he was. Duncan shifted his bruised shoulders, but only his right arm moved. The left was numb, either from lack of movement or repeated blows.

"You be lucky today, Scot. His lordship is come to see you again. Twice in the same day." Crites pulled his filthy jacket over his protruding belly and muttered a vile oath when the clasp refused to fasten. "You'd best tell him what he wants to know." He poked at one of the gashes still trailing blood down Duncan's arm. "You ain't quite recovered from the last time he came to see you."

Duncan fisted his bound hands and readied himself for more abuse. He hadn't survived months of battling the cursed English only to die in a stinking dungeon cell this close to home.

A cold shiver raced down his spine and he braced himself. He'd lost track of the hours — days — he'd been here. He hadn't moved except for the few moments Crites had untied him each day from the rough, wooden pole in the center of the small cell to let him relieve himself. Or, when the pompous fool had tried to force a bowl of rancid gruel down his throat.

Metal ground in the lock. "Make it easy on yourself, Scot," Crites warned. "You know how fond his lordship is of that strap that hangs at his waist."

A thin line of spittle drooled down the coarse man's chin and he wiped it away with the back of his hand as the heavy cell door opened. With a shrug of his shoulders, he looked at Duncan and smiled a toothless grin. "'Tis a shame for you to lose more of your bonny hide."

Duncan looked neither left nor right as William Bolton, Earl of Rivershorn, strode into the cell then stopped directly in front of him. Even though Duncan's left eye was swollen almost shut, it was impossible to miss the determined glare in the other man's eyes.

"I am most distressed, Ferguson. Crites tells me you ate no food again today." Bolton circled the pole in the center of the room, jabbing each bruise on Duncan's arms and naked chest with the blunt handle of his leather strap. "How will you ever find the strength to tell me where you've hidden the Bishop's Crown if you don't eat?"

A deafening silence permeated the dank cell, and when the sharp crack of Bolton's strap struck Duncan's chest, Crites rubbed his hands together and lifted a corner of his mouth in anticipation.

"I've grown tired of your stubbornness, Scot." Bolton paced before Duncan like a spoiled child on the verge of a tantrum, then stopped and swung out his right hand. The handle of his whip struck Duncan squarely across the jaw. "Where is the Bishop's Crown?"

Bolton raised his hand again and brought the leather strap down with a snap. It didn't take long for a red welt to cross Duncan's upper arm, then angle to his waist.

"You stubborn, pigheaded fool. The crown does not belong to you. Nor does it belong to Scotland. It was stolen from our King and the people of England on Midsummer Day. I will have it back and the band of your bastard Scots that took it."

Bolton paced the small cell like a man possessed. The red on his face darkened to a purple and his glare took on a demented look. "I will have England's crown. It sickens me to think of such a magnificent object in the hands of the vile Scots."

Bolton brought the whip down again. This time the ends of the leather strap hit the dirt at Duncan's feet. Then, he walked around him with deliberate slowness. "You think yourself so in command, Scot. You'll not remain silent for long. I will have the crown."

Duncan glared at the Englishman before dismissing him with a turn of his head. He would see the man rot in hell before he would ever help him find the Bishop's Crown.

Without warning, Bolton turned and flicked his wrist. The whip cracked across Duncan's chest, opening his flesh from his shoulder to his waist.

"You fool. How can you think England will let you have their crown? How can you think England will not retaliate for what your clansmen did?"

Bolton paced back and forth in front of Duncan, then stopped. "Perhaps you'll consider trading the crown for this." He reached into his pocket and held up a large gold and silver medallion encrusted with the Ferguson crest. An eagle in full flight wore a crown of small jewels upon its head.

The breath caught in Duncan's throat. It was impossible for him not to react. This is what he'd risked his life to recover. This, and the crown. After months of fighting at Robert Bruce's side, he'd come home to find all save one of his family dead. His home had been severely damaged, and the medallion that represented the lineage and nobility of his ancestors was now in the hands of a murdering Englishman.

"I thought this might bring you about. You bloody Scots are such a territorial lot. You cling to your customs and traditions with a ferocity that is appalling."

Duncan stared at the medallion. In earthly terms it held very little value. To Duncan, it was priceless. Whoever wore it around his neck laid claim to Lochmore Castle and the surrounding land. The Ferguson medallion had been a part of his family's history since the first Ferguson, a Celt, had stepped on Scotland's soil. The relic had been passed down to each head of the clan, and as long as Duncan was alive, no one other than he would wear the medallion.

Bolton dangled the pendant before Duncan like a bone before a starving mongrel, then wrapped his fingers around the precious metal and raised his fist in the air. "I want the Bishop's Crown." His voice was a low hiss. The cold glint in his eyes gave evidence to his insane obsession. For an eternity, Duncan leveled his gaze with unwavering hostility. But said nothing.

"Fool!"

The leather thongs slashed across his shoulders and back once, then twice, then stopped. Duncan held his body rigid and steadied his glare on the Englishman, refusing to look away.

With deliberate slowness, Bolton lifted the cord over his head and let the crest drop against the deep red of his velvet jacket as if he were proud to have it there. The medallion, never before worn by anyone other than a Ferguson, now rested on the breast of the hated English. Duncan's stomach roiled and he swallowed the bile in his throat.

"Tales of your skill and bravery have spread all through England, Ferguson. Even to your fellow Scots you have become quite a hero. Mayhaps these tales are naught but the exaggerations of drunken soldiers." Bolton trailed the blunt handle of his strap across the strained muscles of Duncan's chest, then over bulging biceps ready to spring. "Mayhaps your impressive size and strength has attracted those inclined to active imagination, but not necessarily concerned with fact?"

Bolton lay the handle of the leather strap against Duncan's cheek and pushed, forcing him to look on him.

"Or, mayhaps, you are not nearly as sly and cunning as tales would have us believe. We'll see how brave you are when your flesh burns with pain and you cannot stop from begging me to end your torture. Then you will tell me where you've hidden the crown."

Bolton lowered the hard leather from Duncan's cheek. "Could it be you need even more persuasion, Scot? Something more important than a medallion to loosen your tongue?" The grin on his face was evil as he bellowed out his order. "Bring her here."

Two large guards stepped into the room. A small girl stood between them.

Duncan couldn't breathe. No air would fill his body. The English bastard had his sister Brenna.

Her legs buckled, unable to support her limp body. With great effort she lifted her head, her large, brown eyes looking at him with a silent pleading that ripped his heart from his chest. Her haunting stare begged for help and Duncan struggled to free himself from the leather straps that held his hands behind his back.

"Leave the lass be. She does na know anything about the crown." The wind to his chest came in short, jagged gasps and shards of blinding white light flashed before his eyes. He burned with a rage unlike anything he'd ever felt before.

"Brenna, lass." Duncan stared at the black circles around his sister's empty eyes and saw nothing more than an open appeal for his help. "Brenna, you will be aright. I will na let anything more happen to you."

Duncan looked at the rent in his sister's gown and the scratches on her body and silently cursed all Englishmen to hell. For one so young, she had already lived a lifetime of torment.

Bolton walked over to Brenna and cupped her chin in his hand. The act was vile and Duncan's reaction explosive. Her soft whimper filled the room but Duncan could do nothing to help.

"I think I will take your sister with me."

"Nay!"

"Then give me the crown."

Duncan ignored the fire in Bolton's eyes. "I do na have it!"

Bolton flicked his wrist and a long slash opened another gash on Duncan's chest and stomach, then another and another. Bright red blood trickled down Duncan's body. His stomach clutched in a painful, burning grip.

"Your sister will come with me to England. You have until the eve of the New Year, Scot. She will be safe until then." Bolton stroked Brenna's cheek then glared at Duncan so there was no mistaking his meaning. "If I don't have the Bishop's Crown in my hands when the bells chime with the New Year, I will give your sister as a present to every soldier in England."

Duncan struggled with the straps that bound him and fought the anger that burned within him. "If you take her, I promise you will not live to see the New Year."

"You will stop me?" Bolton threw his head back and laughed, then turned to the two guards. "Take her to England."

With a flash of fury, Bolton brought the whip down over Duncan's flesh again. "You will get your sister back when I have the Bishop's Crown. Not before."

Duncan watched the guards drag Brenna's body from the cell. Bolton remained. The salivating expression on his face turned Duncan's stomach. He would kill the bastard. So help him, he would.

Duncan struggled with the bonds that held his hands behind his back but could not loosen the leather straps. God help him. He did not breathe again until the outer door closed and he could no longer hear his sister's muted cries for help.

Bolton fingered the medallion. "I will return. Think of your precious talisman around my neck and consider what it will cost you to let it lie there. Think of your sister in the hands of my soldiers. When you are ready to give me the Bishop's Crown, I will give you back your precious trinket and your sister."

With that, William Bolton turned on his heels and walked with an arrogant gait from the dank cell.

Duncan leaned his head back against the rough timber that had held him captive for days. He would kill Bolton for taking his sister. If he had to, he would die before he would willingly let the Ferguson crest adorn such a vile creature. And his death may be required in the end.

God help him. He didn't have the Bishop's Crown.

...

"Crites. Crites, move your arse." A faceless voice from beyond the cell door alerted Duncan and roused his snoring jailer. "Bolton sent down a tankard of ale as reward for the fine job you done with the prisoner."

Crites stumbled to his feet. He shook his head then staggered to the door and took the pint being handed him through the small opening. He puffed out his chest like a proud peacock and smiled a wide grin with what was left of his brown, rotting teeth.

Duncan silently cursed the fool on the other side of the door for disturbing the guard. As long as he slept, Duncan was afforded at least a little respite from the club Crites was so fond of leveling on his flesh.

"By the saints! I could tell the earl had his eye on me when he came down earlier. He knows a good and loyal subject at a glance." Crites took a deep swallow of ale and wiped his mouth with the back of his hand. With a haughty stride, he swaggered in front of Duncan and aimed the club at his middle.

"Take heed, Scot. The master don't let a good job go unrewarded. He takes care of them that does right by him." Crites shoved the long club at Duncan's stomach then took another swallow and belched.

"I'd wager he won't return to England without me. You and your heathen Scots will be freezin' your arses in this God forsaken land, and I'll be livin' in grand style on

English soil. If you're still suckin' air that is." His boisterous laughter filled the cell. Crites took another swallow and shoved his club into Duncan's middle again.

"Take a warning from one who knows. His lordship is losing patience with you, Scot. If you don't tell him where you hid that crown he's after soon, you'll be laid out with your toes cocked to the sky and—"

Crites clutched his hands to his throat. His face turned a deep purple as he gasped for air. The tankard of ale crashed to the floor, the remaining liquid soaking into the dirt. Then, he crumpled into a heap beside it, a wide-eyed look of panicked disbelief on his face.

Duncan stared at the man's chest, unable to tell if he was still breathing. He hoped so. He wanted to kill the bastard himself.

Duncan held his breath and waited. A deafening quiet blanketed the small cell. Then the key turned in the lock and the door opened. Bright light from a torch filled the room and he squinted his eyes until his vision adjusted to the brightness.

A woman, slight in stature with hair the color of burnt honey, walked toward him. Her pale blue dress hung over her form, so loose Duncan thought she wore the ill fitting gown on purpose to hide the curves beneath. The breath caught in his throat. Her open beauty held his gaze and he couldn't take his eyes from her face.

With shoulders lifted and chin raised high, she placed the torch in the holder on the wall and closed the distance between them. Duncan focused his gaze on her vivid blue eyes and deepened the frown on his face. He expected her to lower her gaze or at least stop and come no further. He was used to that reaction.

She did neither. She stared at him with unwavering boldness then followed one step with another until she was so close he could smell the rose water she'd bathed in.

"Are you Duncan Ferguson, laird of Lochmore Castle and clan Ferguson?"

He glared at the English woman as if by looks alone he could strike her down. Her reaction was to steel her shoulders and ask her question another time. This time in Gaelic.

Duncan cocked one eyebrow. "I am." He answered in English.

"You are familiar with Ian MacIntyre, laird of Kilgern Castle?"

"I am."

"Can you tell me where he is?" Her question was almost a demand.

Duncan took as deep a breath as his ribs would allow. He could only guess the identity of this beautiful woman. Ian had talked of nothing else but his smiling English wife with flaxen hair and eyes as blue and fathomless as the North Sea. His description had not begun to do her justice.

"Nay. I came in search of the Ferguson medallion which is rightfully mine. I had hoped Ian would be back from the fighting, but the minute I crossed the border onto MacIntyre land, Bolton's men took me captive. I have graced your dungeon too long, milady, and when next I see your husband, I will be sure to tell him I was not pleased with the hospitality in his absence."

She twisted her hands again in the folds of her gown

and Duncan was impressed with the wifely concern he sensed in her.

"When did you last see Ian?"

"I have na seen him since the fighting at Dryburgh."

"Is he still alive?"

He wished to God he knew. "I canna swear to it." Duncan noticed a reaction. He detected a catch in her breathing before she twisted her hands in the folds of her gown. "How long has the bastard Englishman been here?" he asked.

"His men stormed the keep five days past. There were too many to defend against. The earl is searching for the crown."

"Aye."

Long, dark lashes closed over her blue eyes for a moment before she spoke. "Are you a friend of Ian's?"

"Aye. As close as brothers and more. I owe him my life."

She gave a short nod before she spoke. "On behalf of the laird of clan MacIntyre, I beg to ask a favor on that debt. I have need of your—"

The cell door flung open and William Bolton burst into the room. He hesitated only long enough to glance at Crites' crumpled body on the floor, then lift his deadly gaze to the woman. Two men, mammoth in size and armed with ready swords followed close on his heels.

"Alas, my lady," Bolton said, clenching his hands into white-knuckled fists. "Again you cause me concern. I do not look kindly upon anyone murdering my servants."

Bolton studied the lady with a menacing glare. A glare that made Duncan's stomach turn in revolt. "Step away from the Scot." She stepped back and he made a wide circle around the pole to which Duncan was bound. "I could scarce believe the news that you had left your comfortable chamber to come visit the cold dungeon."

Duncan took note of Bolton's hands. The left still clenched into a fist at his side while the right caressed the hilt of his whip. Duncan's heart beat at the base of his throat in warning. The Englishman was on the verge of madness and Duncan feared what he would do.

The lady must have sensed it too, for she tucked her hands deeper into the folds of her skirt and took a step nearer his side as if it were possible for him to protect her. Duncan twisted his bound hands, praying for a miracle. But there was none.

"Three nights past I thought my steward was mistaken when he said you were seen sneaking back to your room. Then, we captured the Ferguson. I didn't think there was any significance to his appearance and your disappearance. Until now." Bolton gripped the handle of his whip and released it from the notch on his belt. "Could it be that you sneaked out of the keep to meet in private with our brave laird?"

Bolton held out the handle of his whip and lifted Lady MacIntyre's chin. "Could it be that while your husband is fighting to protect his home from the dreaded English, you, my dear lady, are so lonesome that you warm the neighboring laird's bed?"

Duncan pulled at his hands behind his back, struggling to release the leather straps. A low growl came from the back of his throat as anger raged within him.

In contrast, Lady MacIntyre slowly raised her hand and pushed the hilt of the whip away from her face. "You are disgusting, my lord. I am ashamed to call you English."

A blue vein popped out on Bolton's neck and the muscles in his jaw worked frantically. "Why are you here to see the prisoner, my lady?"

"I am merely curious, my lord. I heard talk from the servants and came to see if what they said was true."

"And what talk did you hear?"

"Nothing you would wish to hear, my lord."

"What talk!"

With a slight shrug of her shoulders, the lady lifted her chin and faced the earl. "It's rumored that no matter how harshly the mighty Earl of Rivershorn tortures the Ferguson, the English lord is not man enough to bring the lowly Scot to his knees."

Bright flashes of warning went off in Duncan's head. By the saints! What was the woman doing? It was one thing to possess spunk, but such a reckless display of her bravery could get them both killed. Ian had described his wife as meek and demure. Duncan prayed to see a glimmer of either of those qualities.

With a lift of her chin, Lady MacIntyre turned her back to the earl and walked toward the door. Duncan held his breath, wishing her to safety. The two guards took a step together to block her exit.

"I wish to leave, my lord. You have no right to keep me."

"I have every right, my lady. Forgive me if I am in error, but there is naught you can do about it. Now," Bolton said, forcing Lady MacIntyre to step back. "Why did you come here?"

She took a step closer to Duncan. "I told you. I was curious."

"And your curiosity is the reason Crites is lying lifeless on the ground? I think not, my lady." Bolton fingered his whip, running the hard leather thong over his palm. "I think you and the Scot are lovers and you came to the dungeon to set him free."

"And I think you are a fool, my lord."

The whip in Bolton's hand slashed through the air, making a mark across Duncan's chest. It missed Lady MacIntyre by a breath.

"Do you know what else I think, my lady?" Bolton paced the small room, letting the strap run through his fingers. "I think perhaps *you* have the Bishop's Crown."

She lifted her shoulders in a taunting gesture. "You are right, my lord. As you can see, I am wearing it."

Bolton grabbed the lady's chin between his thumb and forefinger and squeezed. "I am not the fool you think, my lady. Maybe you don't have the crown, but perhaps you can be used to persuade your Scot lover to tell me where it is."

She pushed his hand away, and Bolton raised his fist as if to strike her.

Duncan went wild. "Nay! I tell you. I do na know where it is!" He pulled against his bonds with as much strength as he could find.

As if Lady MacIntyre realized the danger, she stepped closer, pressing her back against his chest. He felt her stiff form against him, but she at least was wise enough to hold her tongue.

"I do na have the crown, Bolton." Duncan's voice roared in the confines of the small cell. "I do na know where it is."

"Lies! After the crown was stolen by the Scots, it was

given to the Ferguson priest. We found him on his way back from Kilgern Castle, but he would confess nothing before he died. Since the crown was not at Lochmore Castle, it has to be here. Either you or Lady MacIntyre have hidden it."

Duncan looked down on the lady. The impassive expression on her face told him nothing. Only her slight trembling as she leaned against him gave evidence of her fear. "Milady?"

Her face lifted at his soft word. He tried to read the look in her eyes. Confusion? Indecision? Fear? Was she searching for an answer? Duncan had one ready. "Give him the crown, lass."

"Would you give him the crown, my lord?" She spoke in Gaelic.

"I would rather die first, but I am Scot. You are English. Give him the crown."

Dark, thick lashes rested on her flushed cheeks, then she breathed a shaky sigh. She turned to face Bolton. "I would have a kiss first from my Scot."

Duncan stiffened.

Bolton roared a vile oath, then cracked his whip in the air. "Bloody hell! The wench is in danger of losing her life and she begs for a kiss from her lover."

Bolton's hand twisted on the hilt of his whip as if he couldn't wait to flay flesh and spill blood with its crack. "By all means, my lady. You may kiss your lusty Scot. And then I will have my crown."

She slowly turned until their gazes locked. Duncan's voice was little more than a whisper, heard by no one but her. "Nay, my lady."

She whispered back. "Yes." She stood on her toes to kiss him.

Dear God, he couldn't return her kiss. She was another man's wife. A man he loved like a brother; a man he owed his life.

He turned his face away from her.

Her fingers gently touched his cheek, forcing his gaze to return to her face. The pleading in her eyes more than he could bear. "A kiss, my Scot. I beg you."

Duncan hesitated, then lowered his head and covered her mouth. She reached for him. It was as if once their lips touched he was helpless to deny her. Later he would get on his knees and beg God's forgiveness for his sin, but all he wanted at this moment was to touch her and feel her mouth under his.

His mouth opened and she parted her lips beneath his. She wound one arm around his neck and the other trailed a path to his bound wrists. Her touch burned his flesh; set him ablaze.

He ground his lips against her, wanting more of her, but the feel of warm metal being pressed into the palm of his hand cooled his senses. He stilled, his lips still caressing hers; his mouth drinking from her sweetness.

Duncan clasped the metal in his fist and rubbed his thumb over the embellishment. He could feel the raised span of an eagle's wings and the three small stones blazing the crown atop the eagle's head.

The Ferguson medallion.

Somehow she had taken it from Bolton. The crest his ancestors had fought and given their lives to protect. If he died today, it would be with the Ferguson medallion touching his flesh.

Duncan lifted his face to gaze into her eyes. "Thank you, milady." She raised her hand and cupped his cheek in her palm. His face was rough with three days' growth, but she caressed his flesh as if she'd touched him often. As if to touch him was of importance to her.

"God protect," she whispered in Gaelic. "I have failed."

"'Twas naught you could do."

She took a deep breath then turned to face Bolton.

"I would have my crown now, Lady MacIntyre." Bolton stepped forward and held out his hands as if the lady could miraculously make the object appear and place it in his grasp. Her words stopped him short.

"You will not get your crown from me, my lord."

"No!" Bolton erupted in a rage beyond any Duncan had yet witnessed. His face turned a mottled red while a dozen or more bluish veins popped out over his neck and forehead. With a viselike grip he clamped his hand around her arm and threw her to the ground at Duncan's feet. The knife she had concealed in her hand fell to the floor, and Bolton kicked it out of her reach.

Duncan realized a fear greater than any he'd experienced on the battlefield. At least in battle he'd had the free use of his hands and could move toward or away from the enemy. Here he was helpless, unable to protect the mistress from Bolton's insane rage.

"Milady." Duncan spoke in a loud clear voice and focused his gaze on the woman kneeling at his feet. "You have not failed. Only your death would mean failure. You will not be blamed for giving up the crown."

She looked up at him, her deep blue eyes filled with

pain and torment. Duncan silently pleaded with her to abandon her attempt to save the Bishop's Crown.

"I cannot."

"I will have the crown! It's here and I will have it, or you, my lady, will wish to hell you had never deceived me so." Bolton raised his hand and the leather strap cut through the air with a snap.

Her shoulders jerked and Duncan heard her gasp. He watched in horror as a long red stripe stained a frayed tear across her back. "Give him the crown, milady." Duncan struggled at the straps that bound him to the pole until he felt warm blood trickle down his fingers from the cuts around his wrists. What in God's name was she doing? "There is no need to do this, lass. Give him the crown."

She hung her head and moved it from side to side.

Bolton muttered a vile curse, then issued an order to his guards. "Tie her. Against the wall."

Duncan fought against the straps that bound him. "Nay!" Dear God, he prayed, don't let him do this.

One of Bolton's men picked her up and pushed her against the wall while the other secured her wrists. When finished, they both stood back.

"I want the crown, my lady."

Duncan raised his eyes to heaven, imploring God to help him. "Give him the crown, milady. I beg of you. Give him the crown."

Her voice was small yet firm; her words in Gaelic so Bolton would not understand; her meaning a cut through his heart. "I am no more able to give him the crown than you are."

His heart flew to his throat as he focused his gaze on

the small figure. She'd closed her eyes and stood with her cheek pressed against the cold, damp stone wall. When the first snap of the whip cut through the air, her body jerked and a tiny gasp echoed in the cell.

Duncan fought to get loose with all his might. Violent waves of anger crashed against his ears. His head spun in black confusion. Again and again he bellowed for Bolton to stop, but his demands went unanswered. With unerring accuracy, the whip snapped, flaying her flesh until her gown was soaked with blood.

"My lord! My lord! Hurry. We must leave."

Bolton's steward burst into the cell and the earl flicked his wrist for the final time. "What now, Garret?"

"Ferguson's men. They've crossed the stream and are almost to the top of the ridge."

"Have my men get ready. We'll fight them here."

"It's too late. The men are already leaving."

"Leaving?"

"Yes, my lord. The Fergusons have not come alone. There's a huge army behind them. We must leave now or there will be no chance to escape."

Bolton gave a vile curse, then fled the small cell, his steward and the two guards in his wake.

Duncan dropped his head back against the rough pole and let his chest heave as he struggled to fill his body with air. He worried not that his own body was bloody and bruised. He cared only for the brave lady who had kissed his lips and caressed his cheek.

He wrapped his fingers around the metal in his fist and held it tight. William Bolton would die. 'Twas a vow he made to God on his honor as a Scot.

Chapter 2

"Holy Mother of God!"

Malcolm MacInnes of clan Ferguson burst through the cell opening with sword drawn and dagger ready. Gregor and Balfour flanked him, one on either side. The sight of them together with the Ferguson plaid over their left shoulders was a vision Duncan had waited to behold.

For more than an hour he had pushed away the darkness his mind wished to consume him and stared at the limp figure hanging from straps on the wall while he waited for his clansmen to reach them. He had welcomed the soft moans she'd made at first. At least he knew she still lived. But there had been no sound from her still body for a long time now.

Malcolm and Gregor rushed to cut their laird from the pole, then supported him when he leaned against them. Balfour went to Lady MacIntyre but stopped, not certain how best to free her.

"Do na touch her." Duncan stood with the help of the two men, thankful they were both more than average in size. There were not many he'd trust to support his massive bulk. "I will take her."

"You do na have the strength to hold yourself, Duncan Ferguson," Malcolm scolded. "I've been at your right hand for all this time. Let me do your bidding here, too."

"Not in this. No one will hold her, save me."

Malcolm nodded to his laird, then stood at Duncan's side where he had been for ten years and more as Balfour cut the straps holding her.

Lady MacIntyre crumpled into Duncan's arms and he held her slight form to his chest. He felt a soft whisper of air from her lips when he rested her head under his chin.

"Please, my lord. Do not leave me… in the dark. Not… in the dark." The sigh she uttered against his neck was weak, but it was all Duncan needed to hear. She was still alive.

"Nay, milady. I will na leave you in the dark."

Blood still ran down his arms and the open slashes on his chest and back burned like the fires of hell, but Malcolm's steadying hand was there to support him.

"Is she still breathing?" Malcolm's question was sincere. By looking at her it was impossible to tell for sure.

"Aye. She will na die. I will na let her."

Duncan looked down on her and a gnarled hand twisted his heart in his chest. None of the lashes had touched her face. He didn't think he could stand knowing her beauty had been marred because of him. "Gregor, find Angus. Have him bring his salves with him."

The young clansman nodded, then ran to do his laird's bidding.

Twice on their way from the dungeon, Duncan staggered, and twice more he halted to catch his breath. Sweat ran down his face, stinging the cuts above and below his eyes, but still he climbed one step after another until they were out of the darkness of the dungeon. Neither Malcolm nor Balfour offered to take the English woman from their laird's arms. They knew it would be of no use.

When they reached the great hall of Kilgern Castle, a large number of MacIntyre serfs and clansmen rushed to see to their mistress. Loud, muffled cries of dismay echoed in the large hall as the women dabbed at their eyes and held their hands to their faces. The few men still at the castle, mostly the old and feeble, hung their heads, ashamed they'd been unable to protect their laird's wife.

Only one woman, an English woman by her dress, probably the mistress's handmaiden, braved to go near her lady. Without a word, she glanced at the woman in his arms, and with tears streaming down her cheeks, ran ahead of the Ferguson to lead the way to her lady's chamber.

Duncan carried the mistress of Castle Kilgern up the next set of steps, then through the opening and laid her on the bed. Before he had time to peel the blood-soaked gown from her back, the door to the chamber opened and Angus Kilbride burst into the room. Like a roiling thundercloud that darkened the sky on a clear, spring day, he charged forward, scattering everyone in his path.

He closed the distance in three easy strides and stopped in front of his laird, giving Duncan's wounds an evaluative glance, then gazed down on the bed. Thick, bushy brows met to form a nearly solid line above dark gray eyes that had seen more than his share of wounds in his fifty-odd years. Harsh crevices deepened when a fearsome frown covered his face. He set his bag of salves on the edge of the bed and wiped his hand over his shaggy white beard. "Malcolm, get your laird a seat. I have better things to do with my time than pick the master's large carcass up off the floor."

As if the order had been given by the laird himself, a stool suddenly appeared. Duncan sat while the white-haired giant lifted a frayed edge of the lady's gown.

"Do your knees hit the floor at the sight of blood, woman?" Angus asked Lady MacIntyre's handmaiden.

The servant shook her head.

"Glad I am to hear it." In a loud, booming voice, he issued his orders. He wanted plenty of warm water, plenty of clean cloths and a tankard of ale. A half dozen servants rushed from the room to do his bidding, then he turned and pointed a weathered finger at the door. "The rest of you leave us be and go about your business."

Everyone filed out of the room save Duncan and Malcolm and the mistress' servant called Edith. When they were alone, Angus took his dagger and slit the lady's gown and laid it open.

The breath froze in Duncan's throat and he tightened his fist around the Ferguson medallion.

"Is the bastard who did this still alive?" Angus asked.

"He is."

"Then I will be at your side when you ride after him and it will be my sword that opens him wide after you have run him through. I need to see what kind of heart beats inside such an animal."

Duncan nodded. He couldn't lift his gaze from the lady's back. He had seen enough open wounds and severed limbs in battle to become hardened to the sight of blood, but never had the flayed flesh been that of a woman. A woman who was close to death because of him.

Angus dipped a cloth in the basin of warm water that had been placed on the table by her bed and touched it to her skin. Lady MacIntyre moaned softly. "Keep a hold on your mistress," Angus ordered, then touched the cloth to her skin again.

Duncan wiped the sweat from his face then rubbed the heels of his hands against his eyes. Days of no food, or water, or sleep, plus the toll of his wounds on his body made him light-headed and unable to focus his eyes.

Angus laid a clean wet cloth over her back, then opened his sack and placed three large jars on the table. No one knew the contents of the many jars he carried, and no one was allowed to get close enough while he mixed his potions to guess their ingredients. All anyone knew for certain was that the mixtures contained magic healing powers.

"What think you?" Duncan pushed himself to the edge of his seat and tried to stand. He sank back down and lowered his head to his hands until the room stopped spinning.

"I think the lass was either verra brave or verra foolish to try to save you by herself. I'm not sure you're worth the price she paid."

Duncan rubbed his hand over his face. It was terribly warm in the lady's room. The guilt eating at him made it feel warmer. He owed her. He owed an English.

"'Twas not wise for you to ride to Kilgern Castle alone."

Duncan stiffened his shoulders and glared at the man who had been as a father to him. "I will na answer to you, Angus."

"Aye. You are the laird of clan Ferguson now. You do na need to answer to any man. But you should na have ridden out without your men at your side, and well you know it."

Duncan knew Angus was right.

He should have taken Malcolm and his clansmen when he left Lochmore Castle, but the sight of his slain family and the destruction of his home caused something to snap deep inside him. The bastard Englishman had taken the Ferguson medallion from around his father's neck, and Duncan had come to enlist Ian's help in getting it back. As soon as he'd crossed onto MacIntyre land, he'd regretted his decision and wished to have Malcolm at his side.

"Stop your talking, old man. My father granted you too many liberties with your mouth and now I suffer for it."

"Your father recognized my wise counsel," Angus said, lifting the cloth from her back and touching the first deep cut with the smelly salve.

Duncan rose from his stool when the lady moaned.

"Put your backside down on that seat, milord," Angus ordered Duncan. "There is nothing you can do to help. Malcolm, give your laird this tankard of ale. See that he drinks it all. It will help to soothe his bitter tongue."

Duncan took the tankard Malcolm handed him and drank. He did not care for the sweet taste of the ale, but he had such a thirst he drank it all to the bottom.

"Malcolm, help me stand," Duncan ordered when the lady moaned again in pain. He attempted to rise but was unable to gain his balance. The light in the room slowly dimmed and Duncan leaned back in his seat as a strange sensation washed over him. In a moment more the stiffness and pain eased from his body.

"Malcolm," Angus ordered without ceasing his ministrations. "Do na leave your laird's side. 'Tis time to call for Gregor and Balfour to help you."

Duncan felt his head fall to his chest as if he'd lost all power to hold it up. His legs were weak as a babe's and his arms as limp as a doll's. He struggled to stay in the light, but darkness came at him from every side. "Angus!" he bellowed as the empty cup dropped to the floor. "What have you…"

The laird of clan Ferguson slumped in his seat and Malcolm held him while he called for Gregor and Balfour to help carry their master to a bed. "You know there will be all forms of hell to pay when our laird wakes up, do you na, Angus?"

"Aye, Malcolm. But the mistress is coming back to us. 'Tis better he does na hear her screams."

Malcolm and Balfour and Gregor carried their laird to his room. It took the strength of all three. They stripped him of his boots and after Balfour and Gregor left, Malcolm washed the blood and grime from his laird's body then covered him with the Ferguson plaid. Angus would tend him when he finished with the lady.

Malcolm looked at his friend, deep in slumber, and breathed a heavy sigh. He had grown up with Duncan and loved him as a brother. He had been the first to kneel before him and swear fealty to his new laird when they rode back to Lochmore Castle and found Duncan's father slain. On that day he had sworn to protect his laird with his life. He had almost failed.

Instead, Duncan's life had been saved by the lady. An English. They would wait to see how their laird abided his indebtedness to the enemy.

...

Light from dozens of candles lit the chamber as brightly as if it were day. She wasn't awake, yet she knew the brightness wasn't from the sun. Just as she knew he was with her. She could feel him beside her. Feel his flesh touch her flesh when he held her hand. Hear his soft voice whisper words that bound her to him.

She wanted to die. The pain was so great she wanted to let go of the fragile web that trapped her in his world. But each time she came close to loosening her hold on life, he brought her back. His words pulled her out of the darkness and brought her closer to the light. Light that made the pain easier to bear. But she couldn't stay in the light long before the darkness consumed her again.

...

She pried one eye open a small slit then let it fall shut again. She didn't know how long she'd slept, but sensed it had been days. Maybe more. When she was able to keep her eyes open, she realized she was flat on her stomach. To lift her head without moving any other part of her body almost required more strength than she could find.

She opened her eyes again and watched the flames as they flickered and danced against the stone wall. The movements cast eerie shadows in the silent confusion of her mind that she couldn't comprehend.

He was still here with her. She didn't have to search to find him, she just knew her Scot was there. He'd put salve on her back and held a wet cloth to her lips so she could drink. He'd held her down when she'd thrashed from one side of the bed to the other to escape the pain.

As if he was aware that she was awake, he knelt beside the bed to bring his face level with hers.

He was close shaven now and his clothes were clean, but the bruises on his face still turned his cheeks and eyes a darkish tint of green.

"Good day, milady." He held a wet cloth to her dry lips and she sucked a small amount of moisture. "I'm glad you are awake."

She opened her mouth to speak, but no words would come out.

"Do na try to talk. It's too soon."

He poured a small amount of ale into a metal goblet and an equal amount of broth into another. "It's important that you have some nourishment. Angus said you must take this to get back your strength."

He moved the cups closer and sat on the edge of the bed. "I will lift your head so you can drink. There will be pain when I move you."

He lifted her shoulders and turned her enough so she could get the liquid into her mouth. His movements were tender and careful and though she tried to be brave, she couldn't stop the moan that echoed in the chamber.

He held the broth to her lips first, then the ale. She drank what she could, then turned her head and closed her eyes.

"You've done well, lass. Go back to sleep now and rest."

He lowered her head and placed a light cover over her shoulders. The tips of his fingers brushed against her cheek.

"Good night, milady," he whispered.

"My Scot," she answered and slept.

...

She opened her eyes and looked around. It didn't hurt to move nearly as much today as it had yesterday, and much less than the day before that. She held her breath and listened to the sounds around her.

The chamber was empty. He no longer came to sit with her during the day. Only far into the middle of the night, when no one was about and she was deep in sleep did he enter her room. His presence always lingered until morning when she awoke.

High, muffled giggles drifted to her from the anteroom. The young maid, Eloise, must have been assigned to sit with her this day. The Scottish lass had been hand picked by the Ferguson because she would follow the laird's orders without question, and report every word and movement she made. For a few moments the girl must have sneaked out to be alone with her lover, Cory, while she believed her mistress to be sleeping.

She tried to remember how long it had been since he'd carried her out of the dungeon, most of that time so weak she could barely lift her head. Days? A week? Maybe more. And in all that time she had not been left alone. She knew that had been the Ferguson's order.

She rolled to her side and pulled her legs to her chest. Her wounds were all closed, but when she wrapped her arms around her knees, the skin still stretched tight across her back. She sucked in her breath and held it until the pain went away. Thank God, though, it was nothing like before. More than once she'd prayed God would let her die so she could escape the pain.

Now she had other problems with which to concern herself. She had to get to the place in the rocks.

"Oh. You are awake, milady." A startled Eloise closed the door behind her and straightened her mussed hair. The flush of her cheeks deepened when she neared her mistress. "Would you like me to bring you food? The women prepared an excellent stew for noon meal, and the Ferguson told them to keep some back for your repast."

"Thank you, Eloise, but I'm not hungry. What I am, is tired of this bed. I would like for you to help me dress."

The little maid's face paled. "I can na, milady. The Ferguson said you were nay to leave your bed until he gave the order."

She clenched her fist in the covers and silently prayed Ian would be home soon. Then the Ferguson laird could return to his own keep. The turmoil his nearness caused was too unsettling. He was the most domineering man she had ever met. If she did not get out of this bed soon, she had no doubt she would go mad.

"The Ferguson is not master of Kilgern Castle. I will not let him tell me when I'm ready to leave my bed. He has already kept me prisoner far too long."

"Oh, no, milady. The Ferguson does na wish to make you a prisoner. He is only concerned for your welfare."

"Well, he need not concern himself any longer. My… Ian will be home any day now and everything will be fine." Dear God, she prayed that were true. "Now, help me dress, Eloise."

"Pray, let me get you something to eat first, milady. Then I will help you dress."

She gave in with a sigh. "Very well. Bring me a tray and I will eat first."

The maid smiled and bobbed her head in relief.

"Then I intend to dress and leave this room."

"Yes, milady." With another nervous bob of her head, Eloise left the room.

She struggled to remove the covers and it took her forever to work her way to the edge of the bed. She dangled her feet for a long while before she managed to stand on her own, but she could only remain upright if she gripped the tall poster with all her might.

This was all his fault. She'd never in her life been so weak, and his endless bullying had made her so. He would not allow her to get out of bed so she could get stronger. Well, she could not allow him to keep her abed any longer. Her blood ran cold thinking of what could already have happened in her absence.

The door opened behind her, then closed softly. She lowered her forehead to the smooth post of the bed and breathed a deep sigh. She did not have to turn around to know he was behind her, nor did she have to look to see the frown on his face. She waited for him to speak. The deep rumble of his voice and the burr of his speech were as familiar to her as her own voice.

"You are nay to be out of bed, milady."

"I feel much better today."

"Not well enough, I'm thinking."

She clamped her hands tighter around the bedpost. "You cannot keep me in that bed forever, sir."

He took three steps across the room which brought him close enough for her to smell the scent of horses and leather. Eloise must have found him outside. He certainly hadn't wasted any time coming to her.

Dear God, but he was big. It would have taken an ordinary man five steps to cover the same area, and an ordinary man would not consume so much of the room as he did.

"It's too soon for you to be out of bed, Lady MacIntyre. If your husband were here, he would na let you rise, either."

She turned to face him and staggered when her knees buckled beneath her. Before she had time to reach for something solid, the Ferguson lifted her from her feet and placed her on the bed.

She couldn't breathe, and it had nothing to do with the weakness of her legs. He did that to her. Dear God, she couldn't allow it. "I am only so weak because you've kept me in bed far longer than is necessary. Even Angus says so."

"Angus is as sensitive as a coat of your English chain mail and as delicate as a Highland winter. He'd have thrown you out of bed that first day if you'd opened your eyes for him."

She dropped her head against the pillow and sighed. "He would not have. You would not have allowed it."

"'Tis right, milady, as I will na now."

He stood beside her bed and looked down on her. She should be embarrassed by his nearness, but she wasn't. He'd spent so many hours at her bedside when she'd been ill that for him to be near her now seemed right.

But it wasn't.

"You don't have to be so protective of me. You owe me nothing."

He fingered the medallion hanging from his neck. "I

owe you for what you did. You paid a high price for your actions."

She lowered her gaze, unable to look at him. She'd paid a high price indeed. She'd failed. "I gave you only what was rightfully yours."

"Why did you come to the dungeon, milady. What favor did you want in exchange for my medallion?"

"It's not important."

"It seemed so at the time."

"But it is no longer." She closed her eyes to block the fear. "Have you found him yet?"

One eyebrow on his darkened features raised. "I do na ken your meaning."

"William Bolton. I know you've gone out searching for him. Have you found him?"

"Nay."

"Leave him be, Lord Ferguson. You don't know how far his power reaches."

"I canna leave him be."

"He's protected by the king."

"He is nay protected by *my* king."

A cavern of silence separated them, made more daunting by the fierce glare in his eyes. It worried her. "Many of your fellow Scotsmen will die if you go after him."

"Many men from Scotland have already died because of him, milady."

"But—"

"Enough. Even though you are wed to the laird of clan MacIntyre for a year and more, I see you have na left your love for the English far behind. I think mayhaps you have put the MacIntyre plaid on your body but have not let the MacIntyre Scot into your heart.

"How dare you! It's not to your credit to assume all English are the same as Bolton. Could it be that your hatred lies in the fact that he took something that was yours? Or do you hate all English?"

"If you have need to understand the cause of my hatred of the English, milady, I will show you the graves of my father and mother and two sisters. I found them slaughtered by Bolton and his men when I returned from battle."

"William Bolton killed your family?" *Dear God.*

"Not all, milady. My youngest sister, Brenna, still lives. I found her huddled in a corner on the floor where she'd been since Bolton's men left."

Her stomach clenched, but she refused to lower her gaze from his. Instead, she faced the icy glare of hardened steel focused on her. "Is she all right?" she asked.

"Nay. She is not aright. She was not as lucky as her sisters, Meara and Elissa. She lived. And now William Bolton has her with him in England until I give him the crown."

For the first time since she'd met him, she sensed the building of an uncontrollable violence that smoldered just beneath the surface, waiting to be unleashed. "He would trade your sister for the crown? But you don't have it."

"That matters not to Bolton. All he cares about is getting the crown."

"But the crown doesn't belong to him either. It's England's."

Her statement, though spoken softly, had the impact of a thunderclap. His gaze, which was dangerous and foreboding in the best of circumstances, darkened even more. "Do you think, my lady, that if Bolton gets the crown he'll give it back to England?"

She didn't answer.

"He will not. He knows it is the verra same crown that has adorned the head of every English monarch for more than five hundred years. Its value in stones and gold alone will give Bolton more wealth than anyone in the land. It's a symbol of England's greatness, and Bolton believes its power will raise him to a level equal the King. Bolton will not give it back. His greed is too great."

"How did the crown come to be in Scotland?" she asked.

"It was brought here by some verra brave Scots that died for their efforts."

"And they gave it to your priest?"

"They gave it to my father at Lochmore for safe keeping and he sent it here when Bolton came. Because you're English, he thought it would be safe in your keeping." He lifted the corners of his mouth in a cynical grin. "Is it?"

She lifted her chin to match his formidable expression, and kept her gaze on the dark depths in his eyes. "Why do you want the crown, my lord? If you had it, would you return it to England?"

He didn't try to mask the stark look of hatred on his face. "Nay, milady. I would na give it back to England."

"But there will only be war if Scotland keeps it."

"There will be war even if Scotland gives it back. Your Edward is amassing an army right now. Within the year the English will again cross Scotland's border in their quest for more land and power. Our Scots took the crown to prove to your English they're not invincible. That circle of gold and stones is to England a symbol of her greatness. Our Scots took it to prove how easily that greatness could be taken away."

"Do you think England fears you now?"

"Nay. England will never fear Scotland. But they will never get the crown back either. My father promised to protect the crown, and he died honoring his vow. That oath is now mine. I will have the crown for Scotland just as surely as I will avenge my father's death. Do you understand, milady?"

"I understand you're a very proud man, my lord, but you don't have the crown."

"But it is na far from my grasp. I will na give up until I have it. Do na forget that, milady."

"What about your sister? Bolton wants the crown or he won't give Brenna back."

He hesitated and an expression of anguish crossed his face. "Even Brenna's life is not worth the crown. My sister understands that as well as any loyal Scot. I will get her back without forfeiting the crown."

She let her head fall back against the pillow and sighed. "Why did you come here?"

"To warn Ian and ask his aid to fight against your Englishmen. I thought it best to come alone until I found out if Bolton had laid siege here as he had at Lochmore Castle."

"He didn't. There was no one to fight him here."

"Where was Chalmers? Ian left him to guard Kilgern Castle when he sent the rest of his men to fight the English."

"We buried him two months past. A small band of renegades attacked him while hunting. He and most of the men with him died."

"Were the renegades English?"

"Does it matter?"

"Aye. It matters to me the same as it will to Ian."

She looked down at the covers on the bed. "They were English."

The look in his eyes hardened. Did he see her only as the enemy? It bothered her that he might, and knew it should not.

"Rest now, milady. I'll send Eloise in with your tray." With that he gave her his back and walked to the door.

"Wait."

He halted, then turned and glared at her as if he'd taken great offense at her order. "I cannot lie in bed any longer. Even if you will not allow me to leave my room, at least let me get dressed."

He hesitated a moment then nodded. "Verra well. If you wish." He turned his back on her.

"Wait."

He stopped short. If he disliked her issuing him the first order, he showed he liked it even less the second time. He turned to face her and arched his eyebrows as if it took every ounce of his willpower to hold his temper. "You have another request, milady?"

"Yes. I would like to be left alone. I don't need Eloise or any of the other women to guard me."

"You think of them as guards?"

"What else would you call them? They don't leave my side for an instant and my every movement is whispered in your ear. Even Ian doesn't feel the need to guard his English wife so closely."

His shoulders stiffened. His angry frown deepened. "Your husband is more trusting of the English than I am, milady."

Any false hope that she could compete with him on even footing quickly vanished. "Please. Allow me some privacy." She pointed to the door he held open. "I promise I will not walk out that door without one of your guards with me."

He gave her request more than a moment's hesitation. "Verra well."

When the door slammed behind him, she guessed he already regretted his decision.

Chapter 3

She held the flaming torch above her head as she made her way along the cold, damp stones of the secret passageway that would take her back to Castle Kilgern. Twice she stopped and leaned against the rocks to wipe the sweat from her forehead and catch her breath.

Dear God, give me the strength to get back.

She knew she shouldn't have left her bed. She wasn't strong enough yet. But she had to go to the cottage tonight. She had to make sure everything was all right. It was the first night the Ferguson had not ordered a maid to watch over her. The first chance she'd had to escape. Now she had to get back before anyone noticed she was gone.

She lifted her torch high again and took a few more steps. Surely it couldn't be too much farther? It hadn't seemed this far the other times she'd sneaked out of the castle. But that was before...

She forced herself to take another step, then staggered against the damp wall when a wave of dizziness washed over her. A sharp craggy rock scraped against her tender back and she cried out in pain. With trembling fingers she wiped the moisture from her eyes, then pressed her hand to the ache in her side as she gasped for air. The walls were beginning to close in around her.

She would make it. She had to. If she stopped here, she would never be found. No one would know where to look for her. She would lie on the cold ground until she froze to death. Or worse, her torch could go out and she would be left in the dark. An insurmountable fear wrapped its gnarled hands around her heart and she found the strength to go on.

She pushed herself away from the stone wall and, with one hand anchored against the rocks for support, she inched her way through the passageway until she reached the wooden door that would take her inside the castle. A whisper of a chuckle echoed in her throat through her ragged gasps of air. She was almost there.

She climbed the crude stairs carved from rock and reached for the latch to unlock the secret door that led into her bedroom. After she placed the torch in the holder on the wall, she pushed at the door, then stepped into the brightly lit room. She closed her eyes and leaned back with a sigh of relief.

She'd made it.

"Good evening, milady."

"Oh!" She clamped her hand over her mouth to keep her scream from echoing in the still, quiet chamber. She swung around, her gaze focusing on the Ferguson's broad, menacing form, lounging in the chair on the far side of the room.

The glow from one of the candles on a nearby table reflected off the medallion, giving his face a formidable look. He sat with his arms crossed over his chest. His powerful legs stretched out in front of him, one foot crossed over the other, and the furrows on his forehead sank deep to form an angry frown.

After a long, uncomfortable silence, he sat forward and leaned his elbows on his knees. "I must have been mistaken when I heard you promise you would na leave your room." His voice was soft, deadly. The sharp edge in his tone enough to slice through even the strongest chain mail.

She lifted her shoulders defiantly. "You were mistaken, my lord. I promised not to leave by that door." She nodded to the door on the other side of the room. "I did not promise I wouldn't leave the room."

She heard the harsh intake of his breath.

"So you did." He shifted in his chair, his movements slow and deliberate. When he stood, his full height towered before her.

A wave of nausea washed over her. She wrapped her hands around her arms and rubbed. Her cold, clammy flesh quivered while her face burned with heat.

"You're shivering. You should na have left your bed."

Her vision blurred, her head spun from remaining upright so long.

His gaze didn't leave her for a moment. "If it would na be too much trouble, I would like to know where you went."

"I… I…" She paused, determined not to cower before him. This was, after all, not his home. She owed him no explanation. "It's the middle of the night, sir. How did you know I was gone?"

The room swam before her, and she reached for the edge of a table against the wall, wanting to sit before she fell to the floor. Her legs quivered beneath her and her stomach pitched like a small boat on an angry sea as she watched him come near her. He took one step and then another until his huge body loomed over her.

"I sent Eloise to make sure you were resting peacefully and when she entered your room, she found your bed empty."

"I needed…" She squeezed her eyes shut. By the saints, she could not tell him. She'd promised. There was nothing she could do until Ian returned.

She wiped at the haze covering her eyes and leaned her head back against the wall. She felt so strange. Almost as if… "Please, help me."

Just as she finished the last word, her world went black. As if unable to support her body, her knees buckled and she slumped into his arms. He lifted her to his chest and held her close for a moment, then moved to lay her on the bed.

"No. Don't leave me. Don't leave me alone in the dark."

He grabbed a wool plaid from the bed and wrapped her in the cover, then sat in a large, wooden chair near the fire with her in his arms.

She nestled her face against his chest, waiting for the waves of imbalance to leave her. Huge, strong fingers pushed back the strands of hair that had escaped the netting covering her head. Fingers that had touched her often when she was near death.

"Milady?" His voice a whisper; his touch never ceasing. "Did you leave your chamber tonight to meet your lover?"

Her response caught in her throat. "No, my lord. I did not meet a lover."

She lifted her gaze and stared into his eyes. Such dark, fathomless scrutiny in his midnight eyes. Such confusion; such torment. His thoughts were too obscure to be understood.

She couldn't take his guarded watchfulness any longer, nor the searching in his gaze as he weighed the possibility that she'd lied to him. She didn't want him to think she had.

As if her hand had a will of its own, she lifted her trembling fingers to erase the hint of mistrust she saw. To softly touch the rugged contours of his face and make the doubt go away.

She cupped her palm against his cheek and her world spun in dizzying obscurity as the dark stubble violated her tender flesh. A shiver racked her body as she moved her thumb along the solid cut of his cheekbone, then angled down to follow the rigid strength of his jaw. He didn't push her hand away. She was afraid he might.

With her hands and her eyes and her fingertips, she could do nothing but concentrate on every line and sculptured detail of his countenance, could do nothing but relish the feel of his magnificent features. Her heart pounded frantically in her breast and her breathing came out in short, ragged gasps. His breathing sounded the same. Harsher.

Her finger hesitated on the obvious crease at the side of his full lips. Oh, how she had wanted to touch him there. The crease was so deep and well defined, she knew it would sink into an enchanting crevice if only he would smile.

Which he was not likely to do around her. He seldom did anything other than scowl. And frown.

She lifted her fingers to the furrows on his forehead — furrows that sometimes seemed such a permanent part of his features. She worried to find a way to erase them. She traced her fingers over them again, then moved down the side of his face. To his lips. Full, warm, and firm. Lips that had touched hers once; assuaged a hunger she wasn't aware needed to be fed. A second violent shudder wracked her body, then a third. She could not stop a soft moan that came from somewhere deep inside her.

With undeniable ferocity, he clamped his hand over hers and turned his lips into her palm and kissed her. Then, with a loud, agonizing moan, he turned away from her and dropped his head back on his shoulders. "God forgive me," he whispered.

She couldn't breath. Her chest heaved from his nearness, and deep inside her there was a throbbing ache that needed to be soothed. "There is no need for God's forgiveness, laird. You've done nothing wrong."

The muscles holding her stiffened. "Oh, milady. You are another man's wife. Mayhap that's the way of things in your England, but in Scotland, we canna turn a blind eye to God's laws with such ease."

She leaned her head against his chest and listened to the strong beating of his heart. It was so vibrant and alive. The medallion was there and she touched it. "Would it be a sin for you to hold me until I fell asleep?"

"Aye, milady. It would. But I will hold you."

She snuggled between the plaid and the warmth of his body, and breathed a deep sigh. For just this once, she would dream that she'd found someone who would take care of her.

Just this once.

. . .

Duncan stood on the wall walk and looked out through the wall crenels to watch the dust from the riders' horses as they approached. Ian MacIntyre led the warriors. Even though they were too far away for him to see their plaid, he recognized Ian's large gray mount in front.

"Raise the gate. Lower the drawbridge."

Duncan issued the order as he climbed down the stone steps and mounted his waiting stallion. On his way across the courtyard, he spotted Eloise carrying a basket to the castle and halted her. "Fetch the Lady MacIntyre and tell her that her husband is coming."

"Yes, milord." The maid dropped her basket and ran to the keep. Duncan watched until she disappeared and breathed a sigh. It was finally at an end. He could ride away from Kilgern Castle and forget the woman who haunted his dreams. The woman who was married to his best friend.

The loud clamor of hooves as they crossed the drawbridge echoed in Scotland's crisp, fragrant air, drowning out the voice of guilt and regret that roared inside his head. A dozen or more Ferguson clansmen followed him across the lea, then up a slope. At the top of a rolling hill, he brought his mount to a halt and waited for the laird of Kilgern Castle to reach him.

"Greetings, Duncan." Ian MacIntyre pulled up his horse near enough to be able to reach across and clasp his hand around Duncan's forearm.

Duncan placed his palm over his friend's hand in return greeting. "I'm glad you have returned safe, Ian. You are needed."

"I have heard." Ian's voice sounded tense. "Have you found signs of Bolton?"

"Nay. The coward has fled."

"I stopped at Lochmore Castle yesterday eve and Malcolm told me the English had been there looking for the crown. I am truly sorry about your family. I pledge myself and my men to your aid whenever you choose to go after Bolton."

Duncan nodded. "I've sent word to the MacAndrews, the MacLarens, and the MacGowans. They're waiting to hear when we ride. The MacFarlands and the Sinclairs and the Camerons are standing ready. We will wait until the Kerrs return from Dumfries, then we'll ride to England."

"Are you well?"

"Well enough." Duncan ignored the pain in his side that still ached when he moved or rode his steed. He leaned back in his saddle and filled his lungs with air. He couldn't stand to think of Brenna in English hands one day more than necessary.

"Malcolm has done well in your absence. The bailey wall is almost rebuilt and at least half of the cottages have been repaired. I left what men I could spare to help."

Duncan nodded. He'd expected no less from his neighboring laird and friend.

"Malcolm told me Bolton captured you when you crossed the border. I fear there was something more he would na tell me, but the more I pressed for answers, the further he stepped from what had happened."

"Aye." Duncan took a deep breath. "Bolton has taken Brenna."

"Brenna? Dear God, why?"

"He wants the Bishop's Crown. He will na return her until I give it to him."

Duncan raised his gaze to the sky, unable to look at Ian. He didn't want to imagine how frightened and alone his sister must feel. He didn't want to remember what she had already been through and the nightmares he could never take away.

"Do you have the crown?"

Duncan shook his head.

Ian fisted his hand around the hilt of his sword and shifted atop his horse. "I should have been here. I fear peace between England and Scotland is impossible now. England's greed and Scotland's refusal to submit will forever cause unrest."

Duncan tightened the grip on his reins. "We will never submit. Not as long as there is breath left in one Scotsman. Not even our king can make it happen."

"Aye. But it's not for want of trying. England's King Edward has made more than one attempt to bridge the chasm between our countries. He ordered the Earl of Wentworth to give one of his daughters to William Bolton to marry, and the other daughter to a Scottish laird in hopes that peace would reign along the border. That's how I came to marry my English bride."

Duncan stared at his friend in disbelief. "You were forced to marry the English lass?"

"It was an edict by our king. Robert thought it would

be best if at least one of the English lords bordering us had friendly ties to Scotland."

Duncan's eyes closed to narrow slits. "That means you would have ties to William Bolton."

"Aye. I daresay if the earl would have had one more daughter, you too would have been commanded to take an English bride."

"I would never take an English bride."

Duncan stared at his friend and the look in Ian's eyes told him he would change his mind if his king commanded it. Duncan knew differently. "You did na come back to find your family slaughtered as did I. Ferguson blood will never mix with that of the cursed English after they murdered my family."

"Even for the peace of Scotland?"

"Nay. Na even for Scotland."

A smile lifted the corners of his friend's mouth. "I do na mind telling you I do na regret the choice made for me. I have come to love my Elizabeth. She may be meek and lacking strength, but there is enough love inside her that I will never drink my fill."

Duncan stared at his friend in confusion. Did Ian not know his wife? Duncan would never use the term meek to describe her. Neither did he think her lacking in strength.

"From the day Elizabeth took my name, she has been a Scot."

Duncan swallowed hard. *Elizabeth.* That was her name.

"Your wife, Ian, was verra brave and verra courageous. She stood up to Bolton as well as any warrior."

The expression on Ian's face turned deadly. "Where was Chalmers?"

"Dead. He and most of the men you had left behind were killed in a raid some months past. There was no one to protect your home and Bolton took over without a fight."

"What did he want? What did he think we had?"

"He came for the crown. When Bolton attacked my family, our priest brought it here to Lady MacIntyre for safe keeping."

The look on Ian's face was stark. "Is the crown still here?"

"I do na know. Your wife will not admit that she has it."

"Have you asked her?"

"Bolton tried to make her tell him where the crown was hidden."

Ian's eyes narrowed and the muscles in his jaw bunched. "Was my wife harmed?"

"Aye. But she is well now."

"And the babe?"

Duncan's heart slammed in his chest. There was naught he could say. By the saints, he didn't know she'd lost a babe. "There is na babe, Ian."

Ian lifted an agonizing frown toward the heavens and clenched his fist around the hilt of his sword. He took one deep breath after another until a low, keening moan echoed into the clear Scottish air.

Without another word, Ian turned his mount and raced toward Kilgern Castle. Duncan followed at his side. When they reached the inner courtyard the two lairds jumped to the ground and ran to the steps leading to the keep's entrance.

"Elizabeth!"

Duncan heard the fear in his friend's voice and a stronger wave of guilt slashed through his gut. How could Ian's wife have kissed him like she had? And let him hold her in the night? And touched his face with such tenderness? Did she have no heart? Didn't she know how much her husband loved her?

"Milord! Milord!" Eloise ran through the doorway and collided with Ian, stopping him in his tracks. "She's gone. The mistress is gone."

Ian stared down on her as if the woman had lost her mind. "Lady Elizabeth is gone?"

"Aye. I went to her chamber to tell her you were here and her chamber is empty. I have searched the keep and she is na here. Just like before. She's disappeared."

"Like before? What does she mean, Duncan?"

Duncan didn't take time to answer. He raced ahead of Ian and ran up the stairs two at a time. Her chamber was empty.

"There's a passageway leading from this room," Duncan said. Do you know…"

He didn't get his question uttered before Ian raced in front of him and pushed against the side of a large wooden chest. The chest moved, revealing the entrance to a stone tunnel. Ian grabbed the torch from the wall beside the entryway and didn't stop running until he reached daylight.

"She's gone to the cottage. It's nearest the tunnel. I showed Elizabeth how to reach it should she ever need to escape the castle."

Duncan ran with Ian across the narrow meadow, thick with heather and tiny yellow wild flowers, then through a dense grove of trees, around a small pond, and straight toward a tall stone wall. Duncan thought they could go no farther but Ian stopped, then walked through a wide recess in the rocks. The door to a hut was carved of wood and stood as a barrier from those outside. If Ian hadn't led the way, Duncan wouldn't have seen the hidden fortress.

Ian reached for the latch and lifted. He threw the door open with a loud crash and stormed into the room as if he were overtaking the keep of a warring clan.

When the door flew open, she spun around, then hugged her arms around her waist as a startled cry escaped her lips. The look of fright on her face was unmistakable. Even after she realized she was in no danger, she was not quick enough to erase the confusion in her gaze. Duncan watched, but saw no heartfelt yearning; no gaze of longing; no look of wifely love for a husband long absent.

"Where is she? Where is Elizabeth?"

Duncan stared at his friend in disbelief. What was wrong with him? This was the Lady MacIntyre. The lass with hair of burnished gold and eyes of liquid blue that Ian had talked of every day and every night while he and Duncan had battled the English. The lass who had begged Duncan for a kiss, then given him the Ferguson medallion. The lass who had answered to the MacIntyre name just before Bolton flayed her body with his whip.

"Where is my wife, Katherine?" Ian MacIntyre's voice roared with emotion.

The door to a small chamber opened and a second lass with hair of burnished gold, and eyes as blue as the North Sea stepped into the room. She was a twin to the English woman Duncan believed to be Ian's wife. A twin so close in looks Duncan did not doubt that no one realized she was not Ian's wife.

Ian's wife looked at her husband and covered her mouth to stop a tiny scream, then ran with outstretched arms into his waiting embrace.

Tears of joy flowed down her cheek as she wrapped her arms around Ian's neck and lifted her face to receive his mouth. He kissed her with a passion that said he either didn't remember he had an audience, or he didn't care.

"Are you well?"

"Yes. Katherine took good care of us."

Ian turned around to look at his wife's sister. "Thank you, Katherine. I am forever in your debt."

Duncan looked at the woman. She fisted her hands at her side and blinked back the emotion that glazed her eyes.

"You should have seen Katherine, Ian. When she heard Bolton was coming with his men, she gathered what we needed to hide here. When she was sure we were safe, she went back to the castle and passed herself off as the wife of the laird of clan MacIntyre. She told the servants she had sent your son with her sister to the convent to keep him safe and not one of them realized she was not me."

"You have taken care of my wife well, milady."

Katherine nodded, then looked away from everyone's concentrated gaze. Duncan noticed her small body sag against the wall. He wanted to go to her but he stopped himself.

Elizabeth wrapped her arms around her husband's waist and laid her head against his chest. "Katherine has always taken care of me, Ian. It's in her nature. Not once was I afraid. I knew she would keep us safe."

Duncan looked at Katherine's face. *Katherine.* Why hadn't she told him? Why hadn't she trusted him enough to confide in him? To let him care for her sister until Ian returned? He pushed down the anger that wanted to build within him. All she would have had to do was ask. All she would have had to do was trust him.

He didn't turn away from her and the blush on her cheeks deepened. She braved a look at him one time, but quickly lowered her gaze as if she knew he wanted answers she wasn't ready to give.

"Did Bolton harm you, Elizabeth?" Ian asked.

"No. I was safe here in the cottage." A frown covered Elizabeth's face and she turned her gaze to her twin. "Did Bolton harm you, Katherine? He's an evil man. We will talk to father. Neither Ian nor myself will allow you to—"

"No, Elizabeth. I am fine."

Her answer came out swift and easy and Duncan turned his gaze back to her. Again, she refused to look at him.

"Once father hears how evil Lord Bolton is, it won't matter if the command came from Edward himself, he will never force you to—"

"Elizabeth," Katherine said, rushing to interrupt her sister. "I'm sure your husband is anxious to see his son."

Whatever Katherine's twin was about to say died on her lips. Elizabeth's face brightened and she ran to the small chamber. When she returned, she handed Ian MacIntyre a wiggling bundle, then stepped back while her husband looked at his son for the first time.

Duncan had never seen such a look of pride as was on

Ian's face. The breath caught in his throat when he noticed the wetness in his friend's eyes.

"Look, Duncan. See how strong he is already?" The babe had a grip on Ian's finger and would not release it. "He's sure to be one of Scotland's finest warriors."

"He will be one of Scotland's finest peacemakers," Elizabeth said with the voice of authority. "He will find a way for the Scots and the English to live side by side without war."

"I pray you are right, wife." Ian placed his son in one arm and wrapped the other arm around his wife's shoulder. "I pray you are right."

"I will not let William Bolton marry Katherine, Ian. We cannot give her over to such an evil man."

Duncan's gaze shot to Katherine. Her face had turned deathly pale. A cold hand gripped his heart. "*This* is the sister betrothed to William Bolton? This is the sister your king would force to marry that bastard?"

Ian answered. "Aye."

Duncan turned his glare back to the woman who had already felt the sting of Bolton's whip. "You would marry him? You would marry such a man, knowing what he's capable of doing?"

Elizabeth stepped out of Ian's embrace and faced her sister. "Did Bolton harm you, Katherine?"

Katherine shot Duncan a harsh glance. A glance that told Duncan he didn't understand. That he'd stepped over his bounds. That his words were only upsetting Elizabeth, and Katherine would not have it.

Elizabeth's hands flew to her mouth. "Dear Lord. He did."

The look in Katherine's eyes turned hostile.

"Are you all right, Katherine?" There was panic in Elizabeth's voice. "Oh, no. That's why you didn't come to see me for weeks at a time." Elizabeth turned back to her husband, the frantic look in her eyes edged with despair. "Ian, we cannot let this happen. We cannot let—"

"Stop it!" Katherine turned on her sister, the determined look of resolve strong. "There's nothing you can do to stop the marriage, Elizabeth. It's an edict from our king. Do you know what would happen to father if I went against our king's command?"

Elizabeth shook her head. "You cannot marry such an evil man, Katherine. You cannot."

"It's too late to stop it."

"Ian?" Elizabeth looked at her husband with a pleading look in her eyes.

"I'll give you refuge, Katherine."

Katherine closed her eyes and shook her head. "It would do no good. I would only endanger everyone here if I stayed."

Katherine walked to the arrow slit that let a single ray of sunshine into the room and stood where the sun lit her hair and skin. "Father is one of the king's closest advisors. He's a very important man in England. That makes me special to Bolton. I'm a trophy to him. A prize. He collects what he thinks has great value." She turned to face them. "He wants me for the same reason he wants the Bishop's Crown. He thinks it will give him power."

"But we can—"

"You can do nothing without sacrificing the lives of hundreds of innocent people. I'll handle this problem on my own."

No one spoke. Tiny tears streamed down Ian MacIntyre's wife's cheeks, but even she realized the futility of her sister's plight. It was an edict of the King of England, and it could not be ignored. There was nothing for either of them to do.

"Is there a priest in residence at Kilgern?" Duncan's voice broke through the silence. It was soft and harsh and determined and unyielding.

"Aye," Ian answered. "There is a priest."

"Find him."

Chapter 4

"No!"

Katherine spun around and glared at the huge Scot, hoping that when she looked into his eyes she would not see what she feared. The look was there. So was his determined stance. He stood with his thick, muscled legs braced far apart as if ready to do battle. The cords in his arms bulged as he clasped his hands behind his back, stretching his already too broad shoulders to an unbelievable width. Not one inch of him gave an impression that he would yield.

Katherine shifted her gaze to Ian's face. His hard glare told her nothing — nothing other than that he understood the reason for Duncan's request and would support his friend's decision, even if he did not agree with it.

"Get yourself ready, milady," Duncan issued again.

"I will not. I will never agree to this."

"Agree to what, Katherine?" Elizabeth took a step closer to her husband. "Why do we need the priest?"

"We don't need a priest," Katherine reassured her.

Duncan took another step closer. "It would be best if

you would na argue, milady."

"You cannot do this, Lord Ferguson." Katherine fisted her hands at her sides. "I will not allow it."

Duncan arched his brows. It was a look with which she was already quite familiar. A look usually followed by the rising of his temper.

"You will na allow it?"

"I will not allow it."

"Ian," Duncan ordered. "Get the priest."

"Why do we need the priest, Ian? No one has died, have they?" Elizabeth asked.

"Not yet, wife."

Katherine gave Duncan an icy glare. It didn't seem to intimidate him in the least. She would try a different approach. She would reason with him. "Lord Ferguson."

"You will call me Duncan."

She focused her gaze on him again, a feat not entirely easy given his enormous height and the fact that he had taken several steps toward her. She lifted her chin to focus on his face. "Lord Ferguson."

His right eyebrow spiked high above the black hues of his eyes. She didn't give him time to speak. "You cannot mean to do this."

"You will na be given a choice, Katherine. It will do na good to argue."

"Do you know what will happen if you go through with this ridiculous plan of yours? Every Ferguson in Scotland will pay for your foolishness, plus every Scot that gets in Bolton's way."

"It's already too late. It was too late the moment Bolton attacked Lochmore Castle and killed its laird and his family. Bolton is already an enemy of every Ferguson in Scotland. There is na one of them who will na gladly give his life to see Bolton die."

"But how many of them will give their lives to protect his betrothed? An English woman."

"They will if you belong to me."

"Katherine cannot belong to you, Lord Ferguson," Elizabeth interrupted. "She is betrothed to William Bolton."

"Quiet, lass," Ian whispered, placing his hand around his wife's shoulder and pulling her closer to him.

"But the king has ordered it," Elizabeth argued.

"I do na think Duncan cares much what your king has ordered," Ian countered.

"Your husband is right, milady," Duncan answered, never once dropping his gaze from Katherine's face. "Your king's edict means naught to me."

"But it means much to me, my lord." Katherine's voice trembled with emotion. She couldn't believe he was serious about making her his wife. She had already decided what she would do when she was well enough to leave Kilgern Castle.

She did not plan to become William Bolton's wife. She had made that decision when Bolton had flayed her back with his whip. She would live out her days in a convent rather than marry such an animal. "If I choose not to follow my king's order to marry, it will be my decision, and my decision alone to disobey him. No one else will pay the consequences for what I do."

"What happens to William Bolton is na longer any concern of yours, milady. His fate was sealed when he stepped foot on Ferguson land. All you need concern yourself with is becoming my wife."

"It will not happen, my lord."

"It will happen. You will marry me."

"Why?"

The room hushed to a deafening silence. Not even the baby dared to whimper. Katherine stared at Duncan. She watched the muscles in his jaw tighten and bunch, dared him to speak the truth. "I would ask you why you wish to marry me, my lord? Is it because you have had a change of heart and now find the English less loathsome? Is taking an English wife now a less bitter draught to swallow than it was before you found out I was William Bolton's betrothed?"

His back stiffened and his hands tightened to white-knuckled fists.

"I thought not," she answered, daring him to respond. "Perhaps you feel an obligation to me for retrieving your precious medallion and marriage is in some way payment for what you feel you owe?"

His eyes narrowed and the muscles in his jaw worked with inflexible harshness.

She shook her head. "I thought that was not the reason either," she countered, the tone of her voice bitter. "Perhaps you would marry me for no other reason than because you think I have the crown, and you wish to take me away from William Bolton. You would do anything, even take an English as your wife, as revenge, because she was promised to the man who killed your family. Especially if you thought she possessed the crown."

His eyebrows arched high. Katherine could see her

words had affected him. "I would ask one more question, my lord. Even if I were to become this pawn you wish to make of me, are you sure you can live with English blood forever tainting the blood of every Ferguson from this day forward?"

No one moved. He didn't flinch as he glared at her. For just one small moment Katherine prayed he would deny her accusation; that he would assure her it didn't matter to him that she was English; that he didn't want her just because she had the crown.

The moment passed. He looked away from her and focused his gaze on Ian. "Find the priest. We will wed in one hour's time."

Katherine had to try one more time. "Your hatred for William Bolton is that great? You would sacrifice the lives of your people to keep me from him?"

"You do na know the half of what I would sacrifice, milady."

He turned his back and stormed from the hut.

The air she needed to breathe left with him and she leaned her head against the cold stone wall and closed her eyes. "I cannot marry him, Ian," she said, swallowing the lump in her throat. "I cannot let him use me to feed his hatred for Bolton." She didn't have the strength to look her sister's husband in the eye. She didn't want him to see the fear she couldn't hide.

"You must. He will na let Bolton have you."

"He only wants the crown."

"Aye, lass. He wants the crown. It's a matter of honor. His father died keeping the crown from Bolton, and Duncan will na rest until Bolton is dead and the crown is in Ferguson hands again."

Katherine closed her eyes to shut out the confusion that washed over her. "But I can never give him the crown. I vowed I would not."

"Leave that decision in God's hands, Katherine. He will show you what to do when the time comes. For now put your life in the Ferguson's hands. It's for the best."

Elizabeth rushed to Katherine's side and placed her arm around her shoulder. "It will be all right, Katherine. The Ferguson laird will not let anything happen to you."

"And how many of his people will die to make that so?"

"Every Ferguson will protect you," Ian said as if she should take comfort from that fact.

Katherine turned to face Ian. The tears that threatened to spill from her eyes were no longer of importance. "But is there a Ferguson who will accept me?"

The dark foreboding in Ian's eyes told her he didn't have an answer. She did not doubt that Duncan Ferguson would make whatever sacrifice was necessary to take her away from Bolton and keep the crown for Scotland. Marriage to her would assure him of both.

...

The MacIntyre priest fumbled with the open book in his hands. Katherine understood his discomfort. Even though the fire in the hearth blazed warmly, the air in the room was as cold as the Highland winters were reputed to be. The look on the face of the groom was not much warmer.

God help her. She did not know what to do.

The edict to marry Bolton had come from the king

himself. Yet, she could no more give herself to the man who had beaten her than she could give the crown to the Scot who had saved her.

Katherine bowed her head and prayed for the courage to refuse Duncan. She prayed for the courage to endure a life of seclusion if she was lucky enough to escape Bolton. She prayed for the strength to face her father's disappointment, no matter what her choice.

Katherine raised her head just as Duncan slammed his fist on the table.

"Enough!" he bellowed. Every person in the great hall jumped with a start. "We've wasted enough time, Father. We'll get this marriage over."

The priest rushed to stand on the dais before the window on the far side of the hall, and Ian took his place at Duncan's side. Elizabeth moved to the other side. Only the spot where the bride would stand was empty.

Katherine sat on a wooden chair before the fire and let the warmth seep through her body. She couldn't walk across the great hall and take her place at Duncan's side.

She turned her head away from him when he looked at her, and waited. He would come for her. She had no doubt that he would. Soon his massive frame stood before her. "Do na make this any harder than it need be, English."

She added a special plea for courage at the end of her prayer, then raised her head. The unyielding determination she saw caused her heart to jump in her breast. She steeled her shoulders and spoke with a bravado far greater than she felt. "I have decided I cannot marry you, Laird Ferguson."

Her statement brooked no reaction other than an arched lift to his brows. His voice showed no emotion other than a deadly hint of warning. "You would rather give yourself to Bolton?"

"I will not give myself to him, either. I have decided to seek sanctuary where Bolton cannot touch me."

His mouth lifted in a most mocking grin. "If the kiss we shared in the dungeon is any example of what you intend to deny yourself, Lady Katherine, you are hardly suited for a life of seclusion."

Katherine's cheeks burned as if he'd set them on fire. "That kiss was but the first mistake I made where you are concerned, my lord. I do not intend to add marriage to the growing list."

"Perhaps you think it would be more agreeable to share your kisses with Bolton. Mayhap the touch of his whip is not such a painful memory now?"

"Bolton will never touch me again," she hissed. "I will go where he cannot find me."

He crossed his arms across his chest and leveled her with his most penetrating glare. "There is no place on earth where you will be safe, English. Bolton will seek you out no matter where you go. Even your father will not be able to save you."

A cold hand gripped her heart. What if she failed? What if Bolton found her and forced her to marry him? As if she needed a reminder of Bolton's cruelty, every place on her back where Bolton's whip had torn her flesh burned. Katherine wiped her damp palms against the folds of her gown and wadded the material in her fists.

"Bolton is no longer your concern. I alone am responsible for whatever decisions I make. I alone will suffer the consequences."

His back stiffened. "You are wrong. Anything related to Bolton became my concern the minute the bastard crossed our border and took his sword to the first loyal Ferguson."

The Scot took one step closer until his legs almost touched her knees. His nearness forced Katherine to lift her head at an uncomfortable angle to gaze into his face.

"No matter how confident you are," he said, his voice a soft, deadly whisper, "you have neither the might nor the ability to protect yourself. We will wed so that I can protect you from Bolton."

She lifted her shoulders defiantly. "You wish us to wed so you can take the crown from me," she hissed. "That's the only reason you would take me as your wife."

He did not deny it. He clenched his teeth until the muscle in his jaw knotted. When he spoke, his deep voice rumbled in anger. "Do you think the walls of a convent can protect you when Bolton finds you? You've already experienced his cruelty. How long do you think you will survive when he finds you?"

Katherine felt the blood rush from her face. She was a fool if she thought she could protect herself from Bolton. She was a fool if she thought she wouldn't put those she sought refuge from in danger. But the Fergusons were already at war with Bolton. And the Fergusons would not rest until Bolton was dead.

"Choose, English, and do it now. I will not ask again. You can marry me, or you can sacrifice yourself to Bolton."

Katherine held still as stone for several long seconds, her gaze never leaving the penetrating glare in his eyes. The mind-numbing truth hit her with the force of a battering ram. She did not have the stomach to follow her king's edict. She did not have the courage to face Bolton on her own.

Katherine fisted her hands in the folds of her skirt to block out what her defiance would mean. She set her spine straight and matched his cold stare without flinching. "Then know this, Scot. It will never be as you wish. You will never possess the crown. I will not give it to you." She stood and faced him with more willfulness than his expression told her a woman should possess. She could see it in his eyes. "Nor will you ever possess my heart."

His lips pressed to form a thin, hard line. His hands fisted tight at his side. The anger she read was near the surface, hidden behind the hooded darkness in his eyes. His eyebrows raised in question. "Never is a long time, milady. As impossible to predict as tomorrow."

"Not in this, my lord." Katherine held her ground. She could not weaken. "You will never have what you want."

He stared at her a long time, his countenance darkening even more. A deafening silence stretched interminably between them, and when she could bear his scrutiny no longer, she lifted her chin and curved her lips into a humorless grin. "Has marriage to me lost its appeal, my lord? Is tainting the blood of every Ferguson from this day on too great a sacrifice to make?"

She sat down in her chair and relaxed against the back as if what he decided next did not matter to her one way or the other. "Now the choice is yours, my lord. Do you still want me, knowing you'll gain nothing from your ill-conceived bargain?"

The blazing fire crackled in the silence and she waited

for him to say the words that would end this farce. The words that would condemn her to an uncertain, perhaps even tortured existence.

She said a silent prayer that his decision and God's will would be one and the same. All the while, keeping her gaze locked onto the unreadable coldness in his eyes.

He pulled back his outstretched hand and folded his arms across his chest. Dear Lord, but he was intimidating. The dark scowl on his face did not show a hint of softness. She braced herself for his response.

He stood before her with his feet angled wide and his broad shoulders locked in place. Without emotion, he said, "Let us get this over."

She did not react other than to release the long breath she didn't realize she'd been holding. The Scot would marry her only so Bolton could not have her. And take her to live where she would never be accepted because she was English. He would take her as his wife to repay a debt.

He would take her because he wanted the crown.

Her only other choice was a lonely existence, hiding in fear that Bolton would find her.

If only she would not have kissed her Scot that first time. If only she would not have let him hold her in his arms and comfort her. If only she had not been so willing to trust him. She couldn't think of that now. She couldn't think of that ever again.

She stood at her chair and faced the man she would take as her husband. "There is one thing more, my lord."

He tilted his head and waited.

"You will never again from this day call me 'English.'"

"You are not proud that you are English?"

"I am not proud to be called it when you speak it. You say the word as if it were bile in your mouth. I would rather be nothing."

"You can be Scot."

"I will be nothing."

He nodded. "You will be my wife. From this day on, you will be my wife."

It was decided. She crossed the large room and stood beside him while the priest began the sacrament of holy marriage. Duncan's foreboding presence obviously made the poor man take notice. Katherine understood that. Even after all the hours he'd spent at her bedside, his dark, brooding dominance still affected her.

"Will you, Duncan Ferguson, laird of clan Ferguson, take the Lady Katherine Downing for your wife?"

"I will."

The priest breathed an audible sigh and rushed to his next question. "Will you, Lady Katherine Downing, take Duncan Ferguson, laird of clan Ferguson, for your husband?"

She could not answer. There was one more matter.

The silence seemed endless and uncomfortable. One or two of the Ferguson warriors cleared their throats. Elizabeth, turned to her, waiting for her answer. Ian turned to her.

Duncan turned to her.

She looked up and faced him. "The laird of clan Ferguson has not yet asked me if I would consent to be his wife."

A loud gasp came from Elizabeth. The priest wiped again at the perspiration on his forehead. Ian smiled.

Katherine looked again. Maybe she was mistaken and it wasn't a smile on Ian's face. Maybe it was only a reaction to the pleasant wish that he could wrap his hands around her neck and choke the air from her.

It was the same look she saw on Duncan's face when she looked up at him.

The incredulous expression on his face did not hide his mounting frustration. "You are sorely testing me, woman," he said through clenched teeth.

"I need to be asked, my lord. It's important to me."

For a long time, he said nothing.

She must be asked. When her father came for her, he needed to know that she had not been forced, but had given herself willingly. It might save the Scot's life in the end.

No one in the great hall moved while they waited for the Ferguson to react. She could hear the murmurs behind her as they anticipated his response.

"I would ask you, Lady Katherine Downing. Will you consent to become my wife?"

Katherine closed her eyes and swallowed hard. "I will."

The priest quickly pronounced them man and wife, then wiped at his forehead again.

Katherine turned around with her husband at her side. The Ferguson men Duncan had not sent back to Lochmore stood before their laird, the warrior Angus in the front. There was not a happy face amongst them. Not one.

Even Angus, the Scot who had cared for her, wore a mask of resigned acceptance. Katherine read the sadness in his eyes. The regret.

Angus stepped forward and placed a fist over his heart. "We pledge to you our loyalty, Lady Ferguson. Know that we will protect you with our lives from this day on."

Every Ferguson there placed his clenched fist over his heart, and Katherine bowed her head as she accepted their oath of protection. For that was what it was. All it would ever be. No welcome; no congratulations; no wishes for a long life filled with happiness and the blessing of many Ferguson heirs.

They had promised to protect her, but nothing more. She would be given nothing else. She would never ask for more.

. . .

Duncan checked the saddles on their horses again and waited for his wife to come. She was such a confusion to him. What did she think she would do if he didn't marry her? Fight Bolton on her own and defend the crown from all of Scotland?

He leaned his arm on the saddle and paused for a moment. It was the first time he'd allowed himself to think about his decision to marry her. Damn her willful stubbornness. Her accusations refused to go away. Her vow that she would give him neither the crown or her heart echoed in his head.

No matter how hard he tried, he could not deny he was using her as revenge, but…

In time he would win her trust. He had to. Her trust was the key to gaining the crown.

The fact that she understood exactly why he had taken her as his bride did not give him comfort. He wasn't sure he was pleased his new wife possessed such keen perception. But he'd be damned if he'd let Bolton touch her ever again. How could he let her go after she'd sacrificed so much to give him back the Ferguson medallion? How could he let her go, knowing what her future would hold? How could he let her go, knowing she had the crown?

He pulled on the strap and walked over to the horse she would ride to do the same.

"If you cinch those straps any tighter, Duncan, neither of your horses will have enough air to walk as far as the drawbridge," Ian said.

Duncan looked down at the strap drawn far too tight and loosened it. Then he walked around Ian to loosen the strap on the other horse. "Is my wife almost ready?" Duncan asked, checking the steps to the keep and finding that she still had not emerged.

"Almost, I think, Duncan. She went into the chapel again to pray. Elizabeth went in to get her."

"If hours spent in prayer give her an advantage, Ian, I fear I do na stand a chance."

Ian smiled a broad grin. "You worry your fair wife is enlisting God's help against you?"

Duncan picked up a smooth, round stone from the ground and turned it over in his hand while he checked the steps again. "I doubt she is praying for my good health and fortune."

Ian laughed out loud. "She is indeed a verra brave lass, Duncan. I'm glad. She'll need more than her strong will to secure a place in your keep."

Duncan laughed a shocked burst of disbelief. "That I would like to see. She will na doubt walk in and demand it. Instead of only sending word that I had married, I should have sent a warning for the Fergusons to prepare themselves to be invaded by one small, infuriating female."

Ian clasped his hand around Duncan's forearm, his penetrating gaze filled with warning. "Do not only see the bravery she shows on the outside. Katherine can be hurt, Duncan. On the inside, where she's most vulnerable. I fear it will na be easy for her to live among so many Fergusons."

Duncan hurled the stone in his hand to the dirt. "Do na fear for her, Ian. The lass I married has a will of iron. Nothing will be much of a challenge to her."

"Do you really think that?" Ian asked, frowning openly at his friend. "There's hardly a Ferguson at Lochmore who did na lose someone when Bolton came. There's hardly a Ferguson who will na question why their laird chose an English for their mistress. Including the laird, himself, I fear."

Duncan rebuffed Ian's comment with a hostile glare aimed at his friend. "Do not fear for her, Ian. In time my people will forget she's English."

"Perhaps when their laird does, they will also."

The truth of Ian's words seared his flesh like a hot poker in an open wound. By all that's holy, he'd married his mortal enemy in retaliation against Bolton, and to ensure that Scotland would keep the crown. The crown his father had died to protect. God's blood. He'd sacrificed it all. There would never be a pure Scottish Ferguson from this day on.

Duncan looked to the top of the steps again, his blood boiling hotter when he did not see his wife standing there. By the saints, she was testing his patience.

Ian ignored Duncan's temperament and walked to the

side of Katherine's horse, pretending to check the blankets tied behind the saddle. "What will you do about Regan?"

Duncan looked at him in surprise. "There is naught to do about her. I've never spoken of love or suggested I would take her for my wife. She'll accept her new mistress the same as every other Ferguson."

"Be careful, Duncan. She will na take your news lightly. There's something about your pretty Regan that gives me cause to fear. She has always thought you belonged to her. She may not give you up so easily."

"You worry for naught. Regan has always been there and has been more than willing, but we have never talked of marriage. She knows I do na love her."

"Let's hope so."

The frown did not leave Ian's face, but Duncan didn't have the time or the patience to worry about that now. They needed to be on their way.

He turned back to the steps of the castle. Katherine and her sister stood at the top. She was finally ready. He watched his wife hold the baby close to her then take her sister into her arms again. He knew it was impossible to see so much from this distance, but for a moment he imagined he saw the sun glisten off tears in her eyes.

"See how your wife mothers those around her," Ian said, watching Katherine care for his wife and son. "I'm glad she will live so close. They'll both be a great comfort to each other."

Duncan watched as Katherine walked with Elizabeth, talking the entire way, as if she were giving her instructions to be carried out until they met again. He had no doubts that she would issue her first command within minutes of entering his keep. It was her nature.

Ian held the horses' reins for him. "Go with care, Duncan. Are you sure you would na prefer to spend the night and leave in the morning?"

"Nay, Ian. 'Tis best we leave now. We'll set up camp as soon as we cross onto Ferguson land, then get up early in the morning and ride to Lochmore. I do na want my bride to reach her new home exhausted and in the dark."

Ian nodded then clasped his hand on Duncan's shoulder. "God's speed, friend. I will pray for the best."

"I sent Gregor home with word that I had wed. By nightfall, all should know there's a new mistress."

Ian nodded then reached to take his son from his wife's arms when they neared the horses. Duncan helped Katherine atop her horse, then mounted himself.

"Goodbye, Lady Ferguson," Ian said, clasping Katherine's hands between his own. "God keep you safe." He turned to Duncan. "I'll be waiting for word when you ride to England. We'll bring your Brenna home to you. Do na fear."

Duncan nodded, then turned his mount and rode toward the drawbridge. He kept his pace slow until his wife was at his side, giving his men time to position themselves on all sides. He didn't expect trouble yet. It was too early for Bolton to have heard that he had stolen his betrothed, but it didn't hurt to be cautious. The time would come when he would answer for his actions. Bolton would not let Duncan's insult go unanswered.

The blood rushed through his veins in anticipation of meeting Bolton again. The bastard did not deserve to live.

Chapter 5

Katherine pulled the Ferguson plaid closer around her shoulders. She stuffed her hands deeper into the folds of her gown, hoping to keep them warm. She most likely didn't have to worry whether or not Duncan's clan would accept her. She would probably freeze to death before they crossed the border onto Ferguson land.

At least a half dozen clansmen rode ahead of them on their way to Lochmore castle, and that many behind. The remaining warriors flanked them on either side, and no matter how hard she tried, she could not keep from staring at them. There was an early fall chill in the air, yet not one of them wore anything warmer than the funny little skirt she'd seen on every male from the minute she'd arrived in Scotland, and a loose, flowing shirt with the Ferguson tartan draped over his left shoulder. Even her husband seemed oblivious to the chill.

He rode with a proud lift to his head, the unyielding set to his jaw emphasizing his determination. His dark hair waved back from the rugged features of his face, touching the top of his collar in a fashion slightly shorter than how most of the other Ferguson clan wore theirs. Katherine moved her gaze to the corded muscles on his bronzed forearms. He'd rolled the sleeves of his snow white, linen shirt up to nearly his elbows, the strength he displayed a vague reminder of being held in his arms. The corded muscles of his calves and thighs were even more impressive. There was not a soft spot on his entire body.

A heavy sword rested in a scabbard behind his back, and a smaller sword hung from a belt at his waist. Katherine doubted he would hesitate to use both of them to fight any stranger who dared come near them. She did not doubt he would take an enemy's life without a second thought. The knowledge was strangely calming. Wasn't that one of the reasons she had agreed to marry him? Because she'd been too cowardly to face Bolton on her own.

She brushed such glaring truths aside with a pang of guilt. The disappointed look she knew she would see on her father's face when he found out she had married her Scot loomed before her.

She braved another look at her husband. So far, he had not spoken a word. They'd ridden through meadows arrayed with the purple flowers of heather in full bloom. Then, up gentle, flowing hillsides bedecked with poppies of red and white. To avoid coming too close to where any English could be hiding to ambush them, they'd stayed in the open, skirting groves of gigantic trees that seemed to reach nearly to the sky.

Katherine shifted atop her horse, stretching the places on her back where a few of the deeper scars had not yet completely healed. Her body ached from riding so long. This, too, was the fault of the overprotective Ferguson.

She did not have the stamina she needed to ride so long.

She rolled her shoulders, working out the knot at the base of her neck. As she turned her head, her gaze fell on the man riding beside her. She stiffened when she realized he was watching her.

"Are you tired?"

"No," she lied. She'd rather every limb on her body fell off than let him know she was exhausted. "I simply needed to move."

Katherine could not keep her gaze fixed on him too long. The expressions on his face were too disturbing. Anger. Frustration. Disappointment. These were blatant. Others were more deeply concealed. As if he needed this time in the wide open spaces of the Scottish countryside to come to terms with what he'd done.

"Is the weather always so cold this early? It's not even fall yet" she said, searching for something to say.

He raised his brows. "You think it cold?"

"Yes."

He took the Ferguson tartan from around him and handed it to her. "I fear our Scottish winters will be verra long for you, woman. We'll have to sacrifice many trees just to keep you warm."

She wrapped the tartan around her shoulders and buried her hands in the folds of the material. The thick wool was warm from his body, and when she brought the plaid to her face, she could smell him as if she had her face buried against his chest. Her body shuddered as she thought of being close to him, and she pushed the thought away as quickly as she could. "Are we almost there?" she said, needing to occupy her mind.

He answered without looking. "Nay. We will na be home until tomorrow."

Katherine couldn't hide her surprise, nor her unease. "Your keep is that far away from Ian and Elizabeth? But I thought you lived nearby. I thought it would not take too long to travel back and forth,"

"It is na that far. The journey can be made in half a day, easy."

"Then why will we not arrive until tomorrow?"

"We have na traveled the shortest route. It would lead us through too many dense forests. Too many places where the English could hide. And I do na want to travel at night. Besides, you should see your new home the first time in the daylight."

"Are you worried I'll be disappointed?"

Duncan's mouth turned upward in an unreadable grin. "I do na think you'll be disappointed, woman. It's a grand castle and my mother made it a grand home for her family."

Katherine had another question to ask. A question with which she hoped her husband would not take offense. "Duncan, is your clan very poor?"

He shot her a hard glance. She had no trouble interpreting this look. "Are you worried you will na have enough fine clothes to wear?"

She rolled her eyes, lifting them heavenward. "No. I do not overly care for fine clothes."

"Then why do you worry I am poor?"

She looked around her. "Some of your men are without shoes. Surely, as their laird, you're obligated to provide each man with a pair of shoes. When we get to your castle, you must see to that immediately."

Katherine looked over to him to emphasize her demand and the sigh of exasperation he breathed puzzled her as much as the look on his face.

"You have much to learn, *English*," he said, and the frown on his face told her he found her quite lacking.

She stiffened, not only at what he'd said, but at what he'd called her. She made sure by her look that he knew it. "I asked you not to call me that," she hissed, refusing to drop her glare from the amused look in his eyes.

He lifted his brows. "Aye, you did. I meant…You have much to learn, Kate."

She narrowed her glare. "My name is not Kate, either. No one calls me that."

"No one in England, you mean. You are a Ferguson now. I will call you Kate."

She closed her mouth. It would do little good to argue with him, a fact she was learning rapidly. Besides, perhaps he would forget the name if she ignored it. Or, perhaps she did not mind being called Kate when he said the word.

Her husband moved his gaze to a small glade surrounded by a dense forest of trees. "We will sleep there."

"There? But there's no shelter. Isn't it too cold to sleep out of doors?"

"The men are used to it, and I will make sure you do na feel the cold this night."

An icy shiver twisted its way down Katherine's spine. The violent tremor that shook her had nothing to do with the temperature.

"But surely you don't intend—"

The scowl on his face deepened. "Enough. It was na my preference to sleep out of doors this night, but we did not leave Kilgern as early as I had intended."

She stiffened in surprise. "Are you saying that was my fault?"

"I was not the one who held up the wedding with such a display of stubbornness. Or spent such a long time in prayer after giving my vows." His voice turned hollow and cold. "Were you praying, mayhaps, for a miracle to release you from your vows?"

She turned an icy glare on him and braced a fist against her waist in defiance. "Perhaps if you had given me time to accustom myself to the idea of marrying you, instead of simply demanding that I do so, I would not have taken so long. I was not the one who refused to wait even one day to marry. And I was not the one who bellowed so loudly that even the poor priest couldn't remember half his words."

Katherine gave him as condescending a look as she could muster. "Were you afraid, *mayhaps*, that if you would have had time to think about your vows, you would not have had the courage to say them?"

"It was na courage I needed to say the words, wife, but courage I will need every day for the rest of my life to live with the vows I have given."

His words hit their mark with the accuracy of an arrow fired by an expert bowman. They sliced through the tough barrier she'd erected to protect herself and struck where she was the weakest. The ache in her chest told her so. "You cannot say I didn't warn you that marriage to me would not be as you hoped. I told you what to expect before I said the vows and you cannot demand that I change now."

"Not all you told me can stay as you wish. The day will come when you will have to decide what you will do with the crown, Kate."

"And when I will not give it to you, will I have served my purpose? Will I no longer be of use to you?"

"In time you will realize how important the crown is to me. And to Scotland."

Katherine shook her head. "It will never be," she whispered, not certain she'd spoken the words loud enough to be heard.

"I have made you my wife. For now, we will be content with that."

She slowly lifted her gaze. "Can you be content with it?"

"I will learn to be. Even though you are English."

She dismissed her husband with a turn of her head, concentrating on a small stream babbling in the distance.

. . .

It didn't take long for them to reach the open glade beside the stream where Duncan intended to spend the night. Not nearly long enough for Katherine. She had spent the last hour mulling over the open honesty of the Ferguson's words. No matter how hard she tried to convince herself his not-so-subtle meaning didn't hurt, she could not. He would never forget that she was English. He would never have married her except for one reason. She had the crown.

Katherine pulled her horse to a halt when Duncan stopped, and looked down to the ground. She didn't want him to help her from her horse. She didn't want him anywhere near her, but, by the saints, it was a long way to the ground.

She looked again, then slipped her foot into the strap to lower herself. She slid down the side of the horse, stretching her leg as far as she could reach, praying her toes would hit something solid soon, but they didn't. She had no choice but to let go, and hope her wobbly legs would support her when she landed.

Just as she loosened her grip on the leather saddle, Duncan's strong hands clamped around her waist from behind. He lowered her with a jolt, and turned her until she faced him. "Such impatience could land you in a heap on the ground, milady."

"I am perfectly capable of taking care of myself, my lord," she answered, pushing at his arms around her middle. She didn't want to be this close to him. She pushed again. Harder.

He released her. This time when her legs buckled beneath her, she had the foresight to reach out to something other than his rock solid body for support. Unfortunately, the only thing within arm's distance was her horse. Although holding onto the mare was, in some respects, safer than being held by her Scot, the horse was not nearly as steady. The mare shied to the side as soon as Katherine leaned against her and she again felt Duncan's arms clamp around her.

With one arm, he held her around the waist, and with his other, he lifted her chin with his finger. When he spoke, his face was so close she could feel his warm breath against her cheek. "I think if you will but ignore that stubborn side to your nature, wife, you'll see how enjoyable it is to let me take care of you. Is that not one of the reasons you chose to marry me?"

A cold chill raced up her spine. "If I live to be one hundred years old," she hissed through clenched teeth, "I will never need you to take care of me. And for the life of me," she said, twisting out of his grasp, "I cannot fathom why I thought I must marry you. I must have been a true lackwit. Would that I could go back and undo my mistake."

His mouth turned upward in a mocking grin. "Not a lackwit, milady. The thought of Bolton as your husband frightened you more than having a Scot share your bed. 'Tis not a good sign, though, when you regret your decision on the same day as your wedding."

Katherine couldn't let him stand this close to her. The effect he had on her confused her as much as her inability to keep from marrying him.

She turned and walked away from him. Her legs wobbled unsteadily beneath her but she kept moving across the clearing until she reached the trunk of a tree she could lean against. She anchored one hand against the rough bark and lowered her head until her warm forehead rested against her forearm. By the saints, she was tired. Weary and exhausted and... alone.

"Wife."

Every muscle in her body froze. She hadn't heard him follow her. Katherine lifted her head and slowly turned around. He stood beside her with a small bundle.

"Here is a cloth, soap, and a brush for your hair. You can wash in the stream. Go as far as the edge of the clearing, but do na step out of my sight."

Katherine stared at him, unable to hide the shocked look on her face. "I will have my privacy, my lord. Your men are just on the other side of the clearing."

"They will na bother you, Kate, and I canna protect you if I canna see you. Do na go far into the trees. It's too dangerous."

He shoved the bundle into her hands and turned his back on her as if expecting her to obey his orders without question. He walked to where the other Fergusons were already setting camp and lighting a fire. Katherine glared at his uncompromising back, then slapped the soft bundle against her thigh before storming in the direction of the stream. And the trees. Let him concern himself with his men and leave her alone. She'd not allow him to tell her where she could go.

She stomped through the thick underbrush of the open glade until she reached the water's edge. Sweet Mary, he was a frustration. Her head pounded from his demands, and every muscle in her body ached from being jostled on a horse all afternoon. To make matters worse, the sun had begun its decline and the temperature was beginning to cool. She couldn't make her body stop shivering.

She reluctantly removed the black, red, and gold tartan Duncan had given her from across her shoulders and laid it on the ground beside the water.

The colors of clan Ferguson.

She stared at the plaid. These were her colors now. She had taken them freely and willingly. She rubbed her hands against her eyes. If only she had been brave enough to walk away from her Scot. Then she would not be wondering how she would get the crown out of Scotland, and to her father in England.

Katherine unwrapped the bundle and took out the cloth and soap with which to wash, and dipped them in the stream. The freezing water made her fingers tingle and burn, but she hardly noticed. She had other more pressing problems to face. Including her first night alone with her husband.

She looked over her shoulder. Even though Duncan was busy helping his men prepare camp, she knew he watched her every move. He issued orders, gave commands, and moved among his men with the ease and dignity of a respected laird. It was obvious that those he led held him in high regard.

Katherine focused her gaze on the Fergusons building fires and preparing for the night. How many of them would not come back from their battle when Bolton came to get her? How many of them would die to protect her, only because she had not had the courage to follow her king's edict and marry Bolton?

A weight of guilt pummeled the hollow pit of her stomach. She absently washed her face and the back of her neck, then scrubbed as much of her exposed flesh as she could modestly reach. But she felt no cleaner. No matter which Ferguson's face flashed before her, she knew their sacrifice would be greater than her own.

She finished bathing, then took a dry cloth and rubbed her skin. She raked fingers numb from the cold through her hair before weaving it into the thick plait she wore each night. Perhaps even her Scot would sacrifice his life for her. She clamped her teeth against her bottom lip to stop its trembling. His death would leave her alone to fight not only Bolton, but the Fergusons who would blame her for their laird's death.

Such a thought was mind numbing. She bolted to her

feet and swiftly moved toward the shelter of a thick grove of trees. She needed to be alone. She needed to be away from her husband's watchful glare, from the cold stares of his men.

...

Duncan appointed six men to take the first watch, then collected some bread, cheese, and ale for his wife's evening meal. He took extra blankets, knowing how chilled she was already, and enough wood to build a warm fire in the narrow cave where they would spend the night. He looked again at her small form kneeling by the stream and a heated warmth rushed through him.

By the saints, she was beautiful. But what drew him to her even more than her fair features and sharp wit and keen intelligence, was her willful nature. The fiery depths of her deep azure eyes when her stubborn English pride bristled. The rigid set of her upturned nose and the lift of her proud chin when she readied herself to battle him. The tight line of her full lips when she showed her anger to him. These were all the things he'd come to admire in her. Ian had no cause to fear. She would do well among his Scots.

Duncan breathed a sigh of satisfaction. She would do well as his wife, too. If he could teach her a modicum of obedience. If she would learn to exhibit even a small degree of acquiescence.

He walked to the cave in the rocks and set all but the wood on the ground beside the entrance. He cast a glance in her direction. You would think she would understand why he didn't want her to leave his sight. You would think she would appreciate that he did not want to chance that something might happen to her. Instead, she'd pounced on him as if he'd demanded the impossible.

He cast another glance to where she still knelt beside the stream, raking her fingers through her hair. The sun just setting below the earth bathed her long, golden tresses in a myriad of fiery shades, more exquisite than anything he'd ever seen. When she tossed her hair over her shoulder and let it hang down her back, its length nearly touched the ground where she knelt.

He felt his body grow heavy with desire. Bloody hell. With an impatient sigh, he ducked into the dark cave to start his fire, sure that his English bride would be chilled when she came back.

It didn't take him but a little time to light the fire and arrange the thick branches he'd left outside the cave entrance to be used for their bed. Duncan placed a warm wool blanket atop the soft pine branches and smiled at his handiwork. He stepped out of the cave, anticipating the pleased look on her face when she saw what he'd done.

He looked up. The place where she'd been beside the stream was vacant. She was gone.

Duncan turned his gaze, first to the water's edge near the wall of rocks, then to the dense forest on the other side. His heart skipped a beat. If she'd gone far into the trees, she might be lost. Bolton's men may have been in hiding, and taken her.

Duncan's long, purposeful strides covered the ground leading to the stream. The first wave of fear fired through his body. He successfully released it in the form of anger.

By the saints. He'd told her to stay where he could see her. She'd deliberately disobeyed him. She'd intentionally done what she pleased.

Duncan stopped where she'd been. His tartan lay in the grass beside the stream, along with the cloth and soap. She'd be more than chilled by now. He knew without a doubt that she'd defied his order to stay in the open to prove her independence. His anger — and fear — hitched upward another notch.

He cast a concerned look at the setting sun. The light would not last much longer. Not long enough to search for her if she'd gone too deep into the forest. He picked up the plaid from the ground and quickened his pace.

"Kate," he yelled, hearing his voice echo back to him. "Kate!"

He walked deeper through the trees, following the stream. Surely she would not have strayed from the water. He called her name again, and heard no answer. When he thought his best course may be to go back for his men to help in the search, he saw her.

A strange emotion raged through him, whether anger or relief he did not stop to evaluate. He preferred not to know. He walked over to her, debating whether he wanted to hold her, or shake her. He muttered a curse, and clamped his hands behind his back to keep from doing either.

...

Katherine sat huddled beneath a huge pine tree, her legs tucked close to her chest, her cheek resting on her knees. She'd often escaped to a similar place near her home in England when she needed to think, when she longed for someplace quiet and peaceful, where the problems before her didn't seem quite so monumental. Where the beauty around her didn't make her feel so alone.

She tightened her arms around her knees and squeezed her eyes shut. She was married to the Scot not even half a day and already she'd shown him the defiant side to her nature. Already, she'd given him reason to regret taking her as his wife.

Her father had told her over and over that she was too strong willed and rebellious. He'd tried to break her of her curse, but no matter what he'd done, it had not helped. Her independent nature ruled her actions at every turn. No doubt, her husband would try to cure such willful disobedience too.

She shuddered at the thought, at what means her husband would use to teach her submission. She knew, however, that she would soon find out.

She didn't know exactly how long he'd stood beside her, his towering shadow a consuming blanket of darkness, but it must have been more than just a little while.

She knew, without looking, that he was furious with her. She could feel his anger. He stood with his legs braced far apart, with his hands clasped behind his back, and his shoulders stretched to an unbelievable width. She tilted her gaze upward, looking at the stern expression on his face, confirming the anger she'd only felt — until now.

He impaled her with an icy glare. "Did you na hear me ask you to stay in the open, wife?"

The hard, unyielding tone to his voice sent a shiver of warning down her spine. "Yes, but I needed my privacy, my lord." She lifted her chin in defiance. "And your command did not come out as a request."

"You would have followed it if I had requested you to

do so?"

She shook her head. "I could not. I told you so."

His hands fisted at his side. "You are sorely testing me, woman," he said through clenched teeth. "I am na used to having my orders disobeyed."

"I know." Katherine sat straight and rubbed her hands up and down her arms. "I've never been good at following orders. My father would be the first to tell you so."

She heard the hiss of his breath. For some reason, she felt the need to defend herself. "I needed to be by myself," she announced, hoping her chattering teeth hadn't affected the impact of her words. She rubbed her arms again to warm her flesh.

He didn't answer. He only lifted his eyes heavenward as if the patience he needed to understand her was hidden somewhere in the clouds. "Here," he said, handing her the Ferguson tartan she'd left beside the stream. "Put this around you before you freeze to death and I have only a frozen corpse to take home with me. In time, you will come to enjoy our cool, crisp evenings."

She put the warm woolen rectangle around her shoulders. "Your evenings are not cool, my lord. They're freezing." She tried hard to keep her teeth from chattering.

"You have na seen freezing yet, Kate."

"I cannot wait," she muttered beneath her breath.

She ignored his whispered oath and pulled the soft wool fabric closer.

"Have you had enough privacy, milady, or do you wish to shiver on the cold ground a while longer?"

She looked up at him, his arm already extended as if giving her no choice but to come with him. She hesitated, then reached for his hand, letting him help her to her feet.

"I've prepared a pleasant spot with a warm fire and our food already waiting," he said as he led her back through the trees to the place near the stream where the rocks spiked far above them.

Katherine walked at his side, huddling into the soft wool in an effort to ward off the chill. It was truly a beautiful place. Trees towered on one side, a stream bubbled past them on the other, and a wall of stone created a fortress on a third. There was no way Bolton, or any intruders, could encroach without being heard or seen. It was no wonder he had chosen it.

They walked along the wall of rocks, his hand resting lightly at the small of her back, sending heated pulses from the top of her head to the tips of her toes. She loved the feel of him against her, had from the first time she'd gone to him in the dungeon.

Suddenly, they came to a small opening in the rocks and he urged her ahead of him. Before she could stop her forward movement, he ushered her through the entrance, into a small, narrow room in a dark cave, where they were to spend the night.

Even though a warm, inviting fire blazed before them, there was not enough light for her to see, nor enough room for her to breathe. If the cave had been ten times wider, there still would not have been enough room for her to breathe. From little on, she had not been able to abide such small spaces.

She gasped for air, her chest heaving as it struggled to get the air it needed. *Out.* She needed to escape the small confines of the cave.

She pushed at the hands that held her, clawing until he freed her, then rushed out of the opening and fell to her knees with relief. Her body, which had been so cold only minutes before, now burned with fire. She wiped at the perspiration on her forehead, then wrapped her arms around her middle and rocked back and forth to ease her trembling.

"What is it, Kate?"

She heard him ask the question, but couldn't make her mouth form the words to answer. How could she explain such a weakness? Saints preserve her. She had prayed he would never find out.

Now he would not want her for sure.

"What's wrong, wife?"

"Nothing."

"I can see it's nothing."

He stood before her with his arms crossed over his chest as if he needed to hold them down so they would not strike out at something. She saw his stance out of the corner of her eye and breathed a shuddering sigh. She felt weak, lacking. She knew he saw her the same. "Must you stare at me like that, my lord?"

"Like how?"

"Like you're ready to slay some unseen enemy."

He dropped his hands to his side and stepped in front of her. "What is it you fear, Kate?"

"Nothing. It's nothing."

She lowered her face to her hands. How could she explain it to him? He would think her such a fool. "I only wish to sleep out of doors tonight."

"But it would be warmer—"

"I cannot go back in there." She wrapped her arms closer around her middle.

"Verra well. I will move the blankets and the fire out here under a tree. We will find shelter beneath the stars."

Katherine watched as he moved everything from the cave to the open. He laid the wool blanket atop the branches for their bed and started a new fire, then placed the food he'd wrapped in a cloth nearby. Finally, she had calmed enough to help.

She opened the cloth and laid out the cheese and bread, then poured ale into the only cup that was there.

"Are you aright now?"

She lowered her head.

He silently knelt beside her and waited while she cut a slab of the dark cheese with the dagger that hung from the belt at her side. Their gazes met when she handed him the cheese and a hunk of bread, but he brooked no further questions. They ate in silence, making a meal of what he'd brought, and sharing ale from the same cup.

When they finished, Katherine packed the leftover food and wrapped it in the cloth, and Duncan placed more wood on the fire.

"We will sleep now," he said, placing his scabbard on the ground beside where he intended to sleep. "It's been a long day."

Katherine looked at the bed of thick branches and the blanket he'd spread out on the ground. A lump caught in her throat. This was to be her marriage bed.

"Duncan, I—"

"Go to sleep, wife. Tomorrow will be a long day for us both."

He walked toward his men, leaving her in the flickering shadows of the glowing fire. She watched his retreating back, following him until he was just an outline.

Her chest tightened painfully. He didn't want her.

She knelt beside the bed of branches and said her prayers. When she finished she crossed herself, then lay down.

By the saints, she was cold. Cold, and alone, and — lonely.

With a violent shudder, she curled into a tight ball atop her bed and pulled the woolen blankets under her chin. She stared ahead, watching as her Scot sat on a fallen log beside a blazing fire, talking with Angus and two other men she didn't recognize. With a snap of his powerful fingers, he broke off small bits of a thin branch and threw them, piece by piece, into the fire. There was an unmistakable meaning to his actions. Every snap of the twig an echo of what she saw clearly.

He would not come to her tonight.

Chapter 6

Duncan folded the blanket from what was to have been their marriage bed the night before while Katherine washed in the stream. He wasn't proud of the relief he felt when his wife had been unable to spend their wedding night in the cave and they were forced to sleep out of doors. How could he take the lass's virginity with his men sleeping so nearby? Except, that wasn't the only reason he hadn't made her his wife.

Duncan tossed the last of their belongings into a pile and kicked at the dirt around the fire. God's blood, he hadn't sealed their union because—

He swallowed past the bile rising in his throat. He hadn't been able to seal their union because she was English.

A hard knot fisted in his gut. His father's tall, powerful image flashed before him — strong of character, noble from birth, proud of his Scottish heritage. Would his father have understood his reasons for taking an English as his bride?

Surely the answer was yes. Surely his father would have

done the same.

He threw more dirt onto the smoldering logs, trying to forget the way his bride had refused to look him in the eyes when she'd awakened. Trying to stamp down the anger that simmered just below the surface. Wondering whether she was hurt because he'd been unable to sleep at her side last night. Or relieved.

He looked up as she came toward him. By the saints, she was a sight. She'd bound her hair in a netting of glimmering silver. He remembered how the golden tresses had cascaded to her waist last night in the moonlight. The silver trim on her white gown shimmered in the sunlight, and he couldn't stop his body from reacting to her.

He'd taken her as his bride to protect her from Bolton. Because she'd returned his medallion. And because she had the crown. He owed her. And he wanted what she had.

"How long will it take us to get to your home?" she asked, standing before him, that familiar look of regal confidence in her bearing. He doubted she knew the meaning of the word submission.

"We'll reach *our* home soon. I've sent someone ahead so they will know we're coming."

They walked to where his men waited, and one of his young cousins, Conan by name, came forward to take their bundles. Duncan noticed that Conan's disapproving gaze lingered a mite longer than he deemed necessary. It bothered him that the look on his cousin's face was not friendly, but he told himself it was to be expected. Once they got used to her, they would not see her only as English.

Angus came forward with their horses, his steel gray

eyes as focused and serious as always. "All is ready, Duncan. We should be home ere they set the midday meal on the trestle."

"It will na be soon enough, friend. It seems I've been away from my home a lifetime, and yet, I can na stay long this time either. We'll make our plans to go after Brenna in two weeks' time, whether the Kerrs have returned from Dumfries or nay."

"Your men are ready. Soon we'll have our Brenna back with us." With that, Angus turned to Katherine. "Is your back causing you pain?"

"No, Angus. You are the perfect healer. I could not have asked for better."

The old Scot smoothed a hand over his bushy white beard, a deepening blush darkening his ruddy complexion. The smile on Kate's face could have competed with that of an angel, so consuming was its effect, and Duncan saw a softening to the old man's crusty nature he'd never seen before.

"Take care, lass," Angus said, pointing a crooked finger in her direction. "You can na be too careful," he said, mounting his horse.

"Thank you, Angus. I will remember."

Duncan watched the man who'd been like a second father to him ride away. He couldn't remember ever seeing such a softness in the aging warrior's character before. "You seem to have found a soft side to Angus' nature," Duncan said, fastening the last of their blankets behind the saddle. "He's usually not so amiable."

"As compared to what, my lord? The rest of the Fergusons I've met?"

"You don't feel safe among my men?"

Katherine smiled a cynical grin. "Safety is not my concern, my lord. I've learned that your weather is not all that contains a chill."

"It will take them time, Kate. They do na know you, yet."

"They know enough. They know I'm English."

. . .

Katherine rode at the Ferguson's side as they neared Lochmore castle. Her new home.

She held her back straight, refusing to let thoughts of facing Duncan's people for the first time intimidate her. She took in huge breaths of the clean Scottish air, pretending it smelled of England. She looked at the trees, and the glens, and the hillsides of heather, and convinced herself it did not look so different from home. She closed her eyes and listened to the sounds of the countryside; the birds in the sky, the wind rustling through the leaves, and told herself it was the same breeze that would soon reach her home in England.

For a long time, they rode in silence, up one rolling hill, then another. Through meadows and glades, and across bubbling streams rushing noisily past them, then up a hill even steeper than the ones before. Without warning, Duncan stopped, his eyes riveted on a spot straight ahead. Katherine followed his gaze and stared in awe at the imposing fortress that sat high atop a ridge far in the distance.

Unlike many of the castles she'd seen on her way from England, Lochmore was made of stone rather than wood.

It was also bigger than most, daunting in size and design. Its formidable towers and walls seemed impregnable. It was Duncan's home.

Her home.

Two round towers built along the curtain wall with two three-story towers on either side of the gate boasted both dominance and strength. It was also the first castle she'd seen with a barbican to defend its entrance.

A small group of Ferguson warriors rode from the lowered drawbridge down the steep hill toward them. They were but small figures in the distance, yet Katherine could tell they were all big men. Especially the man in front.

She lifted her chin high. She would not cower before the Scots.

"Your warriors are coming to escort you safely home, my lord." She was glad her voice sounded calm. That was far from how she felt.

"My warriors have been keeping us safe for hours already."

Katherine looked around but saw nothing but trees and craggy hills and rolling meadows. "I do not see them."

"Nay, you can na. They do na wish to be seen."

Katherine looked around again then turned her attention to her husband. The breath caught in her throat. His steady gaze remained riveted on her, his dark look unreadable. Was he watching to study her reaction to his home? Or did the hooded expression on his face conceal a more soul-searching dilemma? "Regrets, husband? Has your rash decision to take an English wife finally come to haunt you?"

He stiffened, and Katherine tried not to let the darkened look in his eyes affect her. It did though. It made his shadowed glare a little more foreboding.

She kept her voice low, her tone casual, so none of the men beside them could hear her words. "Perhaps you can steal me into your castle under the cloak of darkness. I am sure there's a secret chamber where you can hide me where no Ferguson will ever see me. I wouldn't want to be a constant reminder to you or them that their laird sacrificed his honor or the Ferguson name to take an English bride."

His ebony eyes darkened even more, and Katherine thought perhaps she'd spoken out loud his secret thoughts.

"A sharp tongue does na do you credit, Kate. I've seen your bright wit and keen intelligence often, but never have you stooped to play the shrew."

She turned her face away from him and closed her eyes. He was right. She was no good at shrewish behavior.

Her uneasiness wrapped around her like a cloak. It was just that she felt so… alone.

Duncan didn't want her, but wanted the crown. Bolton didn't want her, but wanted the crown and her father's strong ties to the King of England. Duncan's people didn't want her, but wanted a Scottish lass for their laird's mistress.

Katherine tightened her fists around the reins and twisted until her horse skittered nervously beneath her. She would always be a reminder of the atrocities Bolton and his warriors had committed. In time, all would know she had been Bolton's betrothed, and that Duncan had taken her as his wife to feed his revenge against his enemy.

She would not let the Scots defeat her. She was English, and not even Duncan and his clan of Scottish Fergusons could make her forget it. She would stand tall before his people and force them to look hard for a reason to hate her. A reason other than that she was English.

She loosened her clenched hands and watched the group of warriors climb the rise to come near them. "Your men have raised the portcullis and lowered the drawbridge to welcome their laird. It's obvious they're glad to have you back."

"Aye. I've been gone a long time. It's good to be home."

He pushed his horse forward, and Katherine looked down a small slope, then up the second sharp incline to the crest of a high hill where the fortress stood. It seemed… unwelcoming.

She slapped the reins against her horse's flanks and followed behind him. Scores of men stepped out from behind the trees and joined them on the hillside. By the time they reached the crest of the first small hill, there were several hundred Ferguson clansmen surrounding them. The presence of this large an army of Scots riding to greet their laird made the goose flesh rise on her arms.

Duncan reined his horse to a stop and waited for the small group of riders from Lochmore Castle to reach them. A Scot almost as big as her husband, but with hair a lighter shade of brown, and eyes a paler hue, stopped alongside Duncan. The warrior's features were sharp, his nose as angular as Duncan's, his forehead as high and dominant, his face equally as handsome, but in a different sort of way. That is where the similarities ended.

The cut of his cheekbones was not nearly as sharp, the

slant of his jaw not nearly so rigid, and his features not nearly as rugged and defined. But there was still a distinct likeness to the undeniable strength that set Duncan apart as the laird of clan Ferguson, and that likeness made Katherine take note of his presence.

The Scot grasped his laird's forearm in greeting. He raised his sword high in the air and a thunderous roar erupted from the warriors surrounding them.

"Malcolm, this is my wife, Katherine. Kate, this is Malcolm, my friend and right hand in all things."

Katherine raised her shoulders and held her head high, refusing to bend before Malcolm's narrowing gaze.

The Scot put his hand over his heart and bowed his head. "Lady Katherine. Know always that I will guard and protect you with my very life. Just as I swore fealty to my laird when we returned to find his father slain, so do I now swear it to you, his wife and my mistress."

Katherine nodded in acceptance, then curved her lips to a slight smile. Every Ferguson clansman watched with great interest. Not a sound could be heard. Malcolm bowed his head in servitude, but did not return the smile. The gesture did not go unnoticed.

Katherine ignored the warmth that infused her cheeks and nodded in understanding. The line had been drawn.

Duncan was the first to move. He turned to Malcolm. "Ian said that you had done well in my absence to repair the damage done by the English. Is the castle secured and the cottages ready for winter?"

"With the aid of the men the MacIntyre laird left behind, we've repaired the outer bailey wall and the damage done to the front wall of the keep. All the cottages save four are habitable and even those should be ready by week's end."

"What of the lives lost?"

"There were twenty-eight in all, counting Kenneth's wee lass of two summers who was trampled by the English bastard's horse."

Katherine turned her head and tried to swallow past the lump in her throat. *A child.* A mother had lost her babe.

She focused on Duncan, expecting to see the black glare of revenge staring back at her. But he kept his eyes on Malcolm as if he'd forgotten she was there.

"What of food for winter and the weapons we'll need to go after Bolton?"

"We will pray that we do na have a harsh winter for food will na be plentiful this year, but we will have enough to survive. Bolton was in such a hurry to go after the crown that his men did na spend too much time plundering our supplies. They were more interested in searching for what was na here."

Katherine's stomach lurched and she noticed Duncan's hands tighten on the edge of his saddle until his knuckles turned white.

"What of our weapons?"

"Orin has worked day and night since Bolton left to make and repair what our men will need when we leave. He told me just today that if we rode out tomorrow not one of our warriors would lack a weapon to defend himself."

Katherine looked at the expression on her husband's face. It was hard, unyielding. An expression that was familiar to her.

Twice she braved a look at the strange faces around her. If any felt contempt for their laird's new wife, they hid it well. If any felt a warmth for her, they disguised that equally as well.

"Kate?"

Katherine jerked her attention back to Duncan with a start. "Yes, my lord?"

"Are you ready?"

Her mouth was dry. "Yes."

"I will show you your home."

She rode on Duncan's left while Malcolm rode on his right. Angus gave her a nod of confidence, then took his place behind them. Katherine kept her back stiff and her eyes fixed straight ahead as they climbed the steep rise to Lochmore castle. She twisted the reins around her fingers until her hands hurt.

The drumming of the two hundred or more Ferguson men and horses that thundered atop the wooden planks of the drawbridge did not deaden the pounding of her heart in her ears. She did not look at the crowd as they crossed the outer bailey. There were so many of them, and they stared at her as if, because she was English, she was the cause of their heartache.

They continued through the hundreds of Fergusons that crowded the inner bailey. When they reached the steps of the keep, Duncan dismounted, then lifted her from her horse. Katherine clamped her hands around his forearm and held onto him for a moment before she dropped her hands and stepped away. She could not rely on him to be the buffer between his people and his English wife. In this, as in everything that had happened to her since she'd come to Scotland, she was alone.

Four hundred Ferguson men, women, and children

had come to see their laird's English bride. She would show them she did not fear them. Katherine lifted her shoulders and faced them.

She held her head high and stared at the hostile faces before her. Each man, woman, and child wore an expression ranging from critical, to disapproving, to cold indifference.

She was English. She knew she should expect nothing less.

Duncan lifted his hand in the air and the Fergusons greeted their laird with a mighty roar. When the din quieted, he reached for her hand and held it up for all to see.

Another great roar echoed throughout the castle courtyard, and Katherine took a step closer to her husband. When the sound died, Duncan braced his feet and addressed his people in a loud voice that bespoke authority.

"I present to you my wife. She is na longer English, but is from this day on a Ferguson."

A loud roar went up and Katherine felt Duncan's hand reach for hers and entwine his fingers.

"Know you all that the Lady Katherine has found a place with me and her name will be written in the book beside mine for all time. From this day on, the Lady Katherine Ferguson will be the mistress of Lochmore castle."

Every soldier drew his sword and raised it high in the air, then another resounding roar filled the courtyard and echoed off the curtain wall.

Katherine bowed her head and bent her knees low.

Another cheer sounded. They didn't know. Just as Duncan had used her to get the crown, she had used him to escape marriage to Bolton, and now every Ferguson was in danger of losing his life.

When the roar of the crowd quieted, Duncan placed his arm around Katherine's shoulder and led her into the keep. Katherine stopped and stared in amazement at her new home.

The gigantic rooms were even larger than those at Kilgern castle. Katherine breathed a sigh of relief. Duncan was right. She would never fear the dark here, nor would she fear the walls closing in on her.

The great hall of Lochmore castle was built in a circle with three huge fireplaces set into the walls. Katherine smiled. Neither would she be cold. A balcony with many doors exiting into the stone lined the second level. Katherine assumed these each led to the chapel and the laird's private chambers. She wanted nothing more than to find solitude behind one of them, but instead, walked sedately at her husband's side.

"We have waited the midday meal for you, milord. The table is prepared."

Katherine turned around to face the gentle voice that had just spoken.

"Thank you, Morgana." Duncan smiled warmly at the woman nearing them. "Kate, this is Morgana. She has served the mistress at Lochmore castle as did her mother and her grandmother before her. She was my mother's handmaiden, and she will be yours. All you want or need, you will get from Morgana."

Morgana could not be much older than Katherine. She

smiled at the pretty blush that covered the maid's cheeks. When Morgana bowed her head and bent her knees before her new mistress, Katherine held out her hand and touched the handmaiden's shoulder. "I am pleased to have you at my side, Morgana."

Morgana graced her with a smile. Not a huge, open grin, but a small, sincere lift of her lips. A warm rush surged through Katherine's breast. A friendly face. The first friendly face she'd seen since she'd arrived. "I can see I shall want for nothing," Katherine said, smiling back. "May I learn well and stay true to all that has been before me."

There was a pleased look on the maid's face as well as the faces of everyone who had heard Katherine's words. "Would you like to eat your midday meal or see your new home first, milady?"

"You have waited the midday meal. We will eat first, then I will let you show me your laird's home."

Morgana smiled a bright smile. "Come, the food is ready." She led the way to the center of the long table and Duncan sat down with Katherine at his side. Malcolm sat at Duncan's right, and Angus next to Katherine. Gregor, Balfour, and twenty or thirty Ferguson warriors Katherine knew she had met, but whose names she could not remember, joined them.

The mood was festive, the talk lively, but more than once Katherine caught a sideways glance from one of the soldiers or from the women serving the table. The warrior to the far right shot her daggers whenever he looked at her. Perhaps he'd lost a son to the English.

The pretty little server who walked around the table to

refill the cups of ale fixed Katherine with a most hostile glare. Perhaps she'd lost her lover.

The robust woman who brought another platter of bread and cheese to the table paused, then watched Katherine with a hateful stare. Perhaps her home had been burned.

And the young man who sat across from her with the dark, smoldering look. Perhaps his name was Kenneth and it had been his little girl who had been trampled by the English horse.

Katherine did not want to know what went on behind their looks. Perhaps they knew she'd lacked the strength to follow her king's edict and fight Bolton on her own, and now had put them all in danger. She closed her eyes to block out their faces, but they were forever before her.

"You're not hungry, Kate?" The flat line of his voice spoke in a tone void of emotion. He asked his question between bites of food and without a glance in her direction.

"No, my lord. My stomach is not ready for food."

He reached for his cup of ale and slowly lifted it to his mouth. "'Tis best if you make an attempt to eat, lass, lest the women think you're not pleased with their offering."

Katherine raised her gaze to meet her husband's look of concern and stabbed a piece of roasted fowl and brought it to her mouth.

"A drink of ale will help, too." He reached for her cup and handed it to her.

When Katherine wrapped her fingers around the warm metal, he covered her hand and refused to release it for just a moment. Their gazes locked and a heated rush went down to her toes.

"You are safe, Kate."

Katherine could not find words to answer. She didn't worry about being safe. Every Ferguson she'd set eyes upon since she'd said her vows as their mistress had sworn to protect her with their lives. Safety was not a concern.

She closed her eyes and thought about the Ferguson she'd married. From the moment she'd kissed him in the dungeon, he had been the one she'd wanted to hold her. For the first time in her life, she'd met someone she could rely on. Someone who would take care of her.

She pushed the thought away as quickly as it appeared. She could never forget that he'd only chosen her for the crown.

She picked up a piece of meat with her fingers and lifted it to her mouth, then tasted the peas and the leeks and the pears cooked in a sweet sauce, showing as much enthusiasm as she could muster. Each mouthful lodged in her throat and refused to move. She shoved the food around on her platter, making a show of eating without actually doing so.

She did take a bite of the warm bread placed before her, and ate a piece of cheese. She sipped the ale while she listened to the talk of the men around her, but she did not look at them. She didn't want to see the expressions on their faces.

"When you've finished eating, Morgana will show you your chambers." His voice startled her. Duncan reached for another hunk of warm bread then smiled at the girl who refilled his cup with ale. But the smile faded from his face when he looked down at her.

"There is much that needs my attention here and will

keep me busy for the rest of the day. Morgana will answer any questions you may have."

"As you wish, my lord." She shoved her platter away from her and started to rise. Duncan covered her hand on the table. His massive palm warmed her flesh and the possessiveness of his touch sent a disturbing wave of hot liquid surging through her.

He'd not touched her often in the past two days. It was obvious having her as his wife was not as easy as he thought it would be. She could not imagine him experiencing the warmth of hot honey swirling deep in his belly when she touched him. She could not imagine her Scot wanting to hold her in his arms, or press his lips against hers. She could not imagine him wanting to… No, she could not. The way he reacted when she came close told her he did not. Her touch was obviously not such a pleasant experience.

"Come to me if you need anything, wife."

She met his determined stare. "I will not need you, husband." Katherine turned her attention toward Angus, sitting near. "Angus?"

"Yes, mistress?"

"Perhaps after I have seen my chambers, you will show me where you gather your herbs and potions. There is much you know that I would like to—"

"Nay."

Duncan's flat voice startled Katherine and everyone else surrounding them. All eyes turned toward him.

"There is na need for you to learn the potions, wife."

A wide chasm of silence separated Katherine from her Scot. The meaning behind his words a bed of contention. She bristled at his order.

"Is there someone else who knows your potions, Angus?" she asked, her question tinged with a hint of defiance. Every man at the table looked at their laird, then turned their gazes toward Angus.

"Nay, milady."

"Someone should. The day may come when knowing Angus' secret could be of benefit even to you, my lord." She glared at Duncan. He lifted his eyebrows and leveled her with a warning glare that cautioned her to give up. She didn't. "You never know when someone may need to save your bonny hide from the English."

Duncan leaned forward in his chair, grasping a cup of ale in his hand as if it were the hilt of his sword. "You will na bother Angus with your foolishness, Kate. That is all."

"But there is much I can learn from Angus, my lord."

"Enough!" Duncan leaned back in his chair and crossed his arms over his chest, showing the picture of rigid calmness and serenity. "There is na need, wife. If Angus feels he must pass on his mixtures and potions to someone younger, he will pick someone of his own choosing."

"Someone Scot?"

The air sparked with anger. She didn't want his warriors to see her rebellious nature, but she could not meekly submit. Not when no one knew the strength of Angus' healing powers.

For an eternity, she and Duncan locked gazes, neither willing to back down. Katherine slid her chair back from the table and rose. "Morgana," she said without lifting her gaze from Duncan's hostile glare. "I would see my laird's chambers now." She lifted the corners of her mouth in a cryptic grin. "Would that be to your liking, my lord?"

"Tread easy, Kate," he whispered in a voice she doubted anyone save Angus and Malcolm could hear.

The air left Katherine's breast. Why couldn't she be meek and docile? Why couldn't she have a temperament like Elizabeth's?

She suddenly feared she could never be the wife her Scot wanted.

With a proud lift to her chin, Katherine walked the length of the great hall, ignoring the deafening silence that surrounded her. She took each of the five stone steps leading to the exit with deliberate pomp, and stepped into the large entryway where Duncan and his men could no longer see her, then breathed a sigh of relief. There was a door on her right that led to the outdoors — to freedom. The stairs leading to the laird's private chambers on her left. She fought the urge to go right.

Morgana appeared at her side and Katherine looked to read the expression in her eyes. She saw nothing. Only the nondescript openness she'd seen when they'd first met. Morgana, at least, would not be judgmental.

Would that her Scot could be the same.

Chapter 7

For her entire lifetime, Katherine had struggled with her rebellious nature. Her father had punished her again and again so she would learn to curb her wayward tongue and keep her thoughts inside, but she had not learned. All the times he had locked her in the small, dark closet where she couldn't breathe, had done no good. He would have been disappointed again today.

She knew her Scot was disappointed in her. She didn't doubt that Duncan wasn't finished with his censure of her outspokenness.

But couldn't he see she was right?

Angus was no longer a young man, and no other Ferguson knew his remedies. There was a wealth of knowledge to be learned that could prevent the wounded from dying and the ill from suffering. Someone should know his secrets. It hurt that Duncan didn't want it to be her.

Katherine followed Morgana to the second level where the laird's chambers were. She could not dismiss Duncan's attitude. What did he expect her to do with her time? Stay in her chambers every day? Never be a part of life at

Lochmore castle?

No doubt he wished he could lock her away to keep from being reminded he'd taken an English wife. No doubt he preferred to keep her prisoner until she gave him the crown. No doubt he wished he'd never brought her here. Katherine fisted her hands at her side and wished his handsome face was close enough to hit. Well, he could wish for the moon before—

"Did you enjoy your meal, milady?"

Morgana's voice interrupted her thoughts and brought her back to the present. "Very much. I would like to thank the women who prepared the excellent food."

"They would like that," Morgana said, continuing down the long hall, past three closed doors, then to one that stood open. "This is the laird's chambers. It's where you will sleep."

Katherine stopped in front of the open door. "Is the chapel near?"

"Yes. The laird's mother wanted the chapel near her room. She was very devout and spent much time there."

"I will see the chapel first."

Morgana did not enter the laird's chamber, but instead went back to one of the closed doors at the end of the hall. From this point, Katherine could stand at the railing overlooking the great hall to see Duncan sitting at the table below. Angus and Malcolm sat beside him, and one by one, warriors and farmers and tradesmen came to him with their problems and concerns. A dispute over payment for a cow. A boundary disagreement between two farmers. An argument between two women over a rooster. Katherine watched as her husband listened to each petition, then issued a decision.

Next, a father with his sobbing daughter, demanding that the man responsible for the babe in his daughter's belly be required to give her his name.

Duncan listened carefully, then led the young warrior accused of fathering the child to the side of the great hall. She watched with great interest while her husband conferred with the lad. In the end, Duncan clasped his hand on the warrior's shoulder and spoke softly. She wondered what words he gave to the lad.

When they returned, the laird wore a resigned look. The lad kept his eyes lowered and walked to stand beside the girl. There would be a wedding tomorrow.

The judgment must have met with Angus's approval, for a slight smile covered his face, and he smoothed his weathered hand over his bushy white beard before he crossed his arms over his chest.

Katherine stepped back into the shadows. The man she'd married was not just any Scottish warrior. He was a Scottish laird. Born to make decisions. Born to take his rightful place as leader of clan Ferguson and rule with integrity and fairness.

A warm feeling swirled deep in her stomach. There were many facets to the man she'd married. Each revelation became yet another example of his quiet strength and gentle understanding. A reminder of her weaknesses. She was neither quiet, nor subservient. She remembered the argument she'd had with Duncan last night, and their argument just now in front of his men. Her cheeks grew warm as she silently reproached herself.

She turned away from the railing and followed Morgana

to the chapel. She already knew she would spend much time on her knees here.

Morgana held the door open and Katherine entered. Although the chapel was not huge, there was a comforting feel about the chamber. The dancing light from dozens of glowing candles cast moving shadows in a strangely welcoming array upon the wall. Katherine made her way down the center aisle, past the six or eight rows of wooden benches. Each had a hand-sewn cushion on it, an unheard of comfort in many chapels.

The statue that stood on the altar at Lochmore was similar to the statue at Kilgern, only it wasn't Jesus the Shepherd, but Jesus the Crucified, with his nail-marked hands outstretched. The workmanship was beautiful, the spiritual ambiance all-consuming in the small chamber. Strong, serene emotions engulfed her.

She knelt at the railing in front of the altar and bowed her head. She had much for which to be thankful. She had much for which to ask guidance. She had much for which to ask forgiveness. She began by asking for forgiveness. That she needed the most right now.

After a long time, she stood and turned to leave. Morgana sat on one of the benches waiting for her.

"The mistress came here often every day," Morgana said, a faraway look in her eyes. "The laird came with her each evening. It was their habit."

"I pray it will be our habit, too," Katherine said. "It's one I will work to establish."

Katherine followed Morgana out of the room and past the three closed doors. "What are in these rooms, Morgana?"

"Everything that belonged to the laird's parents. The laird has na taken care of their belongings yet and does na want anything disturbed. The room next to it," she said, pointing to the end room, "is Lady Brenna's. It's ready and waiting for her to return."

Katherine looked at the closed door. "It will not be long."

Morgana gave a curt nod, then walked into Duncan's chamber. Their chamber. It was just as she expected. Large and spacious, with a boldly masculine feel about it. The room emitted a masterful dominance she had sensed nowhere else in the keep. Duncan belonged here.

She prayed she belonged here with him.

"I would like to meet the cooks now and thank them for the wonderful meal. Please, take me to them."

"You would go to the kitchens?"

"Yes."

"It's very hot there, milady. Perhaps you should just send a message."

"I have been warm before. Even we English have kitchens in which we cook our food."

Morgana gave Katherine a closed look, then led her out of the keep to a separate building next door. The long, wooden hut where they cooked the meat and prepared the food was enormous. But the first thing Katherine noticed was the bilious smoke rolling from the wide door at the front. "Is there a fire?" she asked, looking for flames.

"Nay, milady. Anna and Margaret are roasting the meat for tomorrow. It always smokes this much."

Katherine took a deep breath, and walked through the thick haze. Even though some of the smoke made an escape through the one opening, it was so dense she had to search to find the workers. There were about fifteen women scattered throughout the room, and it didn't take long for them to realize she was there. They all stood in stony silence and glared at her. Waiting. Evaluating.

Morgana hollered through the smoke. "Anna. Margaret. Your mistress has come to greet you."

Two women turned around from a table laden with vegetables to be chopped. They were two of the largest, tallest women Katherine had ever seen, with arms as thick as small trees and shoulders nearly as broad as a man's. They'd rolled their sleeves up past their elbows, and opened the necklines of their shirts almost to the point of being indecent, yet still looked as if the heat was about to suffocate them. Their look made them appear even more menacing.

Katherine swallowed hard, a little unnerved by their size, then walked confidently toward them.

Both women shifted the surprised looks on their faces to a guarded expression void of any signs of friendliness. Their exchanged glances said they were being forced to face a mistress they obviously hoped never to set eyes upon. They rubbed their hands on their skirts, then wiped away the sweat trickling down their flushed faces while they waited for her to come closer.

Margaret stepped forward first, obviously the chief spokesman for the women.

Katherine lifted her chin. She would not let the Scot's size or the black glare in her eyes intimidate her. The woman must be all of six feet and more. A giant. A hostile giant. "Morgana tells me you are in charge of the Ferguson kitchens," she said, facing Margaret.

"Aye," Margaret answered, puffing out her chest with a deep breath. She propped her fists on her hips, and issued Katherine a challenging look that was as fiery as the oppressive heat in the room. "I have been in charge of this kitchen for more than twenty summers."

Katherine met the woman's gaze and smiled in greeting. The smile was not returned. "It's obvious you hold your position proudly. Your meals display your talents."

"You can save your compliments and your sweet talk, milady. We have talked among us, and decided there will be no *English* dishes prepared in this kitchen. Our laird may not mind your English ways, but you'll not be bringing the way you eat to Lochmore keep. Not while Anna, and I, and the rest, have breath in our body to stop you."

Her statement was blunt, direct, and said with purpose. Katherine held her ground, ignoring the heat she could feel roll off Margaret's body and the hatred she could hear in her voice. "That is as it should be, Margaret. If the food you prepared this midday is an example of your Scottish dishes, I will be well satisfied."

The women stared at her in gaping silence, the doubting expressions on their faces evident. Katherine waited for a sign that they accepted her compliment, but could find none. There were no smiles. No softening of their looks. Not even a glimmer in an eye of the other women crowding around.

An uncomfortable silence stretched into an even greater chasm of cold mistrust. Katherine wanted nothing more than to turn her back on the women and run back to England. Instead, she ignored a trickle of perspiration that burned her eye and lifted her shoulders. "I came because I wanted you to know how much I enjoyed your splendid fare. Since I do not know my husband's likes or dislikes yet, I will rely solely on your knowledge and good judgment to prepare the dishes for which he has a particular fondness."

"That would be our meat pies," Anna said, the words almost bursting from her mouth. "The laird has a special weakness for our meat pies with carrots and peas and Margaret's crust on top."

Margaret cast her coworker a disapproving glare and Anna shrank back as if realizing her blunder too late.

"Then I will especially look forward to your meat pies," Katherine said, ignoring the dark look Margaret still wore.

The chief cook lifted the hem of her dress and wiped the sweat from her forehead, then looked at the other red-faced women. "The laird has never complained."

They all nodded in unison as if Margaret's statement deserved validation. "I'm sure he has not." Katherine steadied her gaze on the smug look on Margaret's face. "As long as we are being so frank with each other, there is also another concern with which I would ask your help." Margaret narrowed her gaze. "Malcolm informed your laird that supplies are not in overabundance this year, but just enough to see us through the winter if we take proper care. Perhaps there is something you can do to increase what we have, or make what is here last a little longer."

Margaret straightened her shoulders as if there was nothing she enjoyed more than a good challenge. "Aye. The men will na go hungry with Anna and me and the rest to see to them."

Katherine nodded confidently. "Your laird will be

grateful for your help." She turned to leave, glad to be out of such a hostile place. She took a few steps away from them, thankful there were not real daggers in their looks, or she would be dead. Because she couldn't leave with them thinking their hostility had affected her, she turned around to give them a final look. Smoke billowed from the far end of the room where half a cow roasted in the mammoth hearth. Open ovens on the sides radiated even more heat. Each woman before her took turns wiping the sweat from her face, while the color of their cheeks turn even more flushed.

Katherine looked around the room. Their kitchen in England had whole sections of the walls that were windows, and could be opened and closed to let in air, and take out the smoke. It didn't seem nearly so stifling there as here. She marched back to where Margaret still stared at her. "Is there a reason there are no more openings other than this one door?" She pointed to the small opening at the far end of the room.

All the women looked at each other as if they were sure there was an answer to her question but they didn't know what it was. Margaret finally answered for them. "It's the way it has always been. There's nothing wrong with it," she defended.

"Yes, there is," Katherine argued. "Someone is going to succumb to the heat."

"Irsa did just last week," Anna volunteered, and everyone turned to look at a young lass of probably no more than seventeen. The girl turned an even deeper shade of crimson, then clutched her hand to her protruding stomach.

"That's because of the babe," Margaret argued. "It was no hotter that day than it is today. Being with child will make you weak."

Katherine didn't know anything about that, but she did know that someone expecting a babe should not be working in such conditions. She took a step closer to Margaret and the other women. "Is there a carpenter here at Lochmore?"

"Aye, Kevin. But he's busy repairing the cottages damaged from when the English raided us."

Katherine ignored her barbed comment. "As soon as he has time, he will come to the kitchens to put in windows along these two walls that you can open and close at will. I think windows at the front will serve well, too. That will open up three sides and let air come in from all directions. It will be up to you, Margaret, to see it's done exactly as you and the other women want."

Margaret bristled, and when she spoke her voice was hard as nails and her words bristled with hatred. "Our kitchen is fine just as it is, milady. We do na need any of your English ways here at Lochmore."

"Whether you think you do or not is unimportant. We will put windows in the walls because it will improve conditions in the kitchens. Not because it is an English way."

"But the laird has na approved such an order," Margaret objected, voicing the concern she could see written on every face in the room.

"I will speak with the laird. If he has any concerns, we have only to put him in this room for an hour or so and he'll not question our request."

Even Margaret couldn't hide her shock and surprise. She opened her mouth to speak, but closed it again as if she couldn't find the words to argue.

"I will explain what I think will work best to the carpenter, and you decide where you want your windows put. I promise you will enjoy your kitchen more when it's not nearly so hot."

Katherine then looked around the group of women until she found the lass Irsa. "Gather your things, Irsa, and follow us to the keep. I'll have Morgana assign you another position. When you have been delivered, you may come back to work in the kitchen if you wish, but not until you present your husband with a fine, healthy babe."

Katherine ignored the shocked looks on the women's faces and walked out the door. She took two steps into the cool, late summer afternoon and stopped to take in several breaths of clean air. "By the saints, I cannot imagine why they would not want to improve their kitchen," she said, rubbing her hand against her damp forehead. "Take me to this carpenter first, Morgana. I want the windows in before too long." Morgana gave her a closed smile then led her to the carpenter's shop.

Katherine took one look at the carpenter's flaming red hair and matching beard, and knew she'd found a Ferguson no more accepting than the women in the kitchen. His steely gray eyes leveled her with open mistrust as she explained in detail her design for changing the kitchen. She discussed and argued, using more persistence and tact than she thought she possessed.

It was not easy to convince the stubborn Scot that windows were more important than a shed for some pigs, but before she left, they'd reached an agreement of sorts. Anyway, she hoped they had. The carpenter seemed to like her no better than anyone else she'd met today, but at least he'd finally listened without criticizing, and even nodded his head a few times.

Katherine left the carpenter's shop feeling a heavier weight tighten around her heart than she thought it was possible to bear. The hostility she'd battled on every front wore her down. The gnawing in the pit of her stomach told her as much.

She wanted to run back to her chambers and shut herself away, but she could not. She would not allow Duncan's Scots to force her into hiding. She would face them with the pride and stateliness her father would expect her to exhibit.

She walked through the inner bailey, ignoring the whispered comments, listening as Morgana pointed out each building and shed. They toured the stables, the armory, the blacksmith's workshop, and the storehouses. The bunkhouses, the granary, the tanner's workshop, and the alehouse.

At each building, Katherine stepped inside and met the workers. She spoke to them, asked questions, then made mental notes of everything done in each area. The names would take her longer to learn. She had never been very good at remembering names.

She'd hoped as they went along the greetings would warm, the stares would be less hostile. They weren't. It would take Duncan's Fergusons a long time to accept an English mistress.

"I think we should go back to the keep now, mistress,"

Morgana said when they reached another row of storage houses. "You had best get settled in your chamber."

"Yes, Morgana. It would be good to get our new mistress settled in her laird's chamber." The husky female voice behind them made them both turn to see who had spoken. From the look on Morgana's face, she wasn't especially pleased to see the young woman facing them.

"Did you need something, Regan?"

"Aye, Morgana. I would like to meet my mistress."

Katherine couldn't help but stare as the dark-haired beauty stepped closer. She found herself looking into the most vibrant pair of green eyes she had ever seen. The beauty's raven-colored hair shimmered as the bright rays of sunlight hit her, casting her lithe form in a glow. She was as dark and alluring as Katherine was fair and commonplace.

"Everyone in the courtyard talks of nothing but our laird's new wife," she said, evaluating Katherine as if she had a right to make a comparison. "Do you hope it will take only a smile and a kind word for us to forget you are English?"

"Regan." Morgana's voice held an unmistakable warning.

"Nay, Morgana. The Lady Katherine should know her smiles will na charm us into forgetting that vile English blood runs in her veins."

Katherine faced her accuser with determination. "I am glad to meet you, Regan, and I have not forgotten that English blood runs in my veins." Katherine took a deep breath and steadied herself to keep her temper in check. It would do no good to get into a fight with one of Duncan's subjects on her first day here. "I do not expect my husband's people ever to forget that I am English. I am as proud of my heritage as you are of yours."

"And is our laird proud that you are English?"

The breath caught in Katherine's throat. She couldn't find an answer. None that she wanted to share.

The girl lifted her head and jutted her chin, then braced her fists against her hips. "Why did our laird marry you? What do you have that is so important he would sacrifice his pride to take an English for his bride?"

Katherine summoned a strength she didn't feel. "You will have to ask your laird that question."

Regan took another step closer and drilled Katherine with eyes that held more hatred than she had ever seen. "He will never love you. Duncan will never love anyone but—"

"'Tis enough, wench." Angus' voice was soft behind them, but the harshness was unmistakable. "You had best get yourself back to your cottage and see to your mother. I hear she is na doing so well."

Angus reached into his pocket and handed her a small vile of white powder. "Give her a small amount of this in a cup of warm ale twice each day. It should ease the pain and make her sleep."

The dark-haired beauty reached for the vile, then cast Katherine another hooded scowl before she sauntered off.

"I am sorry, mistress," Morgana apologized. "I did na think Regan would be so forward."

Katherine watched the Ferguson beauty until she'd passed the inner bailey wall and was out of view. "She's very bitter," Katherine said on a sigh. "I would like to know what keeps her hatred burning so fiercely. Did she lose someone to the English?"

Morgana and Angus both looked at each other and it was Angus who answered. "The man she thought to marry, milady."

"No wonder," Katherine said. "It will take her longest of all to forgive."

"Do na worry about Regan, milady. She will change in time."

Katherine gave Angus a hollow smile.

And perhaps she will never change. Perhaps none of the Fergusons will ever change toward her.

"Take your mistress back to the keep, Morgana," Angus ordered, then turned his attention back to Katherine. "There is a little time before the evening meal and I'm certain you need to rest."

"Thank you, Angus," Katherine said, placing her hand atop the older man's forearm. "For everything."

Katherine didn't know exactly why she felt the need to thank the wizened old warrior with the bushy white beard and the knowing look in his eyes. Perhaps because he had healed her from Bolton's beating. Perhaps because he had defended her from Regan's attack. Perhaps because, although his look was not warm, it at least contained no hatred.

"Go on with ye, now," he said, then turned his back on them.

Katherine walked silently at Morgana's side through the inner courtyard, then stopped suddenly and grabbed the servant's hand. "Go to the keep without me. I have something to ask Angus. I will be back shortly."

Morgana's eyebrows raised high as a fearful look of

concern crossed her face. "Oh, no, mistress. You canna go by yourself. The laird gave strict orders."

"I will be fine. I must hurry to catch Angus before he crosses the drawbridge. Go Morgana," Katherine said, already running after Angus.

"But the laird—"

"I'll be back before your laird even knows I have gone," she yelled over her shoulder.

Katherine left Morgana staring after her with a fearful look on her face, but at the moment she didn't care. The small seeds of an idea had been planted in her head, and no amount of reasoning would change her mind. Katherine looked ahead of her. He was almost to the drawbridge, and Katherine smiled as she watched his strides, still strong and steady. Still those of a young man.

He was too far ahead of her. She wouldn't catch him before he left the safety of the walls, but that didn't bother her. She would have to know the way to his hut if he was to help her like she intended. She would have to know her way outside the walls as well as she would learn her way on the inside before long. She would—

"Stop, mistress."

Katherine took a quick glance at Angus to make sure she knew which direction he went, then turned around to face a lad of no more than fifteen, with golden blond hair and eyes of the deepest blue she had ever seen. "What is it?" she asked impatiently, fearing she would lose Angus if she was detained very long.

"I'm afraid I canna let you walk through these gates, milady. The laird would na like it."

Katherine bristled. "The laird gave orders that I was not

allowed to go beyond these gates?"

"Aye, milady. I think he does na even intend for you to be this far from the keep without someone to guard you."

Katherine gave Angus' fleeting figure another glance then turned her attention to the young lad pretending to be an experienced warrior. "I am only trying to catch up with Angus. If I hurry, I will be safe. You can watch to make sure I am."

"I canna let you, milady."

"You would stop me?"

"I would have to."

Katherine breathed a resigned sigh. She couldn't believe this. "Then you will have to." She looked up, but could no longer see Angus in the distance. With a stomp of her foot and a sigh of exasperation, she stormed past the shocked young man, daring him to try to stop her. She knew he would not dare to touch her. She was his mistress. The laird's wife. But she knew he wouldn't waste any time going for someone who would.

Katherine ran across the drawbridge as quickly, yet as cautiously as possible, then to the right where Angus had gone. She followed the dirt path into the tall, thick trees. Ahead of her was a small hut.

The door of the cottage stood open, inviting her to enter. She called out his name as she ran to the entrance.

Angus came out of the dark opening and stared at her with raised eyebrows. "You left the walls without a guard? Your laird will na be pleased."

She would not give him time to lecture her. "If I come to you, will you teach me your potions?"

"The laird does na want you to learn them."

She repeated her question. "If I come, will you teach me? Please."

He studied her a long moment, then lifted the corners of his mouth slightly. "The laird will na like it."

"I know."

More silence. Then Angus dropped his head back on his shoulders and laughed out loud. "Aye, mistress. I will teach you."

Katherine unclenched the hands she didn't realize were fisted at her side. "Thank you, Angus." She wiped her sweaty palms against her skirt and smiled at the old man. "Perhaps I will come to you tomorrow." She took a step backward. "I must go now, before my laird finds out I have disobeyed him." She spun around to race back to the keep and collided with a body as solid and immovable as a stone wall.

Duncan's soft, deadly voice shattered the silence. Her heart skipped a beat. "It's too late, milady. Your laird has already found out you've disobeyed him."

Katherine lifted her gaze. The angry gleam in his eyes turned murderous. The way he gritted his teeth and fisted his hands at his side was also not a healthy sign.

"I needed to talk to Angus," she said, surprised that her voice sounded as controlled and steady as it did.

"Did not Brandon order you to go back to the keep?"

"Is that the young man I talked with at the drawbridge?"

"Aye. That is his name. If you have need to speak with him further, you will find him cleaning out the castle garderobes from now until next spring."

Katherine squelched a rising surge of guilt. "But it was not his fault, Duncan. I didn't give him a choice."

"He had a sword. He had a choice."

Katherine stared at him in open-mouthed disbelief. She could see Brandon's golden hair and smiling blue eyes. Those eyes would now contain the same hatred as she'd seen on every other Ferguson today.

Chapter 8

Duncan slammed his tankard of ale on the table and shoved back his chair with such force it crashed to the floor. He'd put off going to his chamber until all save a few of the younger warriors in the great hall had gone to sleep. He'd hoped the ale he'd consumed and Malcolm's company would make him forget how angry he was with her. It hadn't.

Duncan crossed the rushes, ignoring the warning lift of Malcolm's brows, and climbed the stairs to his chambers. He thought of Kate waiting there for him. By the saints, she was a frustration. She was the most obstinate, single-minded, stubborn woman he'd ever met. Was there nothing she feared? Was there nothing she did not rush headlong into because she thought it was for the best?

He strode down the long hall to his chamber, each thud of his boots pounding off another reason she'd angered him today. The closer he came, the hotter his blood boiled in his veins. By the time he reached his door, he was even angrier than he'd been when Brandon ran through the great hall to tell him his mistress had left the safety of the castle without an escort.

By the saints. He'd had Fergusons lined up before him all afternoon complaining about something their mistress had done. First Anne and Margaret from the kitchen; then Kevin, the carpenter; then Morgana; and finally Brandon. Didn't she realize the turmoil her ideas caused? The danger in which she put herself?

Duncan shoved at the latch and stormed through the door with the same fervor he felt riding into battle. He expected to find her asleep and anticipated waking her just to give her the scolding she deserved. One she would never forget.

She was not asleep. Far from it.

His wife sat on the edge of the bed. Waiting. The dozen candles she'd lit to brighten the chamber cast her long, loosely woven plait in a golden glow, making her seem soft, contrite. He knew she was not.

She was defiant and rebellious. He'd come to know her too well. The sight of her sitting so demurely was not the Kate he'd married. His Kate had issued orders and made decisions today with clear, calculated thoughtlessness. She intended to create chaos in his life and had done a good job of it. He could not let her rebelliousness go unchecked.

He crossed the room, fighting the ominous foreboding that gnawed deep in his gut, the feeling of impending doom that rumbled like a roiling thundercloud building over Scotland. How could he win her over when her actions were a constant irritant? How could he win her trust when he couldn't even win her obedience? It was only a matter of time until someone came for the crown. He prayed it would be the English. He could fight them to the death as his father had. But how could he slay his fellow Scots to protect the crown his English wife wouldn't give him?

He stood before her, feet braced, arms clasped behind his back. She lifted her deep blue eyes and studied him, as if she had resigned herself to accept his wrath without complaint or argument. She didn't move except to clench her hands tighter in her lap and lift her shoulders in readiness to receive his reprimand.

"Do you have any idea the problems you caused today, wife?"

She lowered her eyes submissively.

"You argued with me in front of my men. Gave orders to rebuild my kitchens without first consulting me. Went outside the castle walls without a guard when you were told you could not. Then, you went to Angus to have him teach you his potions, even though I forbade you to do so. And this is only your first day here!" Duncan slapped his fist against his thigh in frustration.

She opened her mouth as if to say something, then wisely closed it again.

Duncan paced before her stoic figure sitting on the edge of the bed. "Anna and Margaret are convinced you want to change everything to your English ways and have vowed to fight you every step of the way."

"I only wanted to make their kitchen less oppressive in which to work."

"Kevin said—"

"Who is Kevin?" she asked, frowning as she tried to recall the name.

"Our carpenter. He thinks you intend to occupy his time from now until next spring making your changes. He thinks you have no regard for the huts and cottages that must be repaired before the snow falls."

"I only asked him to find time when the cottages were finished. Large windows in the kitchen are needed to take out the smoke and heat. It's not that I want him to rebuild your castle."

"I am laird here, Kate. You should have come to me first."

"As laird, you should have already known your kitchens were hotter than the pits of hell. I only want to improve an intolerable condition."

He could see her struggle to hold her temper. He could tell she was trying with all her might to watch her tongue. It was a battle he knew she had no chance of winning. He had no intention of helping her. "Do you have to charge into places where you are na yet welcome, Kate? Can you na give them a little while to become more accepting of you?"

"And when will that be, my lord?" She bolted from the bed and paced the room like a caged animal. "How long will it take for the people to accept me, when even their laird cannot? They all see that you do not trust me, and that I am guarded like a prisoner. How can I expect anyone to accept me when you have yet to cast an approving glance in my direction?"

"That is na true, Kate. I stood before a priest and took you as my wife. I brought you into my keep and announced to all that you had found a place with me."

"Words," she spat back at him. "You are nothing but a firestorm of contradictions. Do you think I don't know the battle raging inside your head, Duncan?"

"There is na battle."

"Oh, but there is. You thought you had no choice but to marry me because you think I have the crown. And because I gave you back your medallion. I stood up to Bolton in the dungeon and your misplaced Scottish pride won't let you sacrifice me to such a man, knowing what he will do."

"Do na lie to yourself, Kate. You were as fearful as I at the idea of spending your life with Bolton."

"You're right," she admitted, pounding her fist against the cold, stone wall. "But I don't look at marriage to you as a betrayal of my heritage. Or a sin against God."

Every muscle in Duncan's taut body froze. "Nor do I," he denied with blatant vehemence.

"Yes, you do, my lord. You look on our marriage as your greatest betrayal. Not only to your clan and to Scotland, but more than all else, to your father's honor."

"You know nothing about my father's honor. He lived his whole life doing only what was noble. He would have found another way. He would never have married an English just because—"

Katherine turned her face away from him. When she spoke, her voice was soft, edged with a tinge of pain. "Just because she had the crown?"

"I did na say that, wife."

"You did not have to." She leaned against the thick stone wall as if she needed its strength to hold her up. "I married you," she said in a quiet voice, "because I was too great a coward to face the lonely life in a convent. Because I was not brave enough to face Bolton on my own, and because I…I couldn't forget the kiss we shared in Ian's dungeon."

She paused. "I would give anything to be able to undo my mistake and save you from your torment."

"It was not a mistake, Kate. We are together because—"

She spun around to face him. There was anger back in her eyes. "Because I have the crown, and I was Bolton's betrothed. The battle that rages inside you is because you cannot bring yourself to accept the fact that I am English."

She turned and walked to the narrow arrow slit in the wall. A bright shaft of moonlight streamed through the opening, casting a golden glow to her shimmering hair. Damn her. How could this English wife understand him so well? How could she see what he refused to admit to himself?

"Will it always be impossible to want me, my lord?"

Her words slashed through him like a finely honed sword aimed at his heart. She thought he didn't want her. Didn't she know how hard it was for him to deny his desire to take her? Even though she was English.

With long, determined strides, Duncan crossed the room. He reached the place where she was, and turned her in his arms until she faced him. With uncontrolled urgency, he pulled her against him and lowered his mouth to hers. He would show her how little she knew of what went on inside him. He would show her how wrong she was.

Duncan pressed his mouth against hers, drinking from her, taking from her, possessing her. His kiss was deep and thorough, and he was pleased with the way she conformed to him.

He would have her. She was his. He had taken her freely and willingly, and nothing, save death itself, would take her away from him.

Her body burned his flesh like hot tar poured onto cold metal. Nothing separated her from him but the thin material of her night shift, and that was not nearly enough to disguise his desire. He felt the firmness of her breasts through his shirt, touching him, pressing against him. Another surge of molten liquid raged deep into the pit of his gut.

Duncan slanted his mouth over her, deepening his kisses, covering her with a lusty need that overpowered him. He'd wanted her from the moment she'd kissed him in the dungeon. Even when he thought she belonged to someone else, he could not deny the tangible bond that twined them together. He'd agonized over such desires then as they tortured him now.

He opened his mouth atop hers, his tongue skimming her kiss-swollen lips, forcing her to open to him. God's blood, he wanted her. His tongue invaded her mouth, searching, seeking, finding. Raging heat plummeted deep in his belly and he pulled her up against him so she could feel how badly he needed her.

With a ragged sigh of unmistakable surrender, she wrapped her arms around his neck, returning his kisses with even greater fervor.

Duncan skimmed his hands along her sides; down to her narrow waist, lower to her rounded hips, then upwards again until the pads of his thumbs reached the undersides of her lush, firm breasts. He covered her, moving his fingers over the hardened peaks, while his tongue continued its assault on her mouth. She moaned loudly and raked her fingers through his hair, holding him tighter to her.

He wanted to touch every inch of her perfect body. Ached to be inside her. Even if she was English. Ached to plant his seed within her. Even if his heirs would forever be marked with English blood.

... forever marked with English blood.

His hands stopped moving over her breasts. The air froze in his chest. Holy mother of God.

He pulled away from her, staring into eyes glazed with passion, burning with confusion and hurt. He had given her his name, but he could not take her. He hated himself for what he was doing to her. She deserved to be made his wife. But he could not take her.

The heated chamber echoed with the rasping gasps of their heavy breathing. Like a ragged gale in a stormy breeze, her breathing cut through the turmoil. Unsteady. Shuddering.

Duncan raked his fingers through his hair and stepped away from her. He didn't want to see the hurt and confusion on her face. He turned to look out over the rolling Scottish hillsides, bathed brightly in the silvery moonlight. He loved every foot of this earth as dearly as he valued his life. He would die to keep it out of English hands.

"Go to bed, Kate. The room is beginning to chill."

She did not move, but stood alone in the flickering candlelight.

"Go to bed. I will be here until you sleep."

He did not go to her. He couldn't bear to see the expression on her face. The emptiness in her gaze.

He heard her move to the bed, then heard a rustle as she climbed beneath the covers. He crossed his arms over his chest and stared up at the stars in the sky. "I will talk to

Malcolm in the morning to make sure someone goes with you whenever you visit Angus."

She did not give him an answer. He stood in the muted darkness as one after the other of her many candles flickered, then died. In the hazy blackness, the room echoed with only the crackling of the fire in the hearth and the steady beating of his heart.

. . .

Katherine lay beneath the covers and listened to each ragged breath he took. She clutched her arms around her trembling body and curled into a tight ball. She prayed he would go away but he did not. She prayed the tightening in her chest would go away, but it wouldn't leave her either. She moved to the far side of the soft bed and huddled in the corner with her back to him.

He didn't want her.

He'd married her for the crown, and because she was Bolton's betrothed. But he couldn't bring himself to take her as his wife because she was English.

Katherine pushed aside the memory of the passion in his kisses. She brought her fingers to her mouth, her lips still warm and tender. She would never yield to him again like she had tonight. She would never let herself want him like she had tonight.

She could not survive the debilitating pain she'd felt when he'd pulled away. A part of her had died from the hurt of knowing he did not want an English wife.

Katherine squeezed her eyes shut to stop the tears that wanted to come. He would not make her cry. Damn him. He would not make her cry.

She clutched her arms tighter around her middle and ignored the wetness soaking into the pillow beneath her cheek.

She would not let herself care that he didn't want her.

. . .

"Here, lass," Angus hollered in his gruff voice.

Katherine picked up her bag of roots and went to where he was already digging. She had spent every day of the last two weeks working with the old warrior, learning all she could. In a day's time, he would be leaving with Duncan and the other Fergusons to get Brenna.

"See this flower?" he asked, pointing to a tiny purple bud. "This will tell you where to dig to find our angel root. We'll let the roots dry, then grind them to a fine powder. Its powers ease a chill and take down a fever. If, God forbid," Angus stopped to make a sign of the cross, "a plague goes through the clan, a little of this with a mixture of the feverfew is the only potion that will bring down a raging fever. Pray to God we do na need to ever use it."

Katherine wiped the dirt from the roots and placed them in her bag. "Why haven't you shown someone these potions before?"

"The time was na right."

Katherine sat back on her haunches and looked up at him. "Why did you agree to share your knowledge with me, Angus? Duncan doesn't like it. He doesn't think an English should learn your potions."

"You are our laird's wife. It's your duty to protect your people."

Katherine lowered her head. "I think it's a duty I will

not be very good at."

"Aye. You already are. You have always felt the need to protect your sister, have you not?"

"That's different. Elizabeth has never been as strong. She has always needed someone to take care of her."

"Like you take care of all around you. That's why you risked your life to free Duncan from Bolton. You wanted to gain his help to protect your sister and her babe. You will use the powers with just as much care."

Katherine lifted her gaze and looked him in the eyes. "There are others who care, and they are Scot."

"Aye. But they are na the laird's wife."

Katherine did not say the words that would tell Angus that she wasn't either. Not really. Duncan had yet to take her in the way that God intended a woman to be bound to her husband. His Scottish pride would not let him.

During the day, he was considerate and caring and… distant. It was impossible not to see it. She knew everyone noticed. They all watched for some shared sign of affection between their laird and his bride. They found none, and the looks they exchanged said as much.

At night, long after he thought she'd fallen asleep, he came to her room and sat with her. He didn't come to her bed, or hold her in his arms. Or kiss her as he had that first night. It was as if even touching her was too painful.

Each morning, before the sun rose in the sky, he left. She didn't let him know she was awake. But she was.

Angus' voice brought her from her thoughts. "Tomorrow we'll gather the leaves of the stonecrop. I'll show you how to make a poultice to heal open wounds. It's what I put on your back and the laird's chest. Pray to

God we do na need to use it."

Katherine stood up and stretched her limbs. "I'll see you tomorrow, then," she said, and stepped out of the cottage. She looked around for her guard.

Malcolm stood over by a large tree, honing his sword for the battle in two days. Today was his turn to watch her when she went beyond the castle walls. "Are you finished for the day, mistress?" he said when he saw her.

"Yes, Malcolm. I promised Morgana I would be back early. I want to show her what we used in Eng—" She stopped. "I want to show her what we used to make the rushes on the floor smell sweet."

"We would all appreciate that, mistress."

They walked toward the castle in silence. Malcolm was either not a great conversationalist, or he preferred not to talk to *her*.

"Do you have a wife, Malcolm?"

"Nay, milady."

"Is there anyone special who has stolen your heart?"

Malcolm's gaze hardened, and he stared ahead without looking at her. Katherine suddenly felt as if she'd stumbled onto dangerous territory.

"I can never hope to have the lass who has stolen my heart."

"Surely you do not mean that?"

Malcolm didn't answer for a little while but his feet set an even faster pace. "Do na think on it, milady. It is the way of things. Would you like to stop at the kitchen on the way to the keep? I think Kevin is finished with one of the windows."

His abrupt change of topic was a closure to any

discussion concerning his personal life. "I would love to. I can't wait to see what it will look like."

Katherine said no more. Tonight she would ask Duncan who the lady was who had stolen Malcolm's heart. Maybe all was not as hopeless as he thought.

Together they walked to the carpenter's shop. The hostile stares and whispered comments she heard and saw as they passed groups of Fergusons still hurt, but she refused to let Duncan's clansmen know it. She held her head high and walked among them as if she weren't aware of their hatred.

The completed windows for the kitchen were perfect. She couldn't wait to see them all done. Even if Anna and Margaret wouldn't admit that her idea improved their kitchen, she would know it. Every time she saw the windows propped open, she would know the workers were cooler.

Suddenly, her whole day seemed brighter. Today it didn't seem to hurt nearly as much when Carmen Lachlan pulled her little twin daughters behind her skirt before Katherine could speak to them. Nor did it bother her when the old woman who lived in the hut close to Angus stepped to the other side of the bailey, rather than pass too close.

When they reached the keep, Katherine left Malcolm on the front steps and entered the wide opening that led to the great hall. She was looking for Morgana, but stopped when the sound of loud voices reached her. One of the voices was Duncan's. The other she couldn't place, even though she knew she'd heard it before. It was a woman's voice, and the woman was angry.

"How could you bring an English here? How could you marry her, Duncan?"

Katherine stepped away from the opening and pressed her back against the wall. She should leave. She didn't want to hear this.

"You will na talk about your mistress so, Regan."

"Mistress! Ha! She is nothing to me."

"You refuse to give your oath of fealty to your laird's wife?"

"I do! I refuse to accept that she is your wife. I should be your wife. I should be the one to have your name, and share your bed, and bear your children. I am the one you love. Not her!"

"Do na talk like that, Regan. I have never—"

"Nay! Do na say you never said you loved me, or asked me to be your wife. You did na have to. Not after all we shared."

Katherine closed her eyes and let the waves pound against her ears. She should not listen to this. She did not want to hear it.

"Why did you marry the English woman, Duncan? Your hatred for them runs too deep. You will never learn to care for her."

"You do na need to know why I chose the English woman for my wife. Just know that I did. Know that I chose her freely."

"You did not choose her freely. I know you did na. What does she have that you want? The crown?"

Katherine waited for Duncan to deny it. There was only silence.

"Ha! She will never give it to you. She will keep it

hidden until she can give it to her English king, and you will never see it."

"I will get the crown."

Katherine leaned her head back against the stone wall. The crown. Why did everything revolve around the crown?

"Is it true, Duncan, that your English wife was betrothed to Bolton?"

Duncan did not deny it.

Regan laughed, a harsh, bitter sound. "What better way to strike back at the man who killed your father than to turn his betrothed into your whore."

"Enough! Leave me, Regan. And do na come back."

"I will leave, my laird, but you will soon beg me to come back. When you tire of your wife lying cold and lifeless beneath you at night, you will remember how good it was between us, and want me back. I will wait."

Katherine pressed her hand against her mouth, then ran up the stairs to her chamber. God help her.

She closed the door and pressed her back tightly against it. She stood there for a long time, then walked on legs that barely supported her to the small chapel at the end of the hall.

Why did you marry the English woman, Duncan? You will never learn to care for her.

The sun streamed through the two narrow windows on either side of the altar, showering the small room in a muted array of golden streamers. Katherine walked to the front and stared up at the statue of Jesus. A desperate voice echoed deep inside her and she fell to her knees before the altar.

What does she have that you want? The crown?

Katherine dropped her head to her folded hands, trying to forget the boastful tone of Regan's voice, but she could not. Every bitter word screamed in the quiet chamber, a reminder of the chasm that separated her from her husband.

When you tire of your wife… you will remember how good it was between us and beg me to come back.

Katherine clenched her hands tighter and prayed with as much fervor as she'd ever prayed in her life. Then she began her search for the hidden passageway. The time would come when Duncan would demand she give him the crown. She had to be able to escape, should it become necessary.

Chapter 9

Duncan rubbed his temples to ease the throbbing in his head. His conversation with Regan had disturbed him more than he cared to admit.

One by one the Ferguson warriors came through the opening and sat at one of the many long trestle tables, ready to eat the evening meal. Everyone was present except his wife. They would not start without her, and Kate knew it. It angered him that she was not already here, that she would make his men wait to eat.

Duncan searched the room. He ached to hear her rich voice when she spoke. He wanted to stand close to her so he could smell the clean fragrance of roses and heather in which she bathed.

He wanted to touch her, and hold her, and kiss her like he'd done before. He wanted to run his fingers through her hair, and over her skin, and over the soft hidden parts of her body. He wanted to walk with her, and laugh with her, and hold her in his arms until the sun came up each morning.

He wanted her to be something other than English.

He couldn't go on much longer the way he was. Every day he was with her, he wanted her more. Every hour he was without her, he missed her more. Every night he went without loving her, he cursed himself for being more a fool.

He looked up again. Angus was there, but Kate was not with him.

"Where is my wife, Angus?" he said when Angus came near him.

The old warrior's face wrinkled with a frown. "Malcolm came for her earlier this afternoon." Angus turned to Malcolm. "Where did you leave her?"

Tiny nerves prickled on the back of Duncan's neck.

Malcolm looked around the room as if she were hiding somewhere close and they'd missed her. "I brought her here from your cottage, Angus." Malcolm turned back to Duncan. "We stopped to see Kevin on our way. He was in the kitchen with Anna and Margaret."

"Did anything unforeseen happen while you were there?"

"Nay. Nothing any different than any other day. Our people are still not overly accepting of their mistress, Duncan. The air in the hot kitchen near caused a bit of frostbite."

Duncan sat forward in his chair. "Did the women offend their mistress?"

"Nay. Not directly. It's obvious, though, they canna forget she's English."

"Where did you go after the kitchens?"

"We came directly here. I left the mistress on the steps and went to the practice area. Marcus injured himself when he fell from his horse, and Balfour came for me to see if we should send for Angus. He was na injured so bad, and when I came back, the mistress had already come inside. I thought she was with you."

"Was the drawbridge raised after you came in?"

"Aye, and there's a guard at the postern. Neither would let her out. Not after what happened to Brandon."

"The lady Katherine would na go beyond the walls," Angus defended. "She knows how it concerns you."

Duncan raised his eyebrows. Angus did not know how it was between them. Duncan didn't think she would leave on her own, but maybe something had happened to her.

He rose from his chair and walked to where Morgana stood, giving instructions to the new serving girl Irsa. "Have you seen your mistress?"

"Not since earlier this afternoon, my lord. She came back and went to her room. She told me she was tired and wanted to rest."

Duncan turned to Angus and Malcolm who were both at his side. "I'll check in our chamber. She has probably fallen asleep."

Angus and Malcolm shared a smile and watched their laird walk away. "Begin your meal," Duncan hollered over his shoulder as he reached the doorway. He didn't want his men waiting for Kate if she had fallen asleep, but he was not pleased with her for inconveniencing them either. Nor for causing him concern.

He took the steps two at a time, pushing down the niggling fear that ate at him. Kate did not tire easily. It was not like her to sleep in the middle of the day. He hesitated with his hand on the latch, then opened the door.

The chamber was bright. Lit with the flames of a dozen candles. He looked first at the bed, but it was empty. She stood before the narrow arrow slit that overlooked the empty practice yard. She did not turn to face him when he entered.

"The men are awaiting their meal, Kate."

"I am not hungry. Have them begin without me."

He moved closer to where she stood. "It is a custom for the laird and his mistress to eat with the rest."

She spun around, the look in her bright blue eyes brimming with fire. "Then it's time we began a new custom. From now on, their *English* mistress will eat her meals alone in her chamber and the *Scottish* Fergusons can eat in the great hall with their laird. There should be no problem with that, should there, my lord?"

Duncan stared after her as she walked from the narrow window to the table beside the bed. She poured a cup of water then slammed the pitcher back on the table.

"Did something happen today that you need to tell me?"

Her gaze darted toward him, and he felt the stabbing of a thousand pinpricks on the back of his neck.

"No, my lord. Nothing happened today that was different from any other day." She took a sip of her water then focused the intensity of her anger on him. "I have decided that I will visit my sister while you are gone to get Brenna."

"Is that where the crown is hidden?"

The cup froze midway to her mouth. "The crown is safe, my lord. You need not concern yourself with its whereabouts."

"You will na leave the castle while I'm gone."

Fire flashed from her eyes. "Why? Are you worried Bolton will come after me?"

There was a hardness in her voice he didn't like hearing.

"He will not, husband. I am no longer a prize worth having."

"It matters not. You still have the crown and he will never stop wanting that. I will worry about Bolton until I have Brenna back with me and his blood drips from my sword."

"Even after you kill Bolton, your troubles will not be over. Have you thought of what my father will do once he finds out I have broken the king's edict and married you? Have you thought of what our English king will do?"

"Aye, lass. I have thought of that."

"And?"

"It does na warrant the effort to worry about such an insignificant matter as your English king."

"You will not think him so insignificant when his army marches here with my father at his side."

"Enough. We will worry about your king when Brenna is home safe."

"I would like to visit my sister while you're gone."

"And do you intend to return when I come back?"

Her eyebrows raised in question. "Would you care?"

Duncan stiffened. "Aye. I would care. You are my wife."

"No. I have never been your wife."

Her words created an unbridgeable gap between them. He fought to deny them, but couldn't. He struggled to find something to say that would make the meaning of her words less despairing. There was nothing. He cursed the loud knock at the door that would not give him the opportunity to heal the wound separating them. "Aye."

Malcolm opened the door and stepped in. He shut the door tight behind him. "The McGowans are downstairs, Duncan. They've come for the crown."

"Why do the McGowans want the crown?" she asked, her voice as timid as he'd ever heard her. The look of fear in her eyes.

"Their lads stole it from the English. They think they have a right to it."

Duncan refastened the sheath and sword he'd just removed from across his back, and tucked another dagger into his soft, leather boots. When he finished, he turned to Kate. "Will you give me the crown, lass?"

The look in her eyes held more pain than he wished to see in anyone's eyes. Especially for someone who… He would not let himself finish the thought.

"I cannot, Duncan. You know I cannot."

He gave her a brisk nod, then turned to Malcolm. "How many are there?"

"Perhaps thirty."

"Is Fergus with them?"

"Nay. He sent his oldest, Callum."

"Go back and tell them the laird and his mistress will be down presently. Seat them at the table, and give them plenty of food to eat, but do na be overgenerous with the ale. McGowans are hard enough to deal with when they're sober."

"Callum seems peaceable enough," Malcolm said, fingering the hilt of his sword, "but he brought his brother, Geordie, with him. The lad's got a temper that bears watching."

"Get word to Gregor to take some men and secure the

gates. Be sure he's discrete. We wouldn't want our guests to become concerned over their safety."

"Aye," Malcolm said, and opened the door to leave.

"Seat Callum on my left, Malcolm, with room for Kate on my right. Put Geordie opposite me, at your right."

Malcolm gave Duncan an understanding nod, then left the room.

Duncan walked across the chamber, away from the hearth. The room was as chilled as the blood running in his veins. He knew it was only a matter of time before someone came for the crown. If it hadn't been the McGowans, it would have been the MacDougall lords of Lorne and Argyll, bitter enemies of Robert Bruce. He did not doubt they thought possession of the crown would unite the English forces with their own to overthrow the Bruce's power. They would not retreat until they had either the crown — or Kate's head on a pike.

Worse than that, Robert Bruce could have come for it. If Duncan's king, or the king's trusted friend and counselor, James Douglas, had come… Duncan wiped his hand across his jaw. How could he have refused to give the crown to his king?

How could he even think to give up the wife he'd sworn to protect?

"What is going to happen now, Duncan?" Her voice held a determined tone. She still faced each problem with the same dauntless courage she'd shown in Ian's dungeon.

"We will go down to eat with our guests, Kate. Are y' ready?"

She nodded, but her eyes were as large as trenchers when she looked at him, her face as pale as milk.

"Ah, Kate," he said, crossing the room to reach her side. He put his hands on her shoulders and pulled her to him. He felt her tremble.

"I did not mean for it to be this way, Duncan."

"But it is. The McGowans are but the first. You knew it would happen."

"What will you do?"

"I can hardly give them something I do na have, can I, lass?"

"What if they don't accept your refusal, Duncan?"

"Then it would be wise to pray that I am better with a sword than Fergus."

Duncan heard the muffled cry that came from the back of her throat. "Shh, lass. It's too late for regrets. The time to wish for things to be different was when I first asked for the crown. Can you not give it to me?"

"Oh, Duncan. You know—"

Duncan put his finger to her lips to silence her. "We'll make the best of what we have. I promised I would protect you."

Duncan absorbed the trusting look on her face and knew he was going to kiss her. How was it possible to be drawn so fiercely to someone you'd spent your whole life convinced you hated? Why couldn't he control the desire he felt when he was near her?

He lowered his head, and closed his mouth over hers. She held herself stiff in his arms as if she didn't want his kiss, then breathed a shuddering sigh and clung to him. She held onto him and returned his kiss as if she was hungry for it.

"Ah, Kate," he whispered. "What is this power you

hold over me?" He parted his lips and entered her warm, moist cavern. His tongue searched, then found its mate. He'd wanted to kiss her like this since he'd taken her as his wife, but had denied the longing. Now he could not get enough of her. The roar of a thousand claps of thunder echoed in his head, the drone of a mighty rumble building to climactic proportions.

He moved his hands over her, touching her like he'd only dreamed of doing. Holding her like he'd prayed he could. He could no longer deny his feelings that raged out of control. He wanted her. Even without the crown, he wanted her. Even though she was English, he wanted her.

He lifted his mouth from hers and held her in his arms. This was not the time. "Come on, lass. We canna keep them waiting too long."

She lifted her hand and touched her fingers to his cheek. "If the choice were mine, I would give you the crown, Duncan. But the choice was never mine to make."

Duncan cupped her face in his hands and pressed his forehead against hers. "In time, I pray you will find a way, Kate. Our lives may well depend on it."

He held her for a while longer, then released her to take her downstairs. "Kate," he said, walking down the stairs to the great hall. He smiled at the bright red glow to her cheeks, and her kiss-swollen lips that showed the passion they'd just shared. "Mind your words, lass. Let me talk to the McGowans. It will only make things worse if you give them the sharp edge of your tongue."

Duncan almost laughed at the shocked look on her face. He knew she would try her best. He also knew he would be lucky if she lasted until they passed the first trencher of meat.

...

Katherine walked into the great hall at Duncan's side and paused with him at the top of the stairs. She lifted her chin and looked out to the trestle tables filled with unsmiling warriors. Every McGowan face turned to study her. They wore the same disdainful looks she was used to receiving from the Fergusons.

"Keep your gaze down, Kate. Do na let them think you forward."

Katherine focused her gaze on the rushes, but not before she noticed that each man had one hand on the hilt of his sword and the other on the dagger at his side.

"Welcome to Lochmore Castle, Callum. Geordie."

Duncan greeted their guests in Gaelic, which was not surprising. Katherine doubted the McGowans understood English. Very few Fergusons, other than Duncan and Malcolm and one or two others, did.

The McGowan whom Duncan greeted as Callum took a step forward. He stood almost a head shorter than Duncan, his bushy red hair framing a ruddy, flushed face. There was a ready smile on his lips and a twinkle in his eyes Katherine found appealing. If he would not have posed such a threat, she was certain she could have liked him.

Not so his brother, Geordie. From his first leering stare, she felt a strong repulsion to the man. Although a good deal taller and broader than his brother, with blond hair and rugged good looks, the licentious glare in his eyes sent shivers up and down her spine. He stared at her as if he were undressing her, and almost drooled in anticipation of what he would do if he ever got her alone. Katherine lowered her gaze to the rushes again and ignored his stare.

"We are glad you made it home from the fighting, Duncan," Callum said in greeting. "There were many of our Scots who did na."

Duncan nodded in agreement. Geordie lifted his hand to his sword and boasted proudly. "But there were many more of the bastard English whose blood soaked the Scottish ground. I smile when I remember each one I sent to Hades."

Katherine kept her gaze lowered, willing herself not to react. She didn't have to. Duncan reacted for her. He tightened his grip on her hand and pulled her closer. "There were enough on both sides who lost their lives. Even one man is too great a sacrifice."

"Has marriage to the English woman softened you so much, Ferguson?"

Duncan bristled. Katherine felt his muscles bunch beneath her hand. "Death and the loss of so many good friends has changed me. If you think to see if marriage has made me soft, Geordie, I will be glad to use my sword to prove you wrong."

An uneasy wave of friction seeped through the great hall. Each Ferguson warrior readied his stance, moving to guard his back and gain an advantage if a fight broke out with the McGowans scattered throughout the room.

Geordie fingered the hilt of his broad sword, then slowly lifted his hand away. "I meant na challenge, laird. We have all lost friends and family."

Katherine listened but did not hear much regret in his voice.

Callum gave his brother a disapproving look. then took a

step forward. "We will miss your father, Duncan," Callum said, the tone of his voice sincere. "He was a fine laird. Scotland will miss his good counsel."

Duncan nodded in acknowledgment. "The Ferguson fight is na finished. Bolton took Brenna with him. We will ride after her in two days' time."

"You can count on the McGowans to be at your side," Callum added. "We will meet you on our east border when you pass south."

Geordie fingered the hilt of his sword. "It will be a pleasure to send even more of the bastard English to hell where they belong. Would that we could rid the world of every one of them."

"Enough Geordie," Callum warned softly.

Katherine did not react. She didn't want them to know she understood what they were saying, but Duncan must have sensed her anger. He squeezed her hand as a gentle reminder to remain calm. She clenched her teeth until the muscles in her jaw ached, and held onto her temper with the patience of Job himself.

"Have you and your men had enough to eat?" Duncan asked, the tone of his voice strained and hard.

"Aye," Callum answered. "Malcolm made sure we were taken care of well."

Duncan nodded, then led Katherine to the other side of the table. Callum took his place at Duncan's left, and Geordie opposite him on Malcolm's right. Two serving girls quickly brought over trenchers with food and a pitcher of ale to fill their laird and their mistress's goblets. The girl with the ale wasn't fast enough to escape Geordie's reach before he grabbed her to refill his empty tankard.

She gave Duncan an apologetic look and hurried from the room.

Duncan filled his platter and Katherine put but a small portion on hers. While her husband chewed his food as if he enjoyed every bite, Katherine could do no more than shove the roasted fowl and vegetables around on her platter. The air literally sparked with tension. Soon the McGowans would state their purpose for coming, and Duncan would state the reason they could not have the crown.

Or, he would simply tell them Katherine had it and leave them alone with her to see if they could force her to tell them where it was hidden.

Or, he could refuse to discuss the matter and before the tables were cleared, the floor would be littered with dead bodies. Duncan's could be one of them.

A cold sweat covered her body and a chill ran up and down her spine. Whatever happened would be her fault. She gripped the handle of her two-pronged fork and prepared for the worst.

"You'd best eat, lass," Duncan said between mouthfuls of food. He spoke in English so neither of the McGowans understood him.

Katherine jabbed a small piece of carrot, then lifted her fork to her mouth. "It's difficult to eat when one is in the company of such an arrogant ass," she answered, keeping her voice sweet as honey. Duncan's hand halted in mid air as he reached for a piece of dried fruit on a platter in front of him. Malcolm seemed to have swallowed his ale wrong for he coughed most profusely.

She caught the hard look on Geordie's face, as if to

even hear English spoken offended his Scottish pride. She quickly lowered her gaze, thankful that Callum pulled his brother's attention to more important matters.

"It's best to get to the reason we're here, Duncan. We've come for the crown."

Duncan did not lift his head, but stabbed another piece of the roasted fowl and chewed. "You canna have it," he announced, tearing a hunk from the loaf of warm bread and spreading it with honey.

Geordie slid back in his chair and reached for his sword, but Callum held out his hand to stop him. The hateful look on Geordie's face was enough to commit murder. "It was McGowan Scots that died taking the crown," Geordie roared, shoving Callum's hand away. "The crown belongs to us. We demand you give it back."

Slowly, deliberately, Duncan laid down his fork and fisted his hands on either side of his trencher. He lifted his gaze and leveled each brother with a determined look that broached no compromise. His voice when he spoke, emitted a challenge that left no room for doubt. "It was some verra foolish McGowan Scots that took the Bishop's Crown. Not only did they lose their own lives taking it, but their stupidity caused many more innocent Scots to die for a worthless cause."

"How dare you—"

Geordie had his sword only half out of the sheath when Duncan whipped his broadsword from behind his back and slammed it onto the table. The edge of the sword made a deep cut in the wood while the tip of the metal missed striking Geordie by mere inches.

"Enough!"

Geordie froze. Duncan rose to his feet and glared at the young Scot. His towering height dominated the room. He braced his hands on either side of his trencher and faced the McGowans. "When your brave McGowan lads stole the crown from the English, where did they take it for safe keeping? Home? To Fenbyre Castle? Nay! They brought it here. They brought it to Lochmore for my father to protect. For my father to take the risk."

Katherine felt the turbulence in Duncan's body that teetered on the verge of erupting. She could see raw anger in every movement, hear it in every word. Never had she experienced such controlled violence, such restrained intensity as she heard in the quiet fury of his voice.

"My father, and my mother, and my sisters, Meara and Elissa, died because of what McGowan Scots did. When you give my family back to me, alive and unharmed, I will give you back the crown."

The great hall bristled with anger charged enough to light a fire. Katherine waited. Every warrior stood with his hand on his sword, ready to draw blood at the first sign from their laird. Her heart pounded in her breast as she watched to see how many deaths would be caused because of her vow to God.

"The crown is ours," Geordie hissed, the tone of his voice bitter.

"Quiet, Geordie," Callum whispered, then slowly raised his hand in a yielding motion. One by one the McGowan warriors relaxed their stance. "You are right, Duncan. You have forfeited more. The crown is yours by right."

Geordie slammed down his tankard of ale, and shoved his chair away from the table. He gave Duncan a hostile glance, then glared at Katherine with a look equally as hateful. Without another word, he stormed from the room, taking a half dozen McGowan warriors with him.

Katherine watched him leave and felt a relief that was indescribable. Her heart raced as if she'd just been given a reprieve from realizing her greatest fear. And yet, she knew the McGowans were but the first to come after the crown. They were but the first to threaten Duncan.

Callum rose and held his hand out in offering. "We will meet you in two days' time, Duncan. You can count on the McGowans to help you get your sister back."

Duncan took Callum's hand, and clasped his forearm. "You are welcome to stay the night and partake of our food in the morning before you leave."

"Nay. I think it's best if there is some distance between Geordie and Lochmore Castle. He's more than set on having the crown. He has too much of our father's temper to see things in the right light."

Duncan nodded. "You will make a fine laird when the time comes, Callum. Scotland will be the stronger for it."

Callum McGowan turned to Katherine. "You have a fine wife, Duncan. I do na ken the reason you chose an English, but whatever it is, I hope it's worth the price you will be forced to pay. There are many like Geordie who are too filled with prejudice and hatred. They will never search for a way to bond the two countries in peace."

Callum bowed with respect, then left the great hall. The remaining McGowan warriors followed behind him.

"Do you want someone to follow them, Duncan?" Malcolm asked after the last McGowan had left.

"Have Balfour see that they make it past the curtain,

then secure the gates and double the watch. Callum can be trusted. If he has any say, they will na come back tonight."

Malcolm gave a sign to the Ferguson warrior sitting beside him, and Balfour quickly left the room. Duncan reached over and filled his tankard with ale, then poured an equal amount in hers. In no time, the room was bustling with talk of the near skirmish with the McGowans and the excitement of going to fight the English in two days' time.

"Are you all right, Kate?"

She was trembling inside. No, she was not all right. Did Duncan realize what had almost happened? Did he know how close he'd almost come to losing his life? Over a crown he did not have — and a wife he did not want.

She had to get the crown and get it to her father in England. Duncan might not escape so easily the next time someone came for it. She might not escape either if Geordie found out she was hiding it. She wondered how much Duncan would care if she didn't.

She could not forget the words she'd heard Regan say this afternoon, and the boastful tone of her voice. *I should be the one to have your name and share your bed and bear your children. I am the one you love, na her.*

Katherine glanced at her husband. She thought he had not been able to come to her just because she was English. Now she feared that was not the only reason. Why hadn't she realized he loved someone else? Making her his wife betrayed the woman he really loved.

She could not forget the disdainful looks she'd lived with for the past two weeks. Everyone knew their laird loved another — except her.

"Are you ill, Kate?"

Katherine lifted her cup of ale to her mouth and drank. "I am fine." She picked up her fork and shoved a tiny carrot around on her platter. There was a tightness in her throat that would not leave, a void that nothing could fill.

Duncan placed his hand over her fist, and Katherine jerked it back. Heaven help her. She could not allow herself to care for this man. She would not let him pretend he cared for her either. He had not married her because he wanted her, but because she had the crown. He had sacrificed his happiness to get it. Before it was over, he would more than likely have to sacrifice his life, too.

Duncan draped his arm across the back of her chair, and leaned closer. "Not all Scots are like Geordie, Kate."

Her flesh warmed like she'd suddenly come too close to the sun. She didn't want his nearness to effect her like it did. "Aren't they? Listen to your men, Duncan."

Duncan looked away from her, and focused on the conversations of the Ferguson warriors sitting at the tables. There was hardly another topic being discussed than the upcoming battle with Bolton and the English. "There is little difference, Duncan. They are all anxious to fight the English."

"The men are anxious to have Brenna back with us."

Katherine nodded. She didn't want to think of the Ferguson's hatred for the English any longer. She didn't want to think of the lass called Regan. "How long will you be gone?"

"I would think a week. Mayhaps a day or two longer. Is that why you are na eating? You are worried?"

He leaned back in his chair and smiled. Sweet Mary, she was drawn to him. A warm rush swirled deep in her stomach and her breath caught in her throat. How she ached to have him hold her. She'd never felt as safe as when she was at his side. Even when Geordie had reached for his sword she had not been afraid. Not for herself.

"What upsets me, husband, is that you have brought me where I am not wanted, and might not stay alive long enough to care for me."

"You fear for my life?"

She did, but she would never let him know it. "No, husband. I fear for my future."

The smile left his face and Katherine waited to see his anger. There was none. A strange, unreadable expression covered his face while his eyes filled with a haunted yearning. That look was even more disturbing. "I will see what I can do to care for your future, wife." He lifted his cup of ale and drank.

Katherine shoved aside the concern that he would leave in two days' time and might not come back to her alive. Deep down, she wanted his vow that he would come back to her alive. "When you return, I expect to see you sitting atop your horse, leading your men," she said, meeting a look that sent warm shivers all through her body.

"Is that an order, wife, or merely a request?"

She tried to turn away from him, but could not. The intensity of his gaze would not release her. "It is an order, husband. I will not allow you to die and leave me a widow before I have been married a full month."

His lips lifted to form a warm smile, and the riveting of his gaze held her captive with a thousand licking flames of fire. "Malcolm," he said without turning away from her. "You had best guard my back well from the English, or my wife will na be so understanding when we return. She is na partial to becoming a widow just yet."

Katherine bit her lip. She could not allow herself to be so affected by nothing more than a look, or a few soft words and his unsettling nearness.

"I swear, milady," Malcolm said from across the table, "that I will guard your husband's life with my own and when we return he will be sitting atop his horse, leading his men."

Katherine bit her lip harder.

"See, Kate. You have nothing to fear."

She had to leave. She had to put some distance between herself and her husband. She opened her mouth to speak, but no words would come. She swallowed to find her voice. "I will endeavor to adopt your unwavering optimism, my lord, whether founded or not." Katherine clenched her hands at her sides and stood. Her legs were strangely weak. Her insides moving uncomfortably. "If you will excuse me, I am finished and will go to my chamber now."

"No. You will stay here with me." Duncan's harsh command echoed in the large room.

Katherine stopped with a jerk and twisted around to look at her husband. A deep frown covered his forehead and his eyes seemed darker than usual.

"You will na hide in your chamber again, milady."

"Hide?"

"Was that na what you were doing when the McGowans came? Hiding in your chamber because you did na want to be with us?" He stood beside her and lifted her chin with his finger. "Or perhaps it's only your husband you do na want to be near?"

Katherine narrowed her gaze. She glared at him with as harsh a look as she could make. How dare he! "You are the one, my lord, who has made clear the conditions concerning our marriage and the role I am to play as your wife. I am but submitting to the rules you have set down."

"And what rules are those?"

Katherine kept her voice so low, even Malcolm could not hear her words. "For two weeks, you have not been able to bring yourself to be a husband to your English wife." She held up her hands in surrender. "I yield to your choice. Now, I will not allow it."

Katherine stared at the startled expression on Duncan's face until his gaze turned to cold, hard fury. Even she, who feared his temper less than most of the men who'd lived their whole lives with him, was not brave enough to face his anger.

She turned, then walked amid the long rows of trestle tables, keeping her shoulders back and her head high. She made her way out of the great hall, blinking back the damnable wetness that clouded her vision.

She would no more be a wife to him than he intended to be a husband to her.

Chapter 10

Duncan tossed back the remaining ale in his tankard and stormed through the great hall after his wife. Blood thundered in his head as her words echoed in his ears. *For two weeks you have not been able to be a husband to your English wife. Now, I will not allow it.*

Damn her English stubbornness. Damn her English pride. Damn her outspoken English tongue.

Duncan climbed the stone stairs two at a time and reached the long hallway just as the door to his chamber slammed. He took long, angry strides until he reached his room, and threw open the thick, oak door with such force it bounced against the stone wall and came back toward him. He kicked it with his booted foot, then kicked it again from behind to close it after he'd entered the room.

She did not look up, nor was there a hesitation in her movements as she crossed the room to the wooden clothes chest against the wall. She flung open the door and pulled out the white muslin gown she wore each evening when she went to bed, then whipped out the light blue dress she'd worn the day he'd brought her here.

Next, she walked to her small dressing table and snapped up her brush and the silver netting for her hair. When she had everything collected, she stormed toward the door, without even looking at him.

Duncan blocked her path as she reached to open the door. "You will na even think of leaving this chamber, wife." His voice came out as a harsh growl but he didn't care.

"I will do more than think about leaving, *husband*," she leveled back at him. "I intend to stay in the empty chamber near the chapel. And you will not stop me."

"Oh, I will stop you, Kate. And you will na be feeling so pleased with yourself when I do."

Duncan anchored his fists on his hips and glared down at her, giving her a most ferocious look. By the saints, she was a challenge. He had never met anyone more pigheaded in his life. Where did she think she was going? What on earth made her think he would allow it?

He filled his lungs with hot, burning air. She glared back at him, the anger in her eyes mounting. "Step back, Kate," he warned.

She did not flinch, but pursed her lips tighter, fisted her hands around the wadded clothing in her arms and took an equally harsh breath. The flare of her upturned nose was the most appealing thing he'd ever seen.

"I will na let you leave this room, Kate."

With an angry stomp of her foot, she stormed back across the room and threw the clothing to the bed. The brush bounced once, then landed on the tapestry covering the floor with a soft thud. She kicked it in anger. "Why?" She turned on her heels and glared at him. "Why should I stay? You don't want me here."

She paced the floor beside the bed with her hands fisted at her sides and her back as straight as a lancer's spear. "Do you think I don't know that you come here every night and watch me while I sleep?" She pointed to the chair beside the bed. "What are you thinking, laird? How much you wish someone else was lying in your bed?"

She paced the floor again, not bothering to look at him. "Do you think I don't know how demoralizing it is for you to take an Englishwoman as your wife? How it eats away at you and your Scottish pride? I remember the first night you stayed with me. I prayed it would not be impossible for you to…" She breathed a sigh that quivered when she released it. "In the morning when I awoke, you were gone. Until tonight, you haven't even touched me." She spun around to face him. "Am I that repulsive to hold, Duncan?"

The hurt Duncan saw in her eyes twisted his heart inside his chest. He thought she'd been asleep and had not known he'd sat with her each night. "You do na understand, Kate. It's na that—"

"It doesn't matter, Duncan. You no longer have to feel any guilt about tainting the next Ferguson heir with English blood. We will share no bed between us."

"Aye, we will, Kate. You are my wife and—"

"No. I am not your wife. Our marriage has not been consummated."

Duncan looked at the pale coloring of her face and felt the air leave his body. She reached out to steady herself, and he noticed that her hand trembled as she grasped onto the bedpost.

"Our marriage has not been consummated," she repeated,

her voice shaking. "I'm going to London. Considering the special circumstances surrounding our marriage, I'm sure the bishop will—"

"Nay!" Blinding shards of pain slashed through his head, then stabbed into his chest to reach his heart. "You are my wife. I will na let you go."

"What good is it for me to stay?"

Duncan crossed to where Katherine stood and grasped her shoulders. "You will na leave me, Kate."

"Why? You don't want me."

"I wish to God I didn't." Duncan looked at her and understood more clearly than ever before how much he wanted her. He had never wanted anyone more. Every emotion in his body told him so. She was his. He had chosen her.

"I will always be English," she whispered.

"You will always be my wife." He pulled her close and lowered his head to capture her mouth in a blinding kiss.

By the saints, he couldn't lose her. No matter what else, he could not lose the woman who had braved Bolton in the dungeon to try to free him. He could not lose the woman who gave life to every emotion he thought died when he found his parents slaughtered. He could not lose the woman he'd chosen as his wife for all time.

He lifted his mouth and looked into Kate's eyes. She didn't believe him. He could see it written there. He covered her mouth again, drinking from her, teasing, touching, tormenting.

She held herself stiffly in his arms, pushing her arms against his chest, fighting to make him stop. But he would not.

He tried to be gentle, but he could not. She wanted to leave him. He was desperate to make her want to stay.

She turned her head away from him, trying to avoid his kisses. Duncan wrapped one arm around her waist and hauled her up against him. He raked the fingers of his other hand through her hair, cupping her head in his massive grip so she couldn't escape him.

He opened his mouth atop hers, running the tip of his tongue over her lips until she moaned a loud sigh of agony. She opened to him and he entered her warm cavern, seeking, finding. He had this one chance to prove he wanted her as his wife. This last chance to erase the ghosts that had haunted him since he'd found his family slaughtered.

He deepened his kisses, reveling in the hot, searing pulses that caused a burning ache deep in his gut. He needed her. He wanted her. As badly as he'd ever wanted a woman in his whole life. He pulled her up against him and ran his hands over her body, cupping her backside, pressing her fully against him.

Blazing arrows of fire coursed to every part of him. He let his hands roam over her, kneading the heels of his hands against the small of her back. Listening to the soft moans echo in the back of her throat.

He lifted his mouth from hers and took in huge, gasping breaths of air. She panted just as hard. "You will na leave me, Kate," he whispered in her ear, then moved his kisses lower, to the tender spot on the side of her neck. He trailed his kisses downward, pulling at the lacing on the gown she wore. The material ripped and he pulled it harder until her breasts were bared.

Duncan uttered a breathless moan, then kissed her again. He brushed his fingertips against the snowy whiteness of her flesh, reveling in the silky feel of her skin. He kissed her there, moving from one breast to the other.

She clung to him when her knees buckled, and with a loud moan of surrender, she wrapped her arms around his neck and gave herself to him.

She was his wife.

He would forget that she was English, and only remember that she was his wife.

. . .

Katherine lolled her head back on her shoulders and cursed her traitorous body for reacting to his touch. She cursed her traitorous body for desiring his kisses. She cursed her body again, and gave in to the cataclysmic emotions racing through her.

She'd always known his kisses held a special power over her, but she had no idea his touch could do what it did. A burning heat spread from the tips of her toes to the ends of her fingers. Every part of her tingled.

She skimmed her hands over the taut flesh at his sides, then touched the tight cords across his shoulders and down his arms until his muscles quivered in response. She'd been so sure of her decision to leave him, knew it was the only option open to her. Until he'd held her, and kissed her, and touched her like he was now.

His hands pulled at her clothing, ripping what would not come off easily. Cool air washed over her body. She welcomed its relief. Her body burned. His touch did that to her. This was indeed a torment she had never believed possible. Every inch of her flesh where his lips touched and his fingers caressed, blazed. The path his touch forged was as straight as a marksman's arrow, spiraling to the very core of her being.

He stepped away from her and pulled his clothing over his head. Then picked her up in his arms and carried her to the bed. He covered her with his body. The weight of him atop her sent waves of thunder crashing against her ears. The feel of his naked flesh created a firestorm of heat.

She raked her fingers through his thick, dark hair, and pulled his mouth down to hers. She closed her eyes to millions of emotions that rushed through her, hypnotizing her mind, body, and soul. She should stop him. Once he took her, there would be no going back.

His mouth opened over hers while his hands skimmed every inch of her nakedness. He ran the tip of his tongue over her lips until she moaned a loud sigh of agony and lifted her head to meet him. He dared to breach the entrance to her mouth, and she surrendered with something near desperation.

His hands cupped her face on either side while his thumbs rubbed lazy circles on her cheeks. A bolt of molten heat spiraled to the pit of her stomach, to that newly discovered place Duncan had awakened with his first kiss. She could not control the emotions raging within her.

His hands moved over her skin, over her shoulders and down the sides of her body. His long, muscled fingers skimmed the edges of her breasts, the curve of her waist, and the rounding of her hips. She did not know a man's touch could make her feel this way, could make her crave something she couldn't explain.

"You are beautiful, Kate. You are truly beautiful."

He raised above her on his elbows and looked into her eyes, then lowered his mouth to her again. He kissed her deep, drawing from her, giving to her, imploring and demanding from her.

And then his kisses moved. First to the spot below her ear, then down her neck, then to the full rise of her breasts. Katherine grasped her hands around the sinewy cords on his arms and held tight. She needed to touch him. She needed to feel him close to her. She needed more of him.

As if he sensed what she wanted, he covered first one breast with his mouth, then the other. Katherine's head lowered to the pillow as she arched her back to give him more of herself. She couldn't breathe. She couldn't think. She couldn't wait. "Duncan, please."

"Aye, lass."

He positioned himself over her, then kissed her again. His kisses became even more demanding, and all the while he tortured her with his lips, his hands stoked the fire on her skin. He moved over her flesh until she could do nothing but writhe and moan beneath him.

His fingers touched that secret place deep within her, and she arched against him and shattered into a million pieces. She wanted this. She wanted more.

"There will be pain this first time, Kate. I wish it were na so, but it is the way of things."

She felt him come into her and knew he was trying to be as gentle as possible, but heaven help her, the pain was unlike any she had imagined. A ragged moan tore from the back of her throat and she pushed against his shoulders, struggling to free herself.

"Put your arms around my neck and hold on tight, lass."

She couldn't do it. Instead, she turned her head and pushed against him again.

"Put your arms around me."

With a shuddering gasp, Katherine wrapped her arms around his neck and held on with all her strength. Tiny tears welled in her eyes, threatening to spill down her cheeks. She breathed a relieved sigh when his mouth covered hers again and he kissed her.

His tongue urged her to open for him and the moment she did, he thrust his hips forward and entered her. A sharp, searing pain, worse than any she had expected, stabbed through her body. She clenched her fingers on the corded muscles expanding his shoulders as he covered her mouth to muffle her scream.

He clamped his arms around her and held her tight. "Do na move, Kate. Hold yourself verra still and the pain will ease."

Tears filled her eyes, then ran down her cheeks.

He kissed her lightly. "It will never be like this again, lass. I promise." He kissed her again. "Is your pain gone?"

"Nearly."

He kissed her again.

Oh, how she loved his kisses. If he would just be content to do no more. But just as that thought entered her mind, he moved within her. She braced herself for more pain, but it did not come.

"Now I will show you what it will be like," he whispered in her ear.

Ever so slowly, he moved within her until all thoughts vanished from her mind and all reasoning ceased to exist.

Again and again he thrust until he had carried her to a place far above her. Faster and faster he moved, and higher and higher they climbed, until she soared somewhere above even the clouds.

Just as her tears had made the candlelight streak bright white arches above her, so had her passion left a trail of sparkling embers. She shattered to a million twinkling starbursts and simply floated.

Duncan stilled above her, then trembled in her arms. He released a loud moan and collapsed with his face nestled against her neck. Katherine held him tight as he gasped for breath with her.

A heavy sheen of perspiration covered his body, and she skimmed her fingers over the rippling muscles of his shoulders and down the banded cords of his arms. The pounding of his heart echoed in her ears. She lifted her head to touch her lips to his skin.

Everything had changed. With this one act, everything had changed.

From the moment she had accepted Duncan's proposal, she'd thought she could be a wife to him with no risk to herself. She thought she could use him to escape a life of torture with Bolton, profit from his protection, yet keep the one thing he wanted away from him.

She still thought she could. Only now she knew the price she would pay. Now she knew how easy it would be to lose her heart, and how easily Duncan could hurt her if he possessed it.

Katherine blinked away the tears that welled in her eyes. Duncan seemed no more in control than she. As she listened to his ragged breathing, a cold hand squeezed her heart. Leaving was no longer an option. Her small circle of safety had grown considerably smaller.

"Are you all right, Kate?"

"I am more than all right," she breathed.

He rolled to the side and pulled her up against him.

She placed her arm around his chest and snuggled closer. She welcomed the blanket he threw over them.

"I could na let you go," he whispered, then breathed a deep sigh.

Katherine didn't ask why. The answer was better left unsaid.

The fire had gone out in the grate. She should be cold, but she wasn't. She should feel something, but she didn't.

. . .

The Ferguson had taken her as his wife. Even though she was English. Even though he loved another, he had consummated their marriage. Leaving was no longer an option.

Katherine swallowed a cry of despair.

He moved away from her and slipped out of the bed, his absence creating a cold void.

"I must go downstairs to speak with Malcolm," he said lifting his shirt over his shoulders.

Katherine remembered the feel of his muscled flesh beneath her fingers. She couldn't lift her gaze from his body. "Are you worried the McGowans haven't left?" she asked, pulling the covers up to warm the chill his leaving caused.

"It does na hurt to check."

Katherine watched him go, then sat up in bed and

wrapped her arms around her knees. His absence would give her time to be alone with her thoughts. Time to pray for another answer. For God to give her a sign to tell her what to do.

She crawled out of bed and washed in the basin on the stand, then put on a clean gown and went to the chapel to pray. She and her mother and Elizabeth had always spent time each morning and each evening in prayer. It was a habit she had not given up. Now, the time she spent talking to God was even more important than ever. Never had she needed God's help more than she did now.

She took a deep breath and repeated her heartfelt petition that God would forgive her sins, curb her wicked tongue, and watch over Duncan and all the Fergusons who would go to England with him. She added a special request for them to return with Brenna unharmed.

Then, she prayed that somehow she would find a way to get the crown and return it to England.

Before she finished, Katherine clasped her hands tighter and added one more prayer. She pleaded that God would protect her heart from a man who would, when she gave the crown to her father, regret having made her his wife.

She was so deep in prayer she didn't hear the door open behind her. It wasn't until she heard the soft patter of footsteps that she realized she wasn't the only one who had come to the chapel to pray.

She made the sign of the cross, then whispered her final amen. She made to rise, but before she could get to her feet, a jolt unlike any she'd ever felt exploded behind her eyes, sending bright, searing stabs of pain to every part of her body.

She reached for the railing, but her hand grasped only air. Release from the excruciating agony came fast and complete, taking away the hurt, and cloaking her in blessed numbness.

. . .

Duncan opened the door to his chamber and searched the darkness for Kate. He breathed a deep breath, praying he'd done the right thing. She had been going to leave him.

He thought of the way she'd stood up to him. The way she'd fought with him, battled him, and reasoned with him. The way she'd given herself to him with more openness and uninhibited abandon than he thought it was possible to receive from a woman.

He walked toward the bed, aching to hold her in his arms again. To make love to her as he had earlier. His heart clenched in his chest with an uncomfortable sense of longing he pushed aside.

Duncan lit a candle from the torch on the wall outside. He had stayed downstairs talking to Malcolm and Angus far too long and had lost track of the time. Only one more day and he would leave to get Brenna back from England. Only one more day and Bolton would be dead. Duncan closed his eyes and savored the sweet taste of revenge.

He sat on the stool beside the bed to remove his boots, then lifted the candle. Kate had probably fallen asleep long ago. He stood and stared at the empty bed, the covers still rumpled from their lovemaking. A frown covered his face. Without a doubt, she had gone to the chapel to say her evening prayers. She went there every night before she retired, just as his mother had done.

After he returned with Brenna, he would make it his habit to go with her, as his father had gone with his mother. There were many things the two of them would make their habit once Brenna was home...

...and Bolton was dead,

...and Kate had given him the crown.

Duncan crossed the room and walked down the shadowed hallway to the chapel. Last night she had been late coming back from her prayers, too. He'd waited for her, and by the time she returned, she was shivering as violently as a fish thrown out of water.

He opened the chapel door and stopped beside the first wooden bench. His brows shot up in surprise as he looked around the room. He'd been sure he would find her here, but only one short candle flickered in the empty room.

He closed the door behind him and went to the other rooms; Brenna's room, his parents' chambers, the garderobe on this level and the one below. She was in none of them. His heart tightened with a hint of anger.

Perhaps her lovemaking had been an act, and she had taken the first opportunity to run away.

"Morgana," he yelled, walking to the room where Kate's handmaiden stayed so she could be close to her mistress. He covered the distance to her chamber almost at a run, ignoring the blood heating in his veins.

Morgana came to her door, pulling a covering around her night dress. "Milord?"

"Have you seen your mistress?"

"Not since she went to the chapel, laird."

Duncan was already down the hallway to search each room again when he ran into Malcolm. "Is something amiss, Duncan?"

"Kate is na in our chamber. Have you seen her?"

He shook his head. "She has na come down the stairs or we would have noticed." Malcolm matched Duncan's hurried steps as they went back to the room he shared with his wife.

"We'll check each room on this level again," Duncan said, opening the door to the side room, "and if we do na find her we will search the entire keep."

Duncan tried to control the anger building within him. "Send someone to check with the guards at the front gate and the postern."

"Oh, Duncan. She would na try to leave now. Not in the dark."

"Send them," Duncan ordered, his voice sounding strangely calm considering the turmoil building within him.

Duncan checked the chambers another time and Malcolm met him at the chapel entrance. Duncan looked around the empty room then walked to the front. He lifted his eyes to the statue before him. "Do you think it possible that someone could have come for her?"

"Nay, Duncan. The hall has been crowded all night, and Conan spent hours in a dark corner by the door, kissing that comely lass from the kitchen. His mind was occupied with other matters, but not so much that someone could have taken the mistress out of the keep without his notice."

"Where did you see her last, Duncan?" Malcolm asked, resting his hand on the railing next to Duncan's.

"In our chamber, just before I came down to you. There was nothing amiss with her, and—" Duncan stopped and cocked his head to the side to listen. "Did you hear a strange sound, Malcolm?"

Malcolm listened, then shook his head. "Nay," he answered, "but—"

Malcolm stopped too. A soft whimper, barely audible, seeped into the silence in the chapel. Duncan quietly listened. They heard it again. A soft, muffled moan from somewhere near, yet far away.

Every muscle in Duncan's body tightened in alarm. He moved around the railing toward the altar and the whimpers coming from somewhere behind it. A cold, uncomfortable sweat covered his body. Stabs of deadly fear prickled the hairs on the back of his neck.

He heard it again. With Malcolm at his side, Duncan ran to a small storage chamber behind the altar. "Blessed mother, nay," he whispered as he removed the square cut of wood that barricaded the small opening from the outside. "Do na let her be in here. Dear God, nay! She fears small, dark places." Duncan pulled open the door and Kate's pathetic whimper assaulted his senses.

"Bring torches!" he bellowed, and at almost that same instant, Malcolm held up a bright light. Duncan didn't have to enter the tiny room to find her. Kate had her arms clutched around her knees. Her trembling body was curled into a tight ball before the door. Her chest heaved with each low demented moan while her eyes darted wild with fear. Being locked in the small, enclosed darkness had almost driven her to the point of madness.

He reached for her and lifted her up in his arms. She wound her arms around his neck with strength that defied her small frame. "'Tis all right, Kate. You are safe now."

Duncan carried her out of the chapel, past the small group of Fergusons crowded in the hallway. Someone gave him a cover and he wrapped her in it to keep her warm. The men and women parted as he walked past. He read the confusion on their faces.

On everyone's face except for Regan's.

Regan leaned against the stone wall with her hands crossed over her chest and watched as he left the chapel. She raised her eyebrows when he passed, and smiled. The amused look on her face sent a shiver down his spine. Their gazes locked, and Duncan paused. "Leave my keep, Regan. You will na come near my wife until I return from England."

Regan shrugged her shoulders and pushed herself away from the wall. She swaggered down the hall as if she didn't fear him. Duncan gritted his teeth. God help her if she had done this to Kate.

"Malcolm," he ordered. "Send someone for Angus, and have everyone return to their beds. Then come back to me."

"Aye, Duncan."

He carried Kate into their chamber and sat with her on the edge of the bed. He couldn't have pried her arms from around his body if he'd tried.

He pushed the hair from her face, then held her close. Eyes filled with wild terror stared out at nothing and he stroked her flesh with his hands while she trembled in fear. "Kate?" he asked when her breathing had calmed some.

He slowly eased her arms from around him, releasing her death grip. He stared at the blood still smeared at the ends of her fingers from where she had clawed at the door to get out.

"Kate? What happened? Who locked you in the room behind the altar?"

She stiffened against him and refused to answer. A small part of him did not want to hear her answer.

"Did you go there to get something?"

She shook her head then buried her face harder against him. He cupped the back of her head to hold her close, but her soft moan of pain stopped him. He eased his grip and felt the lump there. "How did you get this?"

She closed her eyes and frowned as if the knot on her head slowed her ability to think. "I must have fallen," she muttered with a great deal of effort.

"Do na lie to me, Kate."

"Leave it be, Duncan. It doesn't matter." She tried to push away from him, but he would not release her.

"I'm tired, Duncan. I'd like to sleep now."

She fell against his chest and he pulled her away to hold her straight. "You will na fall asleep until Angus looks at you. It is na wise to—"

"Duncan."

"Aye."

"I think it would be wise to let me up. I don't feel so well. I think I am going to be ill."

Duncan stopped his lecture and handed Kate a pail just in time. By the time Angus arrived, he had her in bed and a little of the color had come back to her face.

"Drink this, milady," Angus said, handing Kate a cup. "It will soothe your stomach."

"Thank you, Angus. I feel much better now."

"Feel her head, Angus," Duncan ordered. "There's a lump as big as my fist at the back."

"It's a very small lump, Angus," Katherine contradicted, as Angus lifted her hair to feel her head.

Angus smiled and Duncan frowned. He did not appreciate Angus' humor.

"It's not as big as your fist, laird, but neither is it very small, milady. Just big enough for you to stay in bed on the morrow."

Duncan nodded his approval. "Angus. Stay with Kate for a moment. I need to speak with Malcolm."

Duncan closed the door behind him as he and Malcolm left the room. "Find Gregor. He will stay here to guard Kate while we're gone. Have him choose what men he'll need, but I do na want my wife alone for a moment. Not even when she sleeps. Her maid will sleep in the room with her, and a guard will sleep outside her door each night. Someone will be at her side every minute of the day."

A frown covered Malcolm's face. "You think someone tried to hurt the mistress?"

"I do na think she locked herself in that small room, and I do na think the lump on her head was caused by any fall. Tell Gregor to guard her closely. I do na want anything to happen while we're gone."

When Malcolm went to find Gregor, Duncan went back to be with Kate. He couldn't believe that someone would want to harm her. That someone could hate her so much they would dare to raise a finger against her.

No one other than Regan.

Chapter 11

"Do you have all the salves and potions you'll need, Angus?"

Katherine looked into the early morning sky and tucked her hands into the folds of the heavy woolen shawl around her shoulders. Duncan was leaving to get Brenna. She looked at the huge army gathered around him and a shiver ran down her spine.

"Aye," Angus answered. "See here?" He opened his sack and showed Katherine the various containers. "Stonecrop, to take care of the wounds. Sorrel for bruises and a fever. Lady's mantle for bleeding."

Angus patted his sack and recited the names of a dozen more powders and salves he had with him. The names were more familiar to her now, but she was so nervous she doubted she would remember much today.

"Keep him safe, Angus," she whispered. She watched Duncan give last minute instructions to Gregor, then check his horse and armor a final time.

"I will, milady. With Malcolm watching his back and me at his side, nothing will happen."

"Kate."

Duncan's voice echoed in the crisp, pre-dawn air and Katherine walked over to where he stood. He tipped her head up with his finger and stared into her eyes. "I want your word that you will na try to leave the keep for anything."

She nodded.

"Answer me, lass."

"Yes, Duncan."

"And you'll do whatever Gregor tells you without question. Understand?"

"Yes."

"Are you sure you are well?"

"Yes. I stayed abed all day yesterday and now I'm fine."

Katherine looked into Duncan's face. He'd taken her again last night. She loved the feel of his muscled flesh against her own. She loved the feel of his naked body atop her. Her cheeks warmed as she remembered the hours they'd spent in each others' arms.

"I'll be home before long with Brenna." Duncan studied her face as if he wanted to memorize her features before he left.

"And Bolton will be dead?"

"Aye. Bolton will be dead, and there will be nothing for you to fear."

"Except my father and my king."

"He is na longer your king."

"And my father?"

"Aye, lass. He will always be your father, but you are now my wife. Your first allegiance is to me."

"I've given you my loyalty as well as my allegiance, husband."

"But you have na given me the crown."

He could not have hurt her more if he'd slapped her face. "It's not mine to give."

"It is na yours to keep."

Katherine closed her eyes and turned her face from him. It was always the crown. The crown always came first.

"I will have it when I come back. You can na keep it from me or from Scotland." He gave her a look that demanded her compliance, then mounted his horse.

She couldn't let him leave like this. Not when he may never come back to her. Katherine ran to his side and touched his leg. "Stay well, my laird."

"I will return leading my men as you have ordered. You have my promise." He turned his steed toward the drawbridge and crossed the inner bailey with his men behind him.

Katherine ran up to the battlement and watched after him until the huge army was no bigger than a tiny dot on the horizon. Then they were gone.

"How touching, English. Do you intend for all who watch to believe the laird's wife will actually miss her husband while he's gone?"

Katherine turned to face the voice. It was Regan.

"It matters little to me what you think, one way or another, Regan."

There was only one set of stairs that led down from the battlement and Katherine turned to make her way past Regan to get to them. She did not want to face her now. Not when Duncan's words still hurt so much. But the dark-haired beauty took a step to the center of the narrow walkway, blocking her path.

"Do na get too comfortable here, English. Once Duncan gets the crown, he'll turn his back and be glad to be rid of you."

Katherine refused to let Regan's words affect her. She lifted her chin and stared back. "And you think he will come to your bed?" Katherine couldn't help the sarcasm that dripped from her voice. She and Regan were no better than two sharp-clawed cats fighting over the same piece of meat.

"I do na *think* he will, English. I am sure of it. Duncan will never be happy with you. All he need do is look at the graves of his family and he'll remember why he can never love you."

Regan took one menacing step closer, and Katherine looked for a way to escape. There was none.

"Regan!'"

Katherine and Regan both looked down from the battlement to find the low voice that had bellowed Regan's name. It had been a warning and Regan glared at Gregor's battle ready stance.

"You've detained your mistress long enough."

Regan gave Katherine a scathing look that sent shivers down her spine then stepped to the side to let Katherine pass. "I would be careful if I were you, milady. A fall from so high could be dangerous."

Katherine braced her shoulders and answered her glare. "I would be equally careful if I were you, Regan. Threats made against your laird's wife from any height could be dangerous."

Katherine stepped past her and walked down the steep steps to the ground. Her legs trembled with every step.

For the second time since she had come to Lochmore, she was truly afraid.

...

Katherine stood on the sentry walkway high on the rampart wall and watched the band of Ferguson warriors make their way over the horizon. Duncan was coming home.

A sennight and three days he'd been gone, and she had tried unsuccessfully three times to escape long enough to get the crown. She had gotten no farther than the front door of the keep.

If Gregor was not there to stop her, one of his many spies was. Morgana had even moved her bed into Katherine's chamber and slept in the same room with her. She'd searched all but the one locked room on the second level at least a half dozen times. She couldn't find a secret passage that led beyond the walls.

Katherine pulled her plaid closer around her shoulders and watched from the battlement to catch her first glimpse of him.

"They'll be here within the hour, milady."

Gregor's soft voice whispered behind her and Katherine looked into the distance to watch them approach. She'd told herself she wouldn't miss him, but she had. She'd missed his gruff voice and his harsh words, and his struggle to deny that he wanted her. "Can you see him, Gregor?"

"Aye. That's his big black horse in front. Just as he promised, the laird is leading the way. Malcolm's bay is to his right and Angus' roan is on his left."

"Where is the Lady Brenna? Can you see her?"

Gregor didn't answer at first and Katherine watched with him as he studied the procession.

"I am na sure, milady. I canna see her horse."

A wave of fear smothered the breath in her chest. "Is she riding with someone, Gregor? Do you think she's hurt?"

"I do na know, milady. They are na close enough for me to see her."

Katherine turned, then headed for the stairs. She refused to believe that Duncan had not been able to rescue his sister. She refused to think that Bolton may have killed Brenna without waiting for the crown. "We must make sure her room is ready and that there is plenty of food and ale for the men. They're probably tired and hungry and …"

Katherine didn't take time to finish her sentence as she ran down the stairs and across the inner bailey. Everyone within the castle walls had heard the news that their laird was coming home and the buzz of activity was frantic.

"Margaret. Anna," Katherine yelled as they passed the kitchen. "Make sure there's plenty of food and ale for the men. Have you any meat pies made up?"

"Aye, mistress," Margaret yelled, wiping the flour from her hands on her apron. "Anna said just this morning she thought we would need extra food. She said she had a feeling when she arose that this was the day the laird would come home with Lady Brenna. How she knew it, I do na know, but she was right."

"Yes. The laird is coming," Katherine said as if to reassure herself it was true. A giddy feeling of expectation surged through her chest. She ran to the keep and up the stairs to her chamber, then to the chamber she had prepared for Brenna.

"Morgana. Have hot water brought up for a bath. The master and Lady Brenna will want to bathe as soon as they arrive."

"Aye, milady." Morgana ran to have the water sent up. There was always a contented smile on Morgana's face, but today she beamed even brighter than usual.

Katherine then ran to each room to make sure a fire blazed in each hearth.

"They've crossed the drawbridge, milady," Gregor yelled up at her. Katherine ran down the stairs and across the entryway, dodging servants who were scurrying to make ready for the men.

She stood on the top step of the keep where she could see the warriors as they approached. Duncan had kept his promise. He was in the lead, with Angus on his left. Malcolm was on his right with the Lady Brenna cradled in his arms.

She was safe. Everything would be all right.

Katherine looked at the riders. They were still a fair distance from her when the first unexpected niggling of concern rushed through her. Her eyes riveted on Duncan and she saw that he sought her out in the same way. She wasn't sure what she expected to see in his gaze, but what she saw alarmed her.

The horses and riders closed the space separating them. Katherine's gaze rested on the small form nestled in Malcolm's arms. Brenna stared blankly ahead, seeing and reacting to nothing.

Katherine shifted her gaze to Malcolm. He was close enough now for Katherine to see him breathe a huge sigh then look over at Duncan in the protective way he had about him.

All was not right.

Next she looked at Angus. The look on his face was serious, worrisome. Her heart jumped to her throat in warning. Angus had his head turned to his laird, watching for…

Katherine looked at Gregor standing beside her and noticed the frown that covered his face. She took one step toward her husband then another, then almost ran the last few feet.

His coloring was pale and there was a sheen of perspiration that covered his face, but it was the look in his eyes that frightened her most. The wild look of unrelenting pain.

"I have come back to you, Kate, as I promised."

"As you promised, husband." Katherine moved closer to him. His eyes closed and he swayed above her on the horse.

"Duncan!"

Katherine reached for him as he leaned and fell to the ground. Gregor was at her side as was Angus, and three or four more Ferguson clansmen she could not name. They lowered their laird, then each of them took a hold and carried him up the steps to their chamber.

Angus bellowed orders but Katherine did not listen to what he said. She focused on Duncan's face, then moved her gaze to the circle of blood at his middle growing larger with each step they took.

The men lay their laird on the bed and stepped back and out of the room. All except Malcolm and Angus.

Katherine moved to one side and placed her hand on Duncan's forehead while Angus and Malcolm moved to the other and removed his clothes. Duncan's face burned with fever.

Katherine brushed a strand of errant hair from his forehead and touched his cheek. "He's badly hurt, Angus."

"Aye, milady. Prepare yourself to be strong if you are going to be any help to me."

Angus pulled open Duncan's shirt, then cut away the blood soaked bandage around his middle. When he exposed the gaping, gnarled flesh, Katherine let out a muffled cry and swallowed fast to keep the little she had eaten in her stomach.

"Take deep breaths, milady, and steady yourself. I have na time for your weak stomach. We must work fast to stop the bleeding or your husband will die."

Katherine reached down to rinse a cloth in a pan of water one of the servants had placed beside the bed and handed it to Angus.

"You must wash the dirt and the blood from his wound, milady."

Her heart leaped to her throat. She was not sure she could touch the raw flesh standing open.

"Wash him or watch him die!" Angus roared.

Malcolm held Duncan's shoulders while Katherine touched his skin with her cloth and began to clean the wound.

"Do na leave even one small speck of dirt in the wound, Lady Katherine," Malcolm whispered, "or the laird will die as quickly as if we had done nothing."

Katherine couldn't find her voice to say any words, so

she nodded, then rinsed her cloth and carefully washed the gaping wound. Duncan moaned and moved his head from one side to the other but she did not stop, nor did she look up from what she was doing.

While Angus mixed his potions and salves, Katherine wiped the blood from her husband's tender flesh. "Don't you dare die, husband," she whispered, "or I will never forgive you. You promised you would not leave me and I would hold you to that promise."

Duncan moaned and opened his eyes and Katherine pulled back her hand from his wound. He tried to speak, but another wave of pain hit him. He clenched his teeth and sucked a harsh breath, then closed his eyes in blessed slumber.

"Do na worry that you are causing pain, milady. Our laird is strong and can take it."

"I cannot stop the bleeding, Angus. What do I do? Her hands shook as she wiped at the blood.

"Is the wound clean?"

"Yes. I think so." Katherine placed her hand against Duncan's forehead. He was burning up. "Help him, Angus. He's so hot."

"Here, milady. Malcolm will lift his head. Get as much of this down him as you can."

Katherine reached for the cup and put it to Duncan's lips. She forced Duncan's lips apart then tipped the cup. Some of the precious liquid ran down the sides of his face but she did not give up until the cup was empty and Duncan had swallowed most of the potion.

"It's gone, Angus."

"Aye. Call some men, Malcolm." Malcolm went to the

door and four huge men followed him in. "It's best you do na watch this, milady."

Angus pulled a long knife from the fire and stepped to Duncan's side. The blade glowed fire red and steam rolled from the hot metal. Katherine's heart thudded in her chest.

"Oh, Angus. Is there not another way?"

"Nay, milady. It must be done. Stand aside until it's over."

Katherine stood with her back to the bed and clutched her hands around her middle. She squeezed her eyes shut tight and wished she could close out the sounds and the smell as well. She couldn't.

She heard the hiss of burning flesh followed by Duncan's roar, then his struggle to escape the pain. Muffled grunts and groans filled the room as the Ferguson clansmen worked to hold their laird still. For an eternity, Katherine felt the pain as if it were her own.

Duncan roared a second time, then Katherine heard only the sizzling hiss and breathed the acrid smell of burning flesh before all was quiet.

"It's finished, milady. We'll sew his wound now." Angus leaned over Duncan's side with a needle and some thread.

Katherine went to her husband's side and wiped the perspiration from his brow. Even though the thread was the finest and the needle the smallest Katherine had ever seen, it still seemed impossible that Angus would sew Duncan's flesh together like some piece of coarse wool.

"Kate."

"Yes, Duncan." Katherine wiped her husband's face with the cool cloth and cradled it in her hands. He was in such pain. "I'm here."

"Bolton was na there. I could na—"

"Don't worry, Duncan. You brought Brenna home with you."

"Aye. Brenna is home."

Katherine reached for his hand as Angus put the first stitch through his flesh. Duncan squeezed his eyes shut and moaned.

Katherine turned back to her husband. "Do what you have to do, Angus. Our laird is losing strength."

"Aye, milady," Angus answered her, putting another stitch in Duncan's flesh, then another.

"You will not leave me, Duncan. I will not let you." She held his hand to her breast and leaned down to whisper in his ear. "If you leave me I will make sure no Scot ever sees the precious crown again. I will take it with me to England and wear it myself. What do you think of that?"

She gave Duncan every reason she could think of why he could not die. By the time Angus had put the last stitch through his flesh, her arm was bruised from her wrist to her elbow where he had gripped her. She didn't know whether Duncan had heard what she'd said, nor did she care. She would have told him the King of Scotland was waiting for him downstairs if it would have helped to save his life.

She whispered in his ear and wiped the perspiration from his brow, and hardly noticed. Angus touched her on the shoulder and took the cloth from her hands. "We'll make a poultice from the stonecrop now, milady. Put this on him, then wrap him with clean cloths."

Katherine took the mixture Angus handed her, then swallowed the lump in her throat when she looked at

Duncan's flesh.

"It is na pretty, but his flesh is na longer gaping open. We will change this poultice twice every day and get as much of this liquid into him as we can. It will help to bring down the fever."

Katherine nodded, then let Angus show her how to dress Duncan's wound. With shaky hands she lifted the cup of catnip tea to his lips and made him drink. "He will live, Angus. I know he will. He gave me his promise."

"Then it will be so. Our laird would never tell you false."

. . .

It had been two days since Duncan had ridden home. At times he'd been so wild with fever it had taken Katherine and Angus and Malcolm to hold him down. Other times he was so still she feared he was no longer breathing. She forced him to drink the healing potion Angus had for him and prayed he would live.

Katherine wiped Duncan's face and body with water that had been kept outside all night so it was almost freezing. Nothing they did seemed to bring his fever down, and he became so violent, Katherine had to call for Angus to hold him. Duncan thought he still battled the English.

"Have you seen Brenna yet today?" Katherine asked, stretching her aching muscles. Duncan slept peacefully, for a while, at least.

"I looked in on her before I came."

"How is she?"

"Much the same. It will take time."

Katherine nodded. "Bolton was not there?"

"Nay, milady. No one was there, save the women and

children and a few old men."

Long fingers of dread twisted her heart in her breast. "Do you know what that means? Bolton has gone to London to enlist Edward's aid in giving him a larger army to fight the Scots."

"Aye. Our laird thinks the same."

"Do you think Bolton knows I'm here with Duncan?"

"Aye."

A cold wave of fear washed over Katherine. She'd known it would come to this. Once Bolton found out she had been taken by Duncan, it would mean war between England and the Fergusons. How many innocent people would die because she had not been brave enough to follow her king's edict? Because she had not been strong enough to walk away from her Scot.

"Do you think he knows I've married Duncan?"

"I do na know, milady."

"It will not be long before he gets here, Angus. A month, perhaps. Maybe only weeks."

"Aye. He will have to make his move soon. Scotland's winters are too harsh to risk exposing his men for long."

Katherine breathed a shallow breath and held Duncan's fist to her breast. She didn't have much time. She would search the room again for a secret passageway that would take her outside the curtain walls. Ian told her once that all Scottish castles had hidden routes for escape. The door leading to them was almost always concealed in the laird's chamber so he could hide his family if the keep were under attack.

She had to get to the crown. She had to have it near her when the king or her father came. Giving England back her crown was the only way she could save Duncan's life and stop the senseless killing of hundreds of innocent people.

Katherine looked back down at Duncan's bruised body. "If there was no battle, how did this happen?" She touched his flesh and caressed his face, then prayed again he would live.

"It was a trap. Bolton knew we would come for Brenna, and he made it easy for us to get her out. We were na expecting them to attack when they did. It was nay until we were back on Scotland's side that we had trouble. About one hundred of Bolton's men ambushed us once we crossed Scotland's border. We were alone then. All the neighboring clans had left us. Although we should have been able to handle the English with little problem, they were na after anyone but the laird.

"They rode at Duncan from the front and surrounded him, cutting him off from the rest of his warriors. He fought brave and left many of the cursed English on the ground, but by the time we could get to him, they had done this."

Katherine rinsed her cloth in the icy water and lay it against his fevered flesh. Then she lifted his head and forced him to drink more of the potion Angus had made to help him.

"Why do you na lay down for a while, lass. You have na left our laird's side for two days. I'll watch him while you rest."

"No, Angus. There will be plenty of time to sleep once his fever is gone."

Katherine lowered Duncan's head to the pillow and placed the cool cloth on his chest. His head thrashed from one side to the other.

"Damn them. Damn them all," he moaned aloud while his hands flayed in the air, fighting the invisible enemy.

"It's all right, Duncan," Katherine whispered, holding down his arms. "You're safe now."

"Damn the English. Vile. Loathsome bastards, all of them."

"Rest easy now, Duncan," Katherine whispered, fighting him with all her strength. Angus reached out to hold Duncan's arms and her fight became a little easier. Duncan breathed an exhausted sigh and quieted his movements.

"Kate. Kate."

"Yes, Duncan."

"Kate. Oh, lass. I canna love an English."

"I know. You do not have to."

Katherine held his arms until he finally collapsed into slumber.

"He does na know what he's saying, milady. It's the fever talking."

"I know." Katherine placed a fresh cloth against his body and bit her lower lip hard to stop the tears. "I have no more leaves to make the potion, Angus."

"I'll go for some, lass. Malcolm is outside if you have need for him to help."

She looked down on her husband, sleeping fitfully and cupped her palm against his cheek. "I'll be fine until you return. Take Malcolm with you, Angus. Don't go outside alone. Bolton's men could be waiting."

"I'll be safe, lass."

"No. I will not chance something happening to you,

too. Promise me you'll take Malcolm with you or I will not let you go. Promise me."

"Aye, lass. I will take Malcolm with me."

Katherine nodded, then lifted Duncan's head again to have him drink the potion that was left. The door closed behind Angus and when all was quiet, she lowered her face to her hands and wept.

Dear God, help her. She had come to care for him. Even though she knew he would never return her love.

She would always be English.

She could never give him the crown.

The first he could not live with. The second he could not live without.

Chapter 12

Katherine turned her head toward the door and listened for Angus and Malcolm's footsteps. All was quiet and she prayed they would hurry. Duncan was becoming more restless by the second and it wouldn't be long and she would not be able to hold him down herself. The fever made him wild and he thrashed his head from side to side and moaned as he pushed the covers from his body.

Katherine pulled them back over his chest and pressed her hand to his cheek to calm him so he wouldn't tear the stitches from his wound. Without warning, his left arm wrapped around her shoulder. He clamped his fingers around the back of her neck and pulled her down against him. His grip was painful. Katherine tried to twist out of his grasp, but he held her tighter.

"Damn you, English," he hissed, his eyes wide open and glazed with pain. He held her face just inches from his and tightened his grip until she thought her neck might break. "Give me the crown."

Katherine tried to pull away, but she could not. He was too strong and his will to fight too great. Before she could protect herself he brought back his hand and struck her. His fist slammed against her cheek and white lights flashed behind her eyes. She struggled to keep the darkness from overwhelming her.

"You have it. You have the crown. Scotland must have it." Duncan brought both hands up and wrapped his fingers around her neck and squeezed. "Give me the crown, English."

Katherine clawed at his fingers clamped around her throat, but she couldn't break his grip.

"I want the crown."

"Duncan, no." Her strangled voice barely came out. She twisted and clawed at him but could not free herself.

Duncan tightened his grip more, cutting off the air she needed. Hot searing pokers stabbed through her. Her chest burned while bright lights exploded in her head. She pulled at his hands again, but knew her grasp was too weak to do any good.

Somewhere in the far distance, a mighty roar shattered through the murky haze and Duncan's hands fell away from around her neck.

Katherine choked and coughed and grabbed her hands to her throat. Her body doubled over in agony and the explosive pain in her head was almost more than she wanted to bear. While her chest took in huge gulps of air, her throat burned with each breath.

"Breathe, mistress. Breathe."

She heard Malcolm's voice. It was familiar, and comforting, and pleasant. It did not hold any of the resentment or disdain she had heard in Duncan's. In his fever, his hatred had found a way to release itself.

Her body hurt, but knowing how much he loathed her made her heart ache a thousand times more.

"Hold on to me, milady, and breathe."

With one hand, Katherine grabbed a fistful of the wool of Malcolm's shirt. With her other hand she protected her face where Duncan had hit her.

"He did na mean it, milady. It was the fever. He would never harm you. You know that."

Katherine did not answer. She touched her fingers to her throat and swallowed. It was as painful on the inside as it was on the outside.

When she could breathe easier, she pushed herself away from Malcolm and walked away. From the other side of the room, she looked at the man who was her husband. He was a stranger to her. She thought she knew him, but she didn't. She knew nothing about him except he was a very proud Scot who wanted the Bishop's Crown, and hated the English.

And hated his wife.

"Get some cord, Malcolm," Angus issued. "We'll tie the laird to the bed."

Katherine's gaze shot to the old Scot's face. "No."

"I can na trust that he will na harm you again. It's his fever. He does na know what he's doing."

"Then we'll have someone sit in the room with me, but we will not tie him to the bed like a mad dog."

Angus nodded, then took the leaves he had brought to the hearth and mixed them with warm ale. He brought back the cup and Katherine lifted Duncan's head to make him drink.

"Kate."

"Yes, Duncan. I'm here. Open your mouth and drink this ale. It will help your fever."

He took a swallow, then another. "Kate. Do na leave me. I do na want you to leave me."

Katherine brought the cup to his mouth again. He was calm and sedate now. Nothing like the violent warrior who had just tried to kill her.

"Rest now, Duncan."

Katherine made him drink until the cup was empty while Angus and Malcolm both stood guard. A faint rustle in the far corner of the room caused all three of them to turn.

Brenna stood in the dark, the black look in her wide open eyes filled with hatred as she stared back at them. She must have been there the whole time. She must have seen it all.

Malcolm took a step toward her to take her from the room, then stopped when she twisted out of his grasp. She glared at Katherine, the look in her eyes as murderous as any she'd ever seen.

"'Tis a pity he did na kill you, English," she said, looking over her shoulder. "I prayed he would."

. . .

Katherine sat at Duncan's bedside and watched his breathing strengthen. For three days she had not left his side for fear he would stop breathing if she wasn't there to threaten him with the crown or remind him he'd promised not to make her a widow. As the sun went down on the fourth day his fever broke and for the first time since he'd returned from getting Brenna, he slept peacefully.

Angus stood behind her and stared at his laird. "Let me put a fresh poultice on your neck, milady, then we will change the laird's bandage so he'll sleep through the night."

Katherine pulled the shawl she wore to cover the hideous bruises on her skin, higher around her neck. She didn't want anyone to see what Duncan had done to her. "He'll be all right now, will he not, Angus?"

"Aye, milady. The fever has left him and he will recover. The laird is strong and it will take more than a sword to his middle to bring him down."

"That's not true, Angus. Your laird almost died."

"You are right, mistress. Even I was more than a little afraid. Now, come here. I've mixed a poultice of sorrel and it's ready to put on your skin."

Katherine put her hand on Duncan's forehead to make sure he was still cool, then sat on the stool by the hearth and took the shawl from around her neck.

"Have the marks gone away any, Angus?"

"Nay, milady. The color is even worse today but the bruises do na feel so warm. Do they still pain you so?"

"Only this one," she said, pointing to the left side of her neck where there was an exact imprint of Duncan's fingers. "This is the only one where the pain has not lessened."

"It's the worst. I should na have left you that night. I should have known it was na safe for you to be left alone."

"Move, Angus. Let me see."

Duncan's voice sliced through their whispers like an ax hewing a small tree. Angus turned, while Katherine grabbed the shawl and pulled it up around her neck. She fumbled to hide her bruises from him.

"Come here, Kate, and let me see."

"There's nothing to see, Duncan." Katherine stayed in the shadows and refused to go near him. "I have hurt myself a little. 'Tis all."

"Do na argue with me, Kate. I do na have the strength to fight you."

"Show him, lass. He'll see you sooner or later."

"It's nothing. See." Katherine lifted the shawl away from her skin and quickly put it back. "The marks will be better in no time. Now, go back to sleep."

Duncan turned to Angus and a silent message passed between them. Angus nodded, and took Katherine's arm. He led her over to the bed, then pulled the shawl from around her neck.

She only had one free hand, not nearly enough fingers to cover the multitude of discolored marks on her skin or the swollen bruise on her face. She let her hand fall so he could see all of her.

She could not look at him. She didn't want to see the look on his face; the look that would put out into the open the proof that he could never abide who she was. Huge, wet tears streamed down her face and she couldn't stop them. She was exhausted. For four days she'd slept very little. Every muscle in her body ached like someone had beaten her. She no longer wanted to pretend to her husband or his clan that she could be the perfect wife for their laird.

"I did that?"

Katherine didn't answer, so Angus answered for her. "Aye. You did."

"Why?"

"It was the fever, milord."

"I would have an answer from my wife, Angus." Duncan's gaze turned to her. "What reason did I give for touching you so?"

The thick wall that had been holding back her feelings crumbled, then broke — along with the tears she'd been holding inside her. She pointed to the bruises on her neck. "These are because I'm English. You cannot abide the fact that you married an English."

Katherine pulled her shawl around her neck and walked to the door. "I'm tired. I would like to sleep now."

Without another word, she left him.

...

Katherine placed another log in the hearth to build a bigger fire to keep the room warm, then turned.

It had been two weeks and the bruises on her neck were almost gone. Although they hadn't spoken of that night again, what had happened remained between them like a festering chasm of discontent. Katherine felt more distanced from him now than ever. The hurt was unbearable.

"I think I will get up today."

"I think you will *dream* about getting up today. Maybe tomorrow Angus will let you out of bed."

"That's what you said yesterday, Kate, and I only agreed out of consideration for your feelings. Today I do na feel so considerate."

Katherine braced her hands against her hips. "You did not get up yesterday, Duncan, because you tried to stand on your own and failed. You think no one saw you, but I did."

Duncan let his head fall back on the pillow and laughed.

"You are too sly for me, wife. I can get nothing past you."

"That is a fact you had best not forget."

Katherine walked over to the bedside table and poured water into a goblet and handed it to him.

"Kate, sit with me a while. We must talk."

Katherine shook her head in denial and pulled her hand from his grasp. She wanted so much to make him understand, but when she turned to face him, she realized that the gap separating them was wider than ever.

"Did Angus tell you Bolton was na there when we arrived?" he said.

"Yes."

"Do you know what that means?"

She couldn't force her voice to answer him. She looked to the floor and nodded.

"It will na be long before Bolton comes here with your king's army, Kate."

She closed her eyes to block out his words, but she knew they were true. She did not have much time. "When?"

"A few weeks. I do na know." Duncan shifted in his bed until he had pushed himself upright. "I need the crown, lass. I need to have it before Bolton comes." His voice softened with the next sentence. "I will na let you give it to him, Kate. I will die before I let Bolton have it."

Katherine closed her eyes and turned her face away from him. "Do not fear, Duncan. Bolton will never get the crown from me."

Katherine could hear the harshness in his voice. "Then why will you not give it to me?"

She gathered her resolve. "It doesn't belong to you. It belongs only to England."

"I will have it, Kate. My father died to protect it, and my mother and my sisters. I must do my part, just as every Scot."

"Even if it means your death?"

"It meant my father's death and I was na here to save him."

Katherine stopped short, and for the first time saw what drove her husband to want the crown. "It's not your fault your father is dead. Can't you see? Had you been here you would more than likely be dead too."

"I can na let his death go for naught, lass. Can you na understand?"

"I understand that if Scotland doesn't give England her crown, many more people will die."

"You would go against your husband to keep the crown? England is still that important to you?"

"No! Peace is that important to me. I would go against my husband to keep peace with England."

For a long time, only silence permeated the chamber. Finally, Duncan spoke, his voice hard, unyielding. "Is the crown hidden at Kilgern Castle?"

Katherine turned away from him.

"In two weeks' time, I will be well enough to travel. We will go to see your sister, and you will get the crown."

Katherine spun around and glared at him. "No! I told you on the day we married I could not give you the crown. I took an oath and I cannot break it."

"You will get the crown and bring it back here. I will give you na choice in this Kate. There is na time left."

A cold chill raced up and down her spine. Several silent moments separated them. Finally his voice cut through the tension.

"You will get the crown, lass. I will at least have it where I can protect it."

Katherine hugged her hands around her arms. What was left for her to do? "Will you promise you will not take it from me?" she whispered, the lump in her throat nearly choking her.

He shook his head. "I promise I will give you the chance to give it to me first."

Katherine walked out of the room on legs that trembled beneath her. She had two weeks.

...

Katherine moved her basket closer to the stream and knelt beside the water. Malcolm had come with her, as were Duncan's instructions. She was not allowed outside the walls without someone at her side. Right now, though, she needed to be alone. She needed time to sort through the desperation and confusion that surrounded her. Time to figure out what she had to do.

She dipped one of Duncan's shirts in the water and scrubbed it with soap. She pretended that each stain represented one of her worries, and rubbed as if it were possible to wash away each problem with simple soap and water.

Each morning and every evening, she got on her knees in the chapel and prayed that God would show her a way. A way to keep the vow she'd given the priest, without losing the man she'd taken as her husband. This morning she had even prayed that God would stop her from giving more of her heart to him. But she knew it was already too late.

Katherine scrubbed the shirt in her hands harder. She

didn't know how she would survive when Duncan turned his back on her.

"If you do na scrub the laird's shirt in a different spot, milady, your husband will walk around with a hole in his back."

Katherine jerked her hands out of the water and looked up at Angus standing above her. She hadn't heard him approach. "My mind is far away and not thinking about what my hands are doing."

"I can see this."

Katherine rinsed the shirt clean, and reached for the next piece and soaped it. "I had planned to come to see you when I was finished. It has been a long time."

"Aye. How is the laird feeling today?"

Katherine smiled. "Much better, Angus. He went downstairs again today. It will not be long and he'll be out training with his men." *And well enough to travel to get the crown.* "He walked to the practice yard yesterday. Finally, Malcolm made him come back. Didn't you, Malcolm?" Katherine looked back at the warrior who leaned against the tree, deep in thought.

Malcolm jerked to attention as if he'd been a thousand miles away. "Aye, milady. He's much better."

Katherine scrubbed the last piece of clothing in the cool water. "Have you seen Brenna today, Malcolm?"

"Aye. I went to see her before we left. She is much the same. Morgana tries to make her leave her room, but she will na. She hides in the darkness like a fey lass."

"Duncan goes each day to see her too. Perhaps he can help."

"Perhaps," Malcolm said, but his tone didn't sound so

sure. Katherine thought of the small figure huddled in the corner of her room and she doubted it too.

"Is there something you can do for her, Angus?"

"I will go see her, mistress, but I think there is naught anyone can do until the lass wants to come back to us."

Katherine rinsed the last of her clothing and twisted it dry. "I'm almost finished here," she said, hanging each article over a low branch or a bush to dry. "I overheard Margaret say the blackberries Duncan is especially fond of are ready to be picked. She said she makes a jam he has a fondness for."

Angus gave a hearty laugh. "I remember last year at this time, Duncan bribed Meara and Elissa and Brenna with a handsome leather belt he had fashioned. He said he would give the belt to the sister who picked him the most berries."

Katherine placed her basket beneath the bushes until she could return to get the clothes. "Who won the belt, Angus?"

"It was Brenna, milady. She returned with almost double the berries either of her sisters had picked, but if I remember right, she had some help."

Angus smiled a broad beaming grin and reached for a leaf from the bush. "Our Brenna has always been a comely lass with a rosy glow to her cheeks and a twinkle in her eyes. With one of her bright smiles, half the laird's warriors jumped to help her pick berries. Is that na right, Malcolm?"

"Aye, Angus. Our Brenna is a rare beauty."

There was a soft hush to Malcolm's voice and Katherine stared at the far away expression in Malcolm's eyes. Brenna was the lass he loved. It was as plain as if it were written across his face. How much he hurt was etched there as well. He must be living an agonizing torture seeing how much she had changed.

"Would you show me where the berries are, Malcolm?" she said, leaving her clothes, and walking back toward the castle.

"Aye, milady. But they are way in the hills." Malcolm pointed to the forest to their right. "You can na go there by yourself. I will take you tomorrow. We'll get our laird all the berries he can eat."

Angus looked up at the gray sky. "Be sure you dress warm, lass. The weather's changing and there will be a blast of cold air to chill our bones by tomorrow."

Katherine stopped and let the damp air hit her face. "I can feel it."

"Aye. It will be colder, especially up high where you'll find the berries."

Katherine didn't mind. It would give her a chance to leave the castle. Perhaps she could find a way to escape. It had been more than a week since Duncan had threatened they would go for the crown, and he was getting stronger by the day. She would soon run out of time.

They walked through the inner bailey, past the kitchen. "It was a good thing you did for our women, milady," Malcolm said. "See, they are open again today."

"It was not a new idea, Malcolm. It's the way our kitchen was in England. It seemed to work there and I only borrowed the idea."

Angus cleared his throat. "It will na be long before our women are convinced having windows was a new idea born in Scotland."

Katherine hid her smile.

"I think it does na hurt to steal England's ideas," Malcolm said with a confident air. "They would do the same, would they not?"

A grin covered Katherine's face. "Yes, Malcolm. They would do the same."

Katherine walked through the front door and stood in the open doorway. She stepped back into the shadows, watching her husband talk to his men; watching as he took care of the clan's important business. He was born to be the laird of clan Ferguson. He'd been taught well. And when the English came for their crown, he would give his life to keep it from them. As his father had given his life before him.

A wave of panic washed over her. She didn't have much time left. She had to find the tunnel that would take her beyond the castle walls, then travel to Kilgern Castle to get the crown. Somehow she had to get the crown out of Scotland and take it back to England. Somehow she had to find the courage to leave Scotland and her Scot.

The last would be the hardest, because once she left, she could never come back to him.

He would never want her back.

...

Katherine lifted her face and watched the clouds race across the sky. Angus had been right. The air would have a biting chill to it soon. Perhaps they would even see snow.

She headed down the path toward the stream to get her laundry. Malcolm was close on her heels, but had slowed to talk to Gregor, while she went ahead to gather her clothing. It wouldn't take her long. Then she could go back to search again for the secret passage that was hidden in one of the rooms in the keep.

With Duncan well enough to spend more time downstairs and out-of-doors, she could now make a thorough search of their room. The secret passageway in the MacIntyre keep had been easier to find. So far, though, she had not found the stone that, when pushed, would open a door leading beyond the wall. The Ferguson escape route was not nearly so easy to find as the MacIntyre's.

Katherine walked toward the bushes where she'd hung her laundry, thinking of which room she would search next. Her footsteps slowed. Something wasn't right.

Katherine stared at the branches where she knew her clothes should be. There were no shirts or gowns hanging there. There were only strips of tattered, dirty rags ground into the mud at the water's edge.

Katherine picked the first torn piece of cloth out of the muck and held it in her trembling hands. It was material from one of her gowns. She picked up the next and examined it. More material from that same gown.

She picked up all the pieces she could find and rinsed them in the water to make sure, but every piece of shredded clothing was from her gown. None had come from Duncan's clothing.

Whoever had done this had slashed her clothing with a knife, and had taken Duncan's shirts with them. The realization of what that meant sent a violent shiver down her spine.

Katherine threw her shredded clothing into the basket, and threw her shawl over the top to cover it. There was no need for anyone to know. Duncan would only assign more

Fergusons to guard her. She would never have a moment alone to search for the hidden passageway.

"Have you gathered your laundry?" Malcolm asked, walking up behind her.

"Yes. I'm ready to go back."

"Here," Malcolm said, reaching for the basket.

"No." Katherine pulled it away. "Thank you, but I can carry it."

There was a frown on Malcolm's face. "Is something wrong, mistress?"

"No. Nothing is wrong."

Katherine breathed a deep sigh and turned the conversation to the berries they would pick tomorrow.

When she said her prayers tonight, she would make certain to pray that she stayed alive long enough to eat some of the jam they made.

Chapter 13

Katherine finished her petitions, then made the sign of the cross and rose from her knees before the altar. She rested her hand against the railing and looked up. The statue of Jesus with his outstretched hands usually comforted her, made her feel safer. Tonight, nothing made her feel safe. Nothing made her feel wanted.

She remembered the shredded clothing she'd found by the stream this afternoon. The warning was abundantly clear. The hatred Duncan's people felt for her was growing.

Candles flickered on the altar, lighting the room in muted dusky shades. She ignored the painful tightening in her breast and fell back to her knees. *Dear God,* she prayed, fervently clutching her hands together in front of her, *don't let them hate me so. Don't let him want me only for the crown.*

She had been Duncan's wife for more than two months, and his people accepted her no more today than they had when Duncan had first brought her here. The glares she received when she came back from the stream today were no softer or more welcoming than they'd been that first day she'd ridden in at Duncan's side. It was as if Duncan's clan all knew she would not truly be a part of their laird's life for long.

Katherine said a final amen, then began again her search for the secret passageway. She walked to the wall behind the altar and ran her hands along the stones. Nothing. Not a lose stone, or a lever to push, or a handle to pull. Nothing that would show her how to get beyond the castle walls.

Satisfied that there was nothing behind the altar, Katherine went to the side wall. She'd searched the chapel before, but maybe, just maybe she'd overlooked something. Maybe tonight she'd find what she was searching for. Her heart beat faster in her breast. She didn't have much time left. Only days before Duncan would force her to go to Kilgern to get the crown. Maybe less before whoever wanted to harm her would accomplish their goal.

Katherine fell to her knees and ran her hand along the stones at the base of the wall. Nothing. She sat back on her heels and looked up. Nothing but a smooth, stone wall. Slowly, wearily, she got to her feet and turned around. Her heart slammed against her ribs, then jumped to her throat. Duncan stood by the door, watching her.

"Are you looking for something?"

Katherine took a step backwards, stopping when her back collided with the wall. "I… I came to say my prayers."

"Have you finished?" he asked, the look on his face unreadable.

"Yes." Katherine focused on the stones on the floor.

"Come here."

"It's late, my lord. I would like to—"

"Come here."

Katherine lifted her gaze to meet his. "I'm tired. I don't

want to argue more about the crown."

His eyes grew darker. The little softness she prayed she would recognize in his features wasn't there. He breathed a sigh before he spoke. "I will na speak of the crown. I would only like to talk to you."

Katherine hesitated a moment, then walked to a bench and took a seat. He sat down beside her, so close his leg pressed against hers.

His nearness caused a strange heat to warm her flesh, then creep to the pit of her stomach. No matter how hard she fought to keep him from affecting her, she failed. His muscled strength caused every nerve in her body to tingle in response. His dominating power made her want to turn to him for comfort. His commanding presence made her want to give herself to him for protection. Except she knew he didn't want her. She knew it was Regan he wished to talk to like this, and hold in his arms, and take to his bed. Regan he would rather have taken as his wife.

Katherine clasped her hands in her lap and waited.

"Are you ill, Kate?"

Katherine concentrated on the stone pattern on the floor. "No. I'm not ill."

"Then why could you na eat your meal again tonight?"

"I wasn't hungry. Nothing more."

She heard him take a breath, releasing the air with a heavy sigh. She wondered what his reaction would be if she told him about the torn clothes she'd found by the stream. Would he even portray a pretense of concern? She wasn't certain, and that bothered her more than knowing one way or the other.

"You have na been hungry for many of the meals our

cooks have prepared of late. Did you na like their food?"

"The food is fine, Duncan. It's just me."

"Your clothes are beginning to hang on your body, wife. I do na want to see them become any looser."

Katherine turned her face away from him. She knew she was becoming thin in the extreme. Perhaps when he compared her to Regan's full, curving body, he found her less than appealing. Perhaps that was why he had yet to take her again since he had healed. Her cheeks burned like they were on fire.

"Why did you come to Scotland, Kate?"

She looked at him, unable to hide her surprise. "I came to be with Elizabeth for the birth of her first child. I was supposed to have wed Bolton, but persuaded father to postpone the wedding until after Elizabeth's babe was born."

"How was it our priest mistook you for your sister?"

Katherine closed her eyes and thought back to the night when the Ferguson priest had come. A cold shiver raced down her spine. "It was the middle of the night when one of the servants came to tell Elizabeth your priest was downstairs. Elizabeth was sleeping soundly. She was still recovering from the birth of the babe and I didn't want to awaken her. When I saw how anxious the servant was, I feared the worst. I was afraid the priest had come to tell us Ian was dead. I didn't want Elizabeth to hear the news like that, so I went in her place."

"And the priest did not ask your identity?"

"No. He only asked if my father was the English Earl of Wentworth."

Katherine thought back to the dried blood staining the

priest's robe and shuddered. As if he could feel the terror she'd felt that night, Duncan placed his arm around her shoulder and drew her close to him. A sudden warmth surged to every part of her body. A strange and comforting peace. Dear God, she wished he would not hold her so. She wished he would not remind her of what she would miss when he could no longer stand to touch her.

"And then what, lass?"

He nestled her close against his side, and Katherine couldn't keep from resting her head against his chest. Couldn't help but breathe in his raw, masculine scent, mixed with leather, and horses, and the smell of the outdoors. Katherine breathed deeply, letting each of her senses have its fill.

"I knew it was only a matter of time until Bolton came in search of the crown. That's what the priest warned me. I hid Elizabeth and the babe, then went back to the keep and passed myself off as the mistress of Kilgern Castle. If any of the servants knew I wasn't Elizabeth, they didn't give me away. They would have gone to their graves to protect their mistress and the MacIntyre heir from Bolton. The MacIntyre Scots had come to love Elizabeth."

He reached over and nestled her hand in his strong grasp. His thumb made slow, lazy circles atop her hand, sending warm pulses deep within her.

"You do na think your Ferguson Scots would be as loyal?"

She said nothing. She knew Duncan wouldn't want to hear her answer.

Duncan's thumb halted its movements atop her hand. "Why did you come to me in the dungeon?"

"I came to ask for your help. I didn't know Bolton had you until he came from the dungeon with your medallion hanging from his neck. He was laughing because you'd become so violent when you saw him wearing it. When he threw it to the rushes on the floor, I waited until he left, then found it. I hoped returning it would gain your help to fight Bolton."

Duncan lifted his hand and clutched his fingers around the medallion that still hung around his neck. "I will always be grateful to you for giving this back to me. I will forever owe you for your bravery."

"You've already sacrificed enough, my lord. I expect nothing more."

He looked down at her, and Katherine lifted her head to meet his gaze. A hand tightened around her heart. All she saw was the pain he couldn't keep from his eyes.

"Oh, lass. How did we come to this?"

"Neither of us had a choice in what we were to do, my lord. You want nothing from me except what I cannot give, and I am willing to give you anything except what you want."

His hand lifted to her face, then he rubbed the back of his fingers against her cheek. The look in his eyes said there was nothing more for which to hope.

"What I have left to give you isn't enough. Is it, my lord?"

He didn't answer.

Katherine separated herself from him and rose to her feet. On legs that threatened to fold beneath her, she walked down the hallway, and into her chambers. He wouldn't come to her again tonight. The look in his eyes told her so.

Katherine set her second full basket of berries on the ground and lifted her shoulders to stretch her muscles. She and Malcolm had picked berries for what seemed hours and all the baskets were finally full. "Are you ready to go home, Malcolm?"

"Aye, milady. Do you think we've picked enough to satisfy our laird's taste through the winter?"

"I'm sure our laird will be pleased with what we have." Katherine looked at the four baskets of berries on the ground and smiled. "We'll both remind him all winter of how pleased he must be with our labors."

Malcolm picked up the two pouches that hung over the horses' saddles and held the first one open while Katherine poured in her basket of berries. There were so many they would be lucky if they all fit.

"Which way is it to Kilgern Castle?" Katherine asked.

Malcolm turned to the right and pointed. "It's over those hills, milady. It's na too far. You just have to follow the stream and you canna miss it."

Katherine looked where Malcolm had pointed and began to formulate her plan. She only had to follow the stream and she would be there.

"Our laird said just this morning that he intends to take you there soon. He said you were anxious to see your sister."

Katherine forced a smile and set the empty basket on the ground. "Yes, I've missed her and cannot wait to see how much the babe has grown."

"It will na be long," he said, picking up a second pouch.

"We'd best hurry back to the keep. The wind has changed and it's getting cooler." Malcolm held the other pouch open for the second basket.

"Does it always turn so cold this early, Malcolm?" Katherine threw the extra shawl she'd brought with her over her shoulders while Malcolm got the second set of saddle pouches from her horse.

"Would it distress you, mistress, if I told you the weather has been mild so far?"

"Oh, Malcolm. If this is mild, I fear I will never survive your Scottish winters."

Malcolm laughed a hearty laugh and handed her the vessel of ale that had been hanging by a rope on her saddle. "Here. This will help to warm you." There was another vessel hanging on Malcolm's saddle, and he took a deep swallow of his ale, then held the pouch while she poured the rest of the berries into it.

Katherine put the vessel to her mouth and drank. She felt the warmth from the ale travel down to the pit of her stomach and rubbed her arms to ward off a shiver. "I don't know who sent the ale to warm us, but I will make sure to thank them when we get back. They must have known it would turn colder before we returned and that we would welcome its warmth."

Malcolm took another swallow of his ale then held the reins to Katherine's horse while she mounted. "Margaret or Morgana probably saw to it. They are thoughtful that way."

Malcolm walked to his horse and put his hands on the saddle. He looked as if he was ready to pull himself up, but his knees buckled beneath him and his forehead fell forward, resting at an awkward angle against the side of his horse.

"Is something wrong, Malcolm?"

"Leave, milady. Get yourself to… Duncan. Ride… fast."

Malcolm's ashen face had a drawn look to it and his slurred words had an unnatural sound to them. "What is the matter, Malcolm?"

"Go… mistress. Now."

"I will not leave you. Are you ill?" Katherine jumped from her horse and ran to his side.

"Get… Duncan."

Malcolm's weak voice came out as soft as a whisper. His feet gave out beneath him and he sank to the ground.

"Malcolm! Malcolm!"

Katherine's heart pounded in her chest and she placed her hand to the warrior's forehead, searching for a cause to his malady. His skin was not fevered but cool to the touch. When she pulled his shirt open at the neck and placed her ear to his chest, she heard the steady pounding of his heart. Even though it seemed to beat slowly, it was still the strong beat of a healthy man. It was as if he wasn't ill at all, but had simply fallen asleep.

"Malcolm, can you hear me?" He didn't move, but lay on the ground in a heap.

"He can na hear you, English."

Katherine jerked her head toward the voice behind her. She breathed a heavy sigh of relief when she looked into the familiar face. She clutched her hand to her breast to calm her breathing. "Oh, thank God it's you. Something has happened to Malcolm."

Katherine touched her hand to Malcolm's forehead

and brushed the strand of blond hair from his face. She didn't know what to do for him. "He all of a sudden fell to the ground and closed his eyes." She ran her fingers over his face and the back of his head searching for any wound that could have caused him to fall, but could find nothing.

"You can na help him, English. Malcolm will na wake up for a while. A verra long while."

"How do you know?"

"I have given him a bit of the potion Angus gives to the ailing. It will na hurt him, if I did na put too much in his ale. If I did, he may never wake up, but that will be a pleasant way to die. Will it not?" She glared at Katherine and the look in her eyes was murderous. "Not like some of the Scots your English have slaughtered."

Katherine looked again into Malcolm's face, unable to believe this was happening. He did not seem to be in pain, but to be sleeping peacefully. "Why? Why would you want to harm Malcolm?"

Her shrill laughter raised the level of Katherine's fear. "Oh, English. I do na want to harm Malcolm. It's you I've come for."

Katherine looked up at the woman, expecting to see concern on her face, but there was none. Instead, an evil countenance covered her dark features and she took another step closer until she stood right beside them. It was then that Katherine saw the knife in the woman's hand.

She kept her gaze focused on the knife while she moved her hand down Malcolm's side. If he were like Duncan, she would find his dirk somewhere around his waist. "But I'm not ill," she said, trying to distract her assailant. "You didn't put the potion in my ale to make me sleep." Katherine found Malcom's knife and wrapped her fingers around it.

"I did na want to make you sleep, English. I want you to know you are going to die. I want you to see death and know it's coming to take you."

A cold chill ran down Katherine's spine and she pulled the knife ever so slowly out of its sheath. She didn't stop until she had it gripped in her hands.

In a movement so swift Katherine didn't see it coming, the girl kicked out her foot. She knocked the knife from Katherine's grasp, then swung out with her own knife and made a slash on Katherine's forearm that cut through the material of her gown and left a crimson streak.

"You canna surprise me, English. I've come to know you too well to expect you to die willingly."

"You cannot do this. Duncan will find you."

Her inhuman laughter made the hairs rise on the back of Katherine's neck.

"My laird will thank me. I'm doing him a favor. He does na want you. Surely even you can see it?" Her malicious smile broadened. "I thought perhaps he'd killed you that night he put his hands around your throat. I watched from the doorway and prayed he would end your life, but Malcolm and the old man came back to save you."

Katherine shook her head in confusion. "You hate me that much?"

"You can na imagine how much I hate you, English. How much I hate watching you take the mistress' place in the castle and giving orders to the servants as if you belonged, as if you were one of us. You can na imagine how much I hate knowing you lie in the master's arms each night and that even now he may have planted his seed in your womb."

She reached out and grabbed the reins to Katherine's horse then pointed her knife. "Get up, English. We have far to go."

"What about Malcolm? You cannot leave him here. He'll freeze."

The woman shrugged her shoulders as if she didn't care, then poked the sharp point of her knife into Katherine's back, giving her no choice but to move. Katherine lowered Malcolm's head to the ground and stood, but before she walked to her horse, she took the extra shawl from around her shoulders and placed it over his body.

"That will na help him once it gets cold, English. But it's one more thing you'll wish you would have kept for yourself once the snow falls."

Katherine lifted herself atop the horse. When she was seated, the woman grabbed her hands and tied them to the saddle. Katherine struggled to free herself, but before she could gain an advantage, the woman jabbed the knife into the flesh at her waist. She smiled when a spot of blood soaked through Katherine's gown.

"Fight me if you want, English. I would just as soon kill you here."

"Then why don't you?" Katherine gasped through the pain.

"Because there would be na doubt that you had been murdered if they find you here with a knife in your chest. I think my laird will sleep better if he thinks your death was an accident."

"Duncan will not let you get away with this."

She cackled a bitter laugh. "He will not care that you're dead. He will only care that he did na get the crown before you died."

The woman gave another shrill laugh then pulled on the reins and the pretty gray mare followed through the trees into the hills.

Katherine turned to look at Malcolm's sleeping body lying on the ground and prayed her shawl would be enough to keep him alive until he awoke or Duncan found him. Even now it was hard to make out his features. All she saw were the first big flakes of snow swirling to the ground, covering his body.

. . .

"I'll be back after the snow settles."

That was all the woman had said before she disappeared into the swirling white.

Katherine struggled to loosen the rope that bound her to the tree where the woman had left her. She'd lost the feeling in her hands and feet long ago. Huge flakes of wet snow pelted her in the face as she worked with the knot.

When the cord finally fell away, she pulled her hands in front of her and stared at the drops of blood that dripped to the snow from her raw fingers. She waited for the pain, but there was none. She felt nothing.

She tucked her numb fingers into the folds of her skirt and took the first step away from the tree, only to realize she didn't know which direction would take her home. When she looked up to the sky, she realized there was not much daylight left for her to find shelter.

A wall of rocks to her right provided the only hope of

protection from the howling wind, and Katherine lifted one foot then another as she plodded through snow that went above her ankles. She leaned against the craggy stones and let the tears she'd kept at bay for the last hour or more spill over her lashes. Tiny ice crystals froze to her cheeks, but her fingers didn't have the feeling to wipe them away. Her heart didn't have enough hope for it to matter.

She curled into a tight ball beside the tiny opening in the rocks, but she couldn't force herself to go deeper into the small, dark space. She no longer cared. All she wanted was to lie down and rest. Perhaps if she slept for just a little while she would be strong enough to find her way home.

She hugged her arms around her middle and closed her eyes, wondering if Duncan would ever find her. The woman's hateful words came back to haunt her and she wondered if her enemy was right. She wondered if Duncan might not even bother to look.

Chapter 14

Duncan sat at his place in the great hall listening with one ear to the complaints of two of his warriors concerning a dispute over a horse. He should not have let Kate go to pick berries this afternoon. His nerves had been unsettled since she and Malcolm had ridden across the drawbridge. And with good cause.

Even though there were men guarding the borders leading onto Ferguson land, it didn't guarantee Bolton and the English would not get past them. If Bolton found Kate, there was no way Malcolm could see to her safety.

He should not have let them go. He should have gone with them. He should have…

Alister burst through the entrance. His flushed cheeks and the worried look on his face sent warning signals racing through Duncan's chest. "My laird. The mistress's horse has come back to the stable alone."

Duncan shoved his chair backward and moved toward the entrance. The loud crash when the chair hit the floor focused every warrior's attention on him.

"Saddle your horses and bring torches."

The Ferguson men jumped from their places around the tables and headed to the exit.

Duncan fought the roaring in his head as he ran from the room and across the bailey to the stable. He'd known something was wrong. She should have been back long ago. Malcolm would never have kept her out this long unless he'd been unable to bring her back.

Painful slashes of guilt ate away at him. He should have kept Kate here to protect her. Just as he should have been here to protect his father and mother and sisters.

When would he learn? When would he know what to do to protect what was his? When would he be able to keep the people for whom he cared most safe? He was their laird. A laird should know. His father had.

Duncan raced through the double doors that led to the stable. His horse was already saddled and waiting for him. He mounted and galloped toward the drawbridge, forcing his warriors to hurry.

She had to be all right. If Bolton had taken her, he'd ride after the bastard this very minute and bring his head back on a spike.

"If we follow the mare's prints in the snow they should lead us to the mistress." It was Alister who spoke, and Duncan glanced down at the lone set of prints that led to the castle.

"Did Malcolm's horse come in too?"

"Nay, milord. Only the mistress's."

Duncan didn't say anything, but glanced down again at the prints as he urged his horse forward. "Bring more torches, Angus. We're losing the daylight."

Angus rode closer with four more warriors. The light

from their torches lit the path a little brighter. They traveled far into the hills, past the place where the women usually went to gather berries, then farther.

"Over here!"

It was Gregor that hollered from far to their right and when Duncan turned he saw what had caused him to stop. Malcolm's horse stood near a thicket, the reins caught in the nettles of a thorn bush, his mouth chomping on grass he'd uncovered beneath the snow.

"He must have wandered off," Duncan said. "Spread out. Malcolm may not be far away."

The men separated and rode forward. It didn't take long for someone to spot Malcolm's snow-covered body lying on the ground.

Duncan's heart jumped to his throat. "Is he alive?" he asked as Angus leaned over Malcolm's still form.

"Aye. He is alive."

Angus lifted the plaid from over Malcolm and threw it to the ground beside the warrior. Duncan picked it up and held it to his chest. It was the plaid Kate had been wearing.

"I can na find any marks on him, Duncan. Not even a lump on his head. It's as if he just went to sleep."

Duncan held the Ferguson plaid tighter and fought the waves of panic that threatened to consume him. "Gregor. Take what men you need to carry Malcolm back to the keep. The rest will come with me."

"Aye, milord," Gregor answered. He kept some men to put the huge warrior on his horse.

Angus gave Gregor instructions as he mounted his horse to follow Duncan. "Have Morgana give him liquids. Do na let her stop feeding him until I return. When he wakes, do na let him sleep again."

"Aye, Angus."

Angus held his torch high in the air to light the way in the snow. "Is the plaid the Lady Katherine's?"

Duncan nodded. It was the best he could do. The thought of Kate lying cold and frozen in the snow wrenched at his heart. "She does na like our winters, Angus."

"The mistress is strong and hearty, Duncan. If she's lost, she'll find a cave in the rocks to stay until we come for her."

"But she will not enter it." Duncan wanted to drop to his knees and roar to the heavens until the rocks and mountains felt his pain. He braced his shoulders and stared at the prints in the snow, then pushed his horse faster. "We have to find her. She will na go into a cave. She will na go in."

Duncan and Angus rode on with Duncan's warriors beside them, holding their torches high.

"If Bolton has taken her…" Angus growled, the remainder of his thought unspoken.

"It's not Bolton, Angus. Bolton would na have left Malcolm lying on the ground still alive. I fear it's one of our own who has done this. Someone who hates Kate and does na want to see her as my wife."

"We should have kept a closer watch, Duncan."

"I know. I should have known when we found her in the chapel she was na safe, but I could na believe one of our own would want to harm her."

"Who do you think would do such a thing?" Angus asked, but Duncan knew the old man already had a name ready.

"I do na know for sure, Angus, but I will na rest until I

find out."

Duncan gripped the reins tighter and held the shawl in his arms. He pushed his horse forward with greater speed.

"Here, milord!" Balfour cried the discovery. "Here!"

Duncan rode to the spot where Balfour had stopped his horse and jumped down to look at the rope hanging from the tree. The snow was packed to the ground where she had stood and his stomach turned when he saw the drops of blood in the powdery flakes. She'd been tied like an animal and left to freeze to death. The rage he felt equaled that of finding the English had murdered his family. Only this time his rage was directed at one of his own. At a Scot.

He followed her faint prints in the snow, running, his movements so frantic he almost tripped over her crumpled body. She was lying on her side, her cheek resting on her folded hands with her knees tucked up close to her chest. Her golden hair fanned out around her face, giving the red cast to her cheeks an even brighter glow.

She looked like an angel lying in the snow. A lifeless angel.

A mighty roar came from deep within him and he fell to his knees to lift her body into his arms. He brushed the snow from her face, and her skin, and her clothes, then pulled the plaid he'd taken from Malcolm over her. Someone handed him a another plaid, and another, and he wrapped each of them around her to make her warm, then stood and held her close to him.

"Let me see her, Duncan." Angus put his weathered hand to her face and felt her skin then found her hands beneath all the covers and rubbed them harshly. She moved her head and moaned a soft sigh, but he didn't stop rubbing. "She's still alive." Angus tucked the covers tighter around her. "Keep her covered until we get her home."

Angus held Kate long enough for Duncan to mount his horse, then Duncan took her and wrapped as many covers around her as he had. He placed a kiss on her forehead and held her close to him as his horse made his way back to the keep.

Duncan looked down at the small woman in his arms and kissed her fiery red cheeks. He'd come to care for her, and he could not stand the thought of losing her now.

This revelation should have surprised him, but it did not. She was his and had become important to him. He'd known it would happen when he took her as his bride. When she'd faced Bolton with him in the dungeon and placed the medallion in his hand.

Then, she'd called him her Scot and captured him with her kiss.

. . .

Duncan watched Kate as she slept beneath layers of Ferguson tartans. He waited to speak until the door had closed on the last of the women who had come to bring fresh water and clean clothes for their mistress.

"Who do you think did this, Angus?"

A bright fire burned in the hearth and the many lit candles around the bedside gave the room a muted glow.

She looked like an angel sleeping beneath the covers, just as she had when they'd found her. He remembered how soft and delicate she'd looked lying in the snow. And how lifeless.

She slept softly in the bed now, her wet clothes discarded

and the cuts on her arm and at her side tended. She had not opened her eyes yet, and Duncan feared she was hurt worse than they knew, but Angus held his hand to her face and assured him she would wake up in time.

"I can na believe one of our own would want to harm her, Angus. They all gave their oath of fealty and swore to protect her."

"Not all, Duncan."

Duncan gripped the tall bedpost. "No. Even Regan would na do this." He didn't want to believe that Regan's emotions had taken such a twisted turn, but he knew jealousy was a powerful motive for love as well as hatred.

"We will know as soon as the mistress wakes. She knows who tied her to the tree and left her to die. If it was Regan, she can tell us." Angus went to the small table beside the bed and poured the heated water the women had just brought into a cup to make some fresh tea.

"Do na use that water, Angus."

Angus turned around to face his laird, the look of incredulity on his face.

"Use only food and water that you bring into the room yourself, friend. We can na trust anyone right now."

"You think someone might try to poison her?"

"Kate was supposed to die and she did not. The killer knows as soon as she awakens she'll give us a name. Our killer must make sure she never opens her eyes." Duncan took some of the potion mixed with water he'd pulled from the well himself and held it to her lips. She swallowed once then turned her head. "We must keep our guard. Our killer does na have much time and she knows it.

"She? You do na think it's one of our warriors, but one

of the women?"

"Aye. A warrior would have killed Kate outright. He would nay have staked her out to die. It's one of our women."

"Then I fear it's Regan." Angus said.

Duncan had to agree, even though he didn't want to.

He did not want to think what he would have to do if it were.

. . .

Duncan stood in the corner of the room near the bed where Kate lay, hiding behind the tall screen where no one could see him, and waited. Angus had made a big commotion when he left, announcing to all within hearing that he would not be back until morning. That the mistress was sleeping peacefully and the laird had gone to an empty chamber to rest until his wife awoke. He gave instructions that the lady Katherine was not to be disturbed until morning.

Duncan leaned against the stone wall, listening to Kate's shallow breathing. He feared their plan to snare whoever had tried to kill Kate might go for naught, but just as the first rays of sunlight colored the dark sky with a faint pink glow, the door to Katherine's room opened a slit and a small, familiar figure stepped into the room.

She walked to the bed and watched Katherine sleep for what seemed an eternity, then raised her hand above her head. Duncan did not wait to see the candlelight reflect off the metal in her hand before he pushed away the screen and catapulted toward her. He knocked the small woman to the floor, grabbed the knife in her hand and threw it across the room.

The door flew open and Angus and Gregor and Balfour rushed into the room and lifted the would-be killer to her feet.

"You should na have stopped me, milord. I would have gladly rid you of your English wife."

Duncan's heart twisted in his chest. "Oh, Morgana. You have done this?"

Morgana and her mother and her mother before her had served the Ferguson mistresses with unswerving loyalty. He couldn't believe she would try to kill Kate. "Why? Why would you try to kill your mistress?"

"She is nay my mistress. She is English."

The look on Morgana's face was filled with such open hostility it took Duncan's breath away.

"I know you did na want to marry her," she cried out, "but only did so for the crown. If she were dead, you would be free to marry a Scot. I was only serving you as my mother did before me."

"That is na true, Morgana. I married her because I wanted her. I want the Lady Katherine to rule my heart and my keep."

"Nay! Your mother is waiting to come back to run Lochmore again, but she can na return as long as Lady Katherine is here. I promised I would get rid of your English wife so she could come back."

"Nay, Morgana. Lady Beatrice is dead. She died with my father, your laird."

The incredulous look on Morgana's face told of her confusion. "They are na dead, milord. And neither is my Hugh or my brother Ambrose or your sisters Meara and Elissa. They are only waiting for me to rid their keep of your English wife."

Duncan held Morgana to him and lifted his watery gaze to the ceiling. She was so young. Barely older than Kate, and already she had lost a husband she had loved dearly, and her father, brothers, and everyone close to her. She had lost them to the English. Maybe in her mind she had to kill Kate to make up for so many deaths.

Morgana looked up at him and Duncan saw the worshipful adoration in her eyes. "You should have seen the look on the English lady's face when she saw that I had come to kill her." The laughter that came from Morgana's mouth was harsh and unnatural. "She thought I had come to help her. From the day you brought her here, she thought I had accepted her. She thought the Fergusons could come to care for her. Now she knows that's impossible."

Morgana turned in Duncan's arms and stared at Katherine's still body lying on the bed. "Now she knows we do na want her here. She knows there is only hatred hidden behind our smiles."

Icy fingers wrapped around Duncan's heart and twisted. When Angus took Morgana from his arms, Duncan let her go.

"Come, lass," Angus said. "I will give you something to make you sleep. You need to rest."

"Aye, Angus. I am very tired." Morgana laid her head on Angus' shoulder and let the old man lead her from the room. "Have I done well?"

"There is na more you can do, Morgana. Na more."

The door closed behind Angus and Gregor, and Duncan turned to his wife, still sleeping on the bed. She had not moved since they'd come back. It was as if she'd willed herself to stay away.

Duncan sat down beside her and lifted her head, then held the cup to her mouth. Katherine took a small swallow of the liquid then turned her head to his chest. He felt the first slight movement and looked down on her just as her eyes fluttered halfway open.

"You came after me."

"Aye, lass. I came."

"She was wrong. She said you would not."

"Aye, lass. She was wrong."

...

Katherine opened her eyes, then closed them again. She did not want to be awake. She wanted to sleep forever, and when she had slept enough here on earth, she wanted God to take her to heaven. But she was awake now, and judging from the furnishings around her she had not gone to heaven.

She was still in Scotland.

She moved her head to the side and looked at Duncan sleeping at her bedside. She remembered him holding her in his arms and forcing her to drink Angus's potions.

The brilliant rays of the sun streamed through the crosslet slits on either side of the bed and through a larger window that overlooked the inner bailey. Light cast the room in a bright glow. She was tired, but at least she was warm. She'd been so cold and so scared. She'd been sure she was going to die. Sure that Morgana would succeed in killing her.

Morgana. The first person she'd met when Duncan had brought her to his home. Morgana, with the friendly smile on her face and honest acceptance in her gaze — and bitter hatred in her heart.

If Regan had stuck a blade into her side and left her to die, it would not have surprised her. She knew the hatred Regan had for her. Regan had not hidden or disguised it. Morgana's hatred had come without warning.

And if Morgana harbored such deep hatred, how many more of Duncan's Fergusons felt the same?

"Will you stay awake this time, Kate?"

Katherine turned her head and looked at her husband. No wonder Regan loved him. He was everything a woman could want. He was strong, and kind, and caring, and proud. So very noble and proud. And deserving of a Scottish wife.

"How long have I slept?"

"Two whole days and into the third. The great hall is filled with people waiting to hear how you are. They are even waiting outside in the bailey until they know."

Katherine turned away from him. Lies. The people of clan Ferguson had probably gathered in the great hall and the bailey to hear if Morgana's attempt had been successful, so they could celebrate around the grave of their English mistress.

"Are you hungry?"

Katherine shook her head. "How is Malcolm?"

"Your cloak kept him warm. He's fine. He would like to see you when you awaken to thank you. He said you saved his life."

"Tell him he is welcome, but I do not care to see him."

"Kate, I—"

"I'm tired now, Duncan. I would like to sleep." Katherine

closed her eyes and turned away from him.

"No, Kate."

The harsh tone of his voice forced her to open her eyes and face him. She'd heard that tone before, and knew he would grant no quarter.

"You will na turn from me, Kate. We will talk about what is wrong."

Katherine stared into the flames of the hearth. The room was warm. On the outside she would heal. On the inside she would never stop hurting. She would never be able to look at one of Duncan's clansmen and not wonder if their smiles were as false as Morgana's and if secretly they too wished she had died.

"Angus said when you opened your eyes, you were to stay awake. He said you were to drink every drop of ale with the potion in it, and that you were to eat the food Margaret had prepared for you."

"I am not hungry."

"When will you be hungry, wife?"

Katherine looked at him and a shudder raced up her spine. If he would just hold her in his arms for a little while, maybe everything would seem better. If he would just tell her that he cared, maybe everything would not hurt so much. If he would just tell her that it didn't matter that she was English, maybe she could believe him.

Maybe she could not.

"What day will you be hungry, Kate? Tomorrow? The next? Or when food will na longer do you any good?"

"Leave me be, Duncan. I am tired."

"I will na leave you be, Kate."

The breath caught in her throat and she swallowed past

the lump it left. "What do you want of me?"

"I want to see the light back in your eyes. I do na want you to wish you had na lived. I want you to be glad that you are mistress of Lochmore Castle. I do na want you to wish you had gone back to England. I want you to wish your laird would hold you in his arms until this nightmare goes away. That is what I want."

Katherine stared up at the high beams in the ceiling. She wanted to say the words but she could not. They would not all be true. Only that she wished her laird would hold her in his arms until this nightmare went away. Those words would be true.

"I know how you feel, Kate. You said it in your sleep. I know it was Morgana who took you into the hills and left you to die. I know what she said to you and why, but it's na true, Kate. None of clan Ferguson feels as she does. They do na hate you or wish you gone."

"Really, Duncan? Should I ask Regan to come here and tell me how she feels?"

"Regan does na matter. She feels as she does because..."

"Because she loves you and knows she would be a better wife for you than your English wife. She feels as all your people feel, but she at least is open with her opinion. She does not keep her silence as you and Morgana and the rest of the Fergusons do." Katherine closed her eyes and turned her face to the wall.

"Do na turn away from me, Kate."

"Can I turn to you, Duncan? Are your words any less false than Morgana's? Do you smile and hold me only because you don't have the crown yet? Do you withhold your lovemaking each night so that I crave the passion we once shared more than the soul I could lose?"

"My smiles and our lovemaking have nothing to do with the crown."

"They have *everything* to do with the crown, Duncan. They have since the day you took me as your wife."

"You do na think I've come to care for you?"

"It would not be wise to care for me, husband. It will bring only pain in the end. On the day I give the crown back to England, I will see how you truly feel. Just as I now see how your people truly feel."

Katherine fisted her hands at her side. Before she realized his intent, Duncan lifted her out of the bed. "What are you doing?"

"I'm taking you to hear how my people feel about you."

He wrapped her in so many covers she could hardly see over the top and walked across the room with her in his arms. He held her securely against him as he descended the stairs.

"I'm not dressed, Duncan. I cannot go where people will see me."

"You are mistress of Lochmore. You will go where your people have gathered in the cold to await word that you are all right."

"Please, Duncan, no. I don't want to face them. I don't want to see their false smiles and hear their false greetings. I'm not strong enough to face Morgana again."

Duncan stopped midway down the stairs. "Morgana is na longer here. You will never have to face her again.

"Morgana was not the only one who felt as she did. There are others."

He held her close for a long second then continued his

way down the stairs. "Give them time, Kate. In time they will learn to love you."

Katherine breathed a heavy sigh, then leaned her cheek against his chest. The medallion rested there. The Ferguson crest that had meant so much to Duncan that he'd risked his life to get it back. The crest she'd taken to him in exchange for his help. To put it in his hands had been the reason she'd kissed him that first time. She put her fingers to the metal and traced the eagle in flight. It had come to mean as much to her as it did to Duncan and she cursed herself because she didn't want it to.

Duncan stopped at the entrance to the great hall and stood with her in his arms so all the warriors of clan Ferguson could see that their mistress fared well. The room was so crowded there was not a place to sit or even to stand. When Duncan stood in the doorway, everyone in the room rose and gave a loud cheer, shouting Katherine's name as they raised their swords or tankards high in the air.

Next, Duncan carried her to the door to the keep and stepped outside. A crowd so huge Katherine could not even see them all had gathered in the cold to await word of their mistress. When Duncan stepped out on the top step of the keep, a deafening roar echoed against the curtain walls.

"Your mistress wants you to know she is well and accepts your prayers and good wishes."

Another tremendous roar echoed in the crisp air and Katherine raised a bandaged hand as the people cried her name. Tears of confusion streamed down her cheeks.

Duncan turned back into the keep and carried her up

the stairs. "Those are the voices I want you to remember, Kate. I want their shouts of concern to drown out Morgana's words of hatred."

Katherine looked up and saw the determined look on Duncan's face. "I was so frightened, Duncan."

"So was I, Kate. I was afraid I had lost you."

"And you would have lost the crown."

"No, Kate. I want both you and the crown."

"You cannot have both, Duncan."

Duncan lay her on the bed and stood back until he could meet her gaze evenly. "I will have both or I will have neither. It's the way it must be, Kate."

Chapter 15

Katherine leaned her shoulder against the cool stones near the window and let her gaze travel to the scene below. One group of Ferguson warriors practiced their skills with heavy metal swords, another with bows and arrows, and a third were engaged in hand-to-hand combat. They prepared long hours each day for their battle with the English.

Spiny fingers of fear clenched her heart and refused to let go. She'd known it would come to this.

Duncan was prepared to defend a crown that did not belong to him. His warriors were prepared to die for a crown they did not even possess. And every Ferguson was prepared to forfeit his life for an English mistress some of them still found it difficult to accept. All because she had not been brave enough to follow her king's edict and marry the man chosen for her. All because in her weakness she had married their laird, and now she did not want to lose him.

Katherine closed her eyes and took a deep breath. It would not be long before Bolton arrived. He would want both the crown and his betrothed. She did not doubt that her father would be with him.

Her father.

Since Bolton had taken the whip to her back in the dungeon, she'd refused to think of her father and what a great disappointment she would be to him. Again.

She turned back to the scene in the courtyard and her gaze automatically searched out the spot where Duncan trained with Malcolm and Gregor and Balfour.

Katherine watched as all three warriors took turns battling their laird. The look on Angus' face as he watched from the side did not show his usual sense of pride or satisfaction. The old man harbored a look of concern. Just as she did, Angus realized his laird fought his warriors as if they were the very devil. He battled in his fight to conquer his wife and her unwillingness to surrender her heart and mind. And the crown.

The breath caught in her throat when Balfour lunged at Duncan, but in the blink of an eye Balfour's huge body flew through the air as if he weighed nothing and landed in a heap at the side. Gregor attacked next, raising his sword, preparing to strike. Duncan spun around and with one deadly swipe, the sound of metal clanged and Gregor's sword flew out of his hands and landed beyond his reach. Duncan made a low growl and threw his friend to the ground, then stood over him with his sword at his throat, looking for the one who would come next. There was a hunger in his eyes that burned with a desire to cause pain — to feel pain — and Katherine knew she was to blame.

Sweat and mud streaked the bare flesh of all four warriors, giving them a serious, more warlike appearance.

Strained muscles and tested tempers created more tension in their struggle. The battle they waged against each other was fierce.

Malcolm rubbed his shoulder as if Duncan's punishing attacks may have already caused an injury, then took a determined leap, knocking Duncan to the ground. Malcolm and Duncan were the most evenly matched, and the two warriors struggled in the dirt, neither giving an advantage. Then Duncan made a decisive move that pinned Malcolm beneath him.

Chests heaved and muscles bunched in a clash of iron wills and brute strength. Without warning Duncan raised his arm and thrust his fist forward. The blow was an unfair assault, a breach of Duncan's practice rules, and the sound of Duncan's fist making contact with Malcolm's flesh brought Gregor and Balfour to attention. They leaped between the pair before Duncan struck again and pulled their laird away.

As if Duncan realized he'd carried his sparring too far, he stood tall with his legs braced and waited for his friend to meet out his revenge. Malcolm would retaliate. All around them expected no less a reaction.

Malcolm sprang from the ground, the look of unleashed fury evident on his face. He doubled his fist and leveled it with all his might until it connected with Duncan's flesh just beneath his right eye. Duncan did not back away but accepted the blow without question.

Katherine turned away from the window. This was the first time she'd seen Duncan lose control of his well harnessed emotions. The first time his frustration and disappointment had affected those around him. Even though Malcolm had received the brunt of his anger, Katherine knew she was the intended victim. Duncan was desperate to get the crown away from her and didn't know how to get it without using force. He was strung as tight as a loaded crossbow and his frustration almost painful to watch. The longer this continued the more dangerous he would become both to himself and those around him.

She had to find the secret passageway that would lead her out of the castle. She had to get the crown and find a way to get it to England. She had to stop waiting for the miracle that would place the crown back in England's hands and still allow her to keep her Scot.

Katherine scanned the stone walls of their chamber one more time and rubbed her hands over her eyes. There was not one inch of the room she hadn't touched or pushed against or moved, and she still hadn't found the opening that would take her outside.

The secret door must be here. According to Ian, Lochmore Castle had a secret escape route just as Kilgern, and it was hidden in the laird's chamber. So why couldn't she find it?

Katherine walked across the room and stared at the beautifully designed tapestries that covered the walls. Every one of them depicted a battle scene or the outdoor picture of a hunt. She walked from one wall hanging to the other, lifting it away from the wall to check the stones beneath. Nothing.

"Is something wrong, mistress?"

Katherine spun around to see her new maid, Mary, watching her. "Oh, no, Mary. I was just looking at these tapestries."

"They're beautiful, are they not?"

"Yes, beautiful."

"The mistress took great pride in her tapestries and has a great many covering the walls of Lochmore Castle."

"Duncan's mother must have been especially fond of animals and the hunt."

"Oh, no, milady. The laird's mother did not fancy these in the least. That's why they hang here. Her favorite tapestries hang in her chamber."

Katherine's arm stopped in mid motion as she was about to touch one of the tapestries that showed a large male deer staring wide-eyed at the Scot who was about to slay him with his drawn bow. "This is not Duncan's parents' chamber?"

"Oh, no, milady. The laird did na want to move into his parents' chamber and chose to keep this one as his own. It was always his chamber."

Katherine's heart pounded in her chest. She'd been looking for the passageway in the wrong room. "Could I see the other tapestries?"

A bright smile lit up the younger maid's face. "Of course, mistress. I'm surprised you have na seen them before. I thought Morgana would have… I'm sorry. I did na mean…"

"It's all right, Mary. Morgana didn't show me her mistress' room. I should have been thoughtful enough to ask."

Katherine breathed a deep sigh. She had been thoughtful enough to ask, but Morgana had told her it was an empty room where the laird had stored his parents' personal possessions. Items he didn't want disturbed. Katherine should have been inquisitive enough to insist that she see them.

Mary led the way to Duncan's parents' chamber and opened the door. Bright sunlight streamed through the two windows, and although this room was no larger than the room she shared with Duncan, the warmth and openness she felt gave this chamber a friendlier feel.

Katherine walked to the nearest tapestry and stared at it in awe. "Oh, how beautiful."

"Yes, milady," Mary answered. "The mistress had a true gift."

"Yes, she did."

Katherine couldn't take her gaze from the rich colors and excellent workmanship. Each design represented a wealth of Scottish folklore combined with the harmony of nature and a love of beauty. There were no battles. No pictures of a hunt. Every scene held her spellbound.

"You may leave me, Mary. I would like to stay here a while." She whispered her orders. To speak louder would have been sacrilege.

"Very well, milady. I'll be near if you need anything. You have just to call."

"Thank you."

Katherine sat on the soft bed and stared at the hangings on the wall and let the tranquillity in the room engulf her. Duncan's mother dwelled here. Her presence filled the room as if she were still alive; as if she still inhabited the room.

Katherine knew she should use this time to look for the secret passageway, but she couldn't move. Her body did not want to lose the closeness she felt to Duncan's mother. For a long time she stared at the hangings and let the contentment she felt here blanket her.

"What are you doing, Kate?"

Katherine did not need Duncan to speak to know he stood behind her in the doorway. She could feel him there. Just as she could feel his mother within the room.

"I didn't know this was your mother's room. Morgana said it was a storeroom."

"I'm sorry. I did na know you had na been in here or I would have shown you myself."

Katherine sighed. "Your mother must have been a remarkable woman."

"Yes, she was. I wish you could have met her."

"I can feel her. She left her calmness and her love for peace in this room. Did your father share her gentleness or was he like you?"

"You do na think I am gentle? You do na think I yearn for peace?"

Katherine looked up at him. He had washed in the stream and mud and grime no longer streaked his skin, but the place on his face where Malcolm had struck him was already discolored and swollen. "I think you have not lived in peace for such a long time you don't realize it's within your grasp."

Duncan stepped into the room and shut the door behind him. The soft thud as it closed echoed in the chamber and Katherine's heart pounded in her chest. She was not afraid of him, she was afraid for him. She was afraid for herself.

"Can you feel my father in this room too?"

Katherine thought, then shook her head. "I don't know.

I think only your mother."

"That's because the two were so united they seemed as one. They thought as one, and talked as one, and acted as one. Their marriage was perfect."

"As ours will never be?"

"That is to be seen. There was a trust between them we do na have. A oneness."

Duncan walked to the tapestry on the wall between the two windows and brushed his fingers over the fabric. "My father was one of the most revered, respected lairds in all of Scotland. His opinion was sought by all, including our own king."

"Is that what drives you so, husband? Are you afraid that your fellow Scots don't respect you as they did your father?"

Duncan shook his head and walked to another tapestry. "Nay, wife. Respect is earned, not given lightly. In time I will earn the respect I am due, just as my father did."

"Then what, Duncan? What drives you to want a crown you know doesn't belong to you?"

Duncan turned around and locked gazes with her. The look in his eyes was hard, uncompromising. "Never in my father's lifetime did he fail at anything. Not in his quest for honesty and truth, nor in the vow he took before God as laird of clan Ferguson to protect all that was entrusted to him. The Bishop's Crown was given to him for safekeeping and he lost it. It was the only vow he made he could na keep."

Katherine closed her eyes and breathed a deep breath. "So you will keep the vow for him?"

"It's my duty. On my father's honor."

"If your father's honor were not at stake, Duncan, could you let me give the crown back to England?"

"Nay, lass. My own vow is as sacred as my father's. As laird of clan Ferguson, I also promised to protect all that was entrusted to me. What was entrusted to my father is the same as if it had been entrusted to me."

Katherine clenched her hands together. "Did you marry me only because you thought I had possession of the crown, and through me you could redeem your father's honor?"

"I owed you a debt, Kate. You gave me back the medallion. It was my duty to protect you from Bolton." Duncan lifted the medal from his chest and wrapped his fingers around it.

Katherine felt as if his admission were a knife plunged into her heart. She'd known the reasons he'd married her from the start, but had hoped that time and what they'd shared would have changed the facts. They hadn't. "Is there any hope for us, Duncan?"

"Our future lies in your hands, wife."

"I must be the one who yields?"

"You must give me the crown."

"Or you will take it from me?"

"Nay, wife. I will na have to take it. If you care for me at all, you will give it to me."

"And if I do not?"

"Then we have na marriage. You will have taken from me all that is important."

"The English will always fight to get back their crown and no Scot will be safe until they do."

"No Scot is safe now, nor have they been since the

beginning of time."

"But do you not want to see this change? Do you not want to be the Scot responsible for the beginning of peace?"

"I do na want to be the Scot responsible for my father's tarnished name. I do na want my father to have died for naught. I do na want to give back the crown, knowing my mother and sisters gave their lives to protect it."

Katherine hugged her arms around her middle and rocked back and forth on the bed. All was lost.

Her whole life she'd been a disappointment to her father. She'd heard it in the tone of his voice and seen it in the look on his face. She'd prayed she would never see that same look on her husband's face, but she was seeing it now. Every day she didn't give him the crown, she became a bigger disappointment to him. In time, there would be nothing more he would want from her.

She thought of her arranged marriage to Bolton and shuddered. Her future with him would have been a living hell. That's why she had clung to Duncan. She'd felt safe with him. He had the strength to protect her and the weakness to want to. She'd felt it when she'd kissed him that first time.

He also possessed the power to destroy her.

This was why she had made the promise to never love him. A promise she had not kept.

She sat on the edge of the bed and fought the urge to run to him. She held back for a very good reason. She didn't trust that he would want to touch her.

"Do what you must soon, Kate. We have almost run out of time."

A tiny little gasp came from deep inside her, a soft

whimper of anguish. Heaven help her. She was bound by a vow that left her no choice. To turn her back on her faith and go against the oath she'd given God would destroy her.

"Help me, Dun—"

"Duncan!"

Malcolm's loud pounding stopped her in mid sentence. For a moment she thought she saw Duncan soften, but before she could be sure, Malcolm threw open the door and rushed across the room.

"Downstairs, Duncan. A messenger from Bolton."

Duncan turned to her. The look in his eyes was hard, almost deadly. "Go to our chamber, Kate. Stay there until I come for you."

Katherine stood and swallowed past the lump in her throat. "But I—"

"Do na argue, lass." Duncan reached for her hand. "I will come for you when it's safe."

He lifted his other hand as if he wanted to caress her face, but dropped it back to his side before his flesh touched hers, then turned away and left the room.

Her heart pounded in her breast and she feared it would explode. As soon as the door closed behind him, Katherine rushed across the room pushing on one stone after another, frantic in her search for the secret passageway.

She must get to the crown. If need be, she would at least have what Bolton wanted in exchange for Duncan's life and the safety of his people.

· · ·

Duncan stared at the man standing before the hearth

warming his hands, then let his gaze study the small army of Englishmen that flanked their leader. Every nerve in his body snapped in warning, yet he wasn't sure why. When he first looked at the strange little man, his initial impulse was to laugh.

The Englishman's shoulders were hardly as broad as Kate's and his bright red hair stood away from his head like it had been groomed by a blind person with a very dull knife.

He wore a short tunic the same color as the pea soup Margaret had served last night for their evening meal, and his hose were identical to the bright yellow ribbon Kate had tied in her hair. He presented a very humorous sight — until he turned around.

The smile formed by his straight thin lips curved into a deadly sneer, and his pale blue eyes bulged from their sockets, glaring in open disdain. He stared at Duncan for a long moment then threw back his head and snorted. It was impossible to miss the derisive tone in his laughter.

"Good God. You are even bigger than the Scots I've already met. I doubted my cousin William's accuracy when he told me you Fergusons had been spawned by giants, but I see he was not exaggerating." The smirk on his face broadened.

Duncan took slow, deliberate steps toward the man until he stood close enough to see every pox mark on his face. Malcolm and Angus plus a score more of Ferguson warriors stood against the walls. Each rested one hand on the hilt of their swords and the other on the small knife tucked into a sheath at their waist. "You do na fear these Scottish giants?" Duncan asked, clasping his hands behind his back.

The messenger laughed again while he lifted the many gold chains from around his neck and let them sift through his fingers. "Strength is not always determined by size, my lord. I have listened to the tales of your bravery in battle and I do not think you the fool William does. You will not kill me and risk having the English army destroy every Ferguson from the face of the earth."

Duncan concentrated on keeping his breathing even. "Do na ever assume you know what I will do, English. It could be the last mistake you make."

"It's you who have made the mistake, Ferguson. It was very foolish of you to refuse to hand over the Bishop's Crown. You made an even greater mistake when you kidnapped my cousin's betrothed."

The pompous Englishman then clasped his hands behind his back and paced before the hearth as if he were lord of the manor. As if he were the one in control of the situation. Duncan felt heated anger tighten the muscles in his chest. "Why has Bolton sent you?"

"I've come to arrange an exchange. You will give me the crown and Lady Katherine, and I will assure the safety of your clan from the English."

"The crown *and* Lady Katherine? She is that important to him?"

The little man paced before him, stopping only to study Duncan with a taunting sneer on his face. "Do you know who you've taken, Scot?" He chuckled as if he alone knew the answer to a great secret. "Lady Katherine is the daughter of the Earl of Wentworth, the chief advisor to King Edward of England. The king does not make a move without first consulting the earl. Wentworth is so powerful, it's almost more important to gain an audience with him than with the king himself."

Duncan raised his eyebrows as if he were duly impressed and the little man puffed out his chest and continued his pompous effusion. "You should realize what you've done, Scot. My cousin intends to have Wentworth's daughter for his bride. Marriage to her will gain my cousin a seat close to the king. If you're not a fool, you'll give over the crown and the Lady Katherine, and we will consider this matter settled."

"And if I do na?"

"Then you and every Ferguson man, woman and child will die."

Duncan stared at Bolton's cousin and held his tongue as well as his temper. What he wanted to do was give the little weasel to his warriors for target practice, then send him back to Bolton in pieces. But he could not. Bolton could carry out his threat, and to mistreat his little puppet would only cause the Fergusons more harm.

"What about the deaths your cousin has already caused?"

"Those were the unfortunate casualties of war."

"Those were the senseless killings of innocent people, and your cousin is to blame. The matter will na be settled until William Bolton is dead."

The small Englishman's eyes sparkled with humor. "That's too bad. I've come to tell you that my cousin and a very large army of King Edward's finest warriors are camped just beyond your border. You have three days to return the crown and Lady Katherine. If you do not obey

William's directives, you can watch the slaughter begin as William annihilates every Ferguson in Scotland."

Duncan stared at the little man as if he were giving much thought to his demands. "I do na think I would like to hand over the Lady Katherine. I have grown quite fond of her, and would sorely miss her company."

A deep red coloring started beneath the little man's collar and slowly crept up his neck, then to his cheeks. "I demand that Lady Katherine be allowed to return with me or the slaughter will begin this very day. We have an army so large—"

In a movement so quick Bolton's messenger didn't see it coming, Duncan picked the man up by his tunic and shoved him hard against the wall.

The English warriors lifted their arms to draw their swords but Duncan heard the loud swish of Scottish swords being drawn at the same time. Both sides stared at each other in stalemate, waiting to see what would happen to their leaders.

"And I demand that you get your lying carcass back to your cousin and tell him I know exactly where he is camped. I can also tell him what he had for his meal last night and which squire he took to his bed. He has no bigger an army than his own men and is hoping the Earl of Wentworth cares enough for his daughter to come after her with a sizable army to aid him."

The roots of the Englishman's red hair turned three shades darker and Duncan swore he could feel him tremble as he dangled his feet off the floor. "You can also tell your cousin if he dares to attack my keep, he will never see Lady Katherine again. If the weaklings that are with him are your king's warriors, then tell them to prepare to die, because if one Ferguson comes to harm, I will come after him. My sword will na rest until I have collected the head of every man riding with him."

With that, Duncan dropped the little man to the floor and watched him splash around until he gained his footing.

"You will regret this, Ferguson," he sputtered, tugging at his tunic and straightening his clothing. "You will regret this."

"All I regret is that I had na yet returned when your cousin came the first time and slaughtered my family. If I had been here that day, he would na be alive now to make such idle threats."

"You will wish you had never laid a hand on the crown or William's betrothed. Lady Katherine's father is on his way, and when he arrives he will storm your castle and rescue his daughter."

"I look forward to meeting Lady Katherine's father. Tell him he is welcome at Lochmore Castle the moment he arrives."

Bolton's cousin turned a deeper shade of red and stomped his foot on the floor in a show of uncontrolled temper. "William will not give up until he gets his betrothed."

"You forgot the crown, little man. Does he na want the crown too?"

"Yes. Of course. But Lady Katherine is just as important to him. Her father is the earl."

Duncan fisted his hands at his side and turned away from the disgusting little man. "Go back to your cousin and tell him he has three days to get out of Scotland. If he is na gone by then, I will gather every Ferguson and neighboring clansmen and we will na return until you are all dead."

"You cannot—"

"Get out, Englishman, and be glad you're leaving alive."

The little man sputtered again, then spun on his heel and stomped from the room, his little army behind him. Duncan waited until he heard the door slam before he took his next breath. "Gregor. Take Balfour with you and make sure he reaches Bolton unharmed. I would hate to have one of our men confuse him with a peacock and kill him before he reaches his cousin."

Duncan waited until he and Malcolm and Angus were alone, then sat in his chair at the long table and rubbed his hands against the throbbing pain at his temple. "What have the men watching Bolton reported today?"

Gregor filled a cup with ale and slid it across the table then filled one for himself and Angus. "Timothy rode in shortly before the English to tell us Bolton is still alone. His army is nay large enough to attack with any success. Bolton is still waiting for Lady Katherine's father. They send scouts every few hours to check. So far, they've come back alone."

Duncan took a long swallow of ale. "If I did na think it would cause a war with Kate's father, I would attack today."

Malcolm sat straight in his seat and propped his elbows on the table. "Nay, Duncan. It's too risky."

Duncan clenched his hand around the goblet. "Three days. I'll give Bolton three days. Na longer."

Both men nodded in agreement, then Angus leaned forward and said out loud what Duncan had only been thinking. "Bolton does na know that Lady Katherine is your wife. What happens when he and the earl find out you've married her?"

Duncan took another swallow of ale, then shoved back his chair and stood. "See that the men get in a couple more hours of training before the sun sets. I need to speak to Kate, then I will be out to train with you."

Angus stood with him. "You need the crown, lad."

Malcolm leaned back in his chair and nodded in agreement. "It's important that we have the crown before the English come."

Duncan kicked his chair with his boot, then strode out of the room and took the stairs two steps at a time until he reached their chamber. He pushed the door open and kicked it shut after its second bounce against the wall. "I will have the crown, Kate!"

His wife slowly turned and their gazes locked. She knew what the crown meant to him and to Scotland. She knew that his father had died to keep the crown. She knew she would destroy any chance they had for a future together if she refused to give it to him.

His heart fell to the pit of his stomach. He could see from the look on her face she was willing to forfeit everything for England.

Chapter 16

Fire blazed in Duncan's eyes and Katherine fought the turmoil that battled within her. A shiver raced down her spine as she watched her husband struggle to control his temper.

With a strangled sigh he walked to the arrow slit and leaned a fisted hand beside the window that looked onto the bailey below. The concentrated sounds of Ferguson warriors training for their battle with the English intruded on the tension-filled silence that surrounded them.

"I wonder how many of my men will na live to see the sun set three days from now?"

The breath caught in Katherine's throat.

"Do you know what I like the least about being laird, Kate? I dislike the most when I have to bring back the dead body of a friend and have to tell their family I failed to keep their loved one safe. It's only because I know they died with honor in their fight to protect Scotland that I can sleep at night."

Duncan turned away from the window and leveled his hooded glare at her. "If England gets back her crown, all who died protecting it will have died for naught. My father will have died for naught. If I let you give the crown to England, I will have betrayed my father's honor and have failed Scotland."

Katherine's voice cracked as she found the courage to say the words that would seal their fate. "I cannot give you the crown."

Duncan grabbed a clay pitcher sitting beside him and heaved it through the air. It shattered against the wall behind her and broke into tiny pieces that prickled against her skin when they hit.

"How can you na see your way to give me the crown? You're my wife! Have you na come to see what it means to me?"

"Please, don't ask, husband. The choice is not mine to make. It never has been."

He reached out for her and grabbed her by the arms. "Then whose? Whose choice is it to na give me the crown? England's? Is England still that important to you?"

She saw the desperation in his eyes. Heard it in his voice. He was frantic to have the crown but didn't know how to get it from her. "It's not England. I do not favor England any more than I favor Scotland. I took an oath before God. I cannot break it."

"What oath?"

"The oath I gave to your priest the night he died. I promised to protect the crown."

"You have protected the crown, wife. There's nothing more you can do."

"That was not all I promised. I placed my hand on your priest's bible and swore I would give the crown to only one man. I swore it."

"Which man? To whom did you swear you would give the crown?"

Duncan's grip on her arms tightened and her breathing came in harsh, agonizing gasps.

"Who?"

"My father."

The muscles in Duncan's jaw tightened and the fury in his voice evidenced his rage. "No! Our priest would na make you swear to give the crown back to England. He would na!"

"He did. The priest sent by your father made me swear I would give the crown to England or lose my soul."

Duncan dropped his hands from around her arms and Katherine slumped to the floor. "I swore to God, Duncan." One sob after another racked her body as she gasped for air. "Your Father Kincaid held my hand on his bible and made me swear to God that I would give the crown to only one man. My father, the Earl of Wentworth."

"Why? Why would he do such a thing?"

"I don't know. Maybe peace was that important to him. He knew if Scotland kept the crown, there would be war. Maybe it was because he didn't want to see innocent people die for a crown that did not belong to them.

Katherine took a deep breath and said what she hoped Duncan could accept as the reason. "Maybe it was because your father gave your priest the order."

"Never! My father died to keep the crown from England. He would not tell our priest to give it back to them."

"Perhaps your father did not die protecting the crown

from England. Perhaps he died keeping it from Bolton."

"It's the same."

"It is not! Bolton is evil and would use the crown for evil. My father will return it where it belongs."

Duncan turned on her as if she'd spoken blasphemy. "Nay! My father's honor is at stake. I must have it to save his honor. I must have it."

The desperate look in his eyes sliced through her and her heart twisted in her breast, then broke. "I cannot give it to you." Katherine's harsh whisper stammered through the violent sobs that shook her body. "I gave my word. I swore to God. I cannot break my vow. Not even for you."

Katherine looked at him through her tears. The expression on his face mirrored her pain. It reflected her torture. It answered the question her heart dreaded to hear. The answer rang as clear and loud as the hollow pealing of a death knell. His next question sealed their fate.

"Have you na come to care for me at all, Kate?"

Katherine swallowed. "Was that your intent these past months? To barter your affection in exchange for the crown?" She raised her head until she could see his face clearly. "I gave you all I could, Duncan. I am sorry if it was not enough."

Katherine concentrated on her husband's face as the muscles in his cheeks tightened and his lips thinned. The frantic look in his eyes frightened her and she turned away from him. The loud slam of the door as he left the room thundered with the same finality as the door he closed on her heart.

An important part of her died.

...

She found the secret passageway. Katherine knelt before the altar in the chapel and repeated the same prayer she'd prayed for months, but God had not seen fit to give her an answer.

She'd begged and bargained and bartered for a miracle that would allow her to return the crown and not lose her Scot, but now it was too late.

In the end, she had no choice but to accept God's will. Now her prayer was that if God would not provide for her to return the crown and keep her Scot, then He would give her the courage to do what she had promised Father Kincaid that night all those months ago. That somehow she would be selfless enough to give the crown to her father even though she knew how desperate Duncan was to have it. Even though she knew without the crown, Duncan would never want her.

She fingered the warm beads in her hands, then added a final prayer that Duncan wouldn't think of her with only hatred in his heart.

Her plan was simple. She only had to reach Ian and ask for sanctuary. Then, Duncan could not touch her. He would not be able to get the crown.

Her heart skipped a beat. She clenched her hand to her stomach and held it there. God's demands were too great. She did not have the courage. She closed her eyes and began her prayer again.

Katherine heard the soft footsteps behind her and knew Regan had arrived. Kate had asked that she meet her.

"Mary said you wanted to see me. Did you think it

would be safer if we met where God could protect you?"

Katherine turned to face the woman who loved Duncan almost as much as she. "I was not concerned with my safety. I asked to meet here because I need a favor from you and I didn't want anyone to overhear."

"You would like a favor of me? That's funny, English. I think I would be the last person you would ask for help."

Katherine took a deep breath. She just had to say the words and it would be over. "I know you don't care for me, Regan, which is—"

The shrill laughter that came from Regan's mouth sounded like blasphemy in the small, sacred sanctuary. "Do na care for you? Oh, English. My feelings have far passed na caring for you."

Katherine fingered the smooth marble beads in her hands. "Then you should find my favor quite agreeable. I would like you to help me leave Duncan."

"For how long?"

Katherine concentrated on the one word she needed to say. The one word that would make what she was doing more real. "Forever."

There was a slight pause before Regan said more. "And go where?"

Katherine could hear the disbelief in her voice. "That's not important. If you help me leave, I promise I'll never come back. You will have Duncan to yourself."

Even in the shadowed candlelight of the small chapel, Katherine could see Regan's eyes open wide. "How can you promise you'll never come back? The laird will na let you leave him. You are his wife."

"When I leave, Duncan will not care if I come back to

him or not."

Regan didn't hesitate long before she asked her next question. "What would I have to do?"

A small, painful breath caught in Katherine's throat and she touched her hand to her breast and swallowed past it. "Tomorrow morning after the laird leaves the keep to practice with his men, I want you to bring a horse to the spot outside the castle walls where the rocks end and the stream curves around the hill. Do you know where that is?"

"Aye."

"Tie the horse to a tree by the stream and leave it. I will find it when I get there."

"How will you get out of the castle without Duncan seeing you?"

"That is my problem."

"Where will you go?"

Katherine leaned her hand against the railing where she'd knelt and gripped the wood for support. "Someplace where Duncan can never find me."

"Why?"

Katherine clutched the beads to her heart. *Why?* "Because..." Katherine's voice broke and she cleared it, but still could not talk. How could she tell this stranger she couldn't stay here, knowing how she'd disappointed him. How could she tell her it was easier for her to live alone for the rest of her life than to live with Duncan's hatred for even one day.

"Do you na love him, English?"

Regan asked the question as if it were impossible to imagine not loving Duncan. "I wish I did not. This would be easier if I did not."

"And does he love you?"

Katherine closed her eyes and blinked back the wetness in her eyes. "No. He doesn't love me. It will not take long for him to forget me and take you back into his bed, Regan."

Katherine waited for Regan to give her answer. It came quickly.

"Your gray mare will be tied to a tree by the stream, English, waiting for you."

Katherine nodded, then walked from the chapel with her shoulders back and her head high — and her heart in pieces.

She'd always known it would come to this. She just didn't think it would hurt so much.

It did.

. . .

Katherine lifted the torch higher and made her way down the long tunnel that would take her outside the walls of Lochmore Castle and far away from Duncan. With each step she struggled to ignore the tunnel walls that closed in on her, suffocating the air from her chest.

This passageway was narrower than the tunnel she'd taken to escape from Kilgern and it seemed longer too, but Katherine knew she was almost to the end. She tried to forget how much her heart ached and walked faster to escape. But she couldn't walk fast enough to get away from the hurt and the emptiness. It was an aching she felt even when Duncan had been in the same room with her.

Last night she'd waited for him, hoping he would come to her. He had not. His absence showed her what their life would be like if she didn't give him the crown.

Katherine continued through the secret passageway, stopping only long enough to catch her breath. She had no doubt that when she made her way to the exit, her horse would be tied to the tree just as Regan had promised. If Duncan noticed she was not in her seat beside him for midday meal, it would probably be with relief that he wouldn't have to look at her until evening.

A familiar stabbing of pain clenched around her heart and she concentrated on opening the locked door just ahead. Bright sunlight blinded her and she shielded her eyes when she pushed on the door. She looked around for the horse Regan had promised would be there and found it tied to the tree just a few yards ahead.

Katherine mounted the familiar gray mare and took one last look at the impressive fortress she'd shared with Duncan for a short time. The place she had called home. She pulled on the reins and rode in the opposite direction. She did not have much time to get the crown and ask Ian for sanctuary before Duncan realized she had left him.

. . .

Duncan lowered one knee to the ground and braced his elbow on the other knee while his chest fought for air. He focused on the two warriors still lying in the dirt ahead of him, then looked to the right to see who was next. There was no one left who would challenge him.

"Give it up, lad," Angus said from behind him. "Your men can na take much more of your punishment. Even if you fight every warrior in Scotland, it will na make you feel better. You can na change what she must do."

Duncan swiped the back of his hand across his face then let his shoulders sag. "She knows how important the crown is to me and she does na care enough to give it over."

"How she feels for you has nothing to do with the crown and well you know it. She took a vow. You told me yourself she swore to God. You would have her risk her soul?"

Duncan brushed the dust from his clothes, grabbed his shirt from the peg where he'd hung it to keep it clean, and took long, determined steps toward the outdoor vat of water where he could bathe. "Nay," he said, stepping into the icy water and scrubbing the dirt and sweat from his body. "I can na ask her to risk her soul. But I can na believe our priest would demand she make such a vow. He knew my father's honor would be lost if he gave up the crown."

"Mayhap you should search hard to make sure your father's honor has been lost."

"Do you think Father could have given the priest the order to return the crown to England?"

Angus paced in front of the wooden barrier. He looked as if he were pondering the idea, considering it as a possibility. "I do na know. Your father loved peace above all else. He may have weighed the options and decided the risks were too great to keep the crown."

"My father loved Scotland above all else, and sacrificed everything to protect his people from the English. I can na believe he would have given the crown to Father Kincaid with instructions to give it to Kate to return it to her father."

"Nay. I do na think Father Kincaid was to give the crown to your Kate. I think he was to give the crown to her sister, Lady MacIntyre. Your Kate took the crown in her place and Father Kincaid did na know the difference."

Duncan rubbed the heel of his hand over his eyes and shook his head. Could he dare believe his father would have made the decision to give the crown back, knowing that loyal Scots had died to take it?

"Kate thinks my father was na protecting the crown from England, but from Bolton. She thinks he believed it would be safer in England's hands than in Bolton's."

Angus handed Duncan a large woolen cloth with which to dry, then held his clothes for him. "We'll never know. I think you'll have to decide on your own what's more important to you. I pray you make the right decision."

Duncan slipped his shirt over his head and breathed a painful sigh. "Dear God, Angus. I wish I'd been here to help Father. I wish I had na been so far away that I could na keep him safe."

"We all wish that, lad. I most of all. I had been at your father's side since I was na more than your age, and never had I allowed anything to happen to him. It was his decision that I go with you when you went to fight the English because he could na abide the thought of anything happening to you. If I had been here…"

"If you had been here, friend, you would be lying in the ground near your laird. I am glad you were with me."

Duncan stumbled over the emotion in his voice and finished dressing, then walked back across the courtyard.

"Have you noticed the lass Regan standing by the stable?" Angus asked as they neared the kitchens. "She's been waiting in the same spot all morning and her eyes have na strayed far from where you are. From the way she's biting at the nails on her fingers I would guess there's something important on her mind. She's been waiting for the right time to speak with you."

A frown covered Duncan's face as he watched Regan pace back and forth then stop to chew her nails and begin her pacing again. Such obvious agitation was uncharacteristic for Regan.

Duncan placed the knife he wore at his side back into its sheath and walked to where she stood. Since the day he'd removed her from the keep, Regan had gone away to lick her wounds like a dangerous animal. Something important had brought her back into the open. He knew from past experience it would be best if he didn't wait much longer to discover what it was.

"Are you waiting to speak to me, Regan?"

The look in her eyes when she turned to face him was different than the confident stare he was used to seeing. A slight frown covered her forehead and her pursed lips bespoke a hesitancy that was uncommon in her.

"Aye. I need to speak with you."

Regan kicked her foot into the dirt and moved the dust that swirled around her slipper. She took a step toward the keep and Duncan walked with her. "Do you remember when we were young, Duncan? You used to race through the glade with Malcolm and Gregor and Balfour beside you, pretending you were the Scots and Brenna and Elissa and I were the English. You would take our strongholds and slay us with your long wooden swords, and announce that you had taken all our land and our riches for Scotland."

A warm smile curved his lips upward as he remembered how carefree life was when they were young. "I remember that Elissa was the only good Englishman of the three of you. She was the only one who knew how to die like a proper warrior so we noble Scots could do justice to our exuberant celebration after we'd stormed your castles and slain you."

"I know. You were so ferocious and brave. I knew then that I loved you and wanted to marry you."

Duncan stopped in the middle of the courtyard and turned Regan to face him. "Regan, cease." His voice was a soft whisper. "Do na talk about this again. I am na free and well you know it."

Regan brought her middle finger to her mouth and bit down on her nail. Her fingers trembled and Duncan felt the first slight twinge of unease. "You have na chewed your nails since we were small and our fathers caught us stealing meat pies from the kitchen. Your father said he could always tell when your conscience bothered you because you bit at your nails."

Regan laughed and took her finger out of her mouth and clenched her fists at her side. "Mayhaps I do have a conscience after all, and it has come out again to torment me."

Duncan's heart beat a little faster and he readied himself for the unknown. "What have you done, Regan?"

"I have been thinking of your wife." Regan fisted her hands in the folds of her skirt and twisted the material.

"What about my wife?"

"Do you remember the night she did na return after she'd gone to the chapel? You found her locked in the small room behind the altar in the dark."

Duncan remembered how terrified Kate had been and how she had clung to him when he'd carried her out.

"Your words and the look in your eyes told me you thought I had closed her in that room, but it was na me, Duncan. It was Morgana."

"I owe you an apology. I did think it was you."

"You do na owe me anything. Even though I did na lock your English wife in the dark, I watched while Morgana hit her on the head and dragged her body behind the altar and into the small room."

"And you left her there?"

"Aye. I left her there. I knew Morgana had na hit her hard enough to kill her, and that you would find her when you went to the chapel for your midnight prayers. I did na see anything wrong in letting her sit in the dark for a while. Until I saw the fear in her eyes when you found her."

Duncan looked into Regan's eyes and he could see the regret harbored there. "I did na know your English wife was so afraid of small places. I did na know or I would have let her out. It's important that you believe that I would have."

Duncan nodded. "I did na think so at the time, Regan, but perhaps you would have." He looked at the worry lines still on Regan's face and knew this was not all she needed to tell him. "Is there more?"

"I need to ask you a question and I need your answer to be the truth."

"It will be. I have never lied to you, have I?"

"Nay. You have never lied to me, even when I prayed you would. Even when I prayed you would say you loved me, knowing the words would not have been the truth."

Duncan clasped his hands behind his back and stood tall. "I could na say them."

"Did you freely take the English as your bride?"

"Aye. I took her freely."

"Why? Because she possessed the crown and was betrothed to Bolton?"

"Nay, Regan. I took her *even though* she was betrothed to Bolton. I wanted her for my bride *even though* she was English."

The color drained from Regan's face and Duncan felt another pang of concern rush to every part of his body. "Is this what you wanted to know?"

"Nay, Duncan." Regan stepped close to him and looked into his eyes. "Do na lie to me now, laird. If your wife were to leave you, how long would it take for you to forget her?"

Duncan's breath caught in his throat. Kate leave him? He could not imagine losing her. She was too important to him.

"How long, Duncan?"

Duncan took a deep breath. "A thousand lifetimes and more. I could never forget my English wife. I have made a place for her here." Duncan held his hand to the spot where his heart pounded even louder than before.

The color drained from Regan's cheeks and the tiny flicker of hope in her eyes faded. "She's my wife, Regan. I will never want another."

"She does na think you care for her. She's certain if she leaves, it will na take you long to take someone else to your bed."

"How do you know this?"

"She told me. She told me all this when she asked for my help so she could leave you."

"Leave me?"

Regan nodded. "She's gone someplace where you can never find her."

The air left Duncan's chest. "Where has she gone?"

"I do na know."

Duncan grabbed Regan by the shoulders and shook her. "Where?"

"I do na know. She left early this morning. I was to have a horse tied to a tree near the stream where the rocks end. She said she would find her way to it after you left your chamber this morning."

Duncan pushed her away from him and ran across the bailey, shouting orders for his men to saddle their horses and follow him.

"She does na think it will matter to you if she never comes back," Regan hollered, running after him. Her words stabbed him in the heart.

Of course she would not think he cared. Why would she? He knew she'd needed him to hold her and comfort her last night, but he could not come to her.

Duncan threw his saddle on his horse's back and rode across the drawbridge. Men gathered from every direction to catch up with him. By the time he had crested the steep hill that led to the rocks beside the stream, Malcolm was on his right and Angus on his left. They both knew without being told what had happened.

He rode after Kate as if the demons of hell chased him. He could not believe he hadn't seen this coming. He should have known it when Bolton issued his threat to return for the crown in three days. The ultimatum put Kate at a much greater risk than him.

He could not believe he hadn't realized she would be

so desperate to get the crown that she would let nothing stop her until she found a way to get away from him. He could not believe he hadn't figured out she was looking for the secret passageway when he found her in his parents' chamber.

He could not believe she would leave him.

What a fool he had been.

Duncan pushed his horse up the steep hill that would take him to the place in the rocks where the door to the secret passageway was hidden. He hadn't forgotten the tunnel was there, he'd just assumed his wife hadn't found it.

Malcolm and Angus and a small army of Fergusons rode at his side and when they reached the stream they found the place where the horse had been tethered. They followed the tracks into the stream then back out when it climbed the bank and headed for Kilgern Castle.

Duncan spurred his horse on faster. He had to get to her before she crossed onto MacIntyre land and reached Ian. If she demanded sanctuary there would be little he could do to get her back. She and the crown would both be lost to him.

A fear unlike any he'd ever felt washed over him. He could not lose the crown.

He could not lose Kate.

Chapter 17

Katherine heard them coming long before she saw them. The ground thundered beneath her, and even the branches on the trees seemed to quiver in fear. If Duncan caught her, there would be no hope. No hope for him, or for his Scots, or for her soul.

She pushed her gray mare to go faster and closed the gap between Kilgern Castle and the sanctuary Ian MacIntyre could offer her. Her throat tightened until she couldn't swallow and the fire in her chest burned with each gasping breath.

She lowered her head and tightened her trembling grip on the thin reins, repeating her prayer that God would not make leaving Duncan so hard. That He would not make it hurt more than it already did.

The sounds grew louder and she knew Duncan and his warriors had gained ground. If she turned around, she would be able to see them. She would be able to see the anger on her Scot's face, and the fury in his eyes.

From up ahead, another low rumble thundered in the air and a cloud of dust rose and swirled before her. She blinked her eyes and prayed she would see the MacIntyre tartan.

Dear God. Please let me reach Ian in time.

MacIntyre warriors were before her and Duncan with his Fergusons behind her. Her heart pounded in her breast, suffocating her as she gasped for air. Dust blurred her vision, making it impossible to focus. The tears in her eyes only made it worse. She couldn't think. All reasoning was gone. Panic clouded her mind with such intensity that she could not pull together two rational thoughts.

She dug her heels into the gray mare's side and rode harder toward the MacIntyre warriors. Ian was in the lead. She had to reach him. She had to ask for sanctuary. God help her. She had to ask for protection from Duncan.

Pounding hooves thundered louder from behind. Duncan was closer. So was Ian. Her brother-in-law was close enough that she could see the worry on his face and the concern in his eyes. When he was almost beside her, Katherine pulled on the reins and brought her mare to a halt.

"Ian—" Her mouth was so dry the words did not want to come out and she tried again. "Ian, I need—" Katherine swallowed hard and tried to form the words through her gasping breaths. "I need—"

"Dear God, Kate! Nay!" The desperation in Duncan's voice was strained with anger. His desolation whipped around her body and covered her in a spiraling cloak of doom.

Katherine turned to face her husband. There was a wild look in his eyes she didn't want to face.

"Do na ask Ian for sanctuary. Please, Kate. Not that."

For a long time no one moved. The wind did not whistle through the grass in the meadow. The birds did not sing in the bushes. The branches did not move on the trees. Only the heaving gusts of the winded horses dared to intrude on the quiet of the Scottish hillside. Nothing had life until Katherine spoke.

"I cannot give you the crown, Duncan. Promise you will not take it from me."

Duncan took a deep breath before he answered. The muscles in his jaw tightened and Katherine could see his struggle. "I will na take it from you. I will wait for you to give it to me. I promise."

Katherine closed her eyes and bowed her head. He still didn't understand. He still hoped for something that could never be.

For a span of time that stretched beyond eternity, Katherine stared into Duncan's eyes, praying that God would tell her what to do. It had taken every ounce of willpower to leave him this time. If she went back now, she didn't know how she would ever find the courage to leave him again.

As if he could see the chaos that raged within her, Duncan nudged his horse forward until he was so close she could feel the heat of his flesh against her. Her breath shuddered as it escaped her lungs. Duncan raised his arm and stretched his hand toward her.

Katherine stared at his open palm and bit her lower lip to keep it from trembling. She wanted to reach out to him. She wanted to be held by him and feel his flesh against her flesh. She wanted to feel safe.

"Take my hand, Kate. Take my hand and let me be the

one to give you sanctuary." He stared at her and his gaze did not waver. "I want to honor the vow I took before God to be your husband, to protect you."

Katherine lowered her head and closed her eyes. She had failed. She wasn't strong enough to turn away from him. She wasn't brave enough to live her life without him.

Ian cleared his throat, then interrupted the uncomfortable stalemate. "Come with me, Katherine. We will all ride to Kilgern and sort this out before you make a decision. I left Elizabeth pacing the floors, waiting to hear why you had crossed onto MacIntyre land without an escort."

Katherine looked at Ian as she struggled to find the courage to ask for sanctuary.

"Elizabeth is worried about you, Katherine," Ian said, almost as a plea. "She has missed you and will be glad to see you again."

Katherine shuddered a sigh then nodded. The courage was not within her.

"Kate?"

Katherine turned her head and studied the hooded expression on Duncan's face, then followed his gaze. His arm was still outstretched, waiting for her to place her hand and her trust in his palm. "Take my hand, Kate."

Katherine hesitated, then placed her hand in his palm. The feel of his skin was callused and hard and possessive. But when he wrapped his fingers around her flesh, a warm rush of unexplainable calm traveled to every part of her body.

"You have only put off the inevitable, Duncan, and made what we both must do more difficult."

"Nay, lass. I did what I had to do to save us."

"And again I was not brave enough to challenge you. If my father were here I would see disappointment on his face."

"And what do you see when you look at my face?"

"Satisfaction."

"That is na satisfaction you see, wife. It's something far more."

Duncan gave her fingers a gentle squeeze then took his hand away from her and a cold void consumed her flesh.

"Come, Kate. Time is almost gone. We must get the crown and return to Lochmore yet today. I do na trust Bolton. He still has na crawled back to England."

Duncan nudged his horse forward and Katherine's mare followed. Ian rode on her other side and Angus and Malcolm and the other Ferguson warriors behind.

"Is Bolton close?" Ian asked after giving orders for his clansmen to ride ahead and tell his wife her sister was safe.

"Aye. He sent a messenger yesterday demanding that I give him the crown and his betrothed."

Ian turned to face Duncan and Katherine caught the look on his face. "He does na know you have married Katherine?"

"Nay. He thinks I took her hostage."

Ian said no more, but Katherine knew his thoughts. They were the same as Duncan's. The same as her own. If Bolton found out Duncan had taken her as his wife, his English warriors would rain down on them and show no mercy. Duncan had ruined the woman betrothed to him, the woman who would gain him influence with the king. Bolton would want revenge.

"Is the crown at Kilgern, Kate?" Duncan's voice echoed harsh in the chilled winter air.

Katherine swallowed past the lump in her throat then nodded. "Yes."

"I will give you time to see your sister, then we will get the crown and return to Lochmore."

Katherine shot Duncan a questioning glance. This was all moving so fast. How could she protect the crown if he went with her? If he was there when she…

"I will na take the crown from you. I gave my word."

It was almost as if he had read her thoughts. Almost as if he knew her fears as well as she did. Almost as if he realized keeping the crown was all that was important to her. As if he didn't have to push her. Yet.

She turned her gaze forward and tightened her grip on the reins as they neared Kilgern Castle. They rode across the drawbridge in silence and before they reached the steps leading into the keep, the door opened and Elizabeth ran out. She paused for only a second, then raced down the stairs to greet her sister.

Katherine dismounted and ran into her sister's arms before Duncan had time to reach her side.

"Are you all right, Katherine? What has happened that you were riding here without an escort? Why did you leave your laird's side when you knew Bolton could be out there waiting for you?"

"Oh, Elizabeth. I've missed you. You don't know how much I have missed your needless worrying and your many questions. It's good to see you." Katherine pulled her sister into her arms again and hugged her tight. She really had missed her. She'd missed being needed. She'd missed feeling wanted.

Duncan didn't need her. He needed nothing except the crown. He didn't want her. He wanted what she could not give him. And yet she loved him. She loved him more than life itself, and would sacrifice anything for him. Anything except her soul and the crown.

Elizabeth grabbed Katherine's arm and moved with her toward the keep. "Come inside, Duncan," she said over her shoulders. "You and your men must be tired and hungry. There is food prepared for all. We will eat while we talk."

Duncan followed them into the keep. "We do na have much time, milady. Kate and I return return shortly."

"And I will go with them, Elizabeth," Ian said.

Elizabeth stopped and faced her husband. "Then I will go with you."

"Nay, wife. You will stay here where I know you will be safe."

"You have already left me alone enough to last a lifetime, Ian. I swore when you came back I would never let you leave without me again. You can say nothing to change my mind."

"The English—"

"It will do you no good to argue, Ian," Elizabeth said, walking ahead of him into the great hall. "If you leave here, I will only follow. English or no."

Ian laughed, took two large steps to catch up with her and put his arm around his wife's shoulder. "I guess you will be just as safe at my side as you will be alone."

"I will be safer, as well you know."

Elizabeth showed Katherine and Duncan to seats at the long trestle tables. Servants brought huge trenchers of roasted meats and breads and cheeses, and set them before them. Katherine put very little on her dish, and twice she caught Duncan staring at her untouched food, then pushing the platter closer to her as a hint that she eat.

"You are as pale as that white gown your sister wears, Kate. We have a long ride back yet today and if you do na eat you will be ill."

"Eat, milady," Angus said from across the table. "It's important that you do na go without food. You know you must have your nourishment."

Katherine dropped the hand that hugged her stomach and lifted her head to met her friend's warm gaze. He had come to know her too well.

"When we return to Lochmore, I will fix you a potion to help settle you," Angus said and gave her a nod that said he knew what she had told no one.

Katherine picked up a piece of warm bread and put it into her mouth. She would eat. It was important that she have nourishment and Angus knew why.

. . .

Duncan watched his wife pick at her food and was thankful Angus' words had affected her. The old man had a special way with Kate, and Duncan was glad she had listened to him. She needed to eat. From the pale look on her face she also needed to rest but they couldn't spare the time. Bolton could be waging war on Lochmore even now.

"It's time, Kate. We must get the crown and go, or we will na reach home before nightfall."

Her fist clenched in her lap and the stark look in her eyes worried him. He wanted to hold her, but he could not weaken. Too much was at stake. His wife's safety. His father's reputation. Scotland's honor.

Ian took Elizabeth's hand and helped her from the table. "We'll be ready when you are, Duncan. I would first like to bid farewell to my son."

"We will na be long, Ian."

Ian and Elizabeth left the great hall together and Duncan stood to urge Kate to do the same. Angus and Malcolm and the rest of the warriors had already finished and were readying their horses for the ride back.

"Come, Kate." Duncan held out his hand to her.

Kate stood without his help, her shoulders high and her back straight. She walked the length of the great hall and turned toward the stairs. Duncan could see the muscles tighten in her body with each determined footstep she took, and when she reached the arched doorway, she climbed the steps that would take them to the second level.

Duncan thought she would stop at the room that had been hers when she had pretended to be her sister but she walked on until she reached the open chapel door. Her steps faltered and when she stumbled, he reached out for her. She put out her hand and braced herself against the wall, ignoring his touch, then walked into the small room and headed for the kneeling bench before the altar.

"Kate, we do na have much time for prayer. We have to start back soon."

"We will, Duncan. Kneel with me this last time."

"Do na say this last time, Kate. Nothing we do now is for the last time and I will na have you think it. Somehow we will work this out between us. Somehow we will find a way."

Katherine lowered herself to the floor and folded her hands. Duncan went to his knees beside her. For a few silent moments, he felt the peace that usually entered his heart when he came to pray. Kate's quiet words shattered that peace.

"Will you stand back and let me give the crown to England? That is the only way we can work this out between us. I took a sacred vow. A vow I cannot break."

Duncan said nothing, he only stared up at the magnificent statue of the Shepherd holding out his arms, blessing his sheep. Didn't she know the crown itself meant nothing to him? That it was his father's tarnished name that was at stake? That keeping the crown for Scotland would atone for the life his father had sacrificed to protect it?

"Was your father much like you, Duncan?"

Duncan thought to answer nay, then stopped. "Aye. He was much like me. Only his will to do what was right was stronger and his compassion for Scotland and all that is hers greater."

Duncan heard her sigh. "He must have been a very great man. Were you ever a disappointment to him?"

"Nay. I was never a disappointment. My father was not ashamed to show his love. I was only a disappointment to myself when I was na here to save him from Bolton's sword."

Duncan clenched his hands until his knuckles turned white. He stole a glance at Kate's still figure kneeling against the railing. "Were you ever a disappointment to your father, Kate?"

"From the moment of my birth. I was to be the son he never had and no matter how I tried, I could never do enough to make him proud of me."

"That does na mean he did na love you."

"No. He just did not want me. I was not manageable and obedient like Elizabeth."

"And he did na like the independence you inherited from him?"

"No. He did not like it."

Katherine bowed her head and closed her eyes. Duncan fought the urge to hold her. He could not imagine ever feeling that his father didn't want him. Her voice interrupted his thoughts.

"It will not be long before my father comes for me. He's one of the king's closest advisors and is a very powerful man."

"We are nay in England, Kate. Here in Scotland your father holds na power at all."

"You will not say that after you've met him."

Duncan turned to look at her. Katherine's lifted gaze focused on the statue. The expression in her eyes reflected her faith, and also her apprehension. There was nothing Duncan could do to alleviate her fears.

No matter what he said, she didn't trust him any more than she trusted her father. She thought her father didn't want her, but only wanted a son. She thought her husband didn't want her, but only wanted the crown. Not all was true, but the part that was threatened to destroy what Kate and he shared.

"It's late and we must return home. Where is the crown, Kate?"

"What you want is here, Duncan. It's here before you."

Duncan followed her gaze to the statue and knew. He

looked at his wife, then up to the statue, then back to his wife. The tortured expression on her face told him he had found the treasure he, and England, and Scotland, had been searching for.

She took a deep breath then bowed her head and made the sign of the cross. Slowly, she lifted herself to her feet.

Duncan could not miss the heaving of her chest nor the arm she put out to steady herself. "Are you ill, Kate?"

"I'm tired, is all."

She held her hand to her middle and took another deep breath. Her pale face held little expression, her movements seemed slow and deliberate. How could he tell her she had nothing to fear? He would protect her even after she got the crown. Even after he had it from her.

"Let's get this over, Duncan. I'll need you to help me."

He stood and followed her to the altar. When they reached the statue, she lifted her trembling fingers and touched the feet of the Shepherd. "You'll have to stand on the altar, Duncan."

Duncan flung his knee over the rim of the altar and stepped up until he was even with the statue.

"Wrap your arms around the statue and turn. I'll hold the base from here. When you feel it loosen, lift. I'll tell you when to put it back. It will be heavy."

"Aye, lass," Duncan said, straining to lift the statue. "It's heavy."

Duncan did what she told him and on the second try he felt a tug, then the body of the Shepherd separated from the feet. He could not believe it.

"How did you hide the crown by yourself?"

"Your Father Kincaid helped me. I didn't know about

this hiding place. He showed me where to put the crown then told me who I was to give it to."

He didn't want to believe her, but what she said must be true. Father Kincaid must have helped her hide the crown, for Kate was not strong enough to lift the statue by herself. Could it be their own Father Kincaid had instructed her to give the crown back to England?

He held the statue and watched his wife lift the object covered with a white cloth from the hollowed-out center of the base. She wrapped her arms around it and held it close to her breast.

Duncan put the statue back in place and stepped down beside his wife. "You have done well, Kate. You have protected the crown as you swore. There is na more that can be asked of you."

"There's more, Duncan, and you know what it is. I knew it would come to this, but I prayed it wouldn't hurt so much."

Duncan looked at the wetness in his wife's eyes and wanted to take her in his arms and hold her, but he could not. His gaze moved to the crown. The crown that had cost his father his life. Everything he had hoped to gain for his father was within his grasp. Everything he had hoped to gain for Scotland was so close he could reach out and touch it. If she would only...

"Dear God, help me," she cried, her voice shattered with emotion. "You think because I have the crown, I'll give it to you. You think I'll prove my love for you by giving you the crown. I've always had it, Duncan. Nothing has changed. I still cannot give it to you."

"And I promised I would not take it from you. Nothing

has changed, Kate. It's still yours to give."

Katherine took a few steps to leave then halted and turned back to face the statue. She held the crown like a mother protecting her babe. "When you came after me, you said you wanted me to honor the vow I took to be your wife. Do you remember the question I put to you on our wedding day?"

Her quiet voice seeped into his body and wrapped around his heart. "Aye. You asked if I would still marry you even though you would never give me England's crown or your heart."

"You made a poor bargain, my Scot."

"Did I? Have you na given me your heart, lass?"

"Yes, but without the crown, my heart is of little value to you. I knew it then as I know it now."

Duncan followed her to where the horses waited. She allowed no one to touch the crown. She would not even give it over to him while she mounted her horse. He thought she would have yielded by now. He thought she would have given it to him by now.

Her words came back to haunt him. His mind refused to believe she had meant them, and did not intend to give him the crown. That she intended to give it back to England.

Duncan looked over at her with the crown locked in her arms. A sharp stab of pain jolted through his body. He could tell from the lifeless expression on her face and the agonizing torture in her eyes, that giving it to England was exactly what she'd meant.

...

"Why did you not tell me the crown was hidden in the chapel, Kate?"

Katherine took a breath to steady herself on her horse and turned to face her sister. Duncan had dropped back beside Ian, giving Katherine a little privacy so she could talk to her sister without being overheard. "I didn't want to concern you with it, Elizabeth."

"You didn't think I was strong enough to protect it, did you? You thought if I knew, I would tell Ian."

Katherine closed her eyes and gripped the edge of the saddle as another wave of nausea washed over her. "I vowed to the priest I would tell no one."

"But the priest thought I was the one taking the vow."

"And I wish to God you had been."

Katherine's harsh voice echoed over the din of the horses as they made their way to Lochmore Castle. Scores of MacIntyre warriors combined with scores of Ferguson warriors surrounded Katherine, escorting her and the crown with one of the most formidable forces she had ever seen.

Duncan and Malcolm had not taken their gazes from her since they had left Kilgern. Angus watched over her like an anxious father, and Ian and Elizabeth had focused on no one but her, along with the warriors who rode with them. They were all there to guard her, to protect her.

And the crown. Especially the crown.

"I'm sorry, Elizabeth. I'm tired. It has made my tongue sharp. I didn't mean it."

"You don't look well, Kate. Is there anything I can do?"

Katherine steadied her breathing and hugged the crown tighter until everything around her stopped spinning. "No.

It's too late to do anything now."

"Oh, Katherine. You know how much it means to Duncan. Do you not love him enough to give him the crown?"

Katherine stared at her sister and worked to swallow past the lump in her throat. "That must be why, Elizabeth." Her voice came out in a hoarse whisper. "I must not love Duncan enough."

"I'm sorry, Katherine. I didn't mean that you don't love Duncan. I just meant…"

"I know what you meant."

"How do you think this will all end?"

"You mean after I give the crown to Father?"

"Yes." Elizabeth lowered her gaze. "Ian says he doesn't know how Duncan will ever… I mean…"

"I know, Elizabeth. Ian doesn't know how Duncan will ever be able to forgive me if I don't give him the crown. How he will ever be able to love me if I go against him." Katherine hugged one arm around the crown and the other around her stomach. "There's no way he can. I've known this from the start."

"But you will not give it to him, will you?"

"I wish it had not been me the priest found that night. I wish to God the priest had given the crown to you."

"Maybe it was meant to be this way, Katherine. You know I've never been the strong one. God knew I would not have had the strength to honor my vow."

Katherine saw Elizabeth's open honesty and heard it in her voice.

"You were always the one who took care of mother and me. We were both weak."

"You're not weak, Elizabeth."

"Yes, I am. Why do you think Father treated me as he did? He knew my shortcomings and therefore expected little from me. He knew your strengths and expected much."

"But it was never good enough."

"No. It was never enough. But only because you were not pleased with what you had to offer."

Katherine put her hand to her face and wiped away the tear that stole down her cheek. "I remember the excitement in the keep when Father would come home from court. Mother would put on her prettiest gown and fix her hair the way Father liked. The minute he sat in his chair you would run across the room and jump onto his lap."

"And you would stand back until he gave you permission to come near."

"I wasn't sure he wanted to hold me. He never said."

"He didn't have to say."

"Then how did you know? I could never do enough to be sure he wanted me. How did you know, Elizabeth?"

"Oh, Katherine. You didn't have to earn Father's love. It was always there for the taking."

"It wasn't there for me. I couldn't find it."

"Have you found Duncan's love?"

Katherine wiped the moisture from her brow and took big gasps of air to breath past the way her eyes could not focus. "I will never earn Duncan's love, Elizabeth. The price is too high."

"You don't have to earn his love, Katherine. He's like father. His love is there for the taking. You have only to reach out to him."

"I cannot. There's a crown in the way."

"Oh, Katherine." Elizabeth held out her hand and Katherine wanted to grasp it but her world spun around her and she had to clasp her fingers to the edge of the saddle to steady herself.

"Katherine, are you all right?"

"I'm fine. I just feel a little strange, 'tis all."

Elizabeth turned around to where Duncan and her husband were riding.

"Don't call for Duncan, Elizabeth. Just stay at my side until this goes away."

"Are you ill, Kate?"

"No. I'm…"

Katherine knew there were more words that needed to be said, but the blanket of darkness that cloaked her mind would not allow them to come out.

"Duncan!"

Elizabeth's voice shattered through the barrier, then strong arms lifted Katherine in the air and settled her down. She felt safe. She felt secure. Duncan's arms were around her.

She wanted to wrap her arms around her Scot's warm body but she couldn't. She would first have to release the cold, metal crown in her grasp. She could not. She had taken a vow and could not break it.

Even in her sleep she could not give up the crown.

Chapter 18

"I am fine now. You may put me down."

Katherine lifted her head from beneath Duncan's chin. The straight line of his lips and the deep furrows across his brow gave him a formidable look. Even with her ear away from his chest she could still hear the rapid pounding of his heart.

"You are na fine. Even a blind man can see that." His strong arms held her fast as he took the steps to their chamber two at a time.

An angry muscle twitched in his jaw and the piercing tint of his eyes darkened. "You didn't sleep at all last night and little the night before, and now that I think on it, I can na remember the last meal you ate. You've struggled and worried until you've made yourself ill."

The angry tone of his soft voice struck a harsh chord. She could not bring herself to look him in the eyes. "Where are Ian and Elizabeth? I must see to them."

"Do na worry about your sister. She can see to herself and to her husband. You have enough to worry about right now."

Katherine closed her eyes and hugged the crown tighter to her chest. She did not remember the last few miles of their journey home nor did she remember crossing the drawbridge into Lochmore Castle.

"You na longer have to protect everyone around you, wife. You na longer have to prove you do na need anyone." He kicked the heavy door of their chamber with his booted foot and it bounced against the stone wall and came back at him. He kicked it again. Harder. "You are na strong enough to fight Bolton by yourself." His raised voice echoed in their chamber. "Do you know how foolish it was for you to leave here to go to Ian?"

He lowered her to a chair and threw back the covers on their bed with such force she shivered from the rush of cold air that whipped around her.

"Bolton could have taken you, and you would be in his camp right now, fighting for your life."

He lifted her from the chair and held her arms in a tight grip. "Is it possible for you put the crown down long enough to ready yourself for bed, or do you na trust me enough to even let the crown out of your grasp?"

Anger and fury radiated from his gaze. She watched the thundering storm that brewed inside him.

She placed the crown on the table beside her and untied the laces at her throat. She couldn't look at him. His rage was too great for her to bear.

With an angry tug, he reached for the gown and pulled it up over her shoulders. A loud rip echoed in the air. With a sigh of frustration, he threw the material on a heap in the corner. "You always think you must do everything yourself. Even in the dungeon you faced Bolton as if you stood a chance of conquering him."

He grabbed her nightdress and dropped it over her head, then picked her up and placed her on the bed. After he jerked the covers up under her chin, he walked to the hearth and dropped another log to make a warmer fire. It fell with a loud whoosh. He turned his head toward her and spoke over his shoulder. "Did you want your crown with you in bed, wife, or do you trust me enough to leave it on the table?"

The air caught in her throat and a cold, hateful hand twisted her heart in her breast. She could not give a reply. She could not even face him.

He answered her anyway. "I will leave it where you can watch it. If you get lonesome during the night you need only to reach for it."

Another log fell on the fire with a deafening thud. "I do na know why you could na just trust me enough to ask for my help. I do na know why you went to Regan. I do na know why—"

"You do not know why I can not give you the crown, Duncan. That is what you do not know."

He hurled the last log to the floor beside the hearth and fired his words at her. "That's right! You are my wife! You know how important the crown is to me. If you cared for me at all, you would give me the crown before Bolton or your father come."

"You know I cannot. I took a vow."

"You were going to ask for sanctuary, Kate. Do you know what that would have meant? Do you know what would have happened?"

Katherine turned her face away from him and closed

her eyes. She would not cry. She would not let him see how his cutting words and the painful tone of his voice ripped her heart from her breast. "I did what I had to do, Duncan."

The roar of his voice bounced off the cold stone walls and came back with a killing vengeance. "And so you chose to leave me? You chose to run to Ian and ask him for sanctuary, knowing it would separate us forever. Why?"

"Because I'm tired of fighting you. Because you still think I'll ignore the vow I gave your priest and will give you the crown. Because I love you and a part of me will die when you don't want me after I give the crown back to England. I can take no more, Duncan. I am not strong enough."

He turned his back to her, then braced his hands against the wall and hung his head between his outstretched arms. The rigid muscles across his shoulders bunched beneath the loose folds of his shirt and his chest heaved with huge gasps of air. Time stretched forever in front of her and she could think of nothing else that would make what she had to do easier.

"Rest now, wife." His strained voice sounded little more than a hoarse whisper. "I will go downstairs and make sure everyone is settled for the night. Someone will bring a tray of food up for you. Do na let it go to waste. You need to eat."

He dropped his arms from the wall and let them hang at his side. Then he squared his shoulders and walked to the door.

"Will you come back to me, Duncan?"

His footsteps halted. His hand froze on the latch. "I do

na know," he finally answered.

With an angry jerk, he opened the door and walked away. A cold void filled the room in his wake. Katherine stared at the empty doorway, then let her head sink back into the pillow and watched the candlelight dance around the huge wooden beams in the high ceiling. This was how she'd always known it would be. This was how she'd known it would end. This was why she'd promised herself she would never loose her heart to him. God help her. She had not kept her promise.

A quiet knock sounded from the hallway and Katherine wiped the wetness from her cheeks.

"I've brought you something to eat and something to ease your stomach." Angus walked across the room with a small platter in one hand and a goblet in the other. He shoved aside the crown on the table and set down the food.

"I don't want anything, Angus. I'm not hungry."

"You do na have a choice in whether or na you want to eat, milady." Angus held out the goblet to her. "Here. Drink this first."

Katherine sat up in bed and took the goblet from him. "What is it?"

"Drink it. It will soothe your stomach."

Katherine took a swallow. The warmth of the liquid spread through her body and she leaned her head back against the headboard and breathed a deep sigh. "Have all the MacIntyre warriors been fed and found places to bed down, Angus?"

"Do na concern yourself with what is about downstairs."

She took another swallow and Angus handed her a

platter and a metal spoon with which to eat. She stared at the thick stew, then looked at Angus, knowing he could read the doubt in her eyes.

"Take a bite of the bread first, milady, and eat the cheese and the fruit that is on the side. The ale should help and maybe you'll even be able to eat a little of the stew."

Katherine took a bite of bread and chewed.

"Have you told our laird you're carrying his babe?"

Her hand stopped midway to her mouth.

"You can na keep it from him for long."

She let her spoon drop on her plate and lowered her gaze.

"Do na stop eating, lass. You need food for the babe."

Katherine picked up a piece of fruit and put it to her mouth. "Do you understand why I must give back the crown, Angus?"

"Aye, lass. I understand. And so does our laird. It's just a painful struggle for him to come to terms with the fact that he may not be able to get the crown back for his father."

"I think Duncan's father wanted England to have her crown. I think his father sent the priest to my sister because he knew it wasn't worth as many Scottish lives as would have died to keep a crown that didn't belong to them."

"Mayhaps you're right, lass. But it will take our laird more time to believe it."

"No. My husband will never believe it. He's too filled with Scottish pride."

Angus handed her the goblet again and she drank, then gave it back to him. "There's no answer, Angus. I cannot do what he wants and he'll hate me for what I must do. I cannot live with his hate."

"He will na hate you, lass. There will be the babe."

Katherine fisted her hands in her lap and held her breath. A cold rush of emptiness washed over her. "I should never have married him, Angus. I knew it that day, but I was so frightened and confused. I didn't have the courage to follow my king's edict and marry Bolton. I had planned to go to the convent and ask for sanctuary but…" Katherine took a deep breath. "I should have gone." She looked up at her friend and held his gaze. "Angus?"

"Aye, milady."

"Promise me you will not tell Duncan I'm carrying his child. Not yet. Not until the crown is no longer between us."

"He will have to know. I will na keep it from him for long."

"In time, he will know."

Angus fisted his hands at his side and squared his shoulders. He furrowed his brow until his thick, bushy eyebrows almost met above his questioning stare. "What are you planning, milady?"

Katherine could not hold his gaze. "I have only one choice, Angus. I've searched for another but there is none."

"You can na take the Ferguson heir away from our laird. I will na allow it." Angus' harsh voice contained a vivid warning.

Katherine shook her head. "I would never take Duncan's child away from him. He will have his heir."

"And will he have his wife?"

Katherine could not stop the one tear that fell to her lap. "He will have what he wants."

"I can na let you do this, milady."

"You can stop it no more than I, Angus." Another tear fell beside the first. "Do you think because of me he will hate the babe?"

"Nay, milady. He will na hate the babe."

"Angus, will you promise me your laird's child will always be cared for?"

"You will be here to care for the babe."

Katherine closed her eyes. "If something were to happen and I could not be here, will you swear to me that you'll make sure he is always cared for?"

"I will help you care for the child. That is what I will promise."

To Katherine that was good enough. She would ask no more of Angus.

"Finish your drink, milady, and I'll leave the platter beside your bed. Close your eyes and rest. For the babe."

Katherine put the goblet to her lips and drank another swallow, then put it on the bedside table next to the crown. She slid down between the covers and closed her eyes and wished her Scot was here with her, holding her in his arms. She wanted just once more to feel him next to her. The memory would have to last a lifetime.

. . .

Duncan looked at the empty bed where his wife should be sleeping and his heart leaped to his throat. He took two hurried steps inside and scanned the room in search of her. So help him, if she had…

He took note of her slender body leaning in the shadows near the window overlooking the courtyard and breathed a sigh of relief. Filtered moonlight streamed through the opening, illuminating her graceful features, and casting an ethereal glow to her pale cheeks. She pulled a cover closer around her shoulders and the thick mass of golden hair hanging to her waist shimmered in the faint light. His body stiffened in response. By the saints, he wanted to rake his fingers through the soft strands, then...

Duncan steeled his shoulders and stared at her, cursing himself for being so weak, cursing himself for climbing the stairs to check on her. He'd sworn he would not come back to her again tonight, but all he could think of while he sat with Malcolm and the other warriors was his English wife.

Hell, he hadn't even been able to drink enough to erase her from his mind. And it was not for want of trying. Instead of the ale dulling his senses, the brew only heightened his emotions. His first thought was how desperate she must have been to leave him. His second was the terror that had consumed him when he realized she was gone.

He walked over to her and stood so close he could smell the clean scent of rose soap. He should have stayed downstairs. It had been a mistake to come up here.

He would just stand beside her. There was nothing more to be said. He would only stand here and feel her near him. But he would not touch her.

A glimmer of silvery moonlight reflected on her hair and he reached out to touch the heavy golden softness. The long tresses sifted through his fingers. He bunched his fist and buried his face in the silky strands. She didn't move. She didn't stiffen or turn away from his touch. He wished to God she had. Then he would have stopped. But she stood still and lifted her chin, exposing her long graceful neck to him. Her eyes closed as if she wanted him to touch her, and his traitorous arm moved with a will of its own.

Duncan lay his hand against her and could feel the

warmth from her flesh. When his fingers curved around her throat, the heat of a roaring fire rushed through his body. Until today he had not believed she'd meant to keep the two promises she'd given him on their wedding day. Until today he had not believed that her vow to give the crown to her father had been more important than her vow of submission to him. Until today he had not believed that she didn't love him enough to give him the crown.

Duncan cupped her face in his palm and stroked her lips with his thumb. Her lips parted and she turned her face to kiss the inside of his hand. He lowered his head and pressed his lips to the soft flesh beneath her ear. He kissed her once, then again, and the cover she held around her shoulders fell to the floor.

They had lived together as husband and wife for months, but not once had he felt such need to possess her. Not once had it seemed so important to show her he wanted her. Maybe she didn't know.

God help him. Maybe she didn't care.

Duncan wrapped his arm around her middle and pulled her close to him. The fit of her body next to him was perfect. With one hand, he caressed her face while his mouth kissed the tender flesh of her throat. His other hand moved up from her waist until it found the gentle rise of her breast.

He heard a sharp intake of her breath when his hand cupped its fullness and her hands curled to tiny fists at her sides. His thumb found the hard nubbin through the soft material of her nightdress, and he rubbed until she moaned and pushed back against him.

How could she have thought to leave him? How could

she have thought to ask Ian for sanctuary?

Two colored ribbons laced her gown around the neck and he reached for them and pulled. The material loosened and fell from her shoulders to pool around her feet. He grasped her by the arms and turned her to face him. By the saints, she was beautiful.

Duncan lifted his shirt over his head and dropped it to the floor, then locked his gaze with hers, trying to read the haunted expression in her eyes. The worry was lost to him. Her breasts raised with each labored breath she took. When he'd cast away all his clothes, he lifted her in his arms and placed her on the bed.

How could she not understand how important it was to restore his father's reputation? How could she not understand how important it was for him to uphold the Ferguson name? How could she not be a Scot after all they had shared?

Duncan stretched above her, then lowered himself until his body covered her. He propped himself on his elbows and nestled closer, then looked into her eyes. The open need and desperation he saw swallowed him like a crashing wave and he feared he was drowning. Never had he told her he cared for her. Never had he spoken of love. He brought his mouth down on hers and touched her lips in a brief meeting.

Oh, please, his heart cried out. *Let her be a Scot.*

He pressed his lips against hers again and drank from her softness. The words she'd spoken the day of their wedding came back to haunt him and he shoved them to the back of his mind to bury them forever.

His passion burned with a fire he could not control and

when she wrapped her arms around his neck and pulled him to her, a thousand shards of lightning struck in the pit of his stomach and seared his resolve. He had to have her. He had to make her his. He had to stop her from doing the one thing that would destroy them.

Duncan kissed her deeply and when she opened her mouth to meet his demands, he invaded her warmth and conquered her weakness until she surrendered. He could not let her erect the barrier that would separate them forever.

If she had not lost her heart to him, as she'd promised on her wedding day, he would win it from her. If she did not plan to give him the crown, as she'd promised on her wedding day, he would take it from her.

Duncan lifted his mouth and looked into her eyes. The raw, unbridled passion he saw fired a new wave of emotions that burned in his veins. In one swift thrust he entered her. She was his. Again and again he took her, desperate to have her; frantic in his need to control her. He drove into her with unrelenting thrusts until he found a release for his fears. With a mighty roar, he spilled his seed and shuddered in her arms.

He collapsed atop her with his face buried against her neck. His chest heaved as he fought to find enough air to breathe, and his back burned from the nail marks his wife had left. He had made her his. Forever and for all time, there would be no doubt he had been the victor. He did not doubt it — until he looked into her eyes.

Her fingers trembled as she traced a line along his shoulders and down his arms. It seemed like a caress, yet the hurt in her eyes took the tenderness from her touch.

Her hand cupped his face then moved over his brows, along his jaw line, and across his cheek bone, yet the disappointment on her face removed any affection from the contact.

Duncan rolled to the side to move away from her, but the tight grip of her arms around his neck stopped him. He lowered his head back against the soft hollow spot in her neck and shut his eyes to block out what had just happened. "I am sorry, wife. I am so sorry."

She combed her fingers through his hair and touched his face with her hands. "Hold me, husband. Just hold me close until morning and do not let me go."

Duncan pulled her against him until there was not a whisper of breath to separate them. She nestled her head on his chest and he lifted a cover over them to keep them warm when the heat in the fireplace died. To keep them close until the heat of their passion died.

. . .

Dear God, it was not what she wanted to remember. There had been so much anger and frustration and regret in their act. His movements had been wild and frantic and desperate, as if he needed to fight something that could be conquered with only brute strength. As if he needed to master someone who refused to submit.

Katherine lay with her arms around him and her legs entwined in his. Her Scot. She had given up all to be with him. All save her soul.

In the end, it would be her only consolation.

Chapter 19

"Duncan! Duncan, wake up!"

Katherine only heard the one loud thud that bounced their chamber door against the stones, and when she opened her eyes, Malcolm was already at their bedside. Duncan pulled her closer to him then pulled a cover over her to hide her nakedness.

"We have company. A lone rider bearing the English king's banner."

The bed turned cold when Duncan left her. Katherine pulled the covers under her chin while her husband dressed with the speed of a practiced warrior.

"Is it Bolton?"

"Nay. It is na Bolton."

The breath caught in her throat. "Father."

Both men looked at her and Duncan reached for the sword he'd left on the table and the long knife he'd placed beside their bed. He put them both in their sheaths at his side. "He brought na warriors?"

"Nay. He is alone."

"Ready my horse and wait for me at the steps."

Malcolm turned and left the room. Duncan followed him to the door then turned to face her. "You have run out of time, wife."

Katherine stared at the crown, then looked at Duncan's beseeching gaze. A glimpse of her shattered future flashed before her. He stood across the chamber and waited for her to give him her decision. Not one muscle on his body moved.

Time and all around her stopped. His breathing halted as he glared at her. If she could have opened the door to his heart, she knew she would have heard his whispered entreaty, pleading with her to give him the crown.

It was impossible to hold his gaze any longer. This was the temptation to which she could not surrender. The priest had predicted it that night, thinking he was warning Elizabeth about Ian's demand for the crown. This was what he had made her swear to on penalty of her soul.

"The crown is not mine to give."

The words fragmented in the air around them. His chest filled with a mighty rush that expanded his shoulders to a breathtaking width. Hands capable of snapping a man's neck fisted at his side, and the fire in his eyes blazed with agonizing intensity. The hurt and disappointment she saw on his face was no more devastating than if she would have slain him with his own sword.

"You have made your decision, wife." His tone was hard. Deadly. "You must now live with what you have decided."

She watched him walk away from her and clutched her hand to the place where his babe rested. Even time would not ease the pain growing inside her.

Duncan sat on his horse high atop the hill with Ian on one side and Malcolm on the other and watched Kate's father draw near them. The English would get their crown. Kate had chosen. He knew now she didn't love him or Scotland enough to yield.

He struggled with the hurt in his chest and considered again taking the crown from her by force. It was a thought he had entertained often. But he knew he could not do it. He'd given his word and he could not break it. Just as she…

No. That was different.

He wanted to fall on his knees and roar to the hills. He wanted to lash out at something — someone — and swing his broad sword until he could no longer lift his arm to attack. He wanted to use power and brute strength to change what he couldn't live with. But physical might would not make right what was wrong. His pain at losing the crown was as great as when he'd ridden through the gates of Lochmore to find his family slain. His English wife had hurt him that much.

He'd never thought it would come to this. He'd been sure in time she would come to love him enough she would give him the crown. He had failed.

Duncan watched until the Englishman was almost upon them. Scores of Ferguson warriors flanked Kate's father on either side. He held his shoulders erect as if it was common to be surrounded by an enemy guard of this size and might. As if he was not concerned in the least to be in the middle of this many Scots.

The English earl brought his horse close enough for Duncan to see the piercing determination in his eyes, then he stopped.

He was broad of shoulder with graying hair that gave his distinguished carriage an intelligent bearing. His rigid posture and the confident look on his face negated any weakness Duncan may have imagined he would have. That and the fact that he had ridden onto Ferguson land alone and unarmed.

Kate's father first looked at Ian and raised a questioning brow. "MacIntyre? I didn't expect to see you here."

"Good day, milord. Your daughter Elizabeth heard you might come and did not want to miss this opportunity to see you."

Next, the earl looked at Duncan. His gaze lingered before he spoke. "Lord Ferguson?"

Duncan felt that in the few seconds the earl studied him, everything about him was revealed. "Good day, milord. You have come without an escort?"

"You would not have ridden to England alone?"

The corners of Duncan's mouth raised slightly. "Nay. Not unless it was my sincere wish to see my Maker on that day."

Kate's father concentrated his gaze. "I have no desire to see my Maker today, laird. I only wish to see my daughter. I'm told she is with you."

Duncan nodded. Without a word, he turned his mount and headed back to the keep. He fought to keep his frustration and disappointment at bay. He tried to come to terms with what Kate would do when she saw her father.

He tried to convince himself his father's honor would

not be betrayed if he lost the crown.

He tried to imagine a life for the two of them after she gave the crown to her father.

He could imagine none of it.

Duncan crossed the inner courtyard and dismounted. The Earl of Wentworth did the same, and together they climbed the stairs and entered the keep.

The great hall was empty and Duncan and Ian and Kate's father sat in chairs at the high table. Malcolm and some of the other warriors took their places at the long trestle tables, and when huge wooden trenchers of bread and cheese and goblets of ale arrived, they ate their morning repast in silence.

"William Bolton has been to see Edward. He's asked the king to grant him an army to fight you, Laird Ferguson." Kate's father spread honey on a warm slice of bread and lifted it to his mouth. He said his words as casually as talk of the weather.

"I thought as much," Duncan answered, taking another helping of roasted pig. "I crossed the border not long after your earl had murdered my mother and father, but he was na there. I assumed he had run to his English king to cry at his feet."

"Bolton thought perhaps you had been slain in the skirmish."

Duncan remembered the ambush and fought his rising temper. "I'm sure that was his fondest desire. I can imagine his disappointment."

"He says you have the Bishop's Crown and plan to keep it from England."

"Did he tell you he took my sister, Brenna, as hostage

for the crown?"

"Yes. He also said you took my daughter Katherine as hostage in spite."

Duncan leveled his gaze on Kate's father and started to form the words that would counter his accusation, but the patter of footsteps crossing the clean rushes on the floor of the great hall stopped him.

"Father!"

The Earl of Wentworth raised his gaze and smiled at the blond nymph running toward him. "Elizabeth." He held open his arms and pulled his daughter into his waiting embrace.

"I've missed you so, Father," Elizabeth said, giving her father another hug.

"And I you. I hear you've made me a grandfather. Is my grandson well?"

"Oh, yes. And Edith says you will be pleased to know he has your temperament. Already he can roar as loudly as you, and is equally as determined in his demands. I am reserving judgment though, because my husband shows so many of these same traits, it's hard to tell."

Ian came to stand beside his wife. "I am na sure, but I think we have been insulted, milord."

"I am sure we have, but I..."

The Earl of Wentworth stopped and turned his gaze toward the wide entrance of the great hall. Duncan had seen her when she'd first walked in, but had only watched as she stood with her hands fisted at her side and her pale face grim and expressionless.

He waited for her to run across the room to her father as Elizabeth had done, but she did not. She stood on the top step and waited to be called forward.

...

"Come here, Katherine."

Katherine lifted her chin and walked across the chamber toward her father. Her knees trembled beneath her until she feared she would not make it to the other end of the long room.

Her gaze focused on the stern, evaluative look on her father's face, then moved to Duncan's vague, hooded expression. The two were so alike. So perfect and noble and honorable. So strong and unyielding and domineering. Why could she never do enough to be accepted by either?

Her whole life she'd searched but couldn't find the key that would make her father love her. What she would do today would gain approval from her father, but would close her husband's heart to her forever.

"Father."

The earl opened his arms and Kate stepped into his embrace. He held her for a moment, then released her and she stepped away.

"Are you well, Katherine?"

"Yes, Father. I'm fine."

"Have you been mistreated?"

"No. I have not been mistreated."

Duncan came to stand at Kate's side and motioned to his warriors. They all filed out until only Ian and Elizabeth were there with them.

"I would like to speak to the Ferguson alone," Katherine's father said, looking at Ian. Expecting compliance.

"I'll take Elizabeth outside for a breath of air," Ian said, clasping his hand around his wife's elbow. "I'll be close if

I'm needed."

Duncan nodded. "We'll be alright."

No one spoke until Ian and Elizabeth were gone, then Katherine's father lifted his shoulders and breathed a deep breath. "You committed a grave error when you brought my daughter here, Lord Ferguson."

Katherine did not look at Duncan's face. She could already imagine the raised eyebrows and slight cock of his head to the right.

"I do na consider it an error."

"By edict of our king, my daughter is betrothed to Bolton, the Earl of Rivershorn. You have taken her against her will and have no right to hold her."

"Your daughter did na come here against her will and I have every right to hold her."

"Are you saying you will not let her leave?"

"Nay, milord. Your daughter is where she belongs. I've taken her as my wife and she will stay with me."

Fire blazed from the earl's eyes and he focused his formidable gaze, first on her then on Duncan. "The church will never recognize your marriage, Ferguson. Even in Scotland, a marriage is not recognized where the bride is forced to say her vows."

"Your daughter was na forced to repeat her vows, milord. She said them freely. As did I."

Her father turned his glare on her. Katherine was not sure if Duncan recognized the disappointment on his face but it was impossible for her to miss. Cold, spiny fingers clenched a fist deep in her stomach and twisted. She felt the warmth drain from her face and prayed she would not embarrass herself and fall to the floor.

"You were betrothed to William Bolton, Katherine. You were issued an edict by your king to marry the Earl of Rivershorn. If the Scot forced you to marry him, it doesn't matter if a priest said the words. The marriage is not binding."

"I was not forced, Father. The Scot asked for my hand before the priest, and I gave it." Katherine could not look at the disbelief on her father's face. She turned her head, but the slight movement tilted the room and she felt her body sway. Duncan's arm reached out for her and pulled her close to him.

"The marriage is binding, milord," Duncan said, the tone of his voice leaving no room for her father to argue. "Edict or na, I would never have allowed her to marry the English bastard."

"You would not have allowed? How dare you! Katherine's marriage was to strengthen the ties between England and Scotland. Your King Robert issued the edict for a marriage between Elizabeth and the MacIntyre to bring peace on Scotland's side. Katherine's marriage would have established peace on England's side."

"Your Katherine would na have lived long enough to establish peace anywhere. Bolton would have killed her. He almost did."

For the first time, Katherine saw her father's composure waver.

"That is a lie, Ferguson."

Katherine sensed the smoldering furor that burned with every breath Duncan took. Her father would never have questioned her husband if he'd known him. He wouldn't have accused him of lying. Duncan had not gone back on his vow to leave the crown with her and it was costing him dearly.

"Turn around, Kate." Duncan's voice was soft and low, his words a hissing sound through clenched teeth.

Kate opened her eyes wide and shook her head. "No, Duncan. You don't have to show him."

"He needs to see. He needs to see what kind of man your king has given an army. He needs to see what kind of man he would have given his daughter to. Come here."

Kate stood before Duncan and looked up into his face. "It does not matter now."

Duncan ignored her. He removed the Ferguson plaid from over her shoulder, then pulled her toward him. Kate placed her cheek against his chest. She wrapped her arms around his waist and begged him again not to do this. Her plea came out as a poor whisper.

He lifted the long knife from its sheath and cut the material of her gown at the back of her neck and ripped it to her waist. Kate pushed her face hard against Duncan's chest when he held the material open.

The sharp intake of her father's breath hissed in the chamber. Duncan kept her back exposed for what seemed an eternity, then wrapped the plaid back around her shoulders to cover her. Thank heaven he held her close for a moment before he released her or her weakened knees would have taken her to the floor.

"Bolton did that?" Kate's father asked. The harsh tone to his voice accented his anger.

"Aye."

"Why? Why would he flog her?"

"He wanted the crown and thought to force her to tell

him where she'd hidden it."

"But she was his betrothed."

"He did na know it was Kate he was whipping, although I do na think it would have stopped him. He thought it was your other daughter, Elizabeth. He was desperate to have the crown. He still is."

Katherine stepped back from Duncan's warmth and pulled the plaid around her shoulders. Her gaze concentrated on the stone floor beneath her feet. She could not look at her father or at Duncan.

"Do you have the crown, Katherine?"

The flat line of her father's voice sent a shiver down her spine. She touched her hand to her stomach to keep down the little food she'd eaten. "Yes."

"The Ferguson has not taken it away from you? He doesn't want it?"

She closed her eyes. The lump in her throat refused to move. The pain in her chest refused to ease. "Yes. He wants it."

"Then why do you still have it?"

Katherine braved a look at Duncan's face. His unblinking gaze stared without warmth at an insignificant spot just above her head. His lips tightened to a straight line and a strained muscle in his jaw knotted. "My husband promised he would not take the crown from me. He would never break his word."

Katherine's father paced before the hearth with his hands behind his back then came to a halt and turned to Duncan. A concentrated frown covered his forehead. "How did you think you would get the crown from my daughter, Lord Ferguson, if not by force?"

Duncan didn't answer and her father repeated his question, this time a little more pointedly. "Did you think if she loved you she would give you the crown?" He waited. "Did you think Katherine so weak she would betray England for love?"

"I was mistaken."

The pain in her chest seemed more than she could bear. Her loss more devastating than she could manage. He didn't think she loved him. All these months, and he didn't know how she felt about him.

Katherine's father paced a few steps away from his spot near the hearth, then halted and faced them. "You were mistaken because you were not able to diminish your wife's loyalty to England? Or, you were mistaken because you couldn't force my daughter to love you? Which one, Lord Ferguson?"

"That is a question only your daughter can answer."

Katherine clutched her hand to her throat to ease the dryness that threatened to choke her. "You know the reason I can not give you the crown, Duncan. You know."

"What is it, Katherine?" her father interrupted. "Do you not love your Scot?"

Katherine choked back a sob. "Yes, I love my Scot. But I gave my word, Father. I swore before God I would give the crown to no one but you. I took a sacred vow."

"To whom did you swear this, Katherine?"

"To the Ferguson priest the night he brought me the crown."

"And you can live with my daughter's decision, Lord Ferguson? You can take Katherine as your wife for the rest of your life, knowing her actions not only betray the

Ferguson name, but all of Scotland? You can still love my daughter even after—"

"She's my wife. I have sworn to care for her. It's a debt I owe. I am honor bound to fulfill it."

"But can you love her?" The volume of his voice increased. The harshness in his tone became more pronounced.

"I can na demand that she break her vow. My sin would be as great as hers."

"But will you love her?" Katherine's father shouted.

"She will have my name," Duncan roared to the heavens. "I have given her that."

Katherine reached for the edge of the trestle table to steady herself and leaned against it. The blood thundered in her head and a hurt more devastating than she could imagine stabbed her in the heart.

"Katherine, get the crown."

The harshness in her father's voice startled her. She'd heard a similar tone often, but never had it been so forceful. Never had it been so unyielding.

"Now!"

Katherine ran from the room, her legs so weak they barely supported her. Her hands shook so fiercely she could hardly keep a grasp on the crown as she carried it back down the open staircase. She made her way across the rushes on the stone floor and shuddered.

She refused to think on Duncan's words. She closed her mind to what they meant. He'd given her his name but would give her no more. His love he would deny her forever. It was a cold, empty existence that lay before her.

Duncan stood in her way. Before she could give the crown to her father she had to pass him. She lowered her gaze, fighting the urge to look into his eyes and ask his forgiveness. She took her first step. His pull on her was too great and before she reached her father, she looked up. The hurt and the pain she saw was too great.

"What was the vow you gave the priest, Katherine?"

She swallowed twice before she could answer. "I swore I would give the crown to no one but my father, the Earl of Wentworth."

"Then give me the crown."

Katherine took a step nearer her father, then stopped. God help her. How could she do this to Duncan?

"Give me the crown, Katherine. You took a vow."

Katherine tried to swallow the torment that wanted to cry out from the depths of her being, but only a tiny, pitiful moan echoed in the silence. Huge tears of agony streamed down her cheeks, dropping to the floor, one after the other. She could not stop them. Her loss was so great she did not care.

"Give me the crown."

Katherine looked into her father's eyes and saw the willful determination she'd recognized from little on. She took another step toward her father and held out her trembling hands.

She gave him the crown.

"You have now honored the vow you gave the priest. You have done what God and man demanded you do. Your soul is not in peril."

The void she felt when her father lifted the crown from her arms consumed her entire body, causing the most agonizing torture to the hollow spot where her heart should be. She had done the one thing her Scot could never accept. She had saved her soul and lost her heart.

"Now, come stand by me and face your Scot."

Katherine shook her head. She did not want to look into Duncan's face and see his anger. She knew what she had done. She could not bear to see his hurt and disappointment.

"Face your Scot."

Katherine turned around but could not lift her gaze to face the humiliation in Duncan's eyes. Violent waves of fear crashed inside her head, shaking her world, drowning her in weary exhaustion.

"The choice is now yours, Duncan Ferguson. If you want the Bishop's Crown, it's yours for the taking." Her father held out the crown in his right hand and grasped Katherine's arm with his left. "You can choose either the crown or my daughter. One will return with me to England. The other will stay here with you.

"The choice is yours. I will give you one, but not both."

. . .

Duncan stared at the Englishman in disbelief, then looked at Kate. The horrified expression on her face wrenched at his heart. The shock and hopelessness plain for all to see.

"You can na expect me to make such a choice. Kate is already mine. Now that she has given over the crown, there's nothing to stop me from taking it from you."

"Yes, there is. Your Scottish pride will not let you steal it from me. I came to you in good faith, alone and unarmed. To take it from me now would be a cowardly act. Your conscience will not allow it."

Duncan steeled himself to control the violent rage that wanted to erupt within him. His chest heaved with deep, burning gasps of air, and still he didn't have enough air to breathe. "My father gave his life to protect the crown for Scotland. You can na expect me to choose one over the other."

"Yes, I can. I will not give over both the crown and my daughter and go back to England with empty hands. You can choose Katherine and lose the crown, or you can keep the crown and lose my daughter."

Duncan looked into Kate's face and saw the total dejection she did not try to hide. The haunted emptiness in her eyes appeared even more devastating when surrounded by the pale shallowness of her skin.

"Choose, my lord. I find it equally as unforgivable to give my daughter to an Englishman who would beat her, as I do to give my daughter to a Scot who will not love her."

Every breath of air left his body. Hot pokers ripped into his chest and made a lethal stab through his heart. He reached out his hands. He wanted to hold the crown that had cost his mother and father and sisters their lives. He wanted to see what it felt like to have what he had dreamed his Kate would give to him.

He closed his eyes and let his head drop back onto his shoulders. He couldn't move. He had lost. Everything he had fought for since he'd come back to find the crown gone and his family slain was within his grasp, yet further away than ever.

He could not keep the crown and lose Kate.

He placed the crown back in Kate's father's hands and turned around to hold Kate next to him. To hold her in his arms and keep her close, without a crown to separate them.

Kate was gone.

"By the Saints! No!"

Duncan looked toward the doorway. Kate was just running to the steps that would take her away from him.

"Kate. Stop."

She did not slow down but continued through the wide doorway and up the winding stairway. Her footsteps padded down the long hall and a door upstairs slammed shut with an irrevocable finality. All was deathly silent. Duncan knew Kate had fled because she doubted his love and didn't want to face him after he'd chosen the crown.

Duncan turned to face Kate's father. "You will have your crown, milord. You above all know how priceless your daughter is. A thousand crowns from England could not even begin to equal her worth."

The earl raised his shoulders and filled his chest. "I'm glad you realize Katherine's value. She has always been more than special."

"That's strange, coming from you. She doesn't think you love her. She thinks you love only Elizabeth."

"She's wrong. I love both my daughters equally but in different ways. Elizabeth was always so much like her mother I could refuse her nothing. Katherine was so much like me I could grant her nothing." The earl lowered his hand and placed the crown on the table near him.

"Have you seen how bright and curious she is?" The earl didn't wait for Duncan to answer but ran his finger over the satin material covering the crown. "And how brave and reckless?"

Duncan remembered how Kate faced Bolton in the dungeon and knew exactly what her father meant.

"As she grew, she became more wise and worldly than a great number of the men with whom my king surrounded himself. I feared for her and found I did not know how to suppress her independent nature. She was more like a son to me, and yet, being a woman, her talents would never be realized. Her brilliant mind would become a dangerous threat to the men who made up my world.

"I thought it best if I could rid her of her outspokenness and teach her acceptable submission. But she still voiced opinions few of my peers were brave enough to utter. I chastised her and sent her to her chamber without meals for her stubbornness and willfulness."

"And you put her in the pit to punish her."

"Yes. I didn't realize how terrified she was of the darkness until it was too late. The damage had already been done."

Duncan read the regret on Kate's father's face and felt a softening toward him.

"She always thought she was a disappointment to me and I didn't know how to show her otherwise." The earl looked up and Duncan saw the sadness in his eyes. "She thinks she has disappointed you, too, because she would not give you the crown. How are you going to show her otherwise?"

"Do na concern yourself with that, milord. Kate will know soon enough I could never exchange her for the crown. She will know how much she means to me."

"Then you had best tell her right away. If there's one thing I've learned about my daughter, it's that she is a very caring person with a heart softer than is good for her. When she's been hurt as deeply as she has been hurt by the choice she thinks you've made, it's hard to tell what she might do."

Duncan glanced over at the empty doorway and took a hesitant step then stopped.

"Go," Kate's father said, filling a cup with ale and sitting in a chair behind the table. "I am going nowhere until I'm sure my daughter wants to stay with you."

"And if she says she does not?"

"Then you will have lost a treasure far greater than the crown."

Duncan gave him a harsh glare, then crossed the room. Before he brought Kate back down to see her father, he would make sure she knew how important she was to him. He would say the words he should have said long ago. That he hadn't taken her as his wife only because she possessed the crown, but because he could not imagine spending the rest of his life without her.

Duncan took the stairs to their chamber two at a time and ignored the harsh pounding of his heart in his chest. Before he brought Kate back down to see her father, he would make sure she didn't doubt his feelings for her. That she knew his mind had been made up from the moment she'd kissed him in the dungeon.

Duncan made his way down the long hallway almost at a run. It was suddenly very important that he see her. That he make sure his Kate was safe. Before he took Kate back down to see her father, he would make sure she knew how much he loved her.

He lifted the latch on the heavy wooden door and

bounded into the room. A cold, empty void slapped him in the face and he knew without looking he would not find her here.

Duncan ran to the chapel, praying she'd gone there as she did every day. Except for the flickering candles on the altar, the room was dark. An all-consuming fear engulfed his entire being, leaving little energy for him to do anything more than force his legs to carry him to the other rooms to search for her.

She had to be on this level. She had not gone down the stairs. He would have seen her if she had.

Duncan ran to the next room, Brenna's room. Empty. He braced his hand against the stone wall to steady his trembling knees and made his way to his parents' chamber. He threw open the door and glanced around the room, praying he would find her here. Fearing he would not.

His eyes stopped their search when his gaze focused on the opening that led to the secret passageway. A thousand voices screamed inside his head. A horde of foul demons from hell lashed out at him. She had left him. She thought he had chosen the crown and did not want her.

Duncan ran across the room and braced his hands against either side of the opening, fighting the lump in his throat that would not let him breathe. He stared down the dark passageway and fought the pain in his chest. He would rather die than spend one day of his life without her.

"Kate!"

The empty sound echoed back to him from the darkness of the tunnel.

"Kate!"

Chapter 20

Duncan raced down the steps of the keep with the furies of hell on his heels. There was no need to issue orders to his men. The determined movements of their laird brought them running from every quarter — from the battlements and the stables and the practice area. Before he reached the outer gate, Ian and Malcolm and Angus were armed and at his side with the remainder of his warriors close behind.

He had to get to the place near the rocks where the passageway exited. He had to reach her before she went too far beyond the stream. Kate was not safe anywhere outside the castle walls. Wild fear thundered in his head when he thought of what might have happened to her already.

If her father had come from England and crossed onto Ferguson land, it was safe to wager that more of the English were nearby. Especially William Bolton.

Duncan pushed his mount harder until he neared the top of the rise that overlooked the place near the rocks where the hidden tunnel exited. He slammed his fist against his thigh in frustration and scanned the area again. She was nowhere in sight.

He turned to the right, the way he knew Kate would go. Back to England. She would think there was nothing left for her in Scotland. God help him. He had failed her. She thought he had chosen the crown. She thought he didn't want her.

He dug his heels into his horse's side and rode only a few feet, then pulled hard on the reins. A massive group of armed warriors carrying an English banner crested the rise. He searched the enemy army, praying he would not see his wife in their midst. It didn't take long to realize his worst fears.

They had Kate.

Bolton had her locked in his arms as if he owned her. As if he had a right to touch her. Bright blazes of fury raged through Duncan's head, blinding him to all but a desperate need to get Kate back. He gripped his fist around the hilt of his sword and took huge, gulping gasps of air. He envisioned the feel of his blade twisting deep in Bolton's gut.

"Do you see Kate with him, Malcolm?" Duncan asked his question without lifting his gaze from Kate sitting in front of the English bastard. He did not dare look away for fear she would be gone when he looked back.

"Aye, Duncan. The English on Bolton's right is mine," Malcom hissed in the crisp, winter air.

Duncan moved his evaluative gaze for a moment as the band of English neared them. "Take heed of the warrior on the left, Angus. His hand hangs awkward at his side. I would na doubt he has a knife hidden there."

"I can see, Duncan. Have no regard for the puny warrior. I will take care of him."

"All of you. Watch me close." The first flakes of snow fluttered down around them and Duncan thought of how chilled Kate must be. He ached to hold her next to him to keep her warm. He ached to touch her and love her until she forgot how much pain he'd caused her. "Ian, you will have the ugly giant riding behind Bolton."

"Aye, friend."

Duncan filled his chest with air and felt his head clear. "Gregor," he called out and the warrior brought his horse close. "Stay here with the men. If we do na all return safe and well, be sure none of the English live to see the sun go down."

The band of English warriors descended the slope at an easy gait, the pompous posture of their leader as he sat atop his horse presented a revolting sight. They were close enough now to see the confident smirk on Bolton's face. Duncan fisted his hands at his side, then reached for the hilt of his sword.

"Duncan." Ian whispered the warning from behind him. "Keep your head. It will do na good to act in haste."

Duncan filled his chest with a blast of cold Scottish air that hissed as it entered his mouth through clenched teeth. Bolton had his arm around Kate's waist, a malevolent smile on his face that made the blood boil in Duncan's veins. "He'll na live to see the end of this day, Ian. I swear it."

"I know, friend. But wait until you have the mistress in your arms before you make a move."

Duncan closed his eyes to block out the picture of Kate sitting in Bolton's lap, then stared at her, willing her to lift her head and look at him. He wanted to see her face and know she was alright. He wanted to show her by his look that he had come to get her and would keep her safe. He wanted to lock his gaze with hers and tell her without words that he loved her. But she would not lift her head to look at him.

Duncan held the air in his chest until his lungs burned. Bolton would not have her much longer.

He watched as Bolton left his main army on the hill and rode down the slope with a half score of his men at his side. He moved in his saddle with a cocksure swagger and a haughty lift to his chin. His hand stayed fixed around Kate's middle until they stopped, then he handed her down to one of his warriors while he dismounted. With a snide grin, he pulled her up against him and stood with her as a shield in front of him.

"I've come to get the Bishop's Crown and my betrothed, Ferguson. As you can see, my betrothed was so anxious for my arrival, she came to meet me. As soon as you hand over the crown, my future bride and I will return to England."

Duncan waited for Kate to look at him but her face remained fixed on the mounting snow that swirled at her feet. She shied away from his gaze as if she had something to hide. "Kate?"

She made him wait a long time before she turned her head. The moment she did, his heart burst within his chest. A large red welt covered her cheek. Duncan swallowed hard to fight the consuming rage that threatened to erupt within him. He prayed Bolton's death would be agonizingly slow.

Duncan tightened the grip on the hilt of his sword to

keep from making a move which might put Kate in more danger. He stared at his wife until she raised her eyes to meet him.

Ever so slowly, her chin lifted. He gazed with unbelievable horror at the haunting emptiness in her blue eyes. The look of abject devastation on her pale face chilled every drop of blood flowing through his body. All signs of life were absent from her dark-rimmed eyes. Any glimmer of hope that had been there before had drained from her face. She had separated her heart from him.

"Release Kate to me now and I will make sure your death is quick, Bolton." Duncan issued his demand through clenched teeth and inched his hand to the knife at his waist.

"Kate? You call my betrothed Kate?" Bolton jeered a demented laugh and tightened his hold around Katherine's waist. "One would almost think you had grown fond of the woman I am to marry, Scot. That cannot be, can it?"

The deadly glare in Bolton's eyes alerted every nerve in Duncan's body. The hostility on his face issued a warning. The man was not human. He was an animal.

"Let her go, Bolton."

"The Lady Katherine was given to me by edict of my king. You have no claim on her."

A shadowed film of sunlight filtered through the blustery clouds that raced over the Scottish meadow. Larger flakes of snow fell around them and Duncan's raised voice boomed through the haze. "Let her go!"

"The English lady is mine, Ferguson, and unless you are prepared to die this very minute, you will give me the Bishop's Crown."

"The Scot does not have the crown, Lord Bolton. It's not his to give to you."

The Earl of Wentworth's voice echoed through the swirling snow like an ominous foreboding of doom.

Bolton darted his gaze to the place from where the voice had come. The earl walked through the Ferguson warriors with the crown cradled in his arms, then came to a halt in front of Bolton. "I have the Bishop's Crown. It's mine to take back to England."

Bolton's eyes opened wide and the obvious fury and anger turned his face a mottled red. Duncan watched him for any sign of danger, waiting for the first opportunity to kill him.

Katherine's father faced Bolton with a determined look that gave no quarter. "You will never get the crown, Bolton. The Ferguson laird gave it to me in exchange for something of much greater value."

Katherine lifted her gaze to meet his. For the first time, Duncan saw a spark of life. He saw her search his face for a reason to hope.

Her father must have seen it too, for he answered the questioning confusion he saw in her gaze. "The Ferguson laird gave the crown to me because it did not mean nearly as much as what he received in its place."

Duncan met Kate's gaze. There were so many unanswered questions in her look. She focused on the crown in her father's hands, then turned back to him. He saw the ragged breath that filled her breast, the gasp of understanding when she realized he'd chosen her over the crown. She struggled harder to free herself from Bolton's grasp, but Duncan gave her a look of warning. The

Englishman was desperate now that he'd lost the crown.

Bolton pulled Katherine back a step as if creating more distance would deny what was happening, would make her his. "You cannot have the crown," Bolton roared. "I want it. I will have it and your daughter as my bride."

"It's too late, Bolton. Lord Ferguson took my daughter as his wife after you beat her and left her to die in the MacIntyre dungeon."

The shocked denial on Bolton's face warned them all to be wary. "No, that was her sister, the one given to the Scottish laird."

"No," the earl said. "It was Katherine. You nearly killed your betrothed."

Bolton went wild. Even Kate must have sensed his imbalance because she tried to pull out of his grasp to get away from him. Bolton twisted her in his arms until she winced in pain.

"Release my daughter, Bolton."

"Never. She's mine. I will have the marriage to the Scot annulled. Words spoken in this heathen country by their pagan priests are not sacred. I can have the words disavowed in short order."

"And what if there is a babe? What if she is already carrying the Ferguson's heir?"

"No! It cannot be!"

Duncan's gaze flashed to Katherine's face and for the briefest second her heart was open to him.

She was.

Kate was carrying his child. The next Ferguson heir. A result of the love they shared.

An emotion unlike any he had ever known engulfed

him. More wondrous, more desperate, more consuming. He would die before he would let anything happen to her.

"Leave her go, Bolton," the earl said. "It's too late. Their vows were spoken before God and you cannot change them."

"The king—"

"The king will not interfere. He will do nothing to help you. I will see that he does not."

Duncan forced himself to remain where he was. He saw Katherine struggle against Bolton, clawing to release his grip, but her efforts were hardly noticed. With frantic, trembling movements, the Englishman's hand reached for the knife at his side. Duncan had no doubt he would use it.

"It's over, Bolton," the earl said, clearly concerned that Bolton was on the brink of madness. "You've lost both your betrothed and the crown."

"No!" Bolton lifted the knife from his sheath at his side and raised it above Katherine's head. "The Scot will not have what the king promised me!"

Before the blade began its downward descent, Duncan threw his dirk with unerring accuracy. The long, pointed weapon found its mark in the center of Bolton's chest, bringing to a halt the beating of his evil heart. The arm poised above Kate's chest froze, unable to continue its downward motion. The weapon pivoted to the ground with a dull thud. Bolton's other arm dropped from around Kate's waist, freeing her from danger.

In the same second, knives from Angus, Ian and Malcolm's hands found their targets and the three warriors nearest Bolton fell to the ground. Only two of the men behind them gave up their lives to defend their leader. The rest dropped their weapons in surrender.

"Kate!" Duncan ran to Kate's side and pulled her into his arms. "Do na look," he warned, cupping her face with his hand and turning her head away from the look of torment on Bolton's face. The stark terror in his wide open eyes evidenced the horrors of hell, and Duncan knew the Englishman had just entered through its portals.

Katherine's father stood before the surviving warriors from Bolton's army then addressed them in a commanding tone. "If you wish to live to see another day, you will pick up your dead and return to England. If not, I will stand back and watch the Scottish Fergusons slaughter you with my blessing."

The remaining English warriors quickly lifted Bolton and the other dead onto the backs of their horses and led them toward England's border. Duncan gave the order for his men to follow to make sure they were gone forever. When Gregor and the others were out of sight, he lifted Kate's head from his chest and looked at her.

"Ah, lass," he said, holding her close. He touched the red welt on her cheek. "It's all right. He'll never hurt you again."

She looked at her father, still holding the crown, then back to Duncan. "You gave up the crown?"

There was a searching look in her eyes. A look that said she needed assurance that he could live with the decision he'd made. "Aye, Kate. Compared to the woman I chose as my wife, the crown means nothing."

Duncan felt Kate shiver in his arms and he leaned down and kissed her on the forehead. "I will take you home now, wife."

The look on Kate's face caused his heart to leap in his

chest. He couldn't quite read every emotion in her gaze, but he prayed he saw at least a glimmer of hope. Something he could hold onto until he could show her how much he loved her.

Duncan mounted his horse, then reached down and lifted Kate to his lap. Her father came to stand before them.

"Are you all right, Katherine?" the earl asked. The concern in his eyes was obvious.

"Yes, Father. I'm fine."

"Good. I have much to say to you, daughter, but I will wait until you're safe and warm in your home."

She nodded, then leaned her head back against Duncan's chest, and he turned his mount toward home. The home he and Kate shared.

"Is it true, Kate?," he whispered as they made their way over the last rise before they reached Lochmore Castle. "Are you carrying my babe?"

"Yes."

"You were na going to tell me?"

"I would have told you, Duncan. I only needed time."

"Time?"

She lifted her head and looked into his eyes. "I needed to know first if you wanted the babe."

"You thought I would na want it?" He couldn't believe she thought he might not.

"I wasn't sure. The babe will be part English."

Duncan took a deep breath. "Aye. He will be part English. And he will be part Scot. We will let only the best of each show itself."

Kate put her head back against his chest and smiled. Duncan leaned down to kiss her forehead, then held her closer to him. His Kate was safe and where she belonged.

...

Katherine sat in a chair near the hearth and let the heat from the fire warm her body. She was cold from the inside out and even the thick covers Duncan had wrapped around her shoulders didn't warm her. Her husband hadn't left her side since they'd returned, and Elizabeth bustled around taking special care of her as if smothering her with attention could erase everything that had happened.

Angus stayed close by, making sure there was a full goblet of his special potion in her hand. With every swallow of the warm, soothing liquid, she felt more of her aches and worries ease.

For the first time since Duncan had returned from England with Brenna, she'd left the darkness and come to the great hall to be with them. Katherine knew her reason for joining them was to find out what had happened to Bolton. And, perhaps she was in hopes that when her brother came back, his English wife would not be with him.

Katherine lifted her gaze to the quiet lass sitting off to the side. She wanted to go to her and comfort her. She wanted to tell her she understood how frightened and alone she had felt being at Bolton's mercy, but she knew her overtures would not be appreciated. She knew Brenna was not ready to accept the English woman her brother had taken as his wife.

She watched as Angus handed Brenna a goblet filled with his soothing potions. She hoped it would help. At least Brenna had come into the open. It was a good first step.

"Will you be all right, Katherine?"

Katherine lifted her gaze to find her father standing before her. With shoulders braced and hands clenched behind his back, he asked his question in a soft, caring voice. The look in his eyes expressed a genuine concern Katherine had seen often, yet never recognized before.

"Yes. I'll be fine."

"It was a very brave and noble thing you did to keep the crown from Bolton. The scars on your back are proof of it."

Katherine lifted her chin and faced her father squarely. "I was neither brave nor noble. I was scared. I knew if I gave Bolton the crown he would use it only for evil. To him the crown represented power, but the power he would yield would be cruel and unjust."

"And you didn't give the crown to your Scot. Even though you love him and knew how much he wanted it."

Katherine shook her head. "I pray in time he'll forgive me. His Ferguson honor was at stake." Katherine paused and clenched her hands tighter in her lap. "I'm a disappointment to Duncan, just as I was to you."

"You were never a disappointment to me, Katherine. Never."

"That's not true. I was always too outspoken and too bold. I saw how you hated it. I tried, but I could not be meek and quiet." Katherine took a deep breath that quivered as she released it. "I could never make you smile and laugh like Mama and Elizabeth did. I didn't know what to do so you would love me like you loved them."

"Oh, Katherine. How I have failed you."

Katherine shook her head. "No, father. It's my shortcoming. I don't know how to be anything but what I am, and it's not good enough. I'm a disappointment to

Duncan just as I was a disappointment to you."

"Nay, lass," Duncan said from behind her, then knelt on one knee by her side and cradled her hands in his. "You have never been a disappointment to me. From the moment you kissed me in Ian's dungeon and placed the Ferguson medallion in my hand, you have been anything but a disappointment to me."

"But I couldn't give you what you needed to restore your father's honor. I couldn't break the vow I'd given the priest and give you the crown."

Brenna stood and all eyes turned toward her. "Giving Duncan the Bishop's Crown would not have been what Father wanted." She slowly walked to Katherine's chair with Malcolm at her side. "Father did na want Scotland to keep the crown. He knew many Scots would die if we kept what did na belong to us. That is why he gave it to our priest and sent him to Ian's wife. He was na proud that Scotland had stolen it from the English king. I know this, Duncan, because when the dying McGowan Scot gave Father the Bishop's Crown, Father wept."

Brenna clutched her hands around her waist and Malcolm put his arm around her shoulder and held her close. "I had never seen Father cry before, Duncan. He cried because he knew in this he had to go against Scotland and give England back the crown." Katherine looked at the confusion in Duncan's eyes and reached for his hand. She entwined her fingers through his, as he had done to comfort her so often before.

"But Father died to protect the crown," Duncan said, the disbelief evident in his voice.

"Nay. Father was murdered. Bolton killed him because

he would na tell him where he had hidden the crown. Bolton killed Mother when she tried to save Father."

Brenna rested her head against Malcolm's chest and the warrior wrapped his arms around her and pulled her close to him. "Father would na have wanted you to keep the crown, Duncan. He would have wanted you to give the crown back to England, just as your wife has done."

Duncan knelt at Katherine's feet and clasped her hands in his. "I love you, Kate. I thought it was the crown I wanted. But I was wrong. I will thank God every day of my life that He sent you to me and that you had the wisdom to follow your conscience."

Katherine closed her eyes and the tears of joy she could not contain spilled down her cheeks. Duncan wiped them away with one of his rough, callused fingers.

"The crown was not mine to give, Duncan. All I have to give is my heart, and that you already possess. It was yours from the moment you held me in your arms and carried me from the dark."

Another tear spilled down her cheek and Duncan wiped it away. "Then you will never be a disappointment to me, lass. There is nothing more I could want than what you have already given me."

About Laura

Laura Landon enjoyed ten years as a high school teacher and nine years making sundaes and malts in her very own ice cream shop, but once she penned her first novel, she closed up shop to spend every free minute writing. Now she enjoys creating her very own heroes and heroines, and making sure they find their happily ever after.

A vital member of her rural community, Laura directed the town's Quasquicentennial celebration, organized funding for an exercise center for the town, and serves on the hospital board.

Laura lives in the Midwest, surrounded by her family and friends. She has written more than a dozen Victorian historicals, five of which are selling worldwide in English, and one which is currently being reprinted in Japanese. She is a Prairie Muse Platinum and Amazon Montlake author.

NOT MINE TO GIVE
is Laura's first Scottish historical

Also by Laura Landon

SHATTERED DREAMS
WHEN LOVE IS ENOUGH
A MATTER OF CHOICE
BROKEN PROMISE
MORE THAN WILLING

Visit Laura at www.lauralandon.com

Watch for Laura's October 2012 releases of

INTIMATE DECEPTIONS

THE MOST TO LOSE

LORD OF VENGEANCE

from Amazon's Montlake Romance

CPSIA information can be obtained at www.ICGtesting.com
Printed in the USA
BVOW010125160413

318227BV00018B/502/P